THE HUNTER

IDW PUBLISHING

Operations:

Ted Adams, Chief Executive Officer • Greg Goldstein, Chief Operating Officer
Matthew Ruzicka, CPA, Chief Financial Officer • Alan Payne, VP of Sales
Lorelei Bunjes, Dir. of Digital Services • AnnaMaria White, Marketing & PR Manager
Marci Hubbard, Executive Assistant • Alonzo Simon, Shipping Manager

Editorial:

Chris Ryall, Publisher / Editor-in-Chief • Scott Dunbier, Editor, Special Projects
Andy Schmidt, Senior Editor • Justin Eisinger, Editor • Kris Oprisko, Editor / Foreign Lic.
Denton J. Tipton, Editor • Tom Waltz, Editor • Mariah Huehner, Associate Editor

Design:

Robbie Robbins, EVP / Sr. Graphic Artist • Neil Uyetake, Art Director
Chris Mowry, Graphic Artist • Amauri Osorio, Graphic Artist
Gilberto Lazcano, Production Assistant

www.idwpublishing.com
ISBN: 978-1-60010-493-0 • 12 11 10 09 2 3 4 5

THE HUNTER. AUGUST 2009. SECOND PRINTING.

IDW Publishing, a division of Idea and Design Works, LLC.
Editorial offices: 5080 Santa Fe St., San Diego, CA 92109.

PRINTED IN KOREA.

RICHARD STARK'S
PARKER

the Hunter

A Graphic Novel

BY
Darwyn Cooke

EDITED by SCOTT DUNBIER

IDW PUBLISHING
San Diego   2009

For Donald Westlake.
They tell me he knew Richard Stark fairly well.

RICHARD STARK'S PARKER:

Hunter

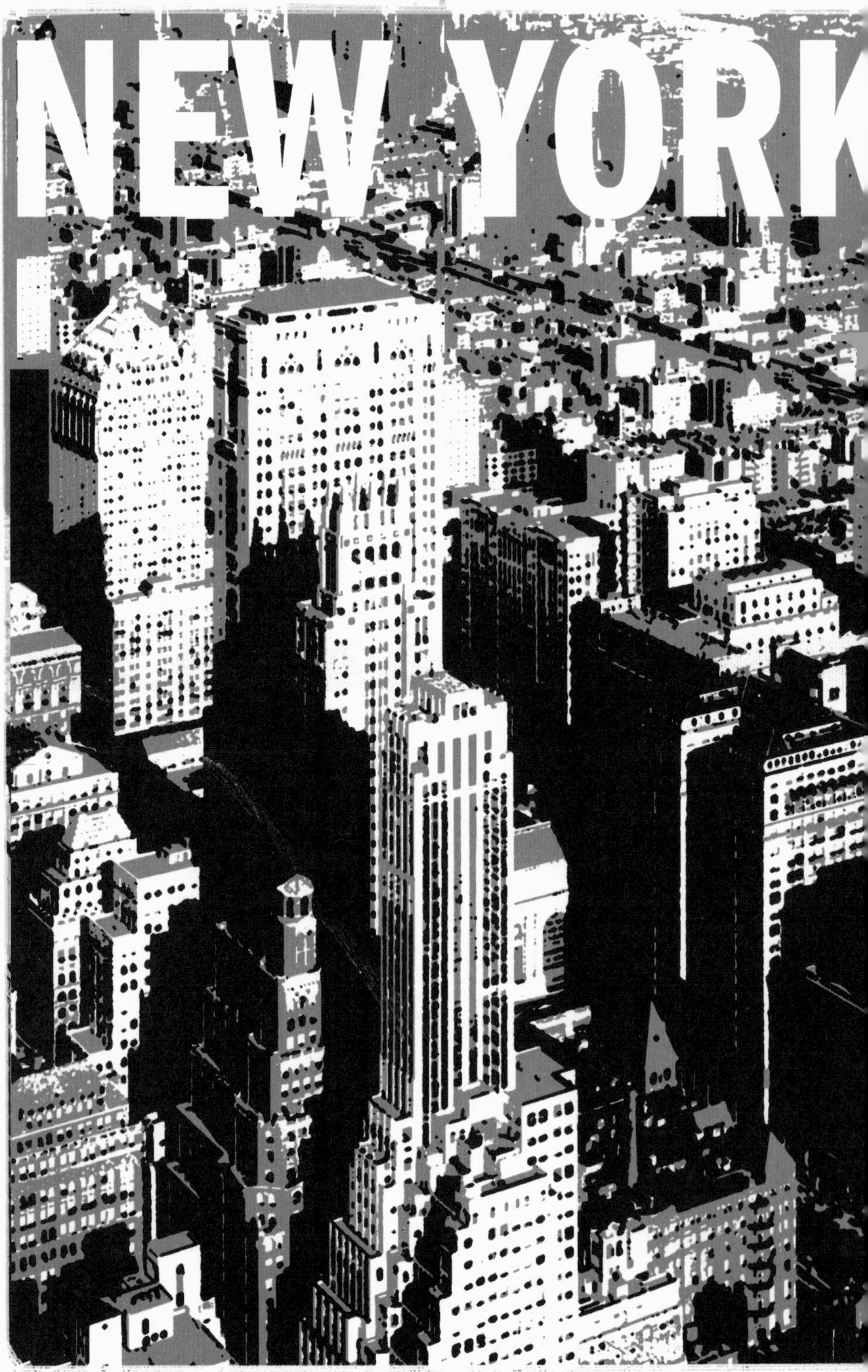
NEW YORK

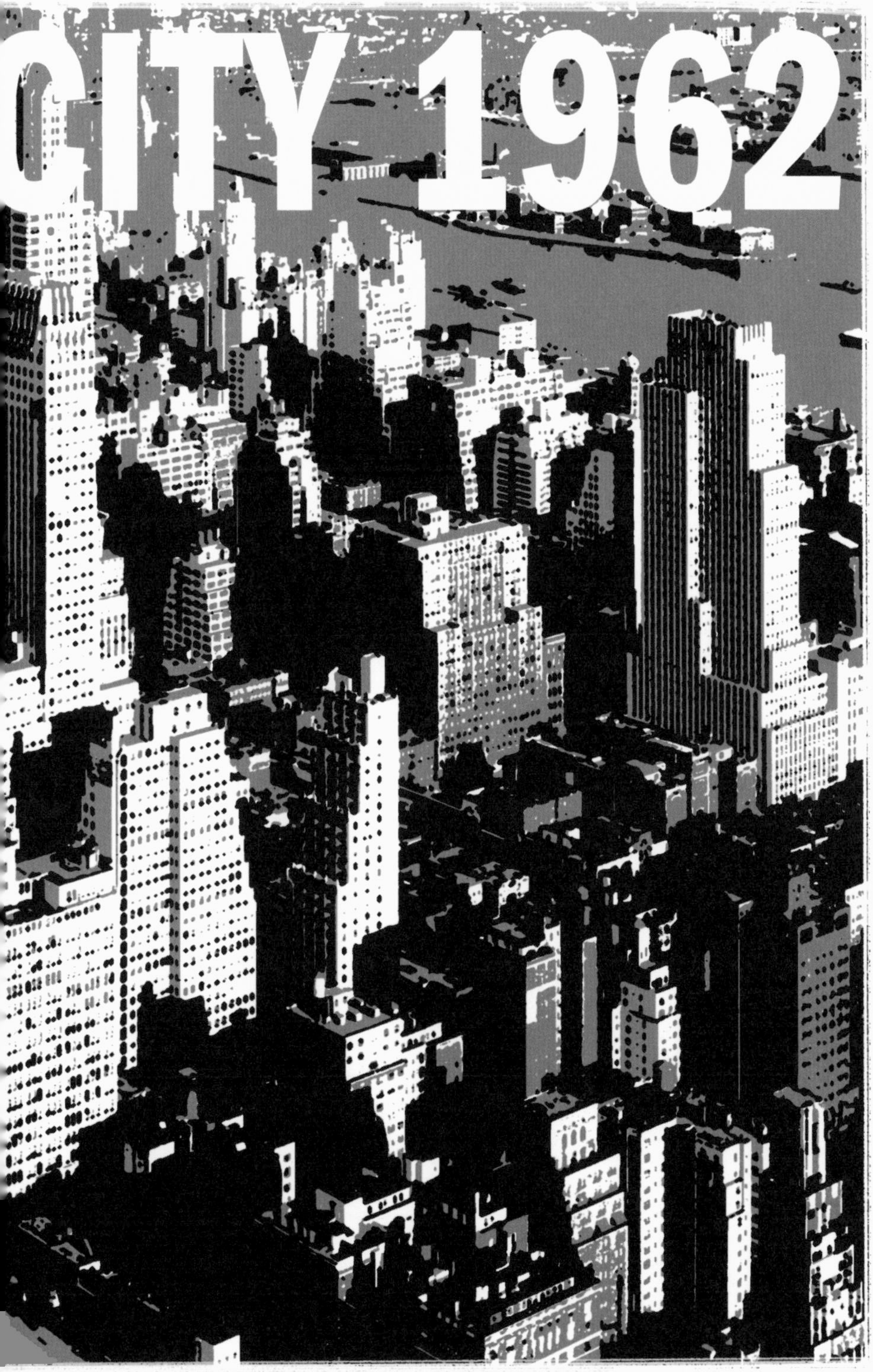
CITY 1962

BOOK ONE

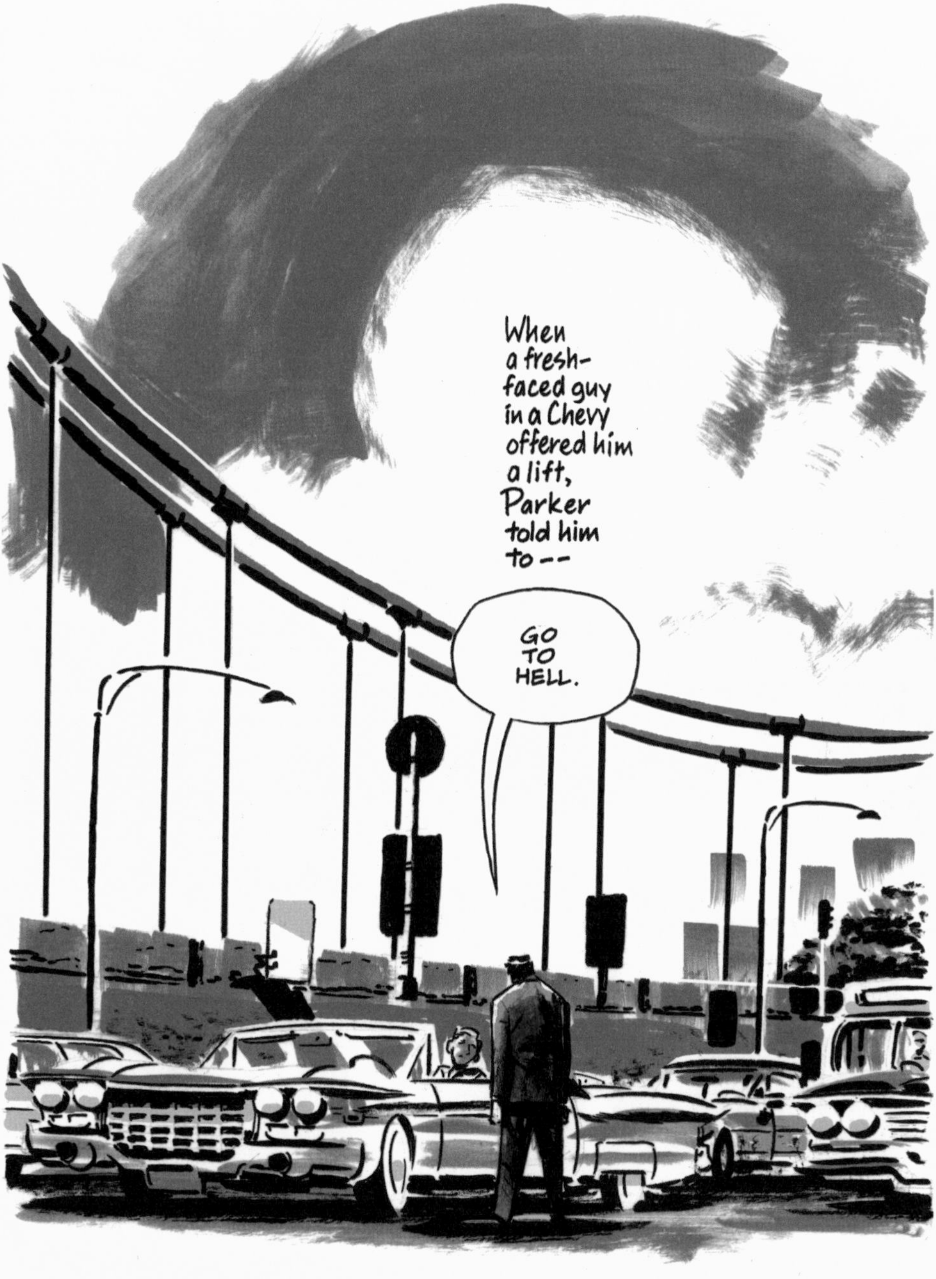
When a fresh-faced guy in a Chevy offered him a lift, Parker told him to --
GO TO HELL.

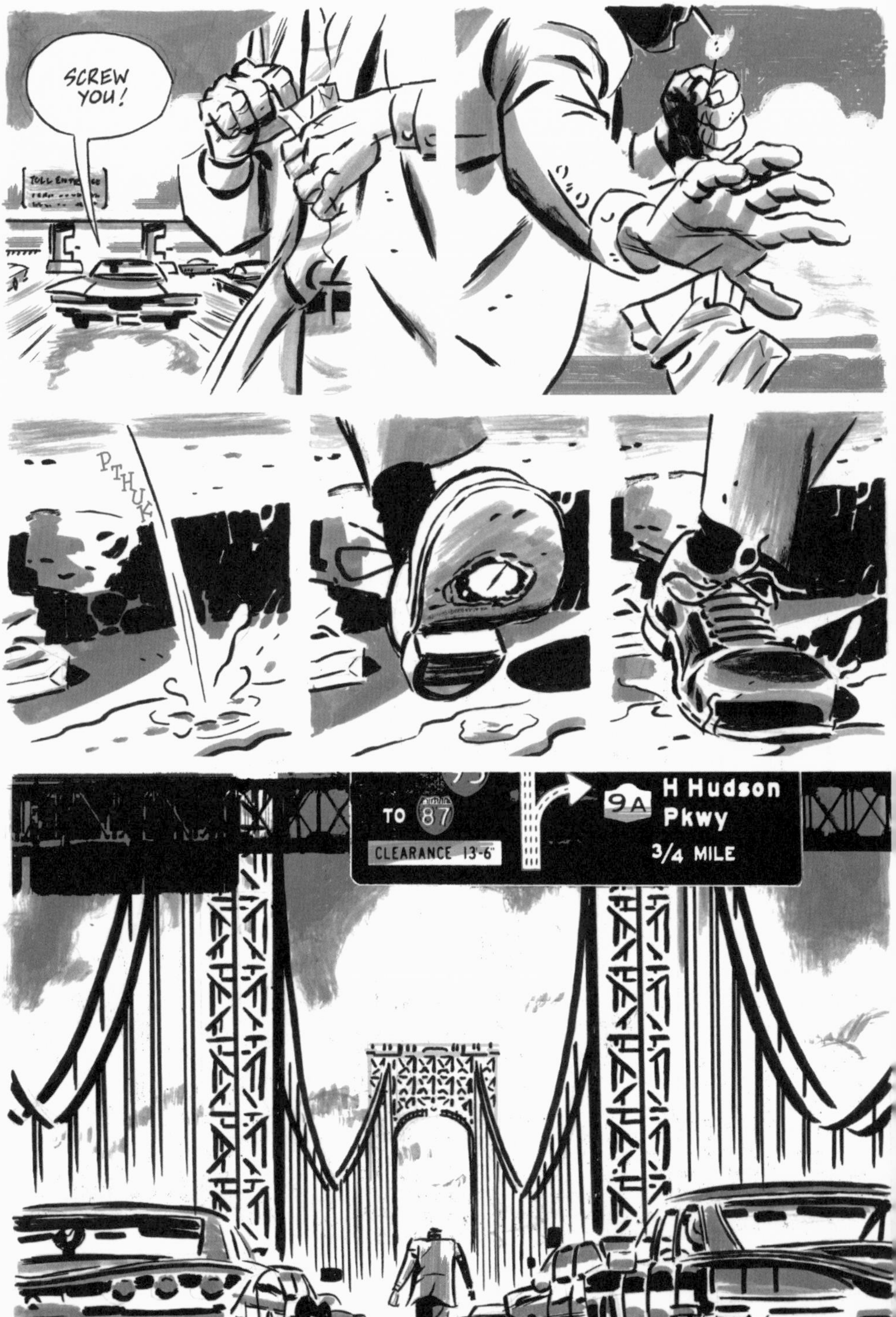
SCREW YOU!
PTHUK
TO 87
CLEARANCE 13-6"
9A H Hudson Pkwy
3/4 MILE

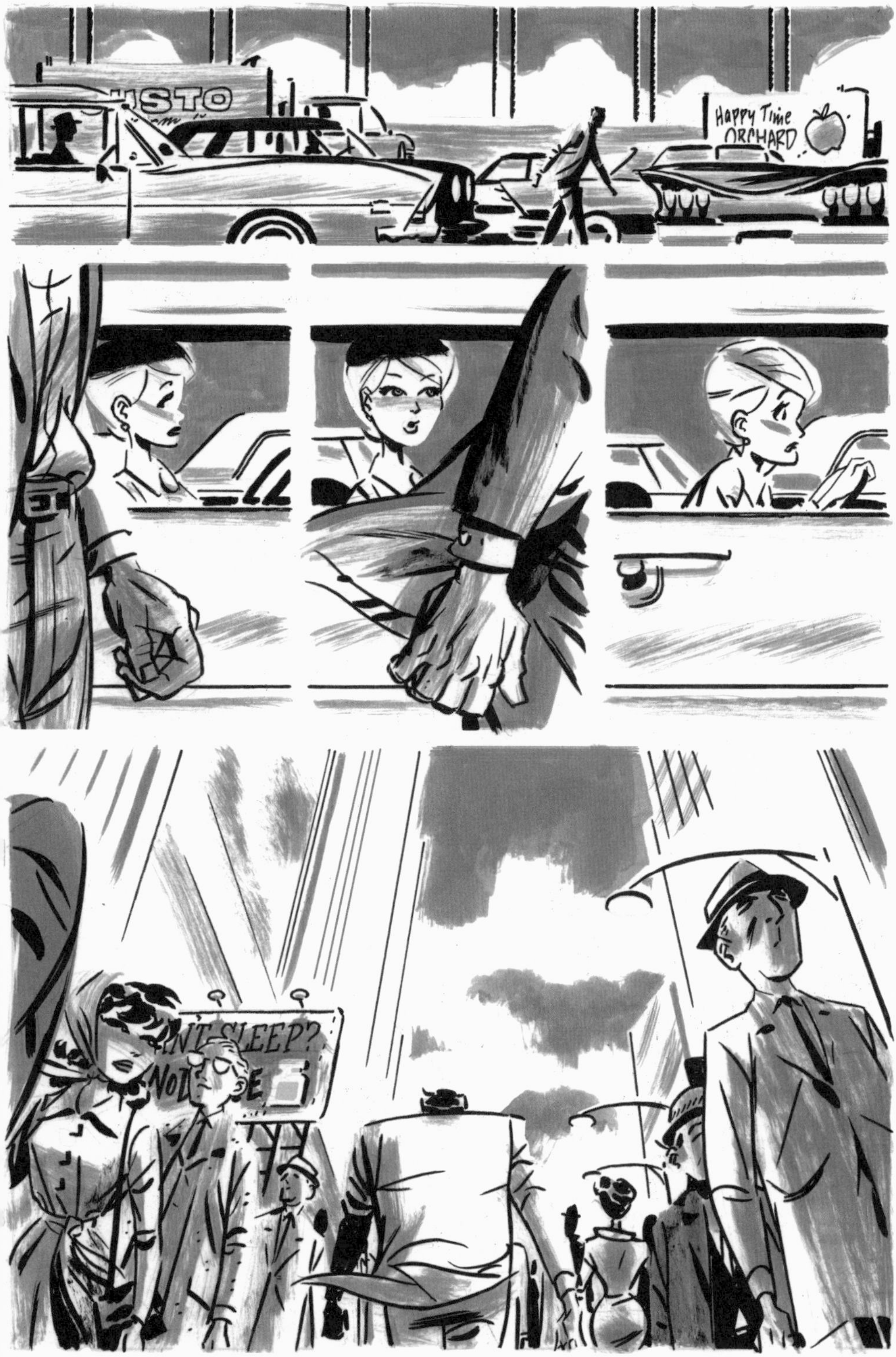
Happy Time
ORCHARD

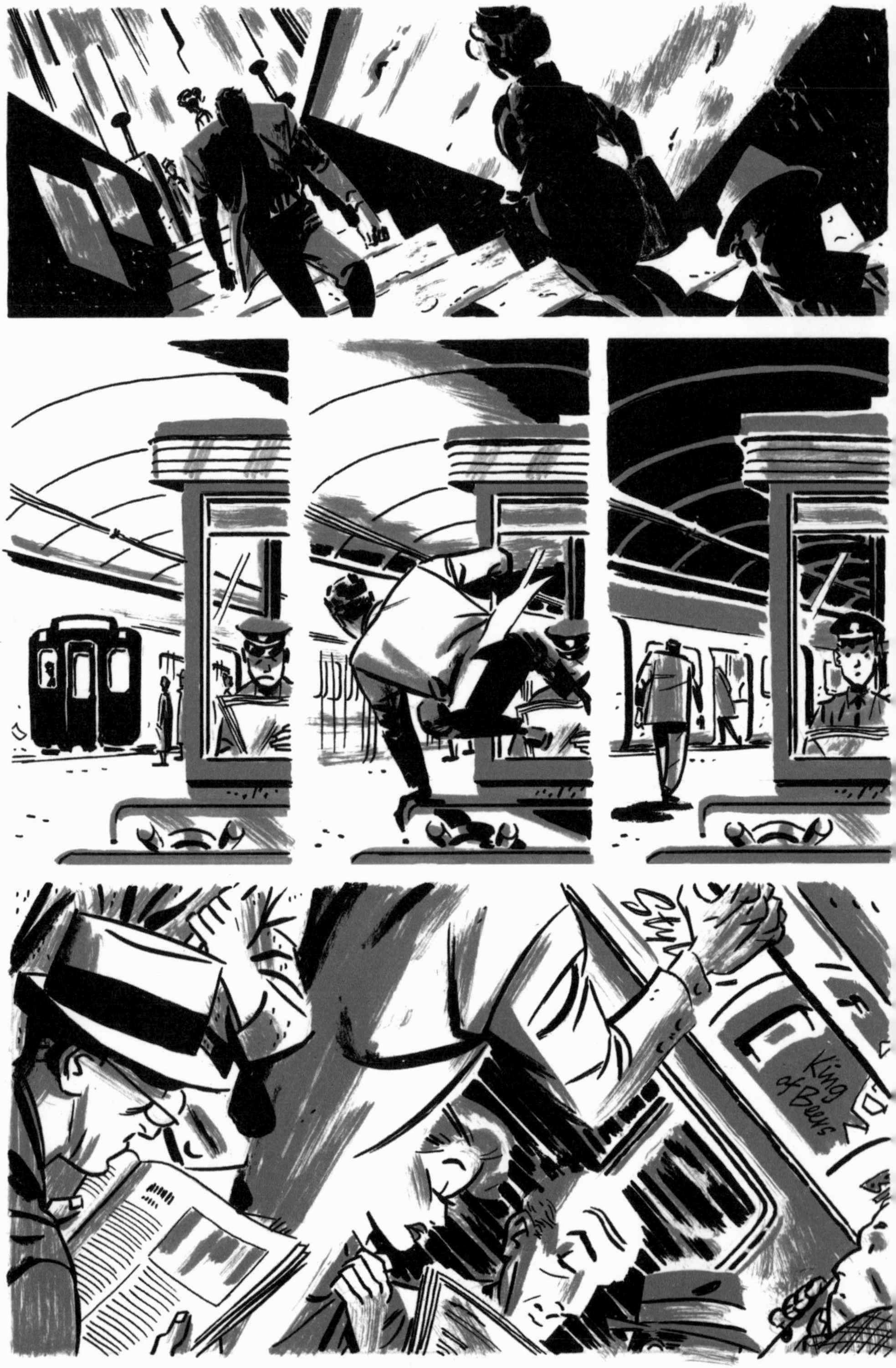
King of Beers

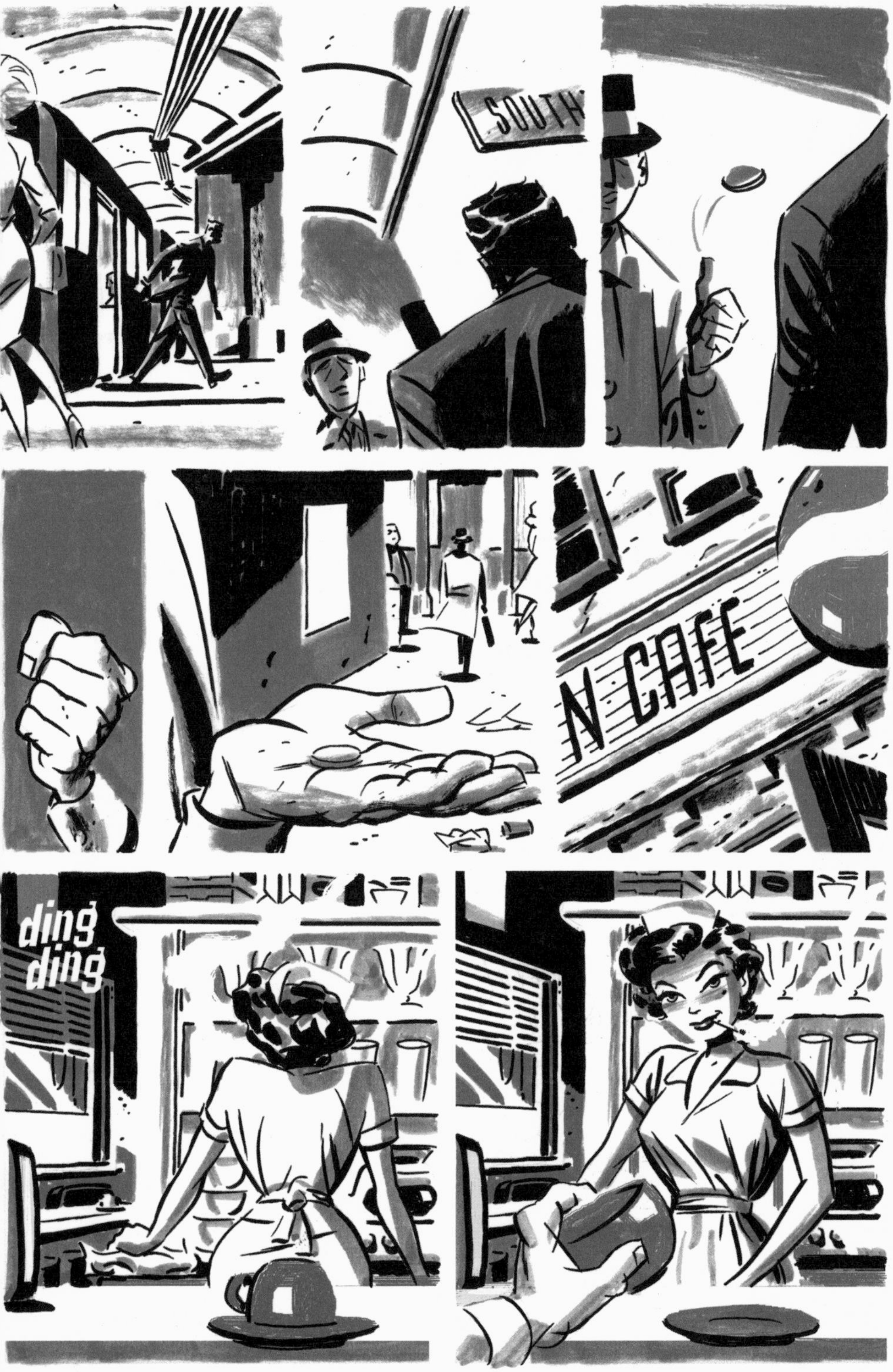
SOUTH
N CAFE
ding ding

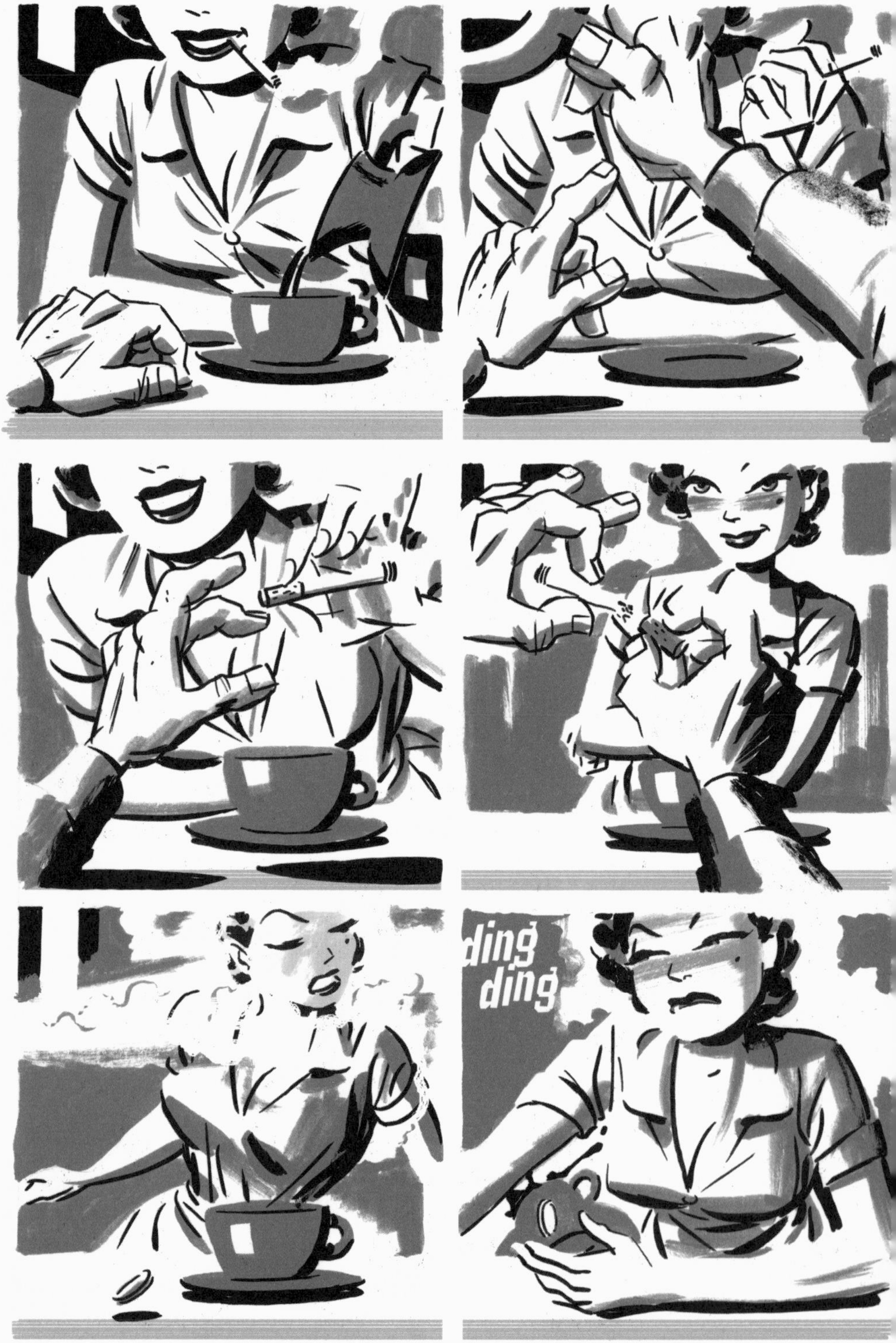
ding
ding

DEPT. OF MOTOR

STATE OF NEW YORK
DRIVER'S LICENSE NO.
FULL NAME
ADDRESS
CITY/STATE

BIRTHDATE | EYES | HEIGHT
SEX | HAIR | WEIGHT

CHIEF HIGHWAY COMM.

NOT VALID UNLESS STAMPED.

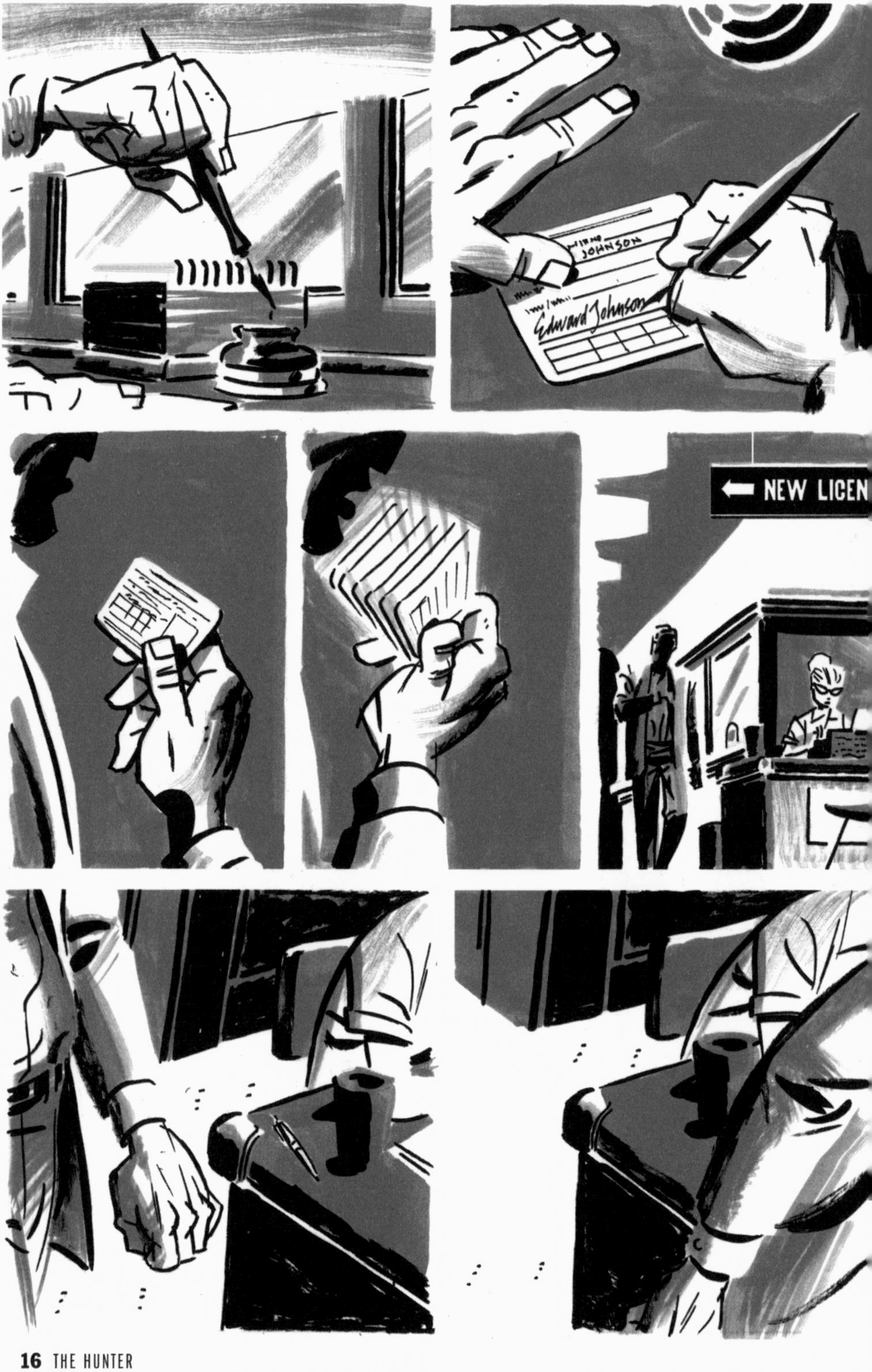
JOHNSON
Edward Johnson
NEW LICEN

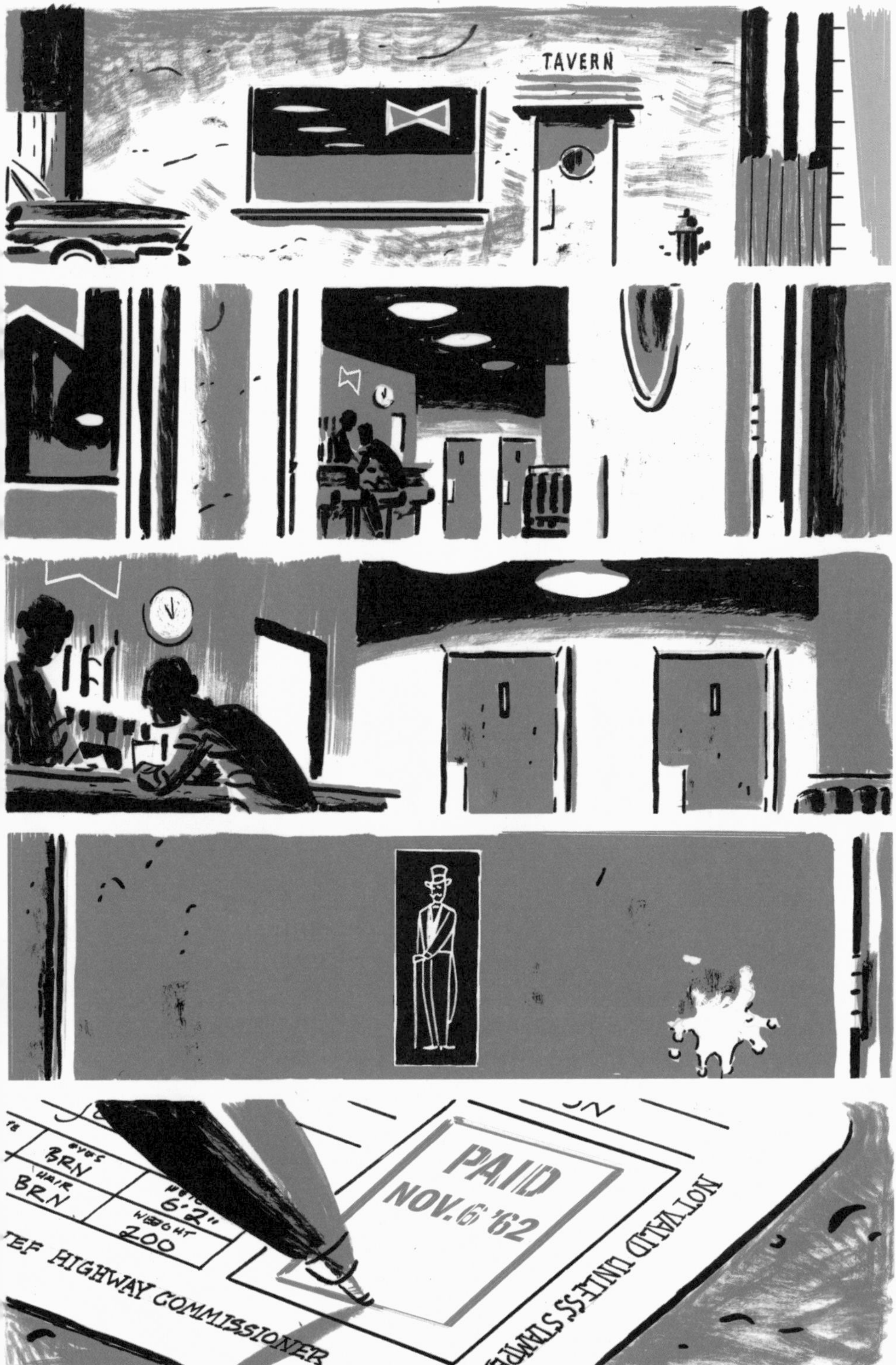

TAVERN
EYES
BRN
HAIR
BRN
6'2"
WEIGHT
200
PAID
NOV. 6 '62
NOT VALID UNLESS STAMPE
EF HIGHWAY COMMISSIONER

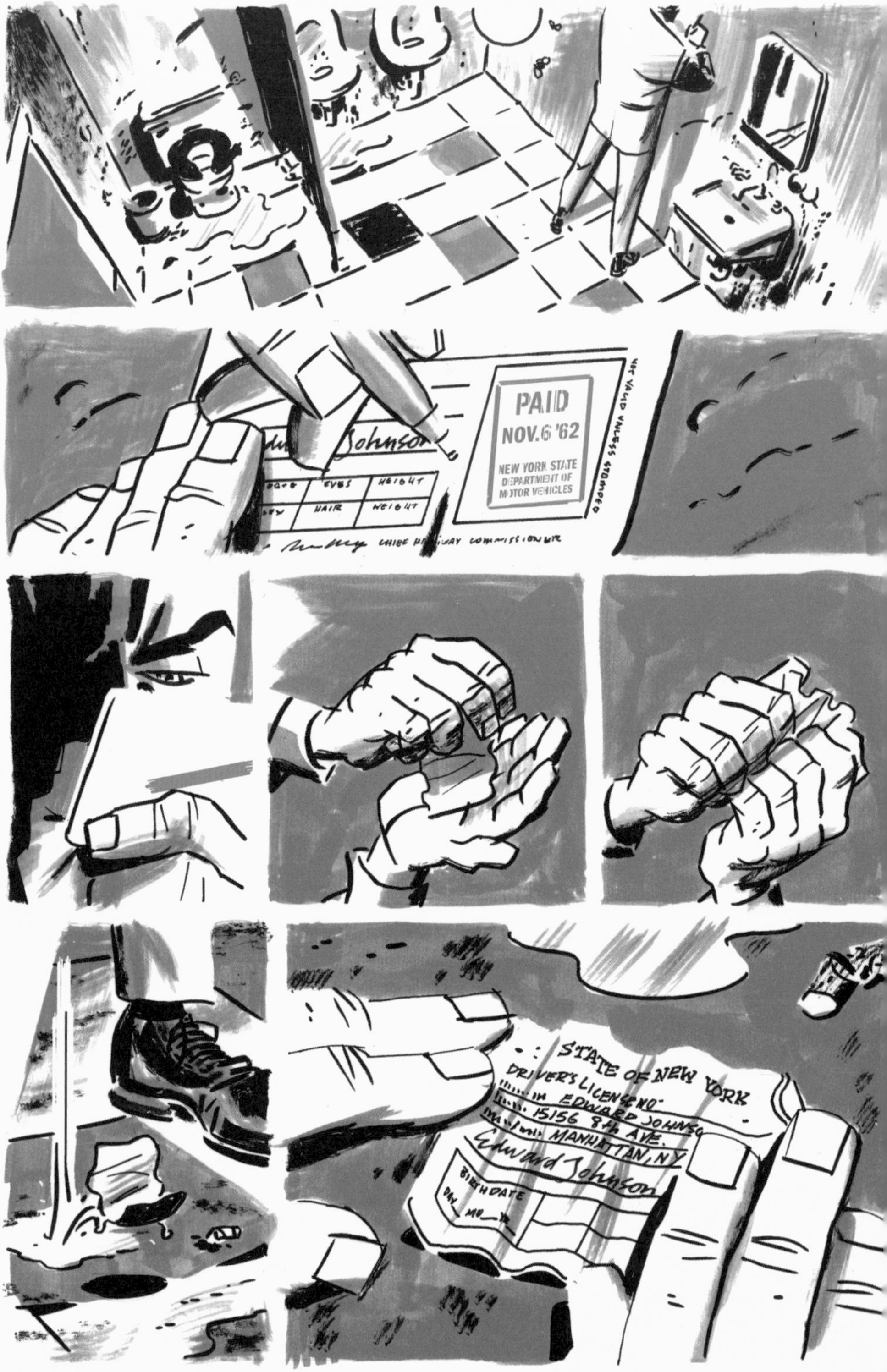
PAID
NOV.6 '62
NEW YORK STATE
DEPARTMENT OF
MOTOR VEHICLES
EYES
HEIGHT
HAIR
WEIGHT
STATE OF NEW YORK
DRIVER'S LICENSE NO
15156 8th AVE.
MANHATTAN, NY
Edward Johnson
BIRTHDATE

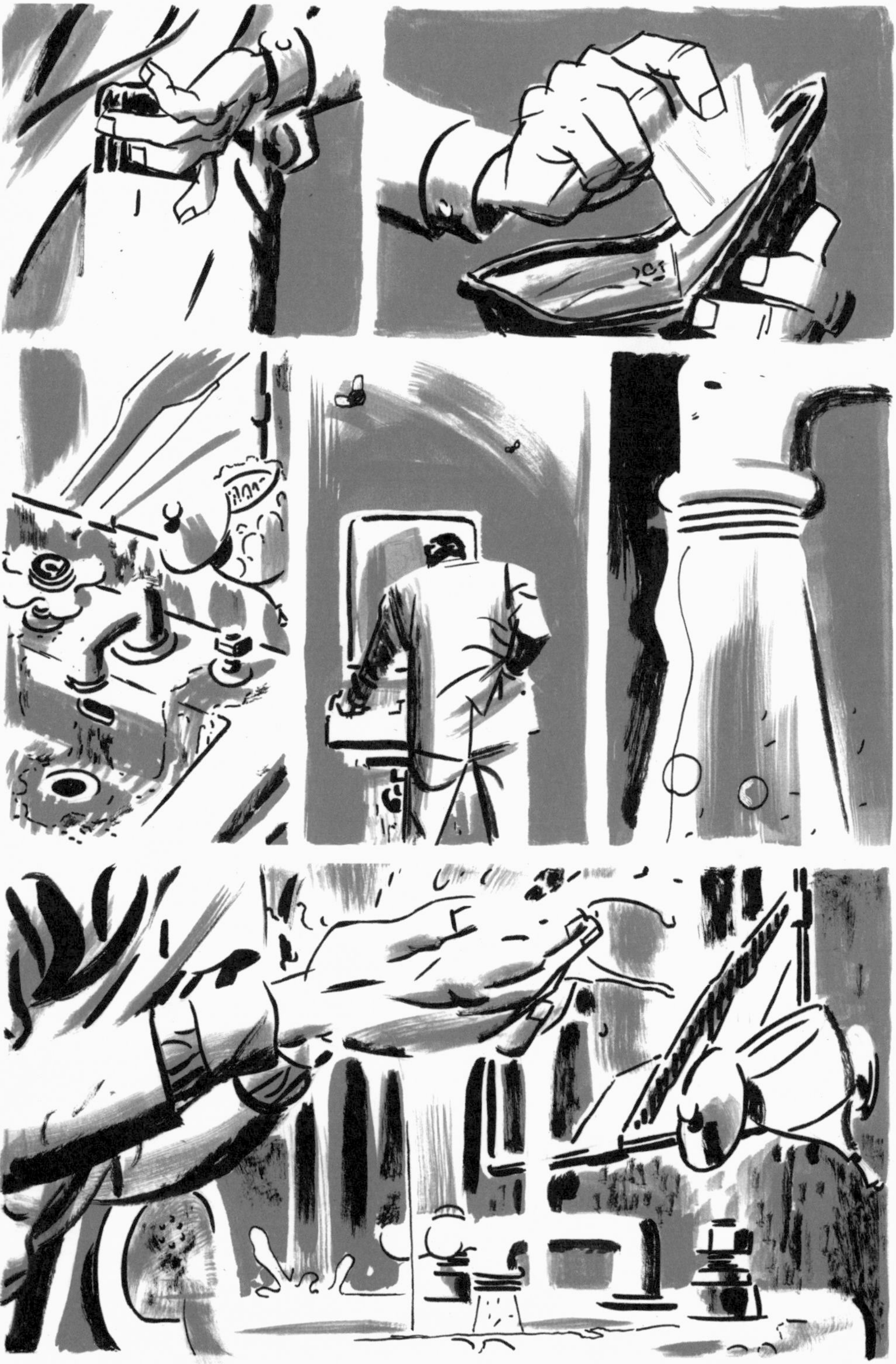

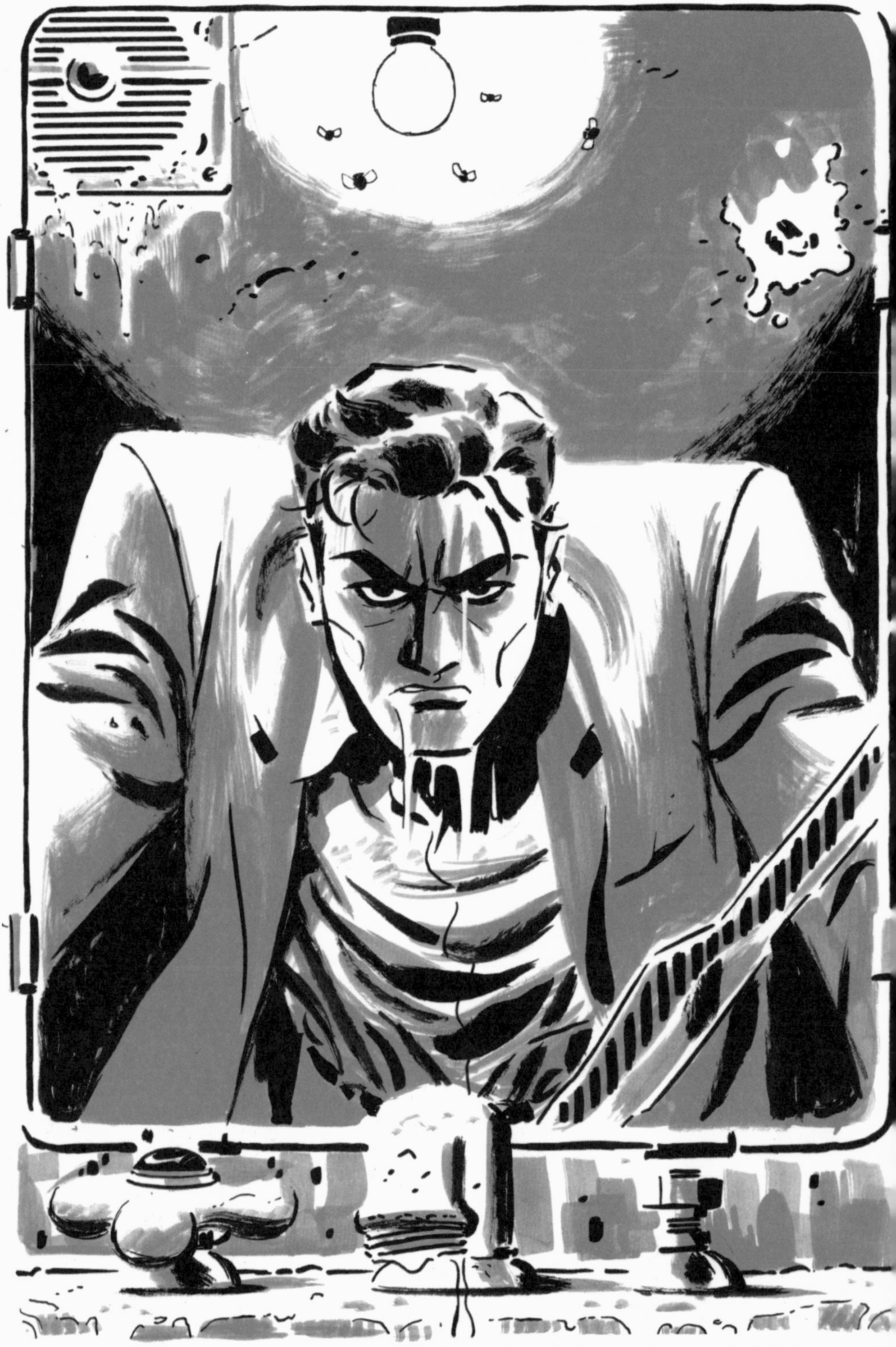

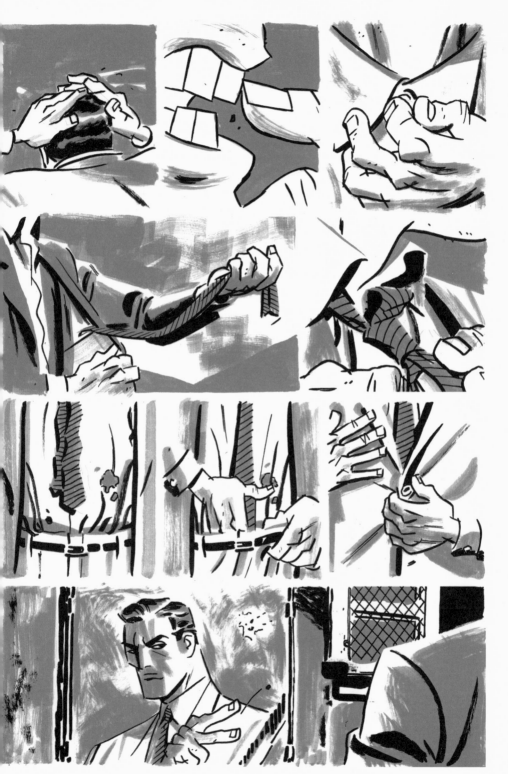

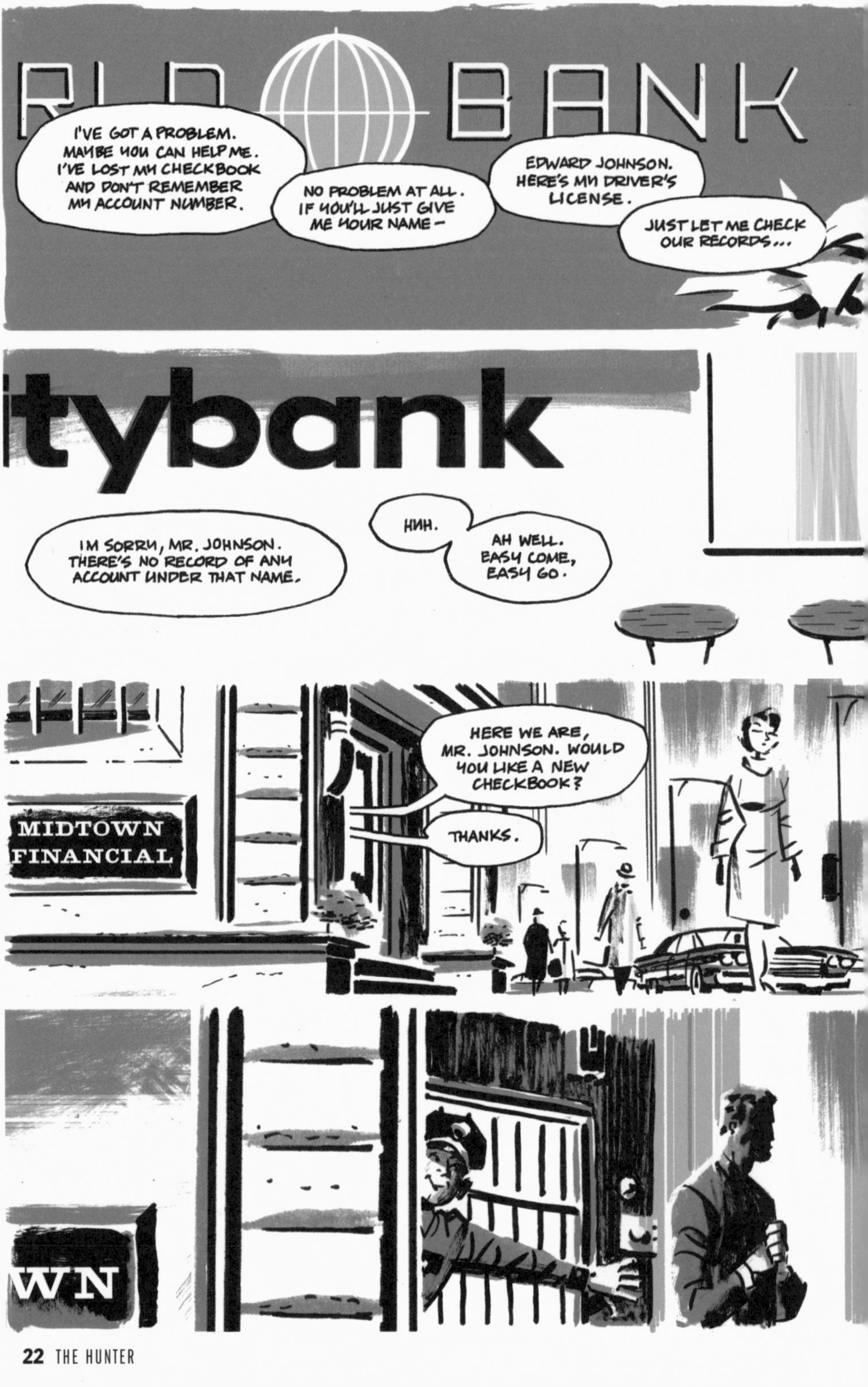

RLD BANK
I'VE GOT A PROBLEM. MAYBE YOU CAN HELP ME. I'VE LOST MY CHECKBOOK AND DON'T REMEMBER MY ACCOUNT NUMBER.
NO PROBLEM AT ALL. IF YOU'LL JUST GIVE ME YOUR NAME—
EDWARD JOHNSON. HERE'S MY DRIVER'S LICENSE.
JUST LET ME CHECK OUR RECORDS...
itybank
IM SORRY, MR. JOHNSON. THERE'S NO RECORD OF ANY ACCOUNT UNDER THAT NAME.
HUH.
AH WELL. EASY COME, EASY GO.
MIDTOWN FINANCIAL
HERE WE ARE, MR. JOHNSON. WOULD YOU LIKE A NEW CHECKBOOK?
THANKS.
WN

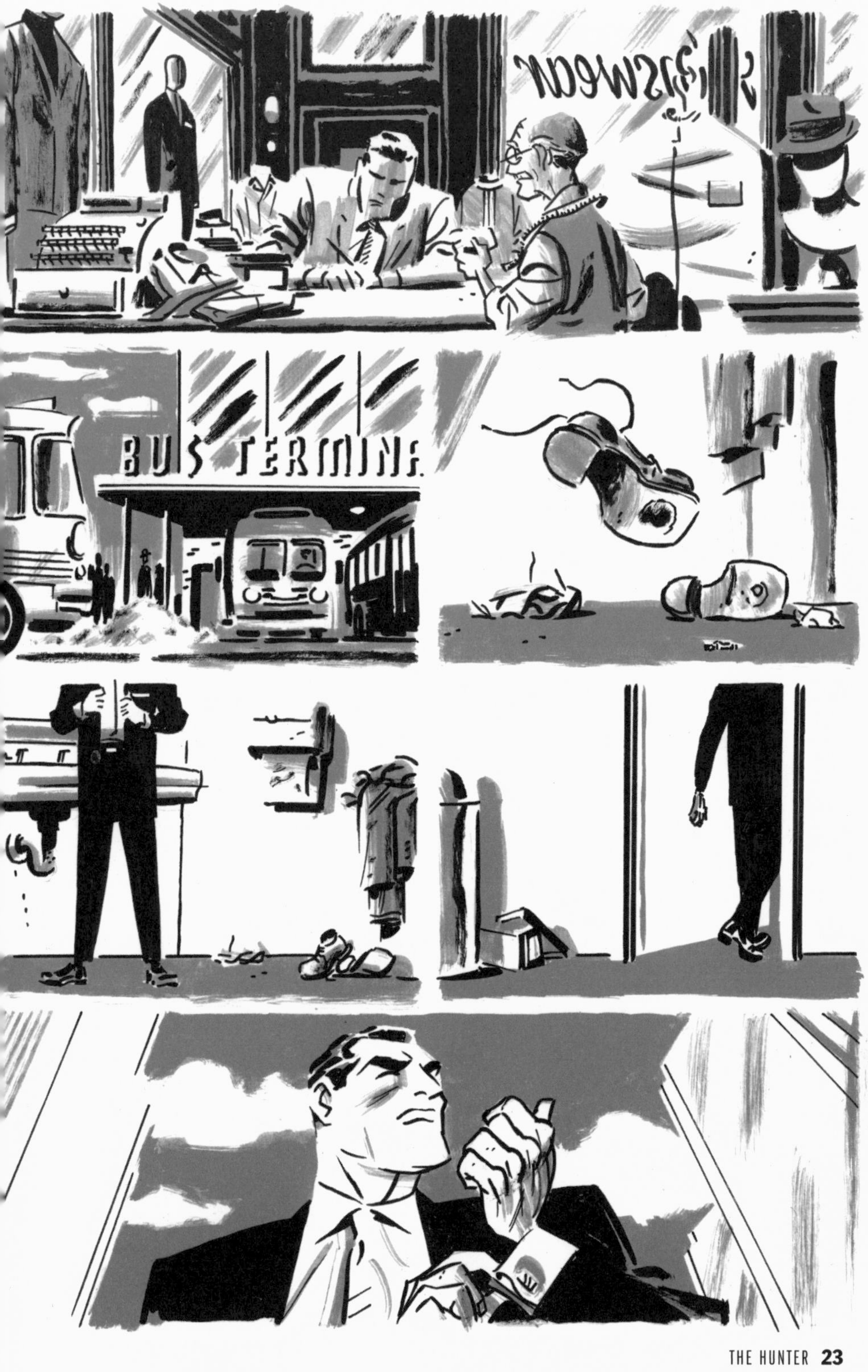
BUS TERMINA

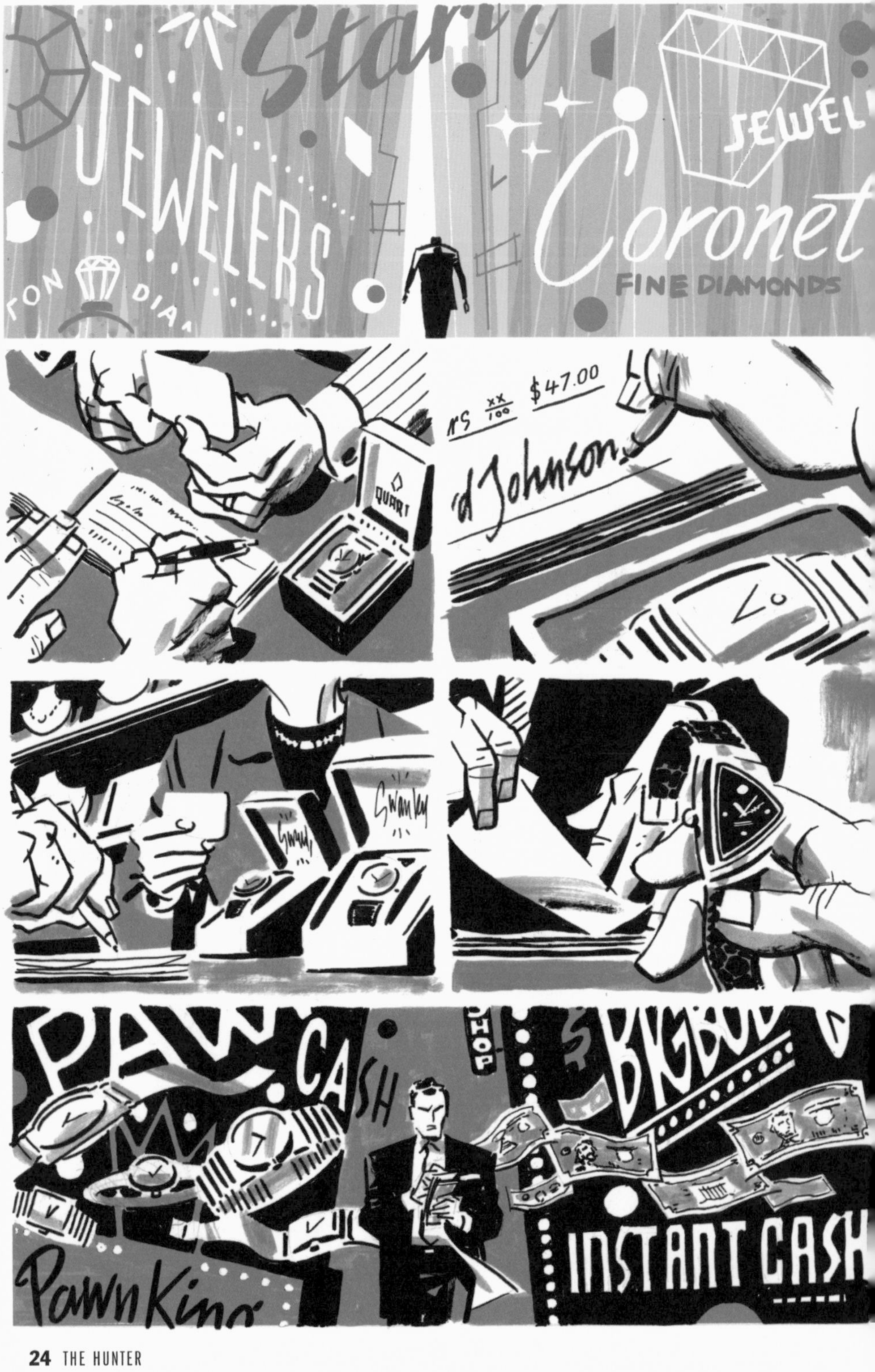
JEWELERS
Coronet
FINE DIAMONDS
$47.00
Johnson
CASH
SHOP
INSTANT CASH

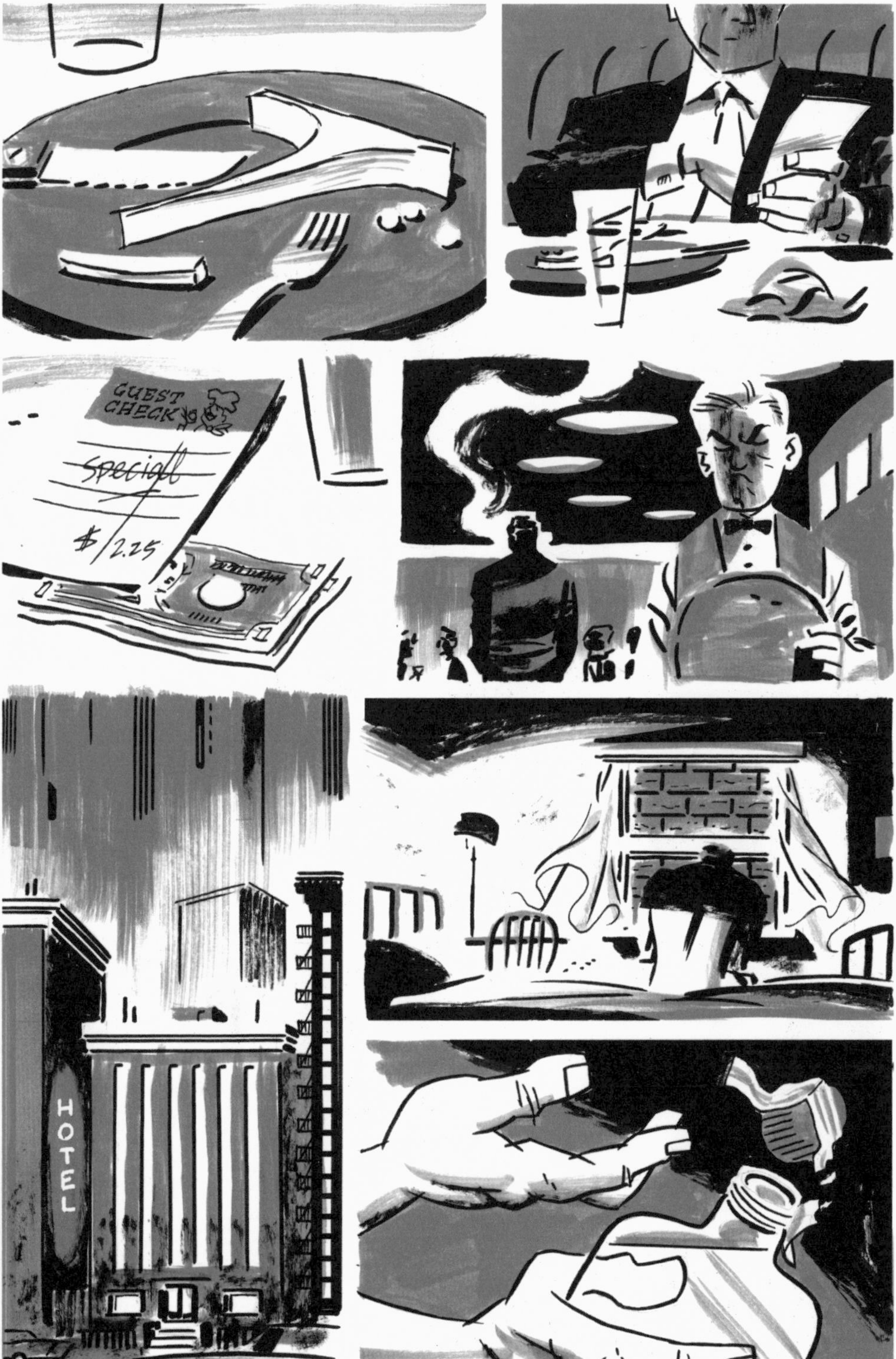
GUEST CHECK
special
$2.25
HOTEL

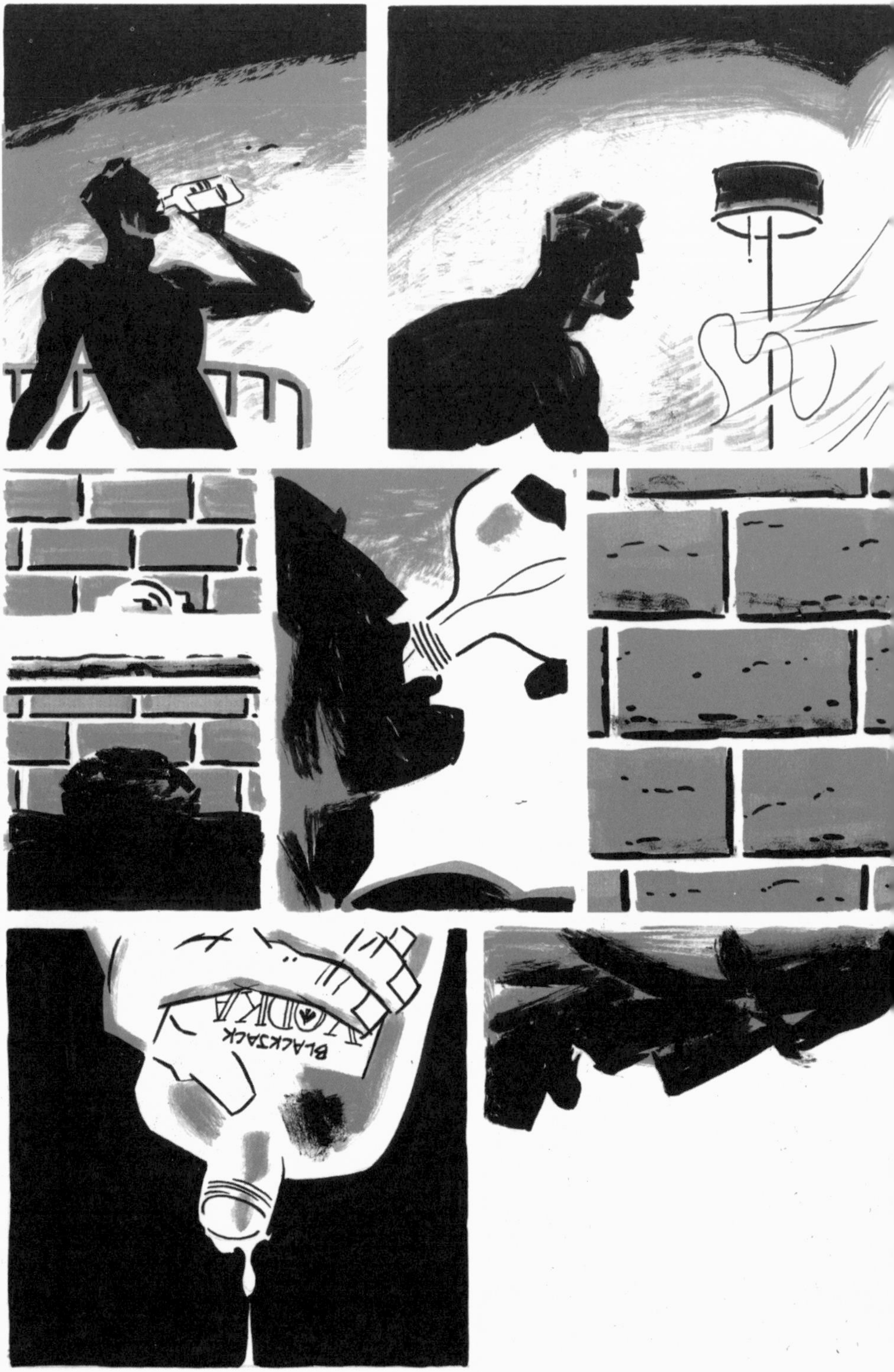
BLACKJACK
VODKA

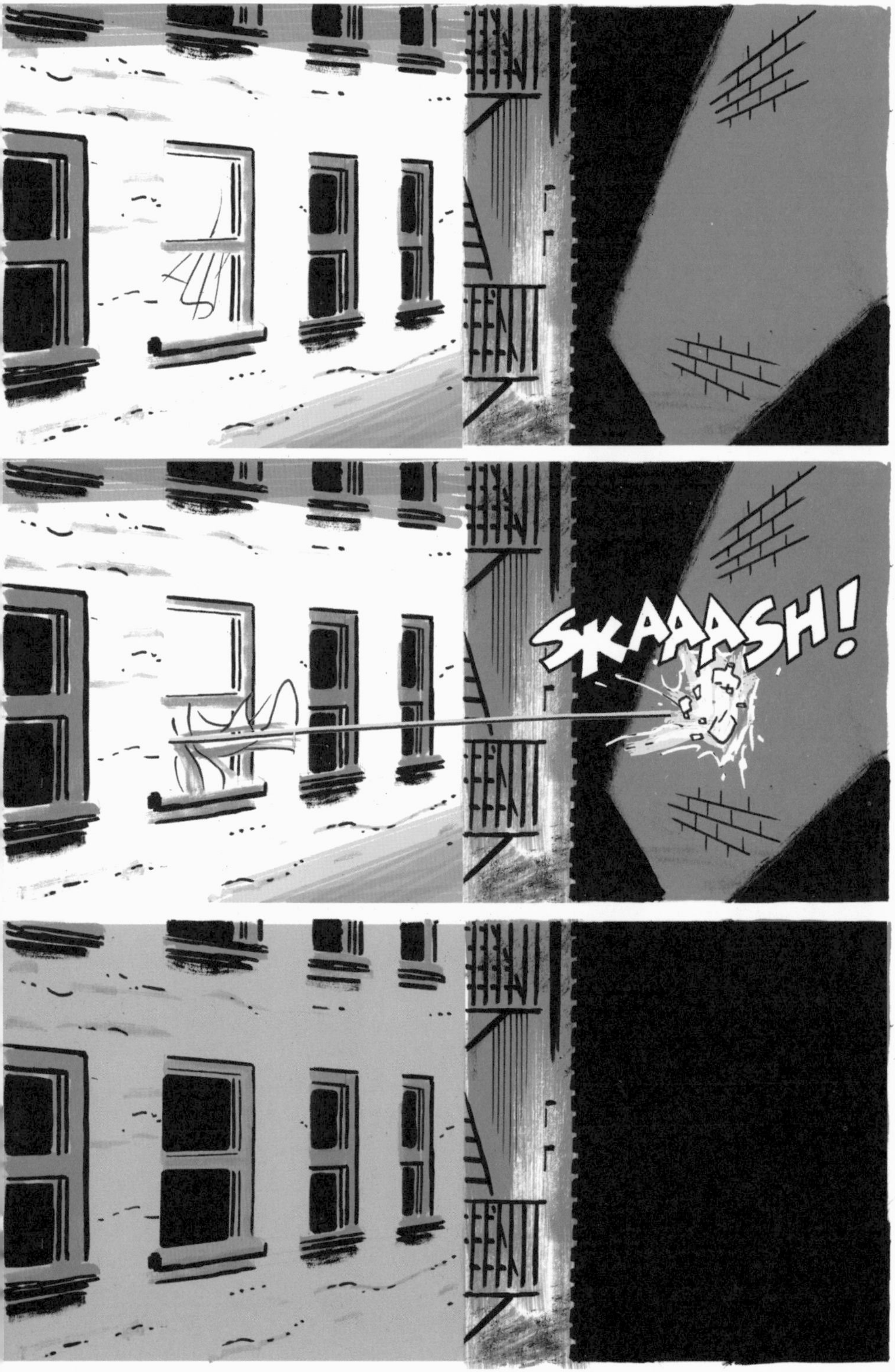
SKAAASH!

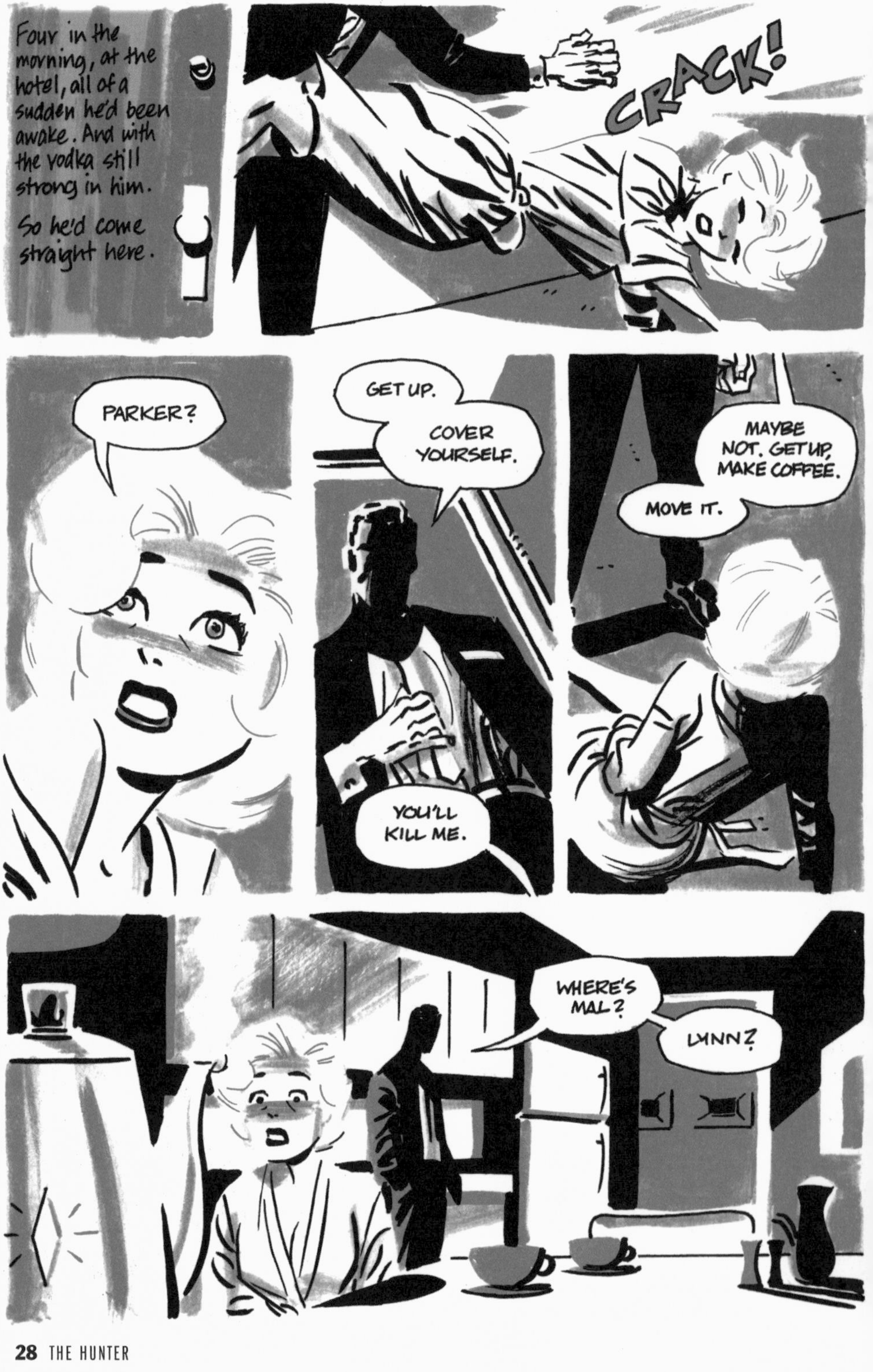
Four in the morning, at the hotel, all of a sudden he'd been awake. And with the vodka still strong in him.
So he'd come straight here.
CRACK!
PARKER?
GET UP.
COVER YOURSELF.
YOU'LL KILL ME.
MAYBE NOT. GET UP, MAKE COFFEE.
MOVE IT.
WHERE'S MAL?
LYNN?

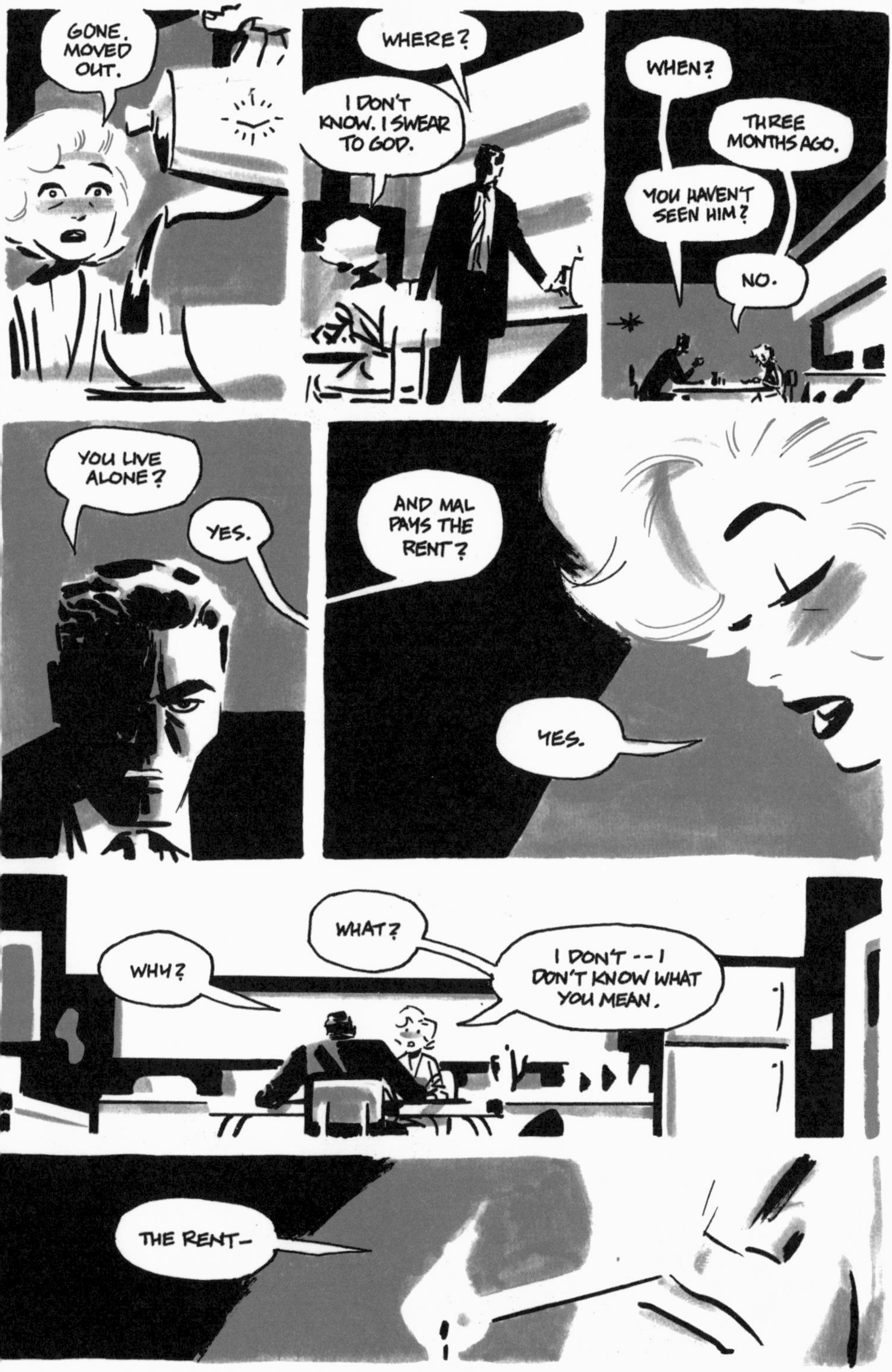
GONE. MOVED OUT.
WHERE?
I DON'T KNOW. I SWEAR TO GOD.
WHEN?
THREE MONTHS AGO.
YOU HAVEN'T SEEN HIM?
NO.
YOU LIVE ALONE?
YES.
AND MAL PAYS THE RENT?
YES.
WHY?
WHAT?
I DON'T -- I DON'T KNOW WHAT YOU MEAN.
THE RENT-

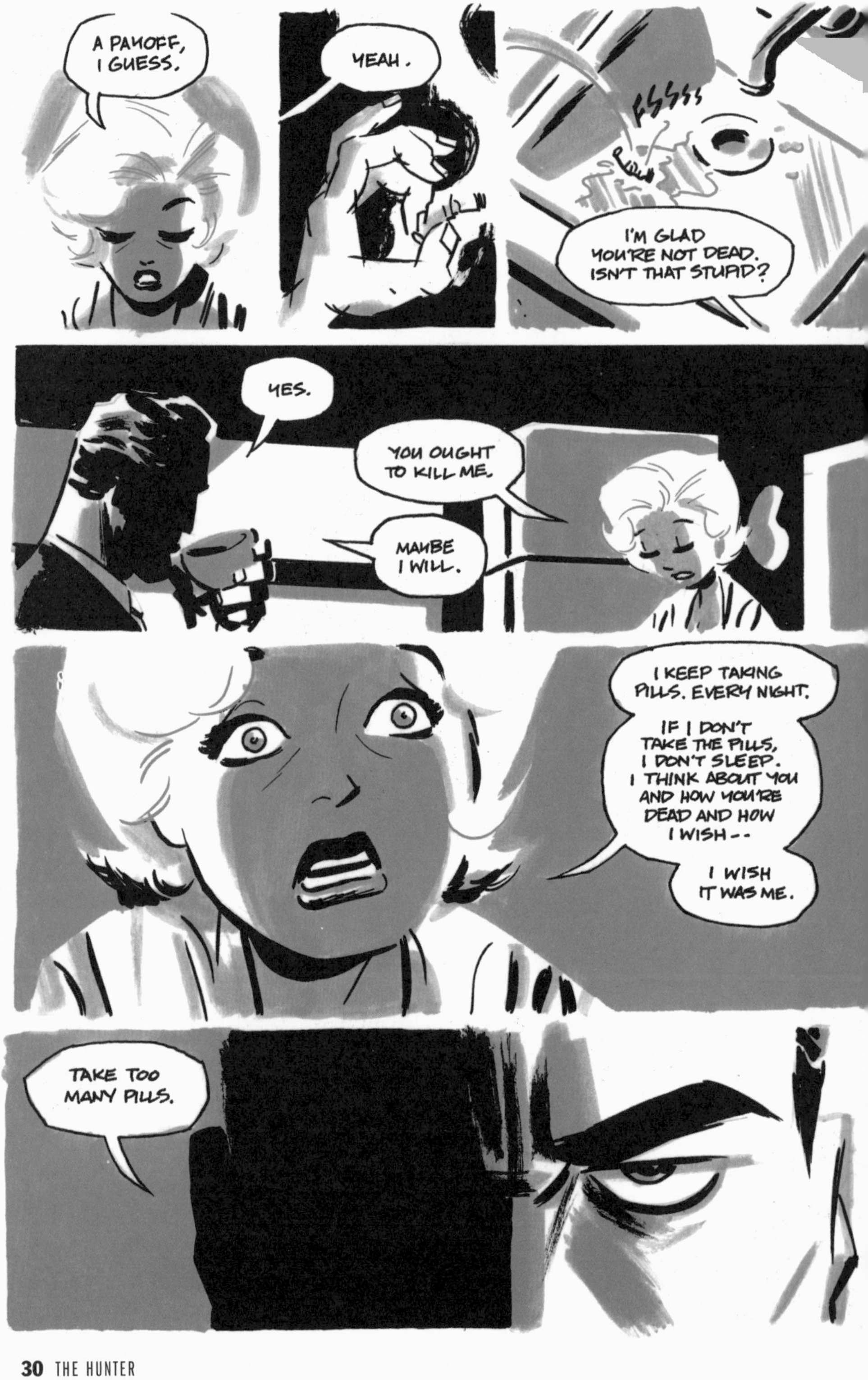
A PAYOFF, I GUESS.
YEAH.
FSSSS
I'M GLAD YOU'RE NOT DEAD. ISN'T THAT STUPID?
YES.
YOU OUGHT TO KILL ME.
MAYBE I WILL.
I KEEP TAKING PILLS. EVERY NIGHT.
IF I DON'T TAKE THE PILLS, I DON'T SLEEP. I THINK ABOUT YOU AND HOW YOU'RE DEAD AND HOW I WISH--
I WISH IT WAS ME.
TAKE TOO MANY PILLS.

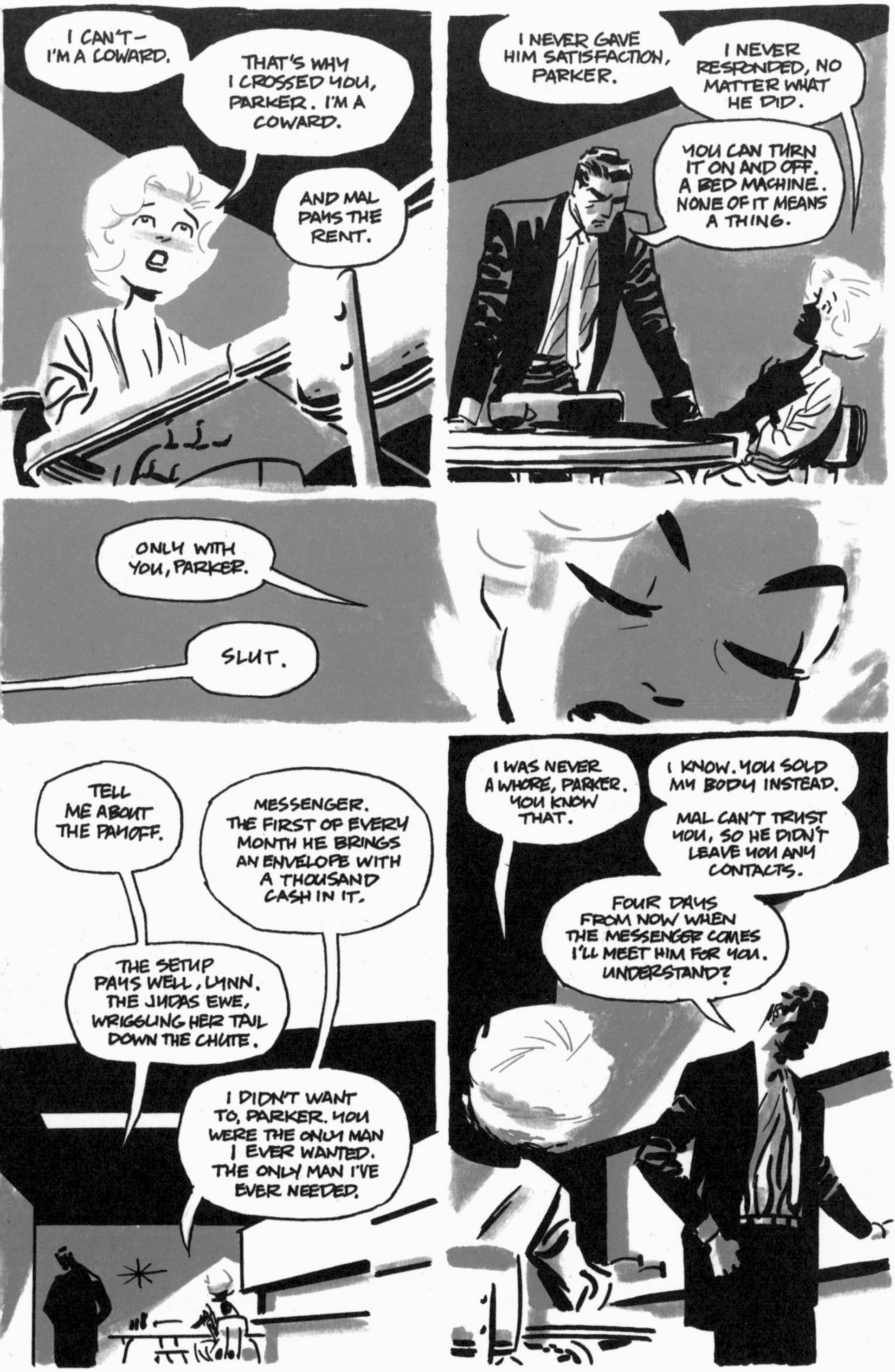
I CAN'T— I'M A COWARD.
THAT'S WHY I CROSSED YOU, PARKER. I'M A COWARD.
AND MAL PAYS THE RENT.
I NEVER GAVE HIM SATISFACTION, PARKER.
I NEVER RESPONDED, NO MATTER WHAT HE DID.
YOU CAN TURN IT ON AND OFF. A BED MACHINE. NONE OF IT MEANS A THING.
ONLY WITH YOU, PARKER.
SLUT.
TELL ME ABOUT THE PAYOFF.
MESSENGER. THE FIRST OF EVERY MONTH HE BRINGS AN ENVELOPE WITH A THOUSAND CASH IN IT.
THE SETUP PAYS WELL, LYNN. THE JUDAS EWE, WRIGGLING HER TAIL DOWN THE CHUTE.
I DIDN'T WANT TO, PARKER. YOU WERE THE ONLY MAN I EVER WANTED. THE ONLY MAN I'VE EVER NEEDED.
I WAS NEVER A WHORE, PARKER. YOU KNOW THAT.
I KNOW. YOU SOLD MY BODY INSTEAD.
MAL CAN'T TRUST YOU, SO HE DIDN'T LEAVE YOU ANY CONTACTS.
FOUR DAYS FROM NOW WHEN THE MESSENGER COMES I'LL MEET HIM FOR YOU. UNDERSTAND?

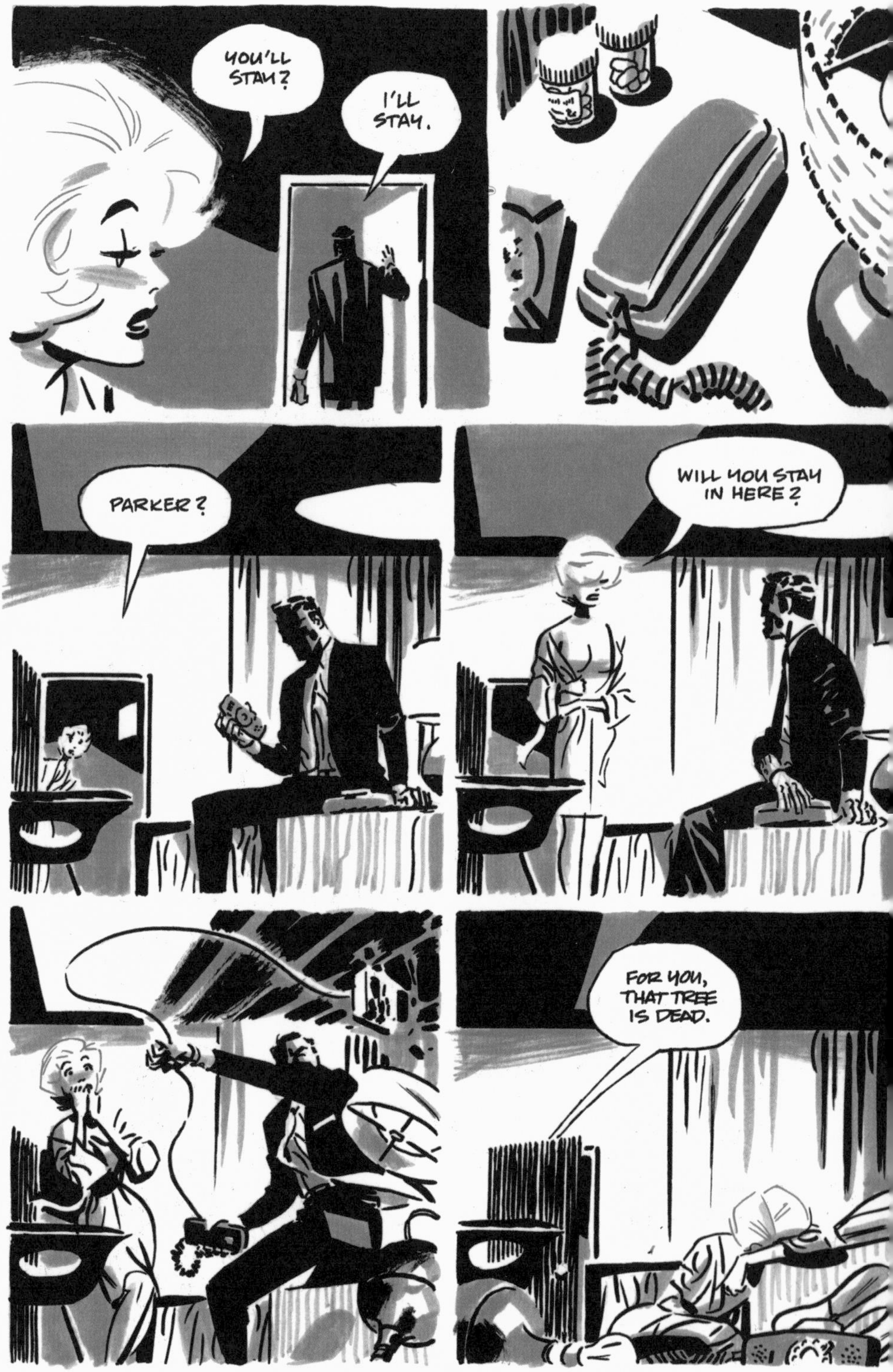
YOU'LL STAY?
I'LL STAY.
PARKER?
WILL YOU STAY IN HERE?
FOR YOU, THAT TREE IS DEAD.

He lied to her.

The tree wasn't dead.

He was afraid of her.

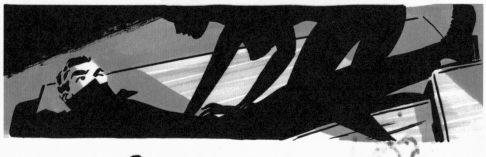

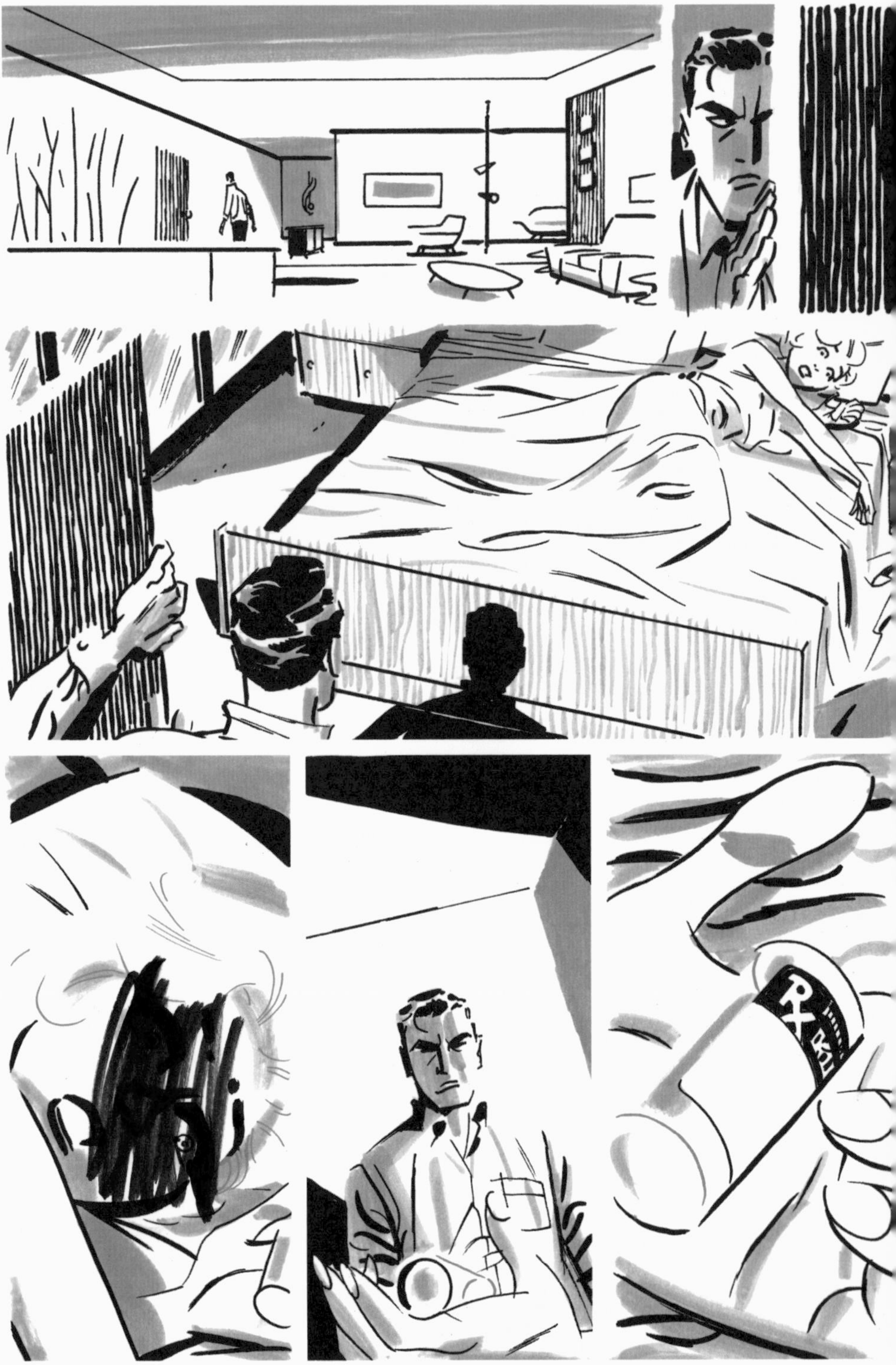

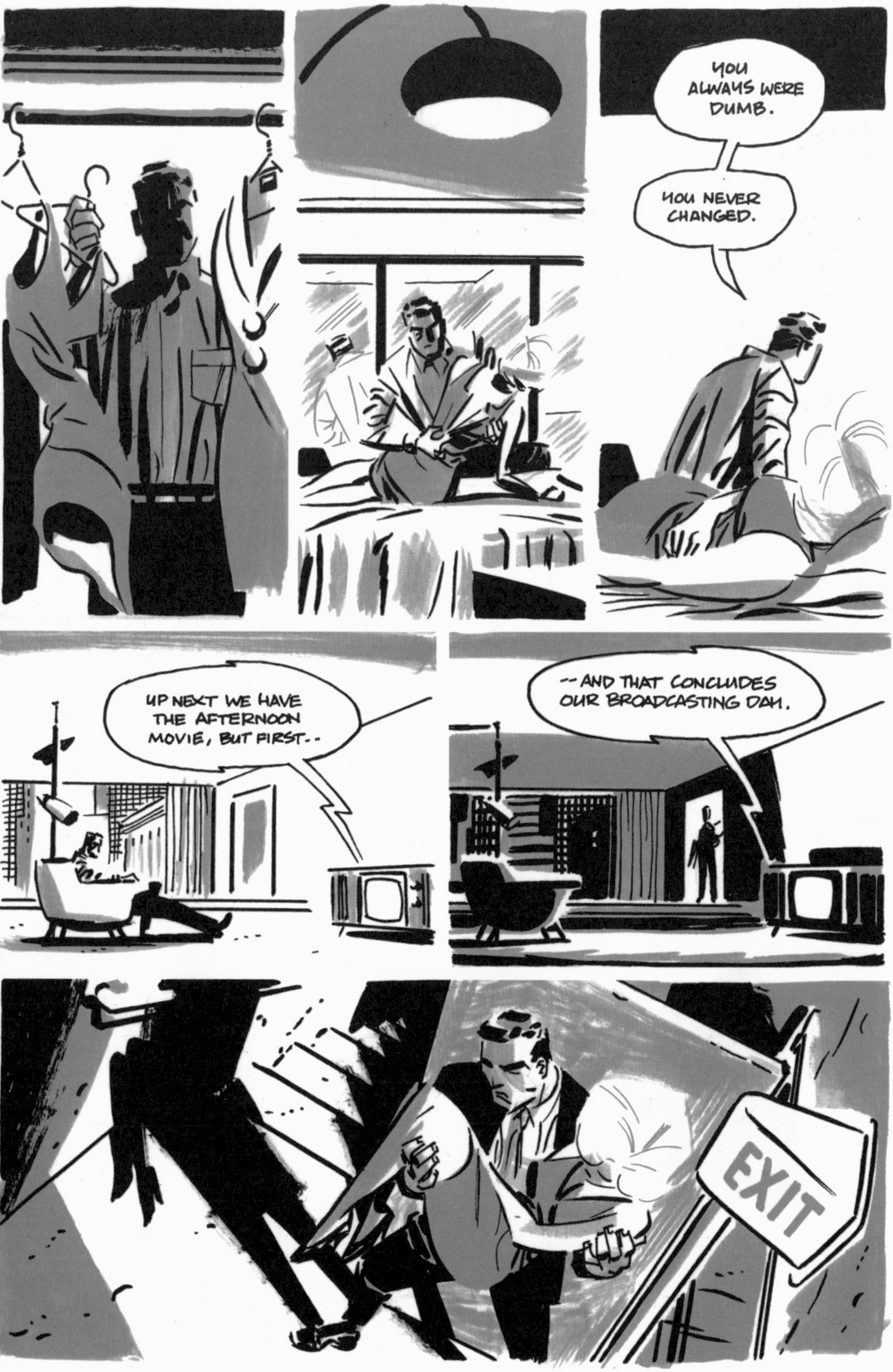
YOU ALWAYS WERE DUMB.
YOU NEVER CHANGED.
UP NEXT WE HAVE THE AFTERNOON MOVIE, BUT FIRST--
--AND THAT CONCLUDES OUR BROADCASTING DAY.
EXIT

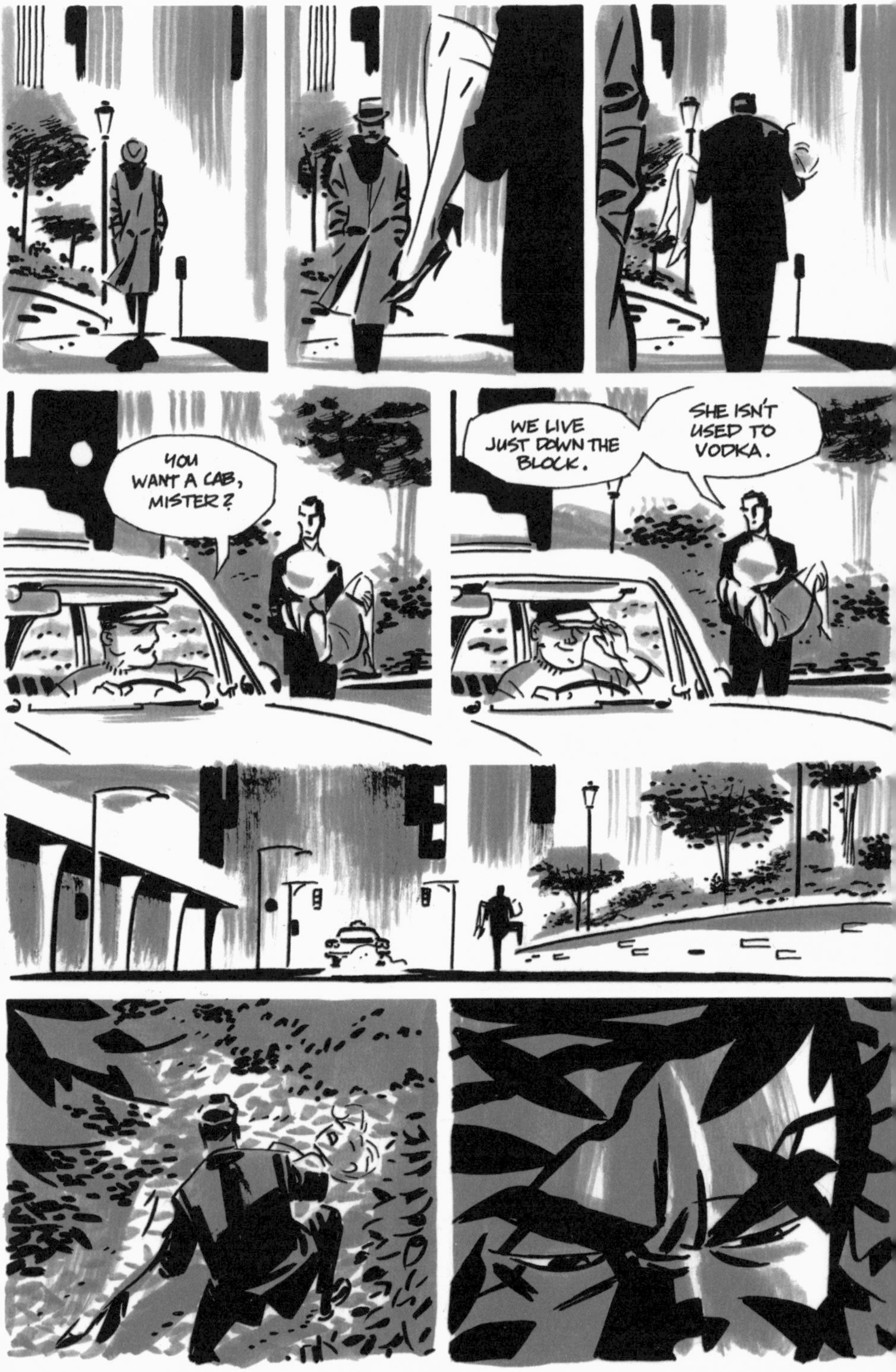
YOU WANT A CAB, MISTER?
WE LIVE JUST DOWN THE BLOCK.
SHE ISN'T USED TO VODKA.

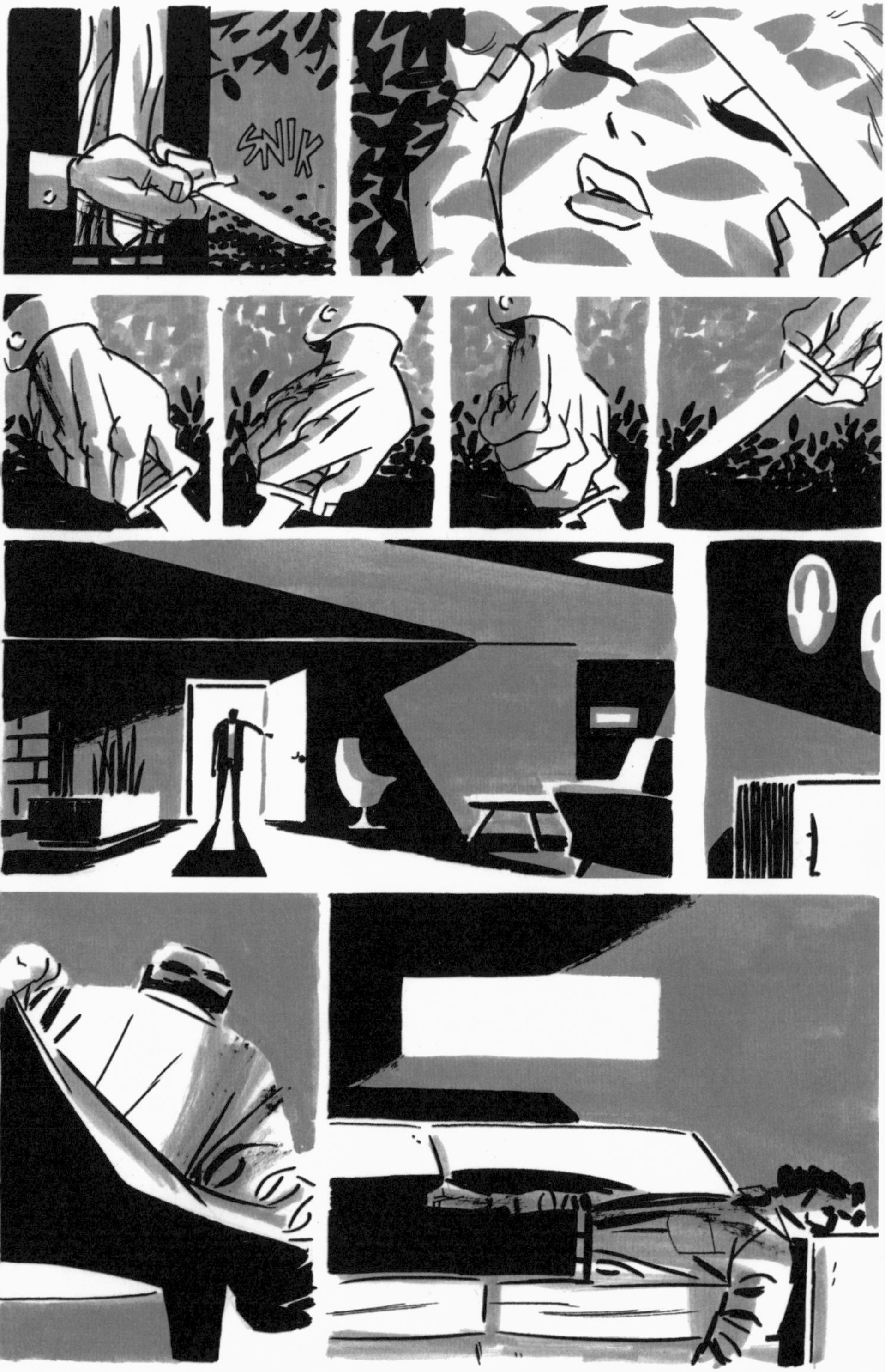
SNIK

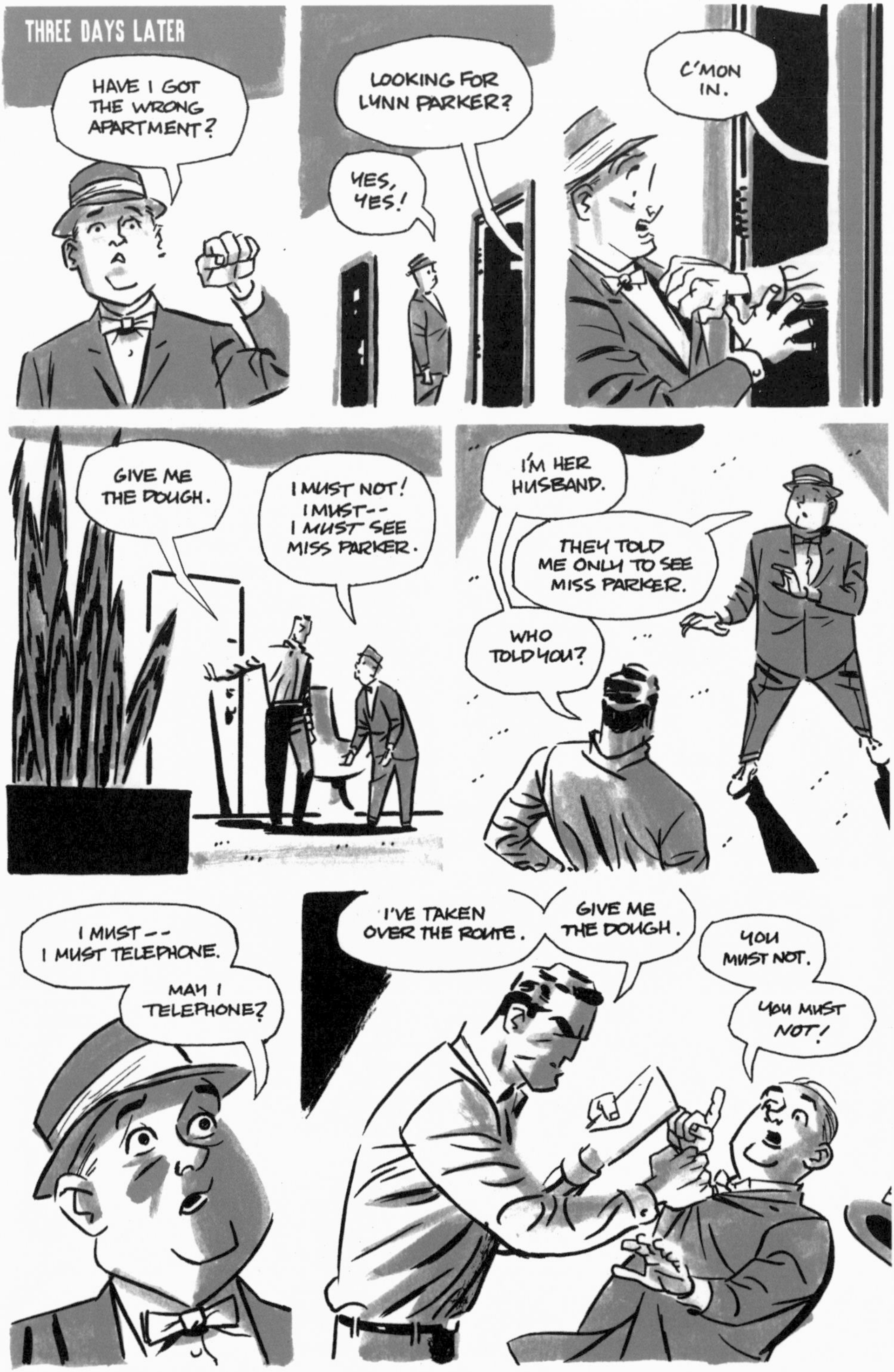
THREE DAYS LATER
HAVE I GOT THE WRONG APARTMENT?
LOOKING FOR LYNN PARKER?
YES, YES!
C'MON IN.
GIVE ME THE DOUGH.
I MUST NOT! I MUST-- I MUST SEE MISS PARKER.
I'M HER HUSBAND.
THEY TOLD ME ONLY TO SEE MISS PARKER.
WHO TOLD YOU?
I MUST-- I MUST TELEPHONE.
MAY I TELEPHONE?
I'VE TAKEN OVER THE ROUTE.
GIVE ME THE DOUGH.
YOU MUST NOT.
YOU MUST NOT!

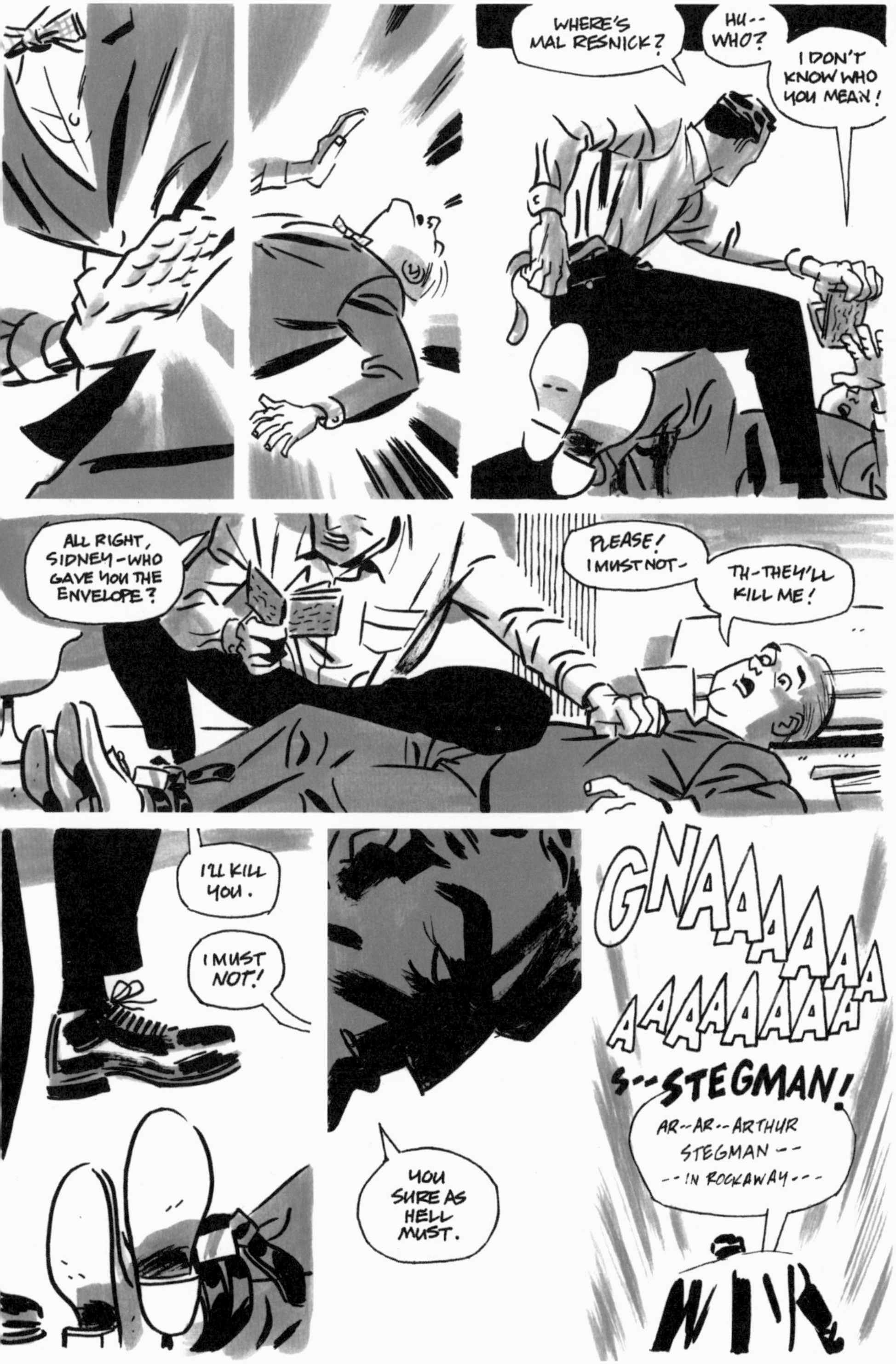
WHERE'S MAL RESNICK?
HU-- WHO?
I DON'T KNOW WHO YOU MEAN!
ALL RIGHT, SIDNEY--WHO GAVE YOU THE ENVELOPE?
PLEASE! I MUST NOT-
TH-THEY'LL KILL ME!
I'LL KILL YOU.
I MUST NOT!
YOU SURE AS HELL MUST.
GNAAAAAAAAAAAAAAAA
S--STEGMAN!
AR--AR--ARTHUR STEGMAN-- --IN ROCKAWAY---

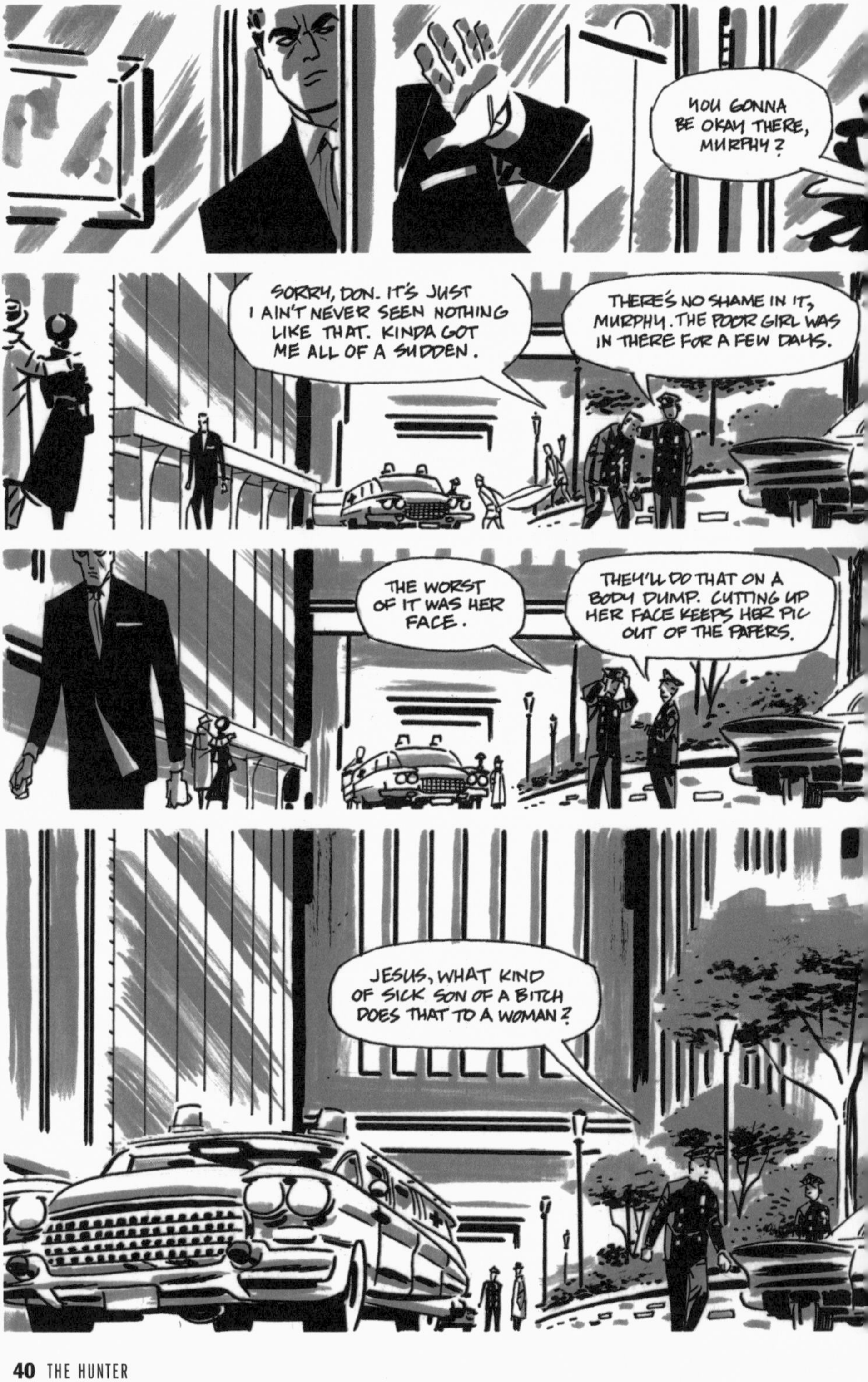

YOU GONNA BE OKAY THERE, MURPHY?
SORRY, DON. IT'S JUST I AIN'T NEVER SEEN NOTHING LIKE THAT. KINDA GOT ME ALL OF A SUDDEN.
THERE'S NO SHAME IN IT, MURPHY. THE POOR GIRL WAS IN THERE FOR A FEW DAYS.
THE WORST OF IT WAS HER FACE.
THEY'LL DO THAT ON A BODY DUMP. CUTTING UP HER FACE KEEPS HER PIC OUT OF THE PAPERS.
JESUS, WHAT KIND OF SICK SON OF A BITCH DOES THAT TO A WOMAN?

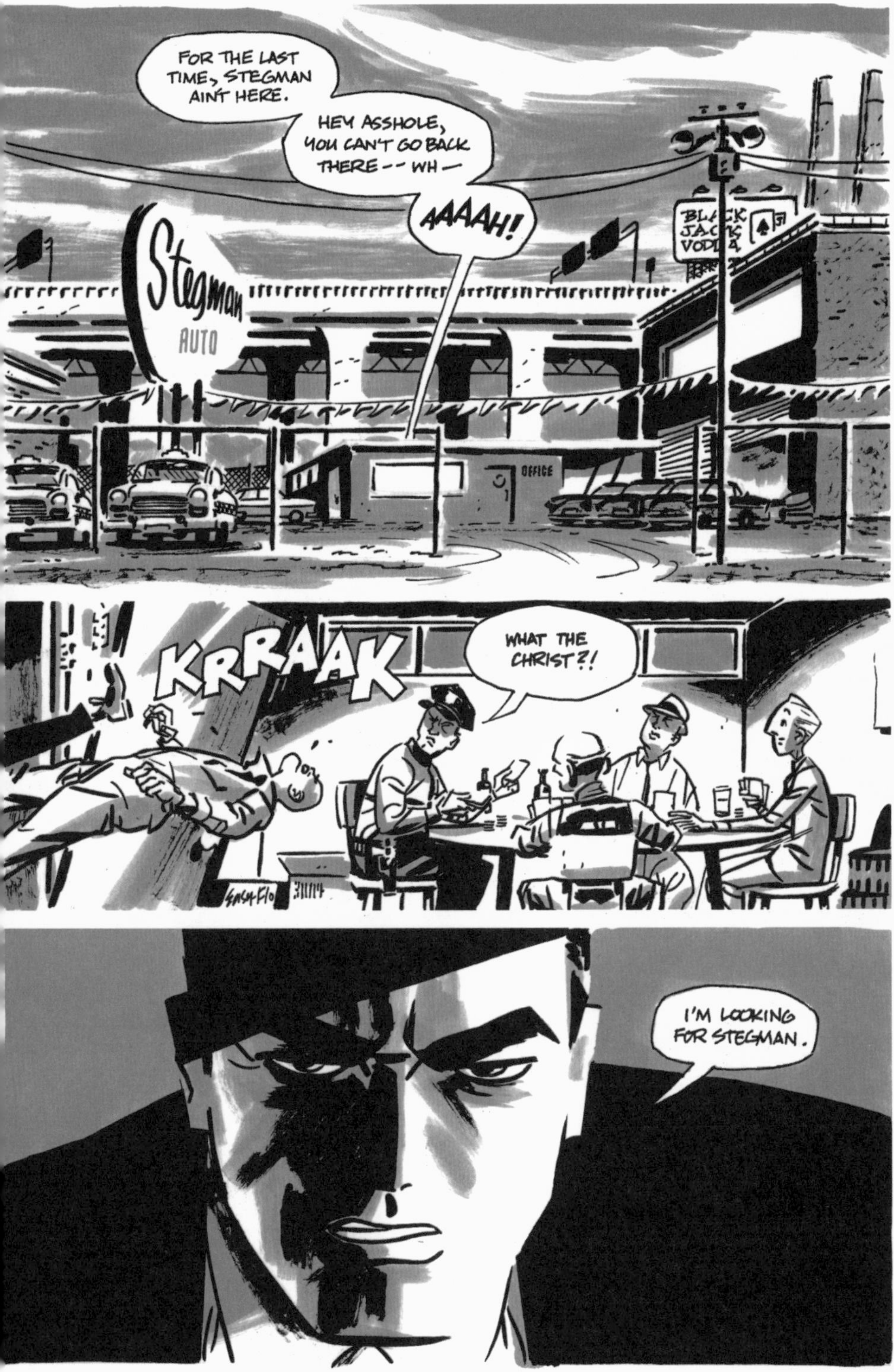
FOR THE LAST TIME, STEGMAN AIN'T HERE.
HEY ASSHOLE, YOU CAN'T GO BACK THERE -- WH—
AAAAH!
Stegman
AUTO
OFFICE
KRRAAK
WHAT THE CHRIST?!
I'M LOOKING FOR STEGMAN.

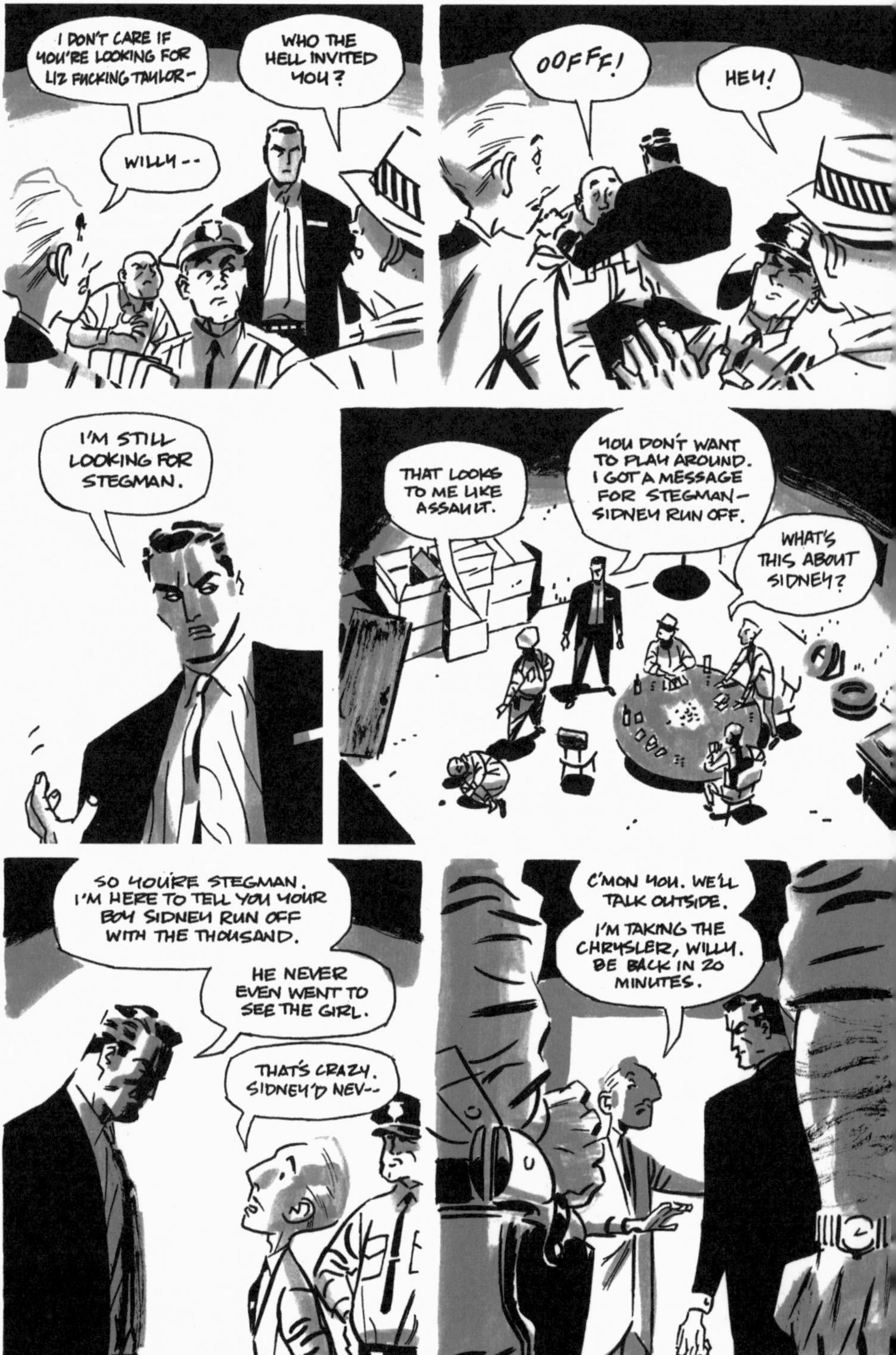
I DON'T CARE IF YOU'RE LOOKING FOR LIZ FUCKING TAYLOR-
WILLY--
WHO THE HELL INVITED YOU?
OOFFF!
HEY!
I'M STILL LOOKING FOR STEGMAN.
THAT LOOKS TO ME LIKE ASSAULT.
YOU DON'T WANT TO PLAY AROUND. I GOT A MESSAGE FOR STEGMAN- SIDNEY RUN OFF.
WHAT'S THIS ABOUT SIDNEY?
SO YOU'RE STEGMAN. I'M HERE TO TELL YOU YOUR BOY SIDNEY RUN OFF WITH THE THOUSAND.
HE NEVER EVEN WENT TO SEE THE GIRL.
THAT'S CRAZY. SIDNEY'D NEV--
C'MON YOU. WE'LL TALK OUTSIDE.
I'M TAKING THE CHRYSLER, WILLY. BE BACK IN 20 MINUTES.

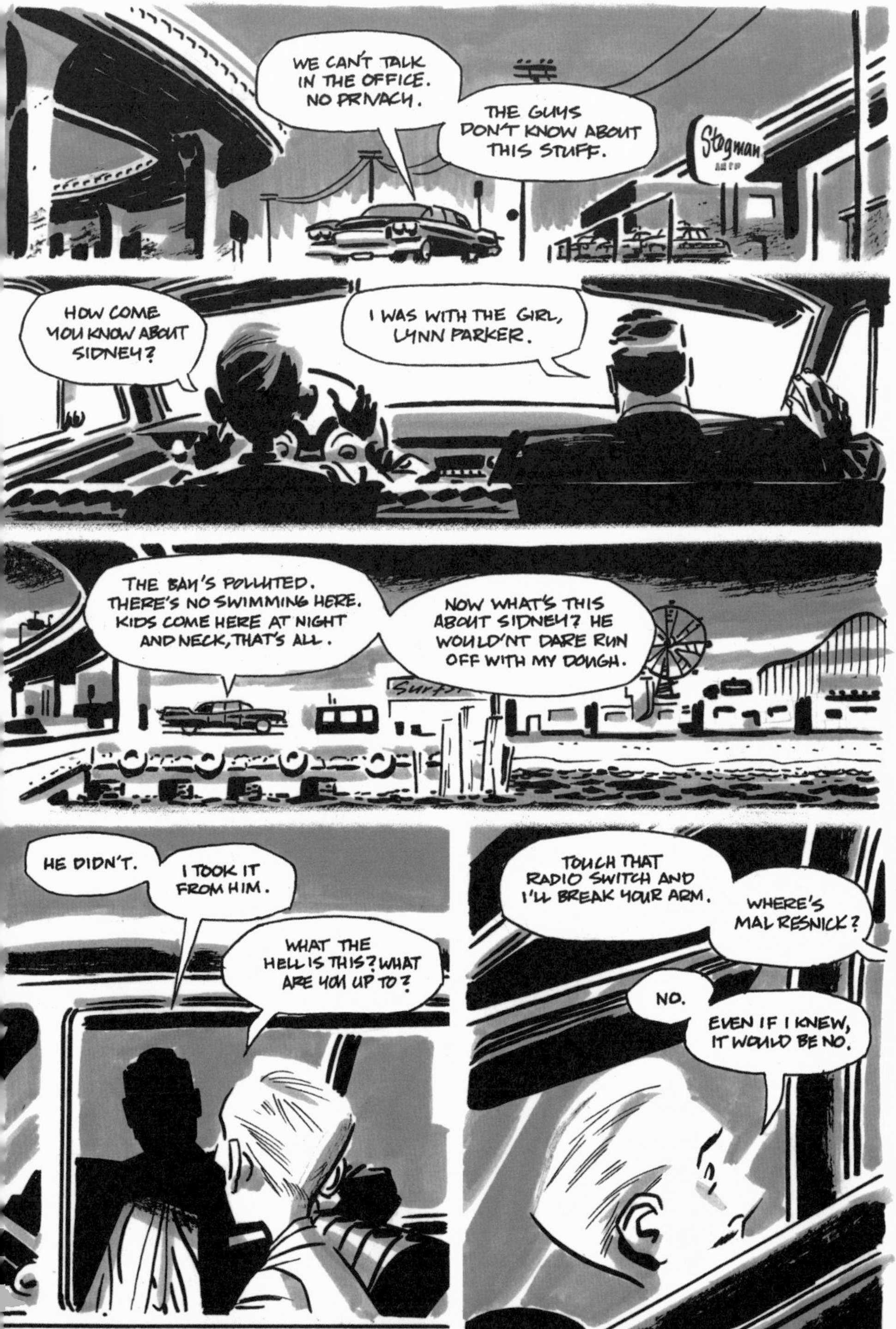
WE CAN'T TALK IN THE OFFICE. NO PRIVACY.
THE GUYS DON'T KNOW ABOUT THIS STUFF.
Stegman
HOW COME YOU KNOW ABOUT SIDNEY?
I WAS WITH THE GIRL, LYNN PARKER.
THE BAY'S POLLUTED. THERE'S NO SWIMMING HERE. KIDS COME HERE AT NIGHT AND NECK, THAT'S ALL.
NOW WHAT'S THIS ABOUT SIDNEY? HE WOULD'NT DARE RUN OFF WITH MY DOUGH.
HE DIDN'T.
I TOOK IT FROM HIM.
WHAT THE HELL IS THIS? WHAT ARE YOU UP TO?
TOUCH THAT RADIO SWITCH AND I'LL BREAK YOUR ARM.
WHERE'S MAL RESNICK?
NO.
EVEN IF I KNEW, IT WOULD BE NO.

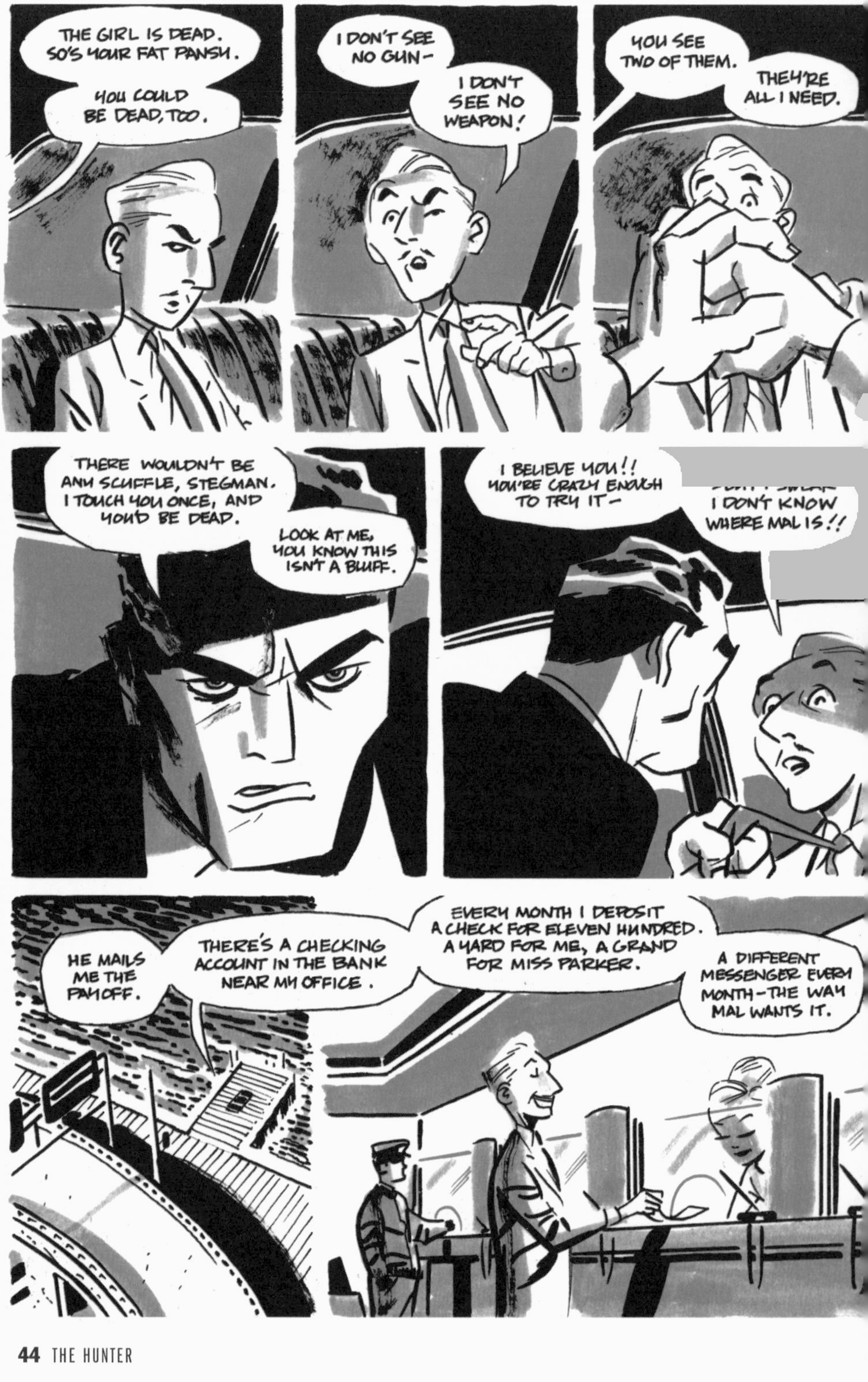
THE GIRL IS DEAD. SO'S YOUR FAT PANSY.
YOU COULD BE DEAD, TOO.
I DON'T SEE NO GUN-
I DON'T SEE NO WEAPON!
YOU SEE TWO OF THEM.
THEY'RE ALL I NEED.
THERE WOULDN'T BE ANY SCUFFLE, STEGMAN. I TOUCH YOU ONCE, AND YOU'D BE DEAD.
LOOK AT ME, YOU KNOW THIS ISN'T A BLUFF.
I BELIEVE YOU!! YOU'RE CRAZY ENOUGH TO TRY IT-
I DON'T KNOW WHERE MAL IS!!
HE MAILS ME THE PAYOFF.
THERE'S A CHECKING ACCOUNT IN THE BANK NEAR MY OFFICE.
EVERY MONTH I DEPOSIT A CHECK FOR ELEVEN HUNDRED. A YARD FOR ME, A GRAND FOR MISS PARKER.
A DIFFERENT MESSENGER EVERY MONTH-THE WAY MAL WANTS IT.

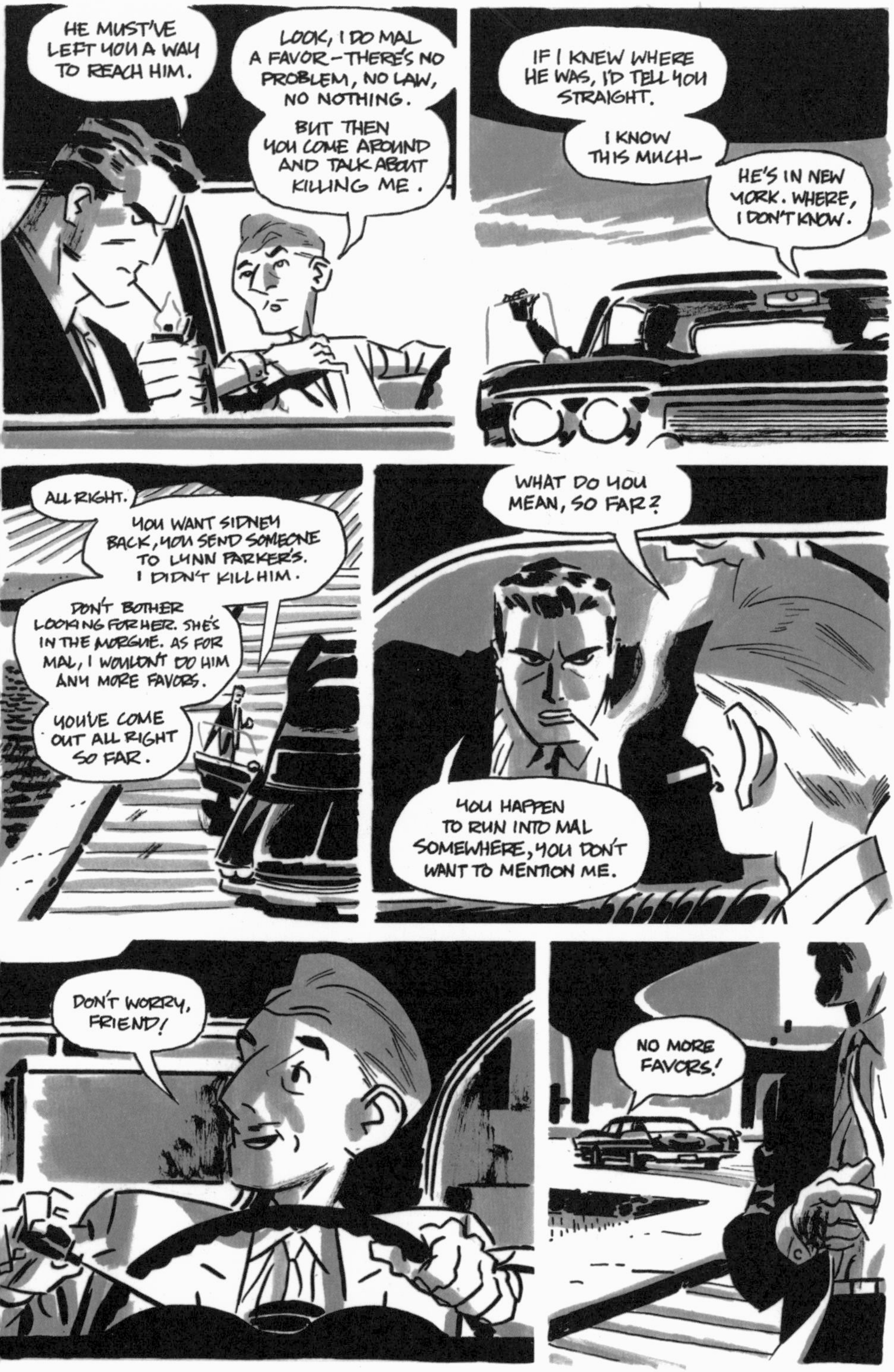
HE MUST'VE LEFT YOU A WAY TO REACH HIM.
LOOK, I DO MAL A FAVOR—THERE'S NO PROBLEM, NO LAW, NO NOTHING.
BUT THEN YOU COME AROUND AND TALK ABOUT KILLING ME.
IF I KNEW WHERE HE WAS, I'D TELL YOU STRAIGHT.
I KNOW THIS MUCH—
HE'S IN NEW YORK. WHERE, I DON'T KNOW.
ALL RIGHT.
YOU WANT SIDNEY BACK, YOU SEND SOMEONE TO LYNN PARKER'S. I DIDN'T KILL HIM.
DON'T BOTHER LOOKING FOR HER. SHE'S IN THE MORGUE. AS FOR MAL, I WOULDN'T DO HIM ANY MORE FAVORS.
YOU'VE COME OUT ALL RIGHT SO FAR.
WHAT DO YOU MEAN, SO FAR?
YOU HAPPEN TO RUN INTO MAL SOMEWHERE, YOU DON'T WANT TO MENTION ME.
DON'T WORRY, FRIEND!
NO MORE FAVORS!

So Mal was in New York –
otherwise Stegman had
been a dead end.

And Lynn was just plain dead.

He hated her. He hated her
and he loved her and he'd
never felt either emotion for
anyone before. Never love,
never hate, never for anyone.

She put him here.

Crossed him and cuckolded
him and jailed him and put his
prints on file. Given him a
continent to cross. She had done it.

No other woman
could have. There
had never been a
woman anywhere
to trouble him,
till her.

Freedom!

There never
would be again.

Freedom!

Lynn was gone
and that left Mal.

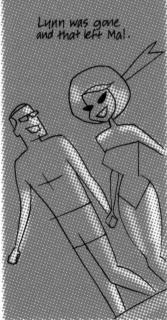

He wanted Mal
between his hands...

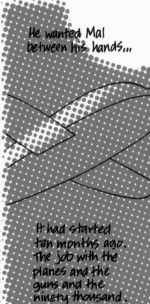

It had started
ten months ago.
The job with the
planes and the
guns and the
ninety thousand.

arker wasn't a syndicate
oy, and never had been.
e worked a job every
ear or so, payroll or
rmored car or banks,
ever taking anything
ut unmarked and
ntraceable cash.

e never worked with
nore than four or five
thers, and never came in
n a job unless he was
ure of the competence
f his associates.
lor did he always work
vith the same people.

le kept his money in hotel
afes and lived his life
n resort hotels — Miami,
as Vegas, Palm Springs —
aking on another job
nly when his cash on
and dropped below
ive thousand dollars.

e had never been
agged for any of his
obs, nor was there
police file on him
nywhere in the world.

Once or twice a year
n intermediary would
ontact Parker about
possible job.
hieves would be invited
n on a job and a neutral
ity would be chosen
or an initial meet.
ometimes the job would
e good and sometimes
t would be bad.

arker had taken Lynn
vith him to Chicago for
ne of these meetings.
The job was bad.
arker walked, even
though his cash reserves
vere low. And that's
vhen Mal came along.

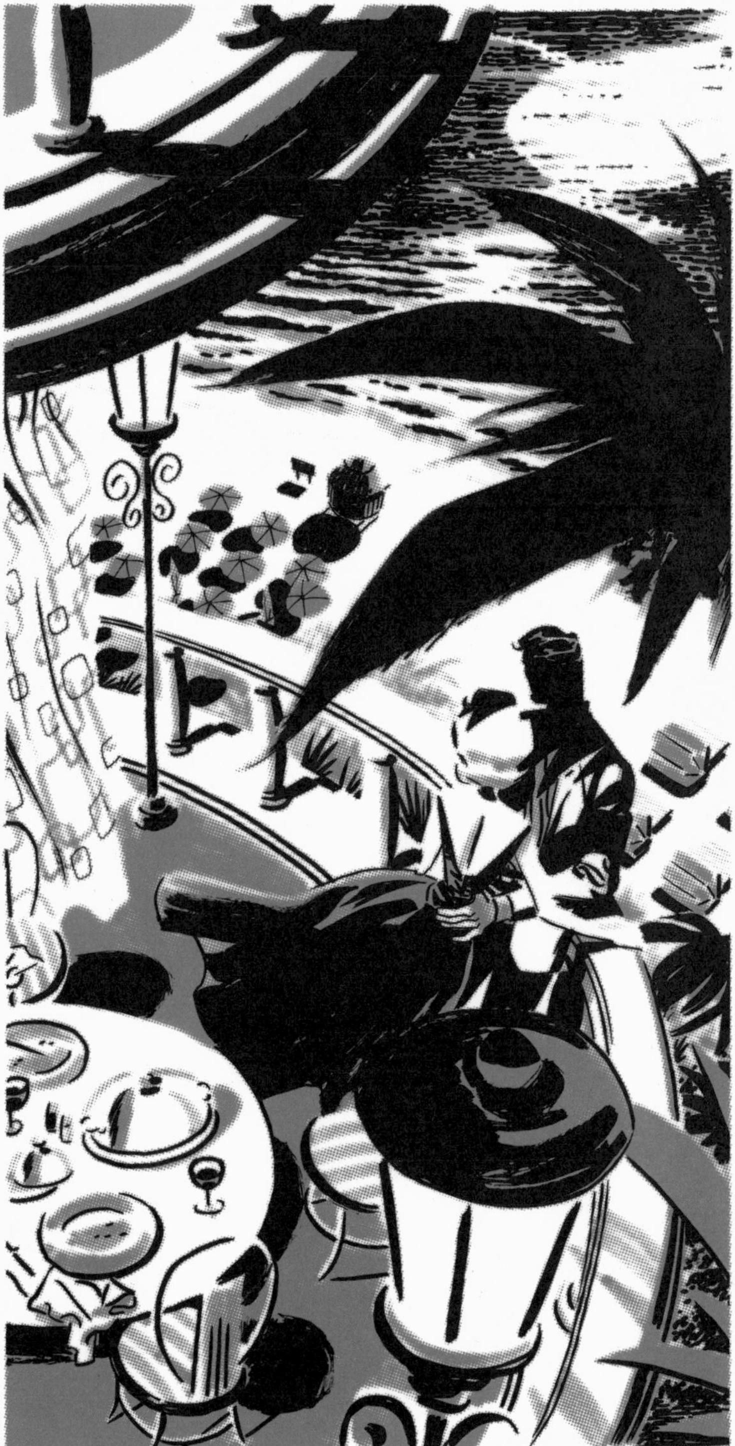

Mal Resnick was a big mouth coward who'd blown a syndicate connection four years before and was making a living in those days as a hack, steering for some of the local business.

The way he loused up with the syndicate, he lost his nerve and dumped forty thousand dollars of uncut snow he was delivering when he mistook the organization linebacker for a plainclothes cop.

They took three of his teeth and kicked him out in the street, telling him to go earn the forty grand and then come back.

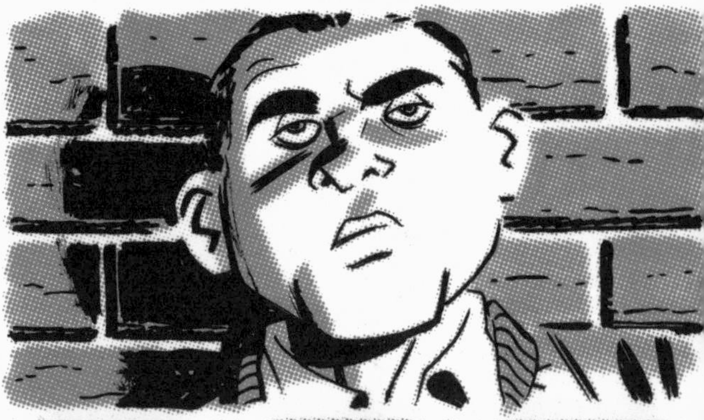

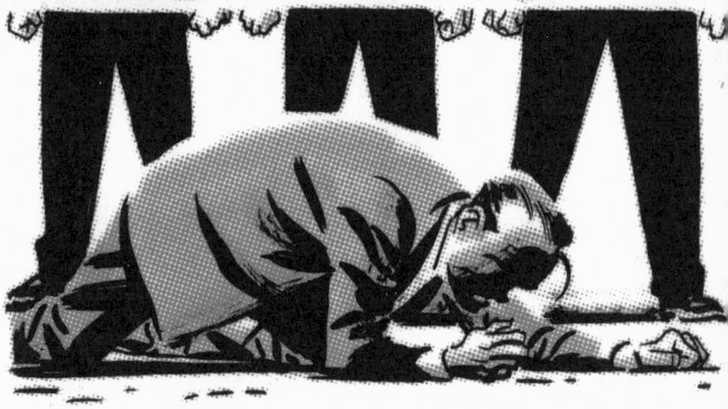

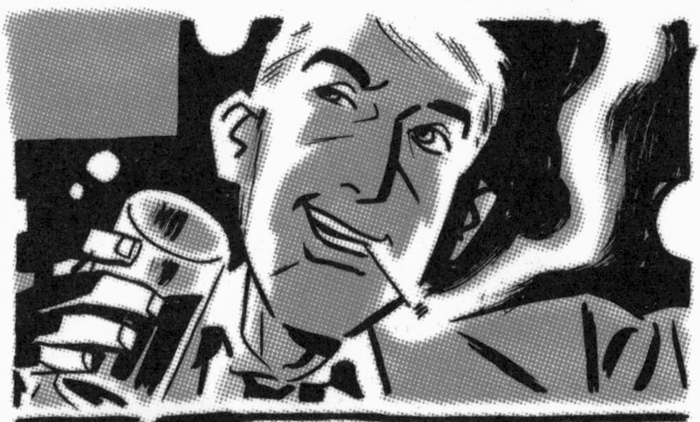

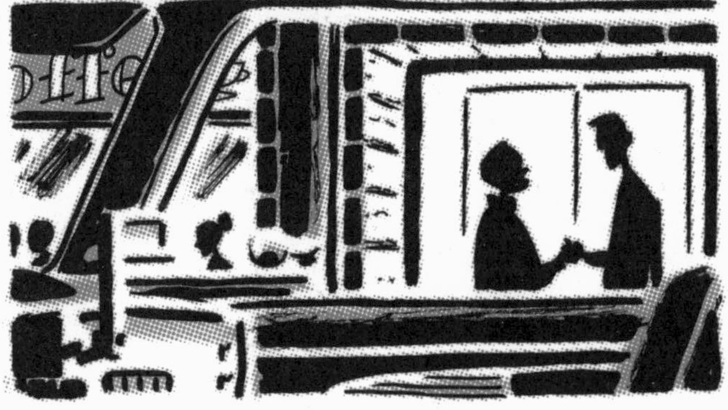

Chester was a hot shot Canadian into smuggling On a few occasions he'd used Mal as an intermediar to move pornography.

Chester was the one who set it up. He'd heard about the arms deal, and saw the angle right away but he was a straight busher when it came to armed robbery.

If Chester had a failing, it was that he believed people were what they thought they were. Mal sti thought of himself as a red hot smart boy with gut and connections so it was Mal that Chester approache Seeing the potential as clearly as Chester, Mal was i

At this point the operation ran into a snag that threatened to hold it up forever. Despite his promises and big words, Mal didn't really know anybody worth adding to the group.

For ten days he stalled Chester, then Parker and his wife hailed his hack just off the loop.

Mal recognized him from a party a few years back, and immediately gave him the proposition.

Ordinarily, Parker wouldn't have bothered to listen but he had come to town for a job that fell through.

Mal's pitch appealed to him. It was a job where there'd be no law on their tail and a ninety grand pie to split.

Mal introduced Parker to Chester, and Parker thereafter felt even better about the operation. Chester was small-time, but serious and intelligent and close-mouthed. There wasn't any doubt that his information could be trusted and he'd be a definite help when the job was pulled.

It was a sweet setup, with a ninety thousand payoff. American munitions were trucked into Canada where it was easy to get them airborne.

The clients were South American rebels with a mountain airfield and a yen for bloodshed. The guns were flown out of the Yukon to Keeley's Island off the California coast. The South Americans fly up to Keeley's and the exchange would take place.

It was a natural for hijacking. There would never be any law called in and there was nothing to fear from a bunch of mountain rebels over a continent away.

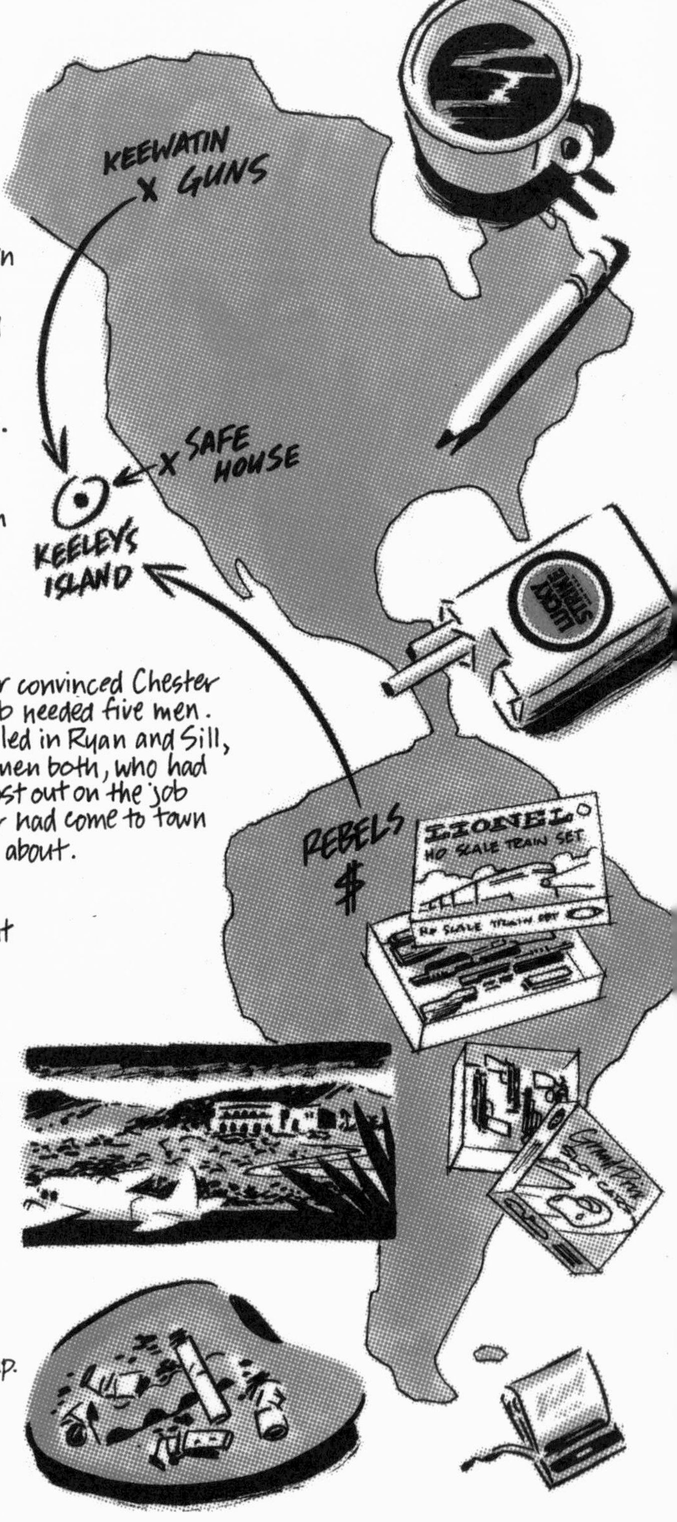
KEEWATIN
X GUNS
X SAFE HOUSE
KEELEY'S ISLAND
LUCKY STRIKE
REBELS
$
LIONEL
HO SCALE TRAIN SET

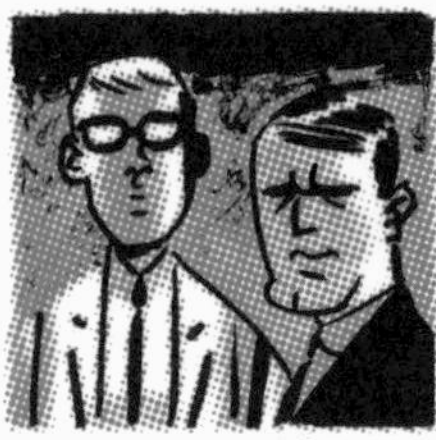

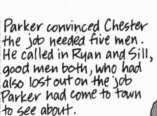

Parker convinced Chester the job needed five men. He called in Ryan and Sill, good men both, who had also lost out on the job Parker had come to town to see about.

They had three weeks to prepare and during that time Parker gradually took over as leader of the string. He arranged for bankrolling the job and set up the rental of a small plane. Ryan could fly, which was critical for the plan.

Lynn and Parker found a remote estate up the coast, long abandoned by it's movie star owner. She had owned a small airplane and the estate had a landing strip. Parker got them guns, and the job was on.

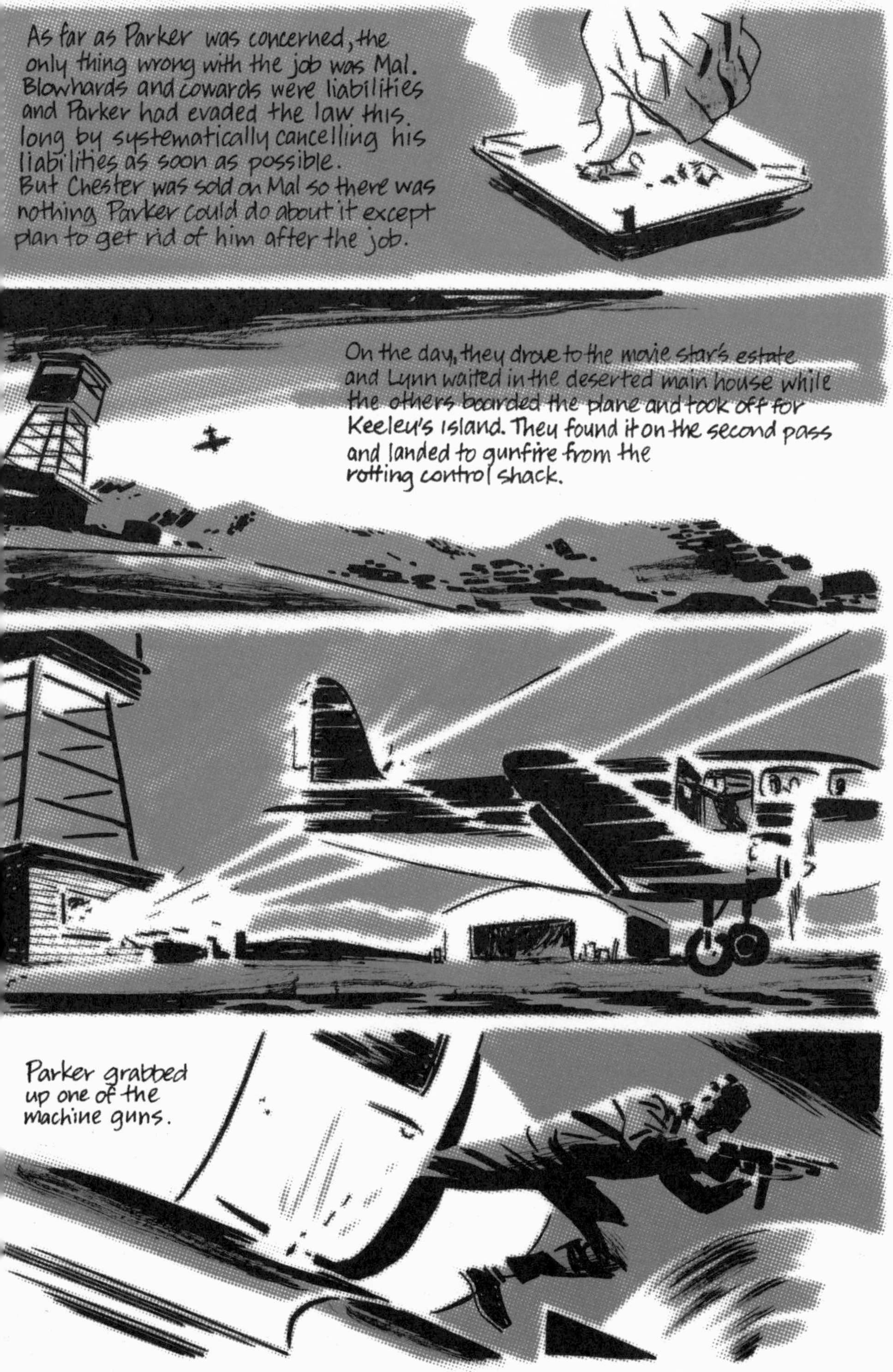
As far as Parker was concerned, the only thing wrong with the job was Mal. Blowhards and cowards were liabilities and Parker had evaded the law this long by systematically cancelling his liabilities as soon as possible.
But Chester was sold on Mal so there was nothing Parker could do about it except plan to get rid of him after the job.
On the day, they drove to the movie star's estate and Lynn waited in the deserted main house while the others boarded the plane and took off for Keeley's island. They found it on the second pass and landed to gunfire from the rotting control shack.
Parker grabbed up one of the machine guns.

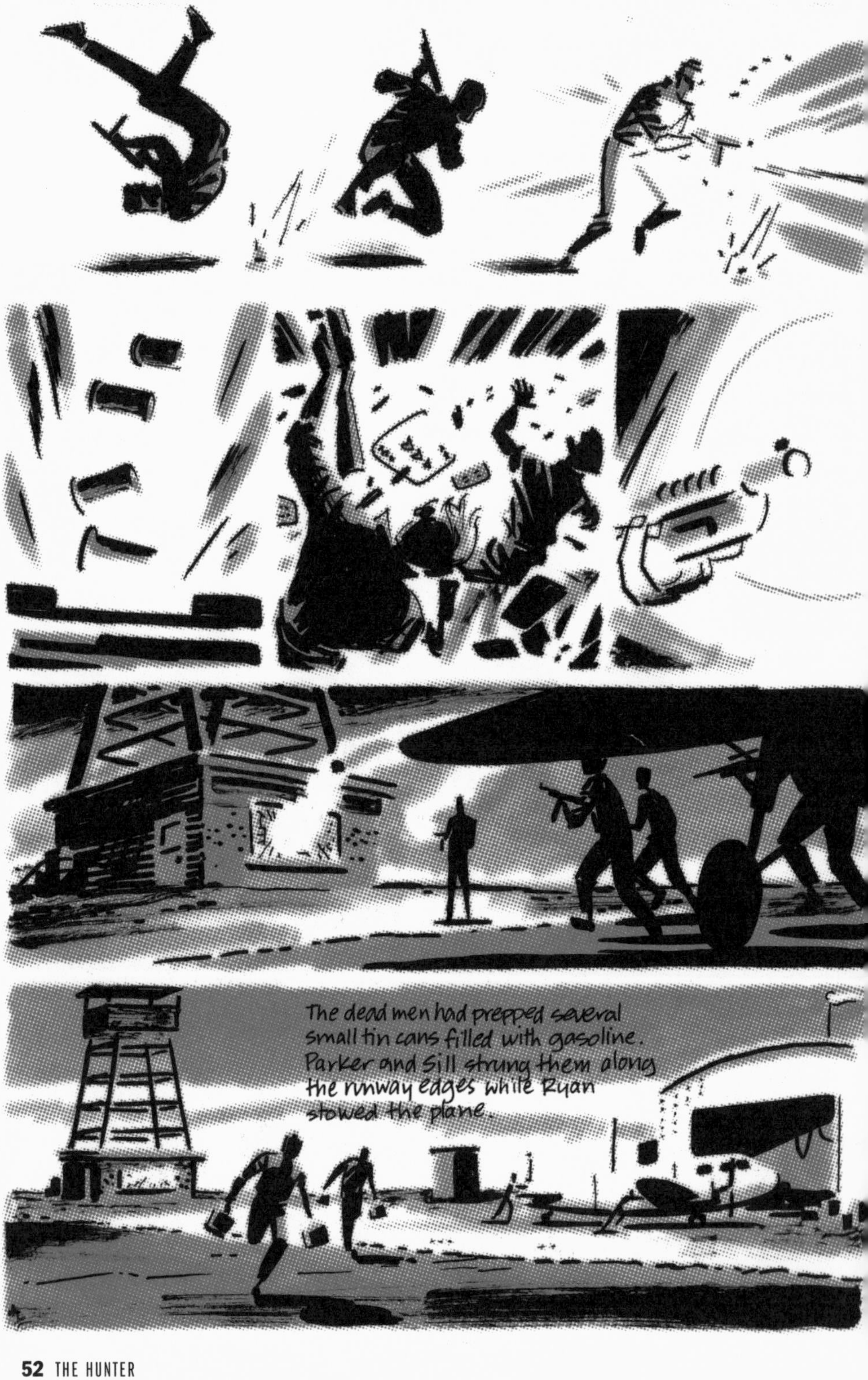
The dead men had prepped several small tin cans filled with gasoline. Parker and Sill strung them along the runway edges while Ryan stowed the plane.

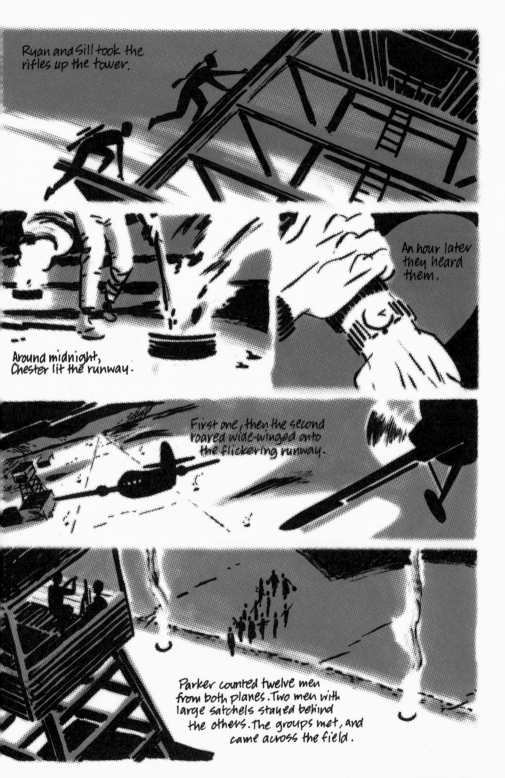

Ruan and Sill took the rifles up the tower.

Around midnight, Chester lit the runway.

An hour later they heard them.

First one, then the second roared wide-winged onto the flickering runway.

Parker counted twelve men from both planes. Two men with large satchels stayed behind the others. The groups met, and came across the field.

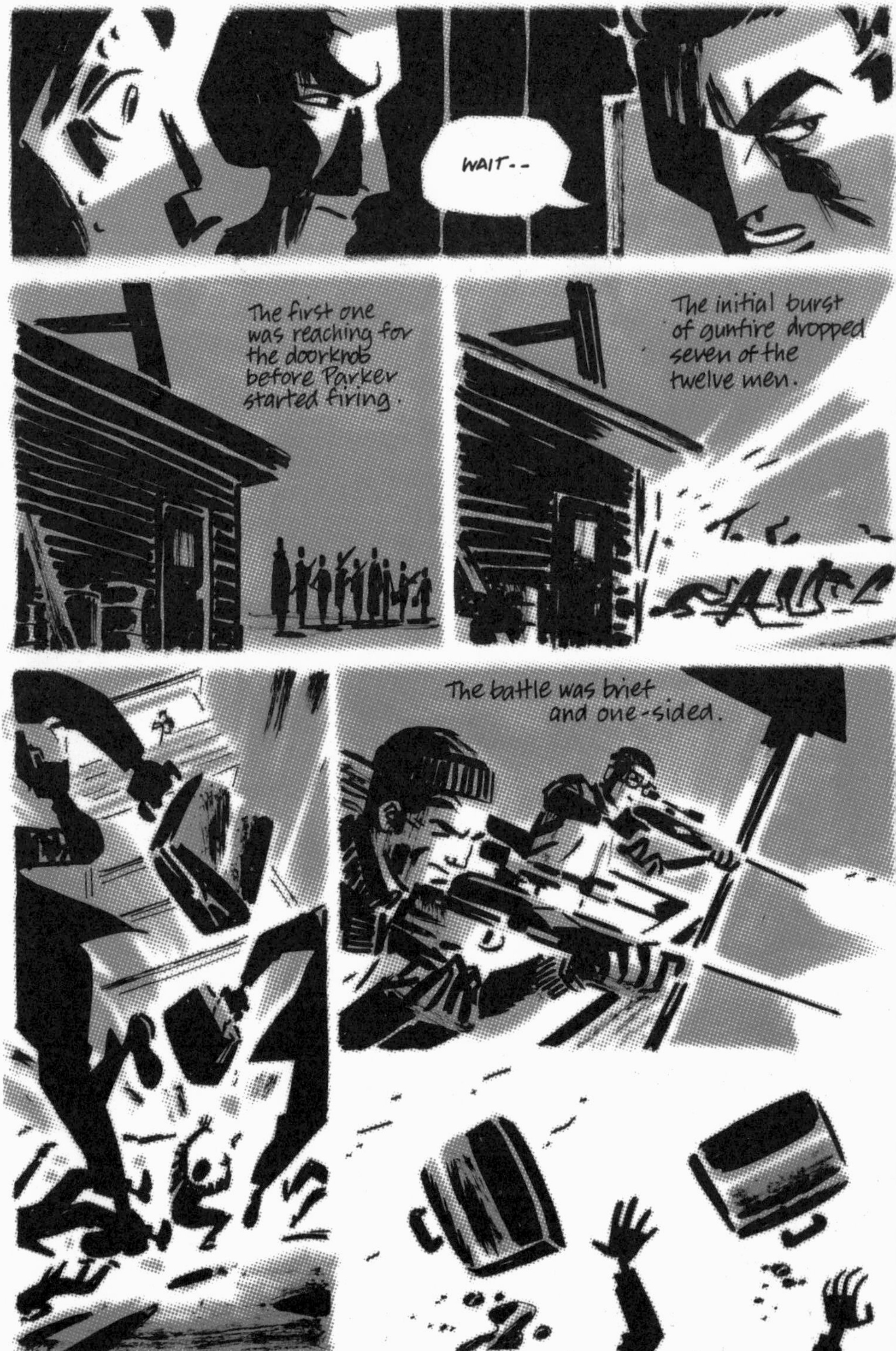
WAIT--
The first one was reaching for the doorknob before Parker started firing.
The initial burst of gunfire dropped seven of the twelve men.
The battle was brief and one-sided.

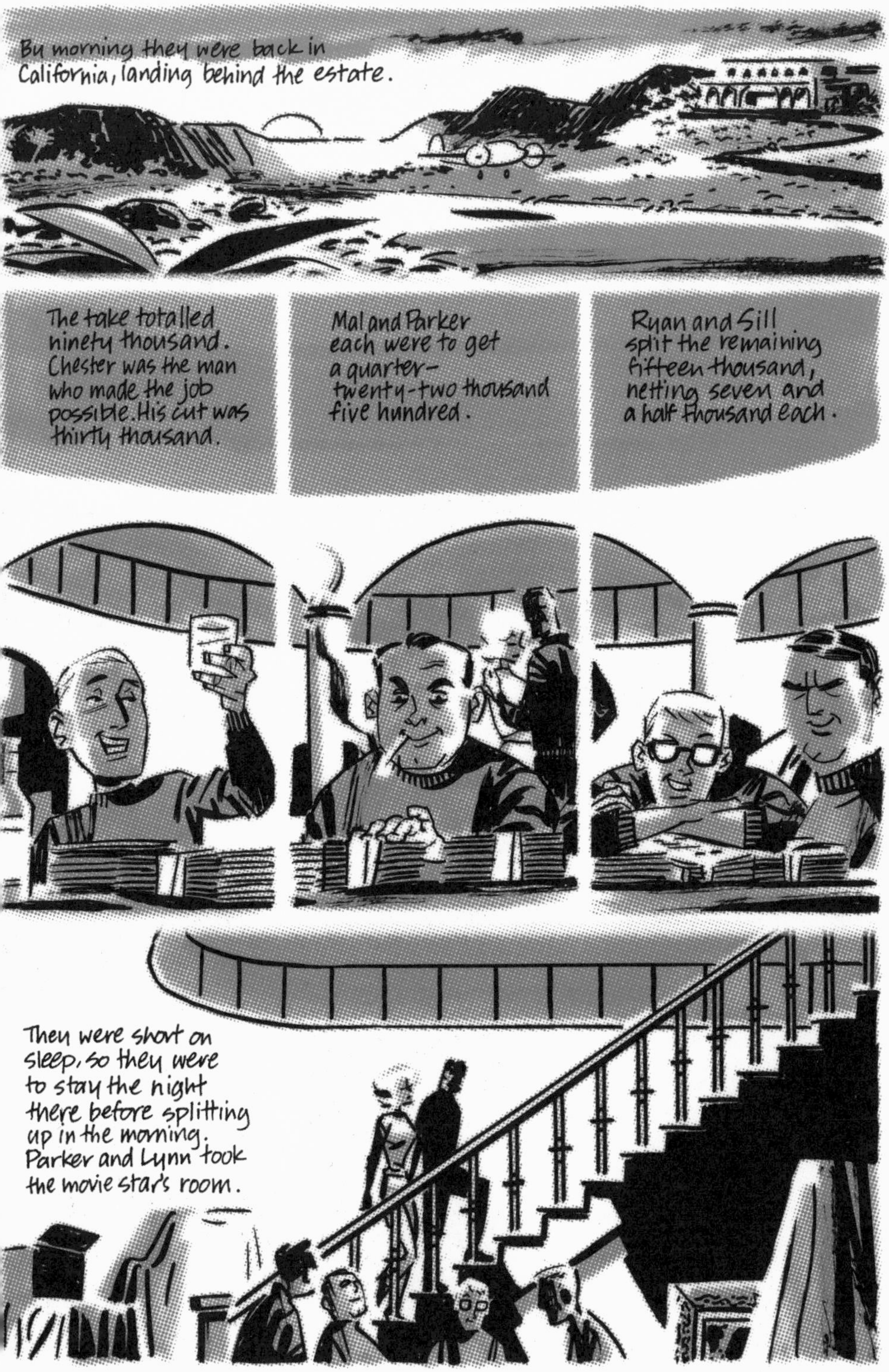

By morning they were back in California, landing behind the estate.
The take totalled ninety thousand. Chester was the man who made the job possible. His cut was thirty thousand.
Mal and Parker each were to get a quarter- twenty-two thousand five hundred.
Ryan and Sill split the remaining fifteen thousand, netting seven and a half thousand each.
They were short on sleep, so they were to stay the night there before splitting up in the morning. Parker and Lynn took the movie star's room.

It was always like this after a job.

He would be fierce, and strong, and demanding, and exultant, allowing his emotions the only release he permitted them.

For weeks after a job they wouldn't skip a night and often it would be more than once a night.

The pattern was always the same, and Lynn had grown used to it, though not without difficulty.

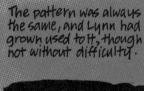

Then gradually his passion would slacken, lessening with their cash reserves until near-celibacy just before the next job.

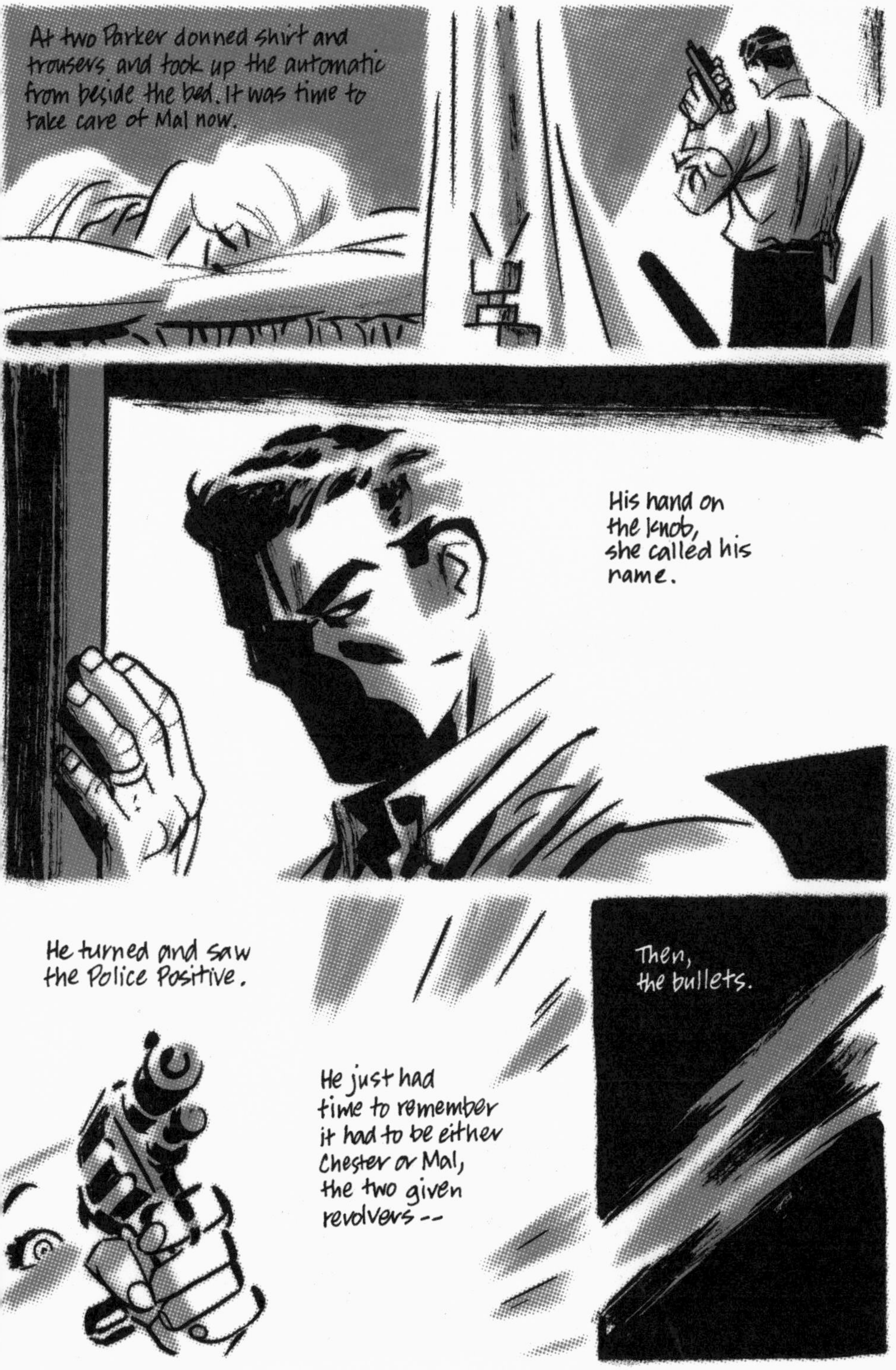
At two Parker donned shirt and trousers and took up the automatic from beside the bed. It was time to take care of Mal now.
His hand on the knob, she called his name.
He turned and saw the Police Positive.
He just had time to remember it had to be either Chester or Mal, the two given revolvers --
Then, the bullets.

He awoke to heat and suffocation.
They'd set fire to the house.

He thought at first the bullet
was in him, but then he realized
what happened. His belt buckle was mashed
into a ragged cup shape. Beneath it
the skin was purplish and he seemed to be
bleeding from his pores.

He stood only because he wanted
to stand, not because it was possible.
He should have left right away but
he had to know which one it was.

He staggered down the blazing hallway.
Mal was gone. Chester was dead, his throat cut.
Sill was dead the same way.

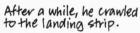

After a while, he crawled
to the landing strip.

He found Ryan there, the back
of his head blown out.
A chill touched him, a reaction
stronger than he was used to
when faced with death.

Parker rested there until
distant sirens forced him to his feet.

He lurched across the
strip and into the woods
on the other side.

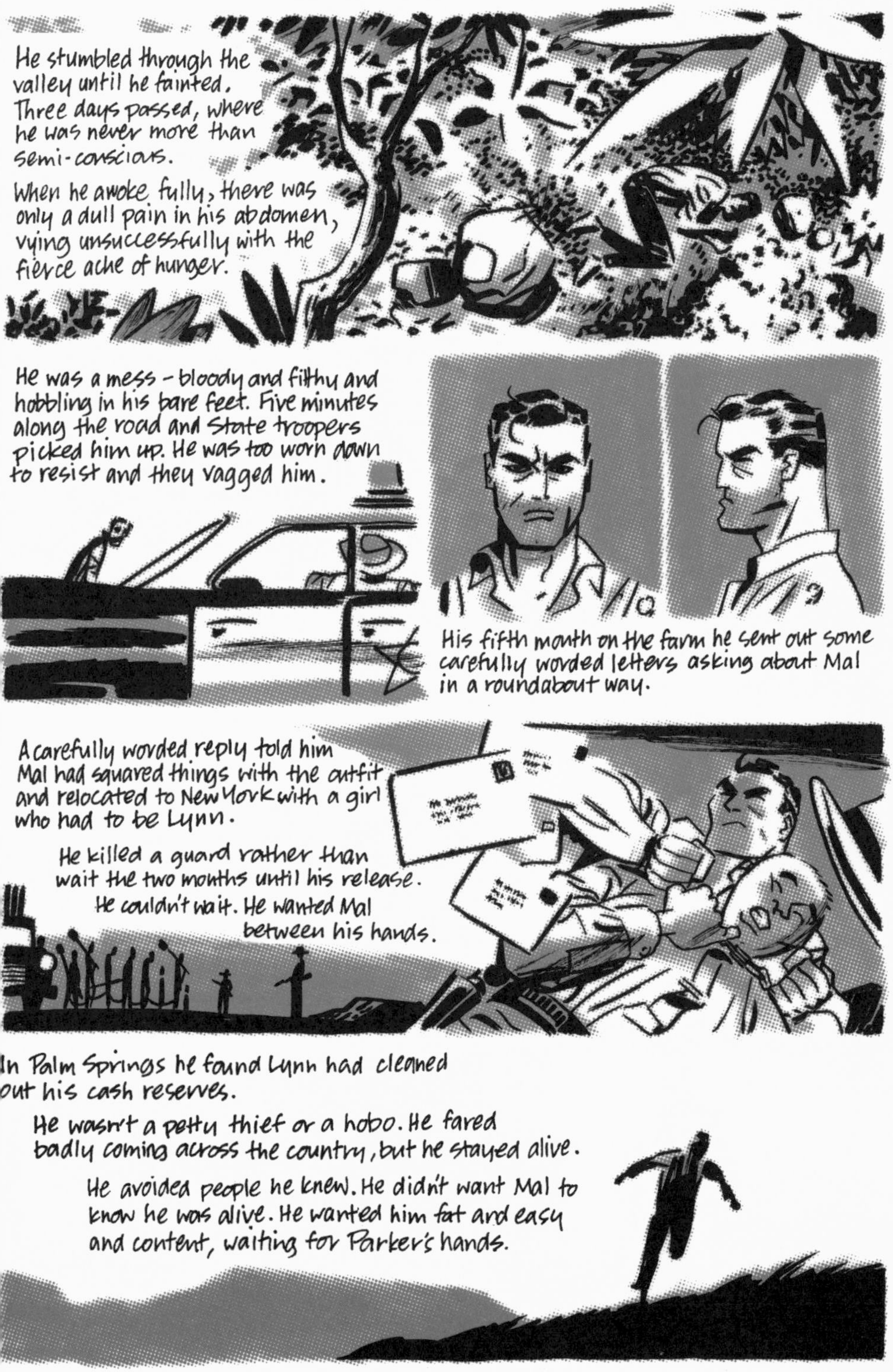
He stumbled through the valley until he fainted. Three days passed, where he was never more than semi-conscious.
When he awoke fully, there was only a dull pain in his abdomen, vying unsuccessfully with the fierce ache of hunger.
He was a mess - bloody and filthy and hobbling in his bare feet. Five minutes along the road and State troopers picked him up. He was too worn down to resist and they vagged him.
His fifth month on the farm he sent out some carefully worded letters asking about Mal in a roundabout way.
A carefully worded reply told him Mal had squared things with the outfit and relocated to New York with a girl who had to be Lynn.
He killed a guard rather than wait the two months until his release.
He couldn't wait. He wanted Mal between his hands.
In Palm Springs he found Lynn had cleaned out his cash reserves.
He wasn't a petty thief or a hobo. He fared badly coming across the country, but he stayed alive.
He avoided people he knew. He didn't want Mal to know he was alive. He wanted him fat and easy and content, waiting for Parker's hands.

BOOK TWO

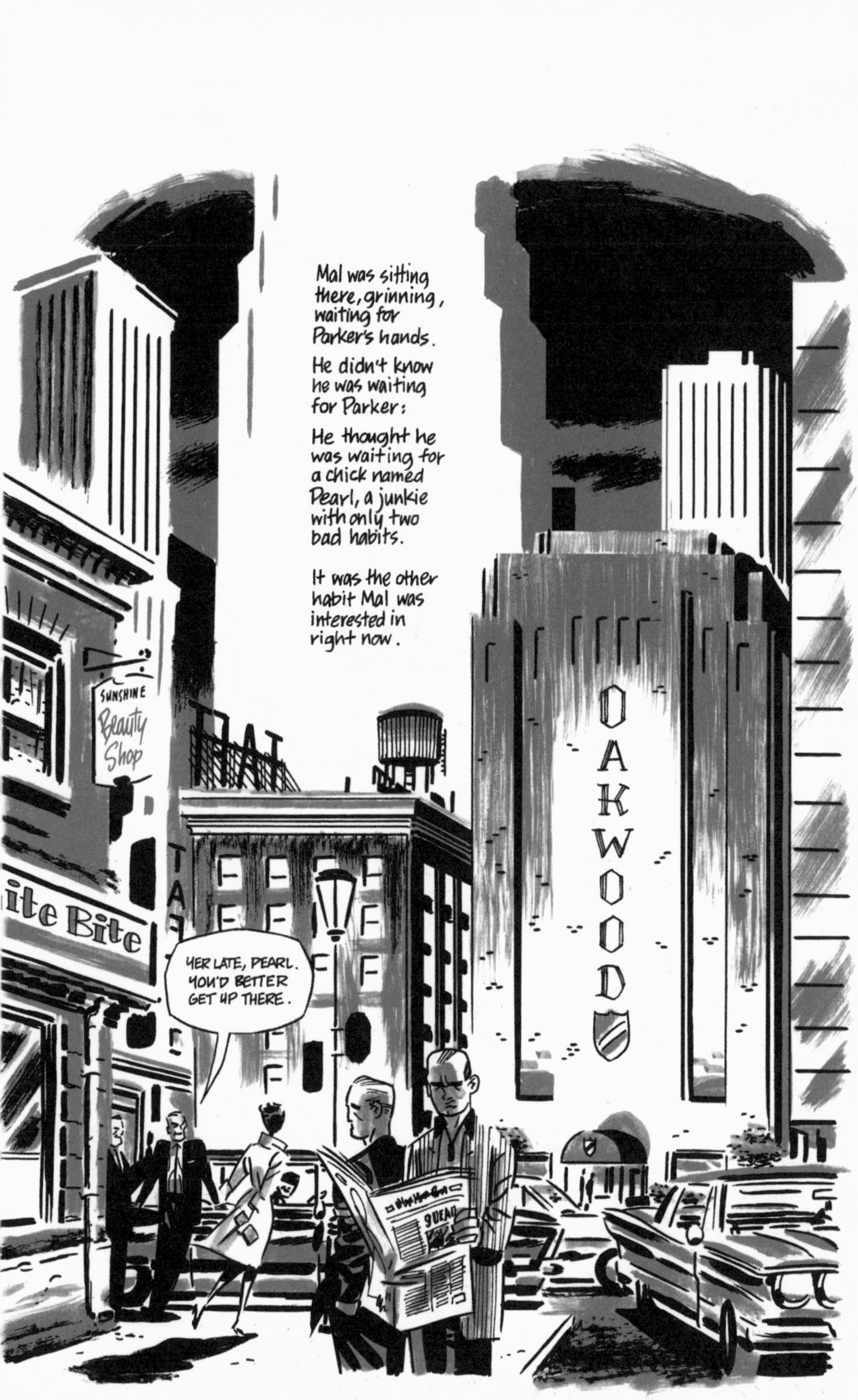
Mal was sitting there, grinning, waiting for Parker's hands.
He didn't know he was waiting for Parker:
He thought he was waiting for a chick named Pearl, a junkie with only two bad habits.
It was the other habit Mal was interested in right now.
SUNSHINE Beauty Shop
ite Bite
OAKWOOD
YER LATE, PEARL. YOU'D BETTER GET UP THERE.

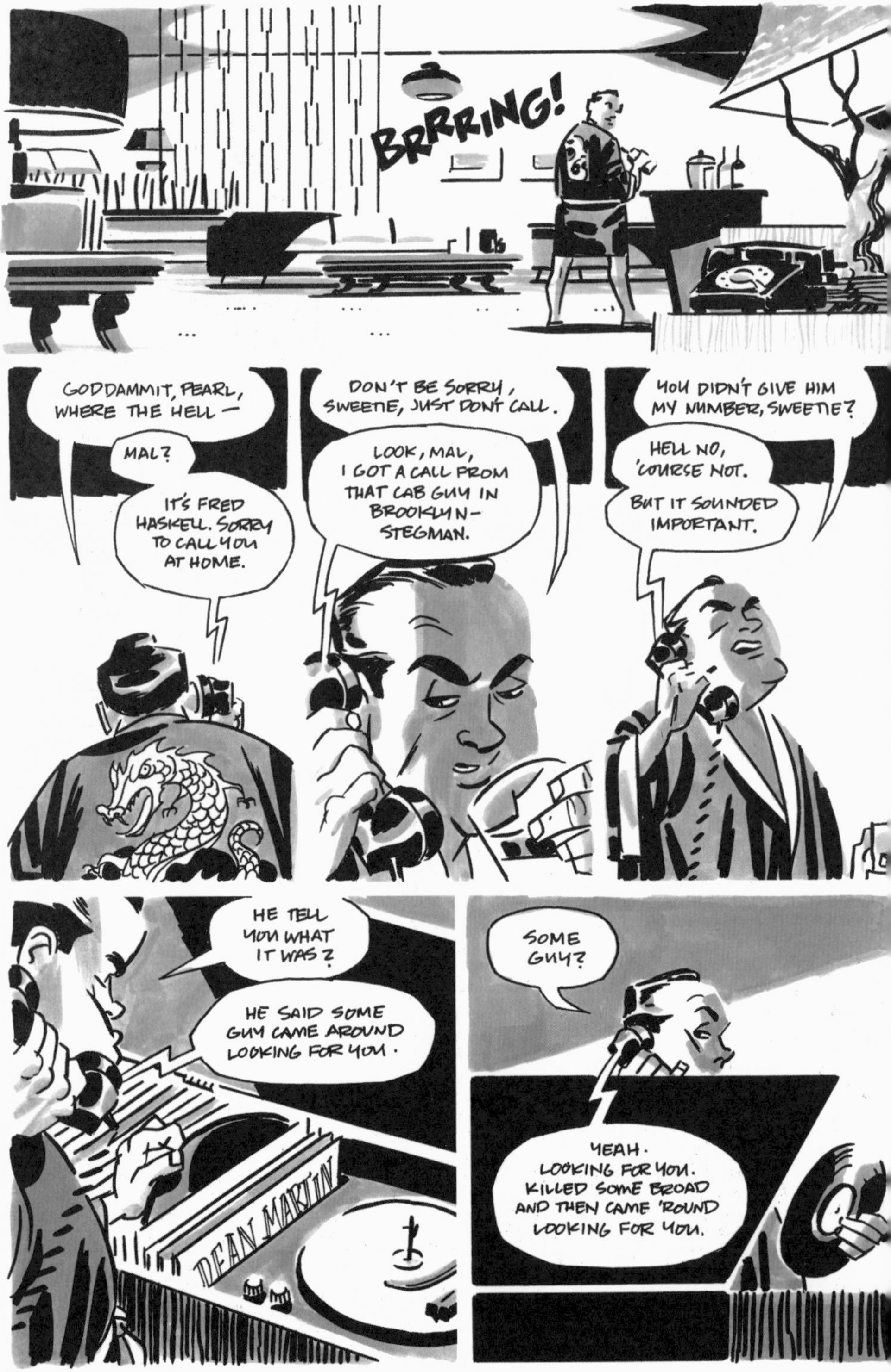
BRRRING!
GODDAMMIT, PEARL, WHERE THE HELL —
MAL?
IT'S FRED HASKELL. SORRY TO CALL YOU AT HOME.
DON'T BE SORRY, SWEETIE, JUST DON'T CALL.
LOOK, MAL, I GOT A CALL FROM THAT CAB GUY IN BROOKLYN- STEGMAN.
YOU DIDN'T GIVE HIM MY NUMBER, SWEETIE?
HELL NO, 'COURSE NOT.
BUT IT SOUNDED IMPORTANT.
HE TELL YOU WHAT IT WAS?
HE SAID SOME GUY CAME AROUND LOOKING FOR YOU.
DEAN MARTIN
SOME GUY?
YEAH. LOOKING FOR YOU. KILLED SOME BROAD AND THEN CAME 'ROUND LOOKING FOR YOU.

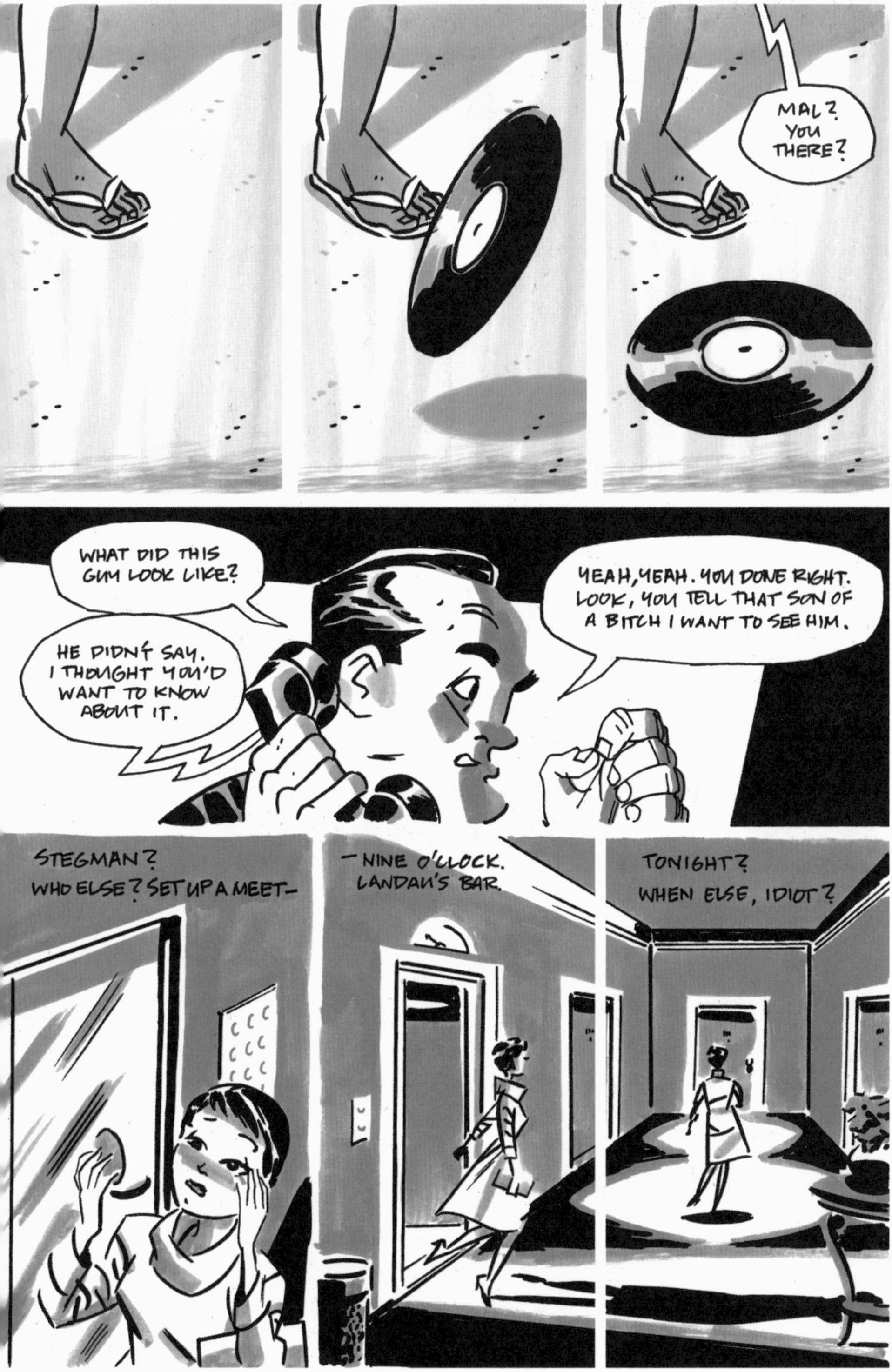
MAL? YOU THERE?
WHAT DID THIS GUY LOOK LIKE?
HE DIDN'T SAY. I THOUGHT YOU'D WANT TO KNOW ABOUT IT.
YEAH, YEAH. YOU DONE RIGHT. LOOK, YOU TELL THAT SON OF A BITCH I WANT TO SEE HIM.
STEGMAN?
WHO ELSE? SET UP A MEET–
–NINE O'CLOCK. LANDAU'S BAR.
TONIGHT?
WHEN ELSE, IDIOT?

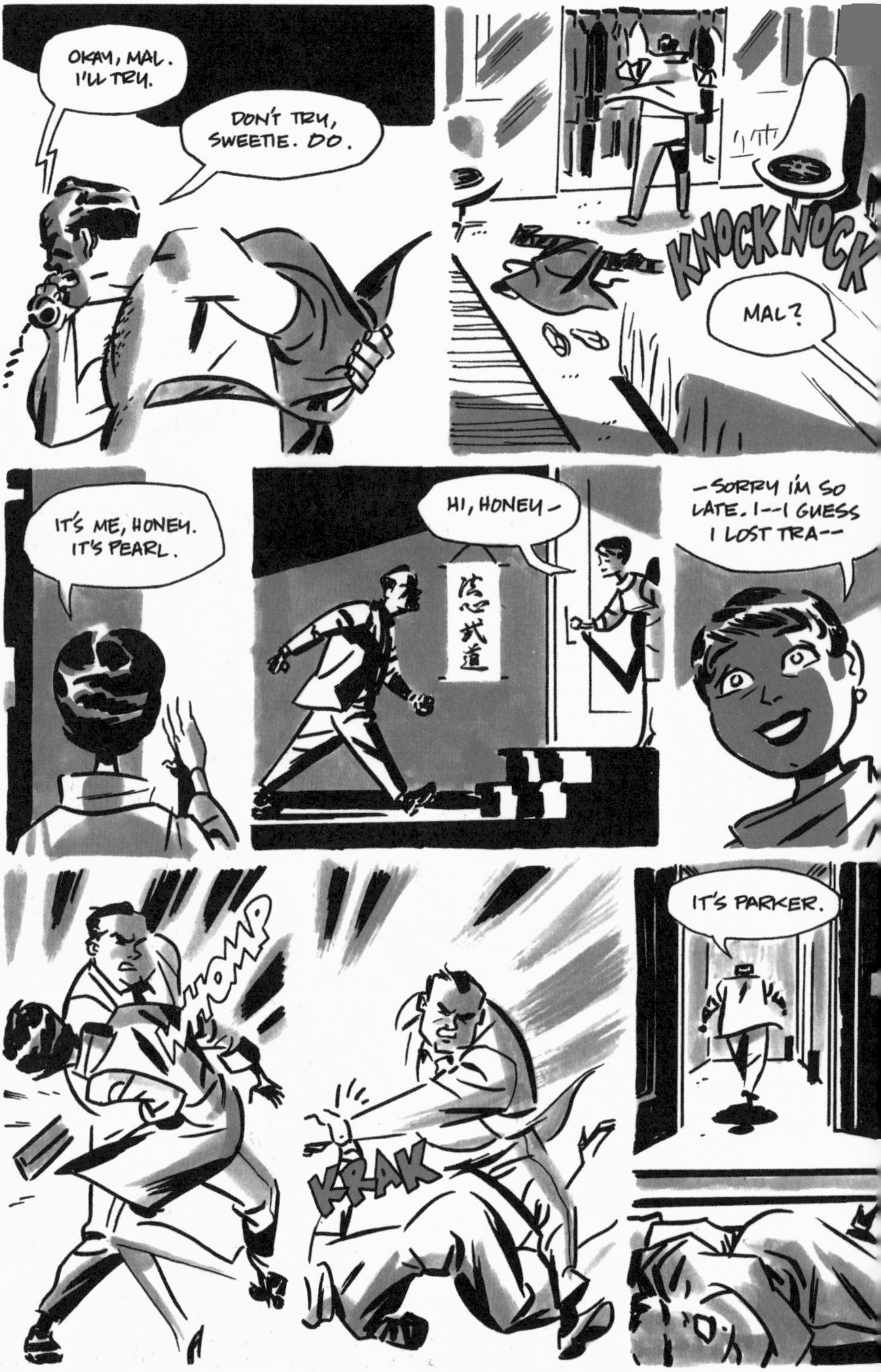

OKAY, MAL. I'LL TRY.
DON'T TRY, SWEETIE. DO.
KNOCK NOCK
MAL?
IT'S ME, HONEY. IT'S PEARL.
HI, HONEY—
—SORRY I'M SO LATE. I--I GUESS I LOST TRA--
WHOMP
KRAK
IT'S PARKER.

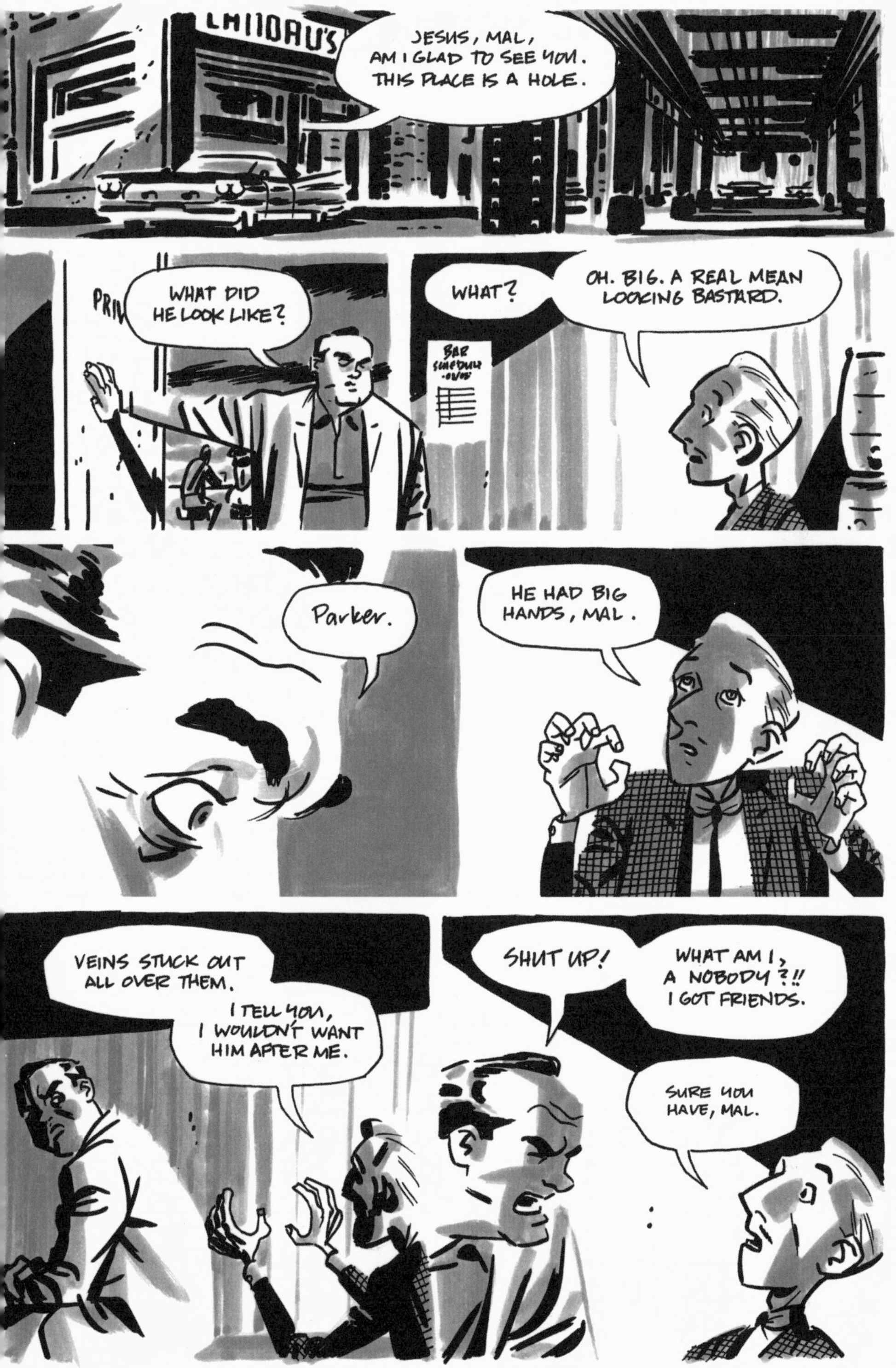
LANDAU'S
JESUS, MAL, AM I GLAD TO SEE YOU. THIS PLACE IS A HOLE.
WHAT DID HE LOOK LIKE?
WHAT?
OH. BIG. A REAL MEAN LOOKING BASTARD.
BAR SCHEDULE
Parker.
HE HAD BIG HANDS, MAL.
VEINS STUCK OUT ALL OVER THEM.
I TELL YOU, I WOULDN'T WANT HIM AFTER ME.
SHUT UP!
WHAT AM I, A NOBODY?!! I GOT FRIENDS.
SURE YOU HAVE, MAL.

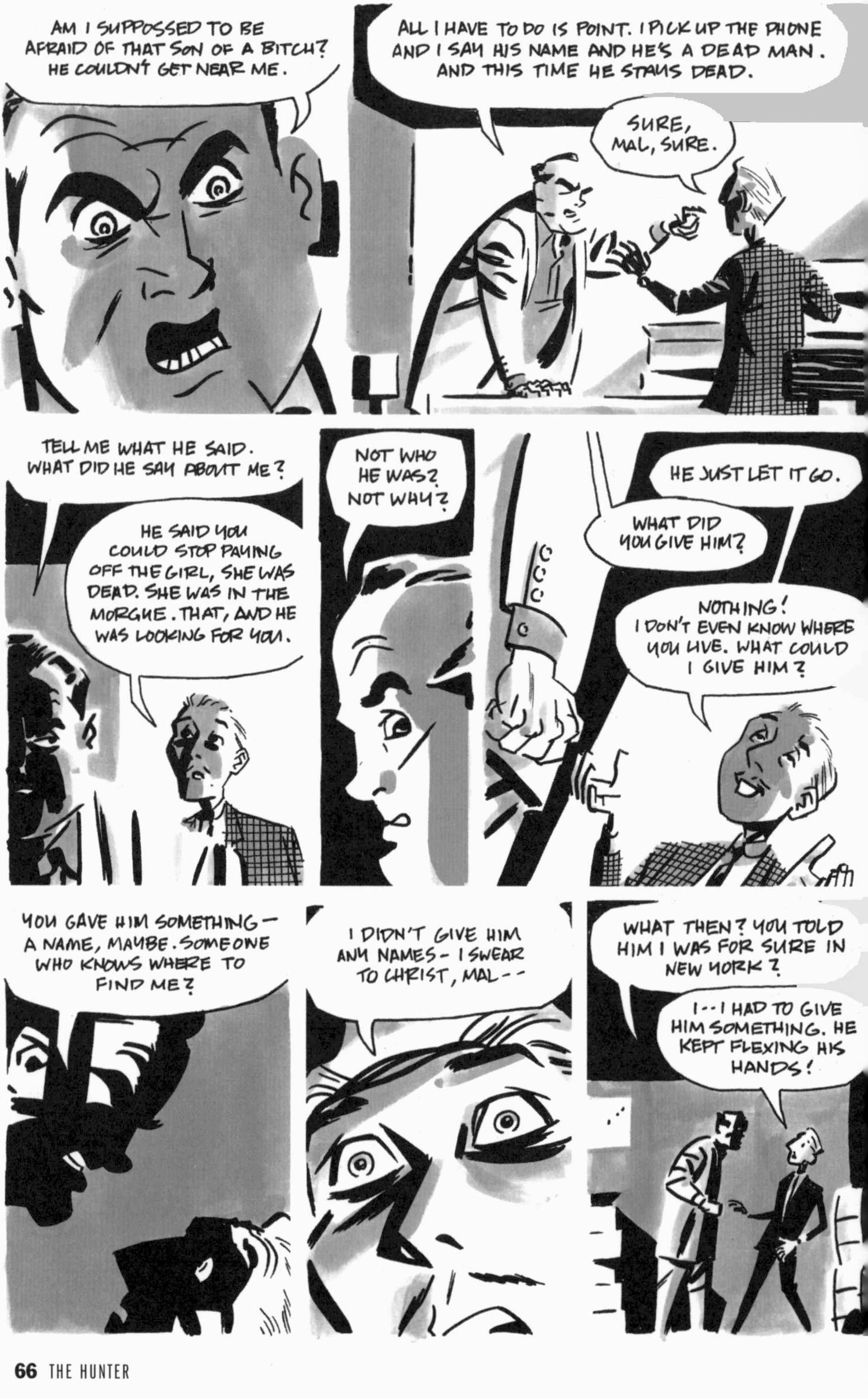

AM I SUPPOSSED TO BE AFRAID OF THAT SON OF A BITCH? HE COULDN'T GET NEAR ME.
ALL I HAVE TO DO IS POINT. I PICK UP THE PHONE AND I SAY HIS NAME AND HE'S A DEAD MAN. AND THIS TIME HE STAYS DEAD.
SURE, MAL, SURE.
TELL ME WHAT HE SAID. WHAT DID HE SAY ABOUT ME?
HE SAID YOU COULD STOP PAYING OFF THE GIRL, SHE WAS DEAD. SHE WAS IN THE MORGUE. THAT, AND HE WAS LOOKING FOR YOU.
NOT WHO HE WAS? NOT WHY?
HE JUST LET IT GO.
WHAT DID YOU GIVE HIM?
NOTHING! I DON'T EVEN KNOW WHERE YOU LIVE. WHAT COULD I GIVE HIM?
YOU GAVE HIM SOMETHING— A NAME, MAYBE. SOMEONE WHO KNOWS WHERE TO FIND ME?
I DIDN'T GIVE HIM ANY NAMES— I SWEAR TO CHRIST, MAL--
WHAT THEN? YOU TOLD HIM I WAS FOR SURE IN NEW YORK?
I--I HAD TO GIVE HIM SOMETHING. HE KEPT FLEXING HIS HANDS!

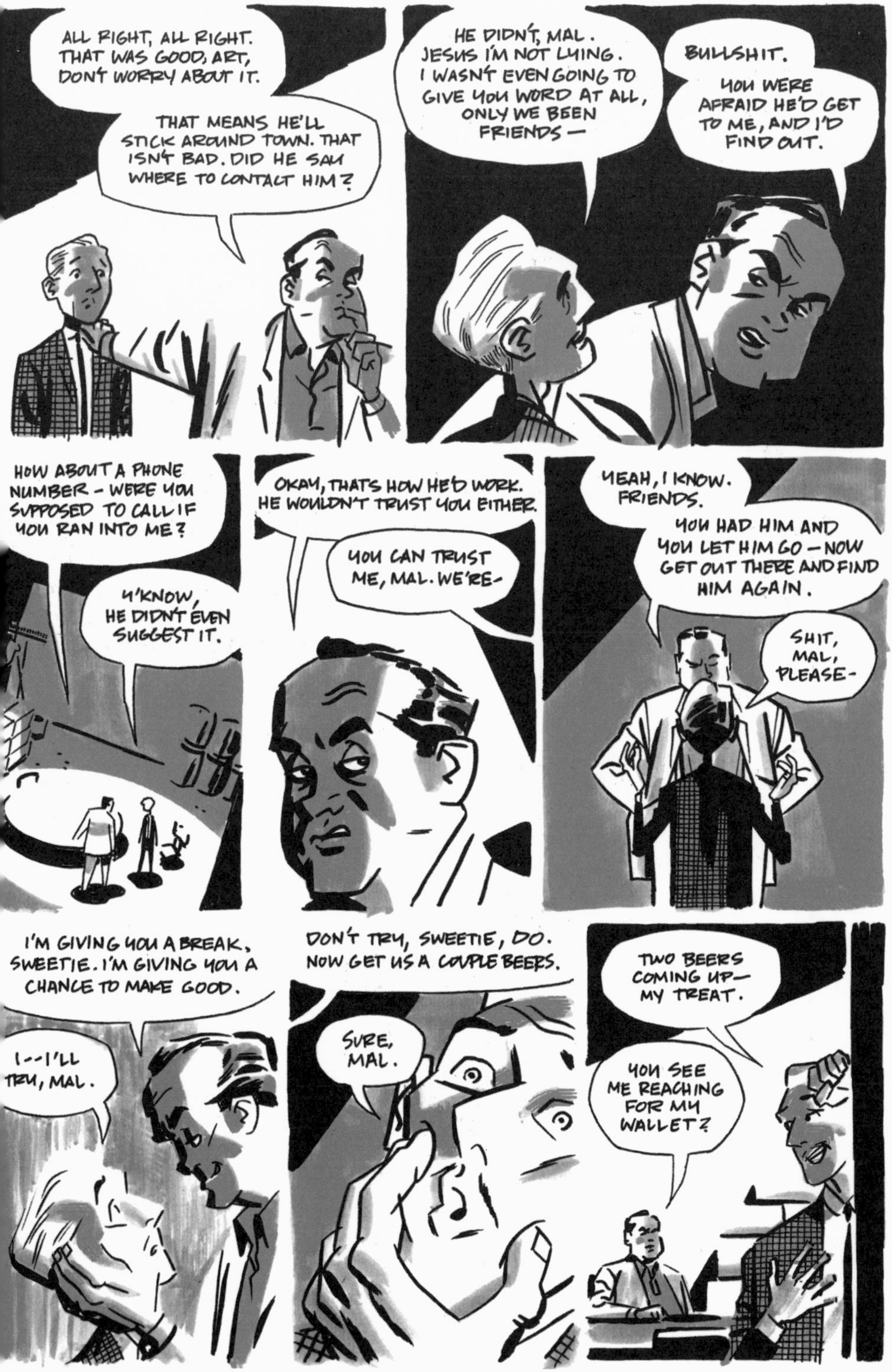
ALL RIGHT, ALL RIGHT. THAT WAS GOOD, ART, DON'T WORRY ABOUT IT.
THAT MEANS HE'LL STICK AROUND TOWN. THAT ISN'T BAD. DID HE SAY WHERE TO CONTACT HIM?
HE DIDN'T, MAL. JESUS I'M NOT LYING. I WASN'T EVEN GOING TO GIVE YOU WORD AT ALL, ONLY WE BEEN FRIENDS—
BULLSHIT.
YOU WERE AFRAID HE'D GET TO ME, AND I'D FIND OUT.
HOW ABOUT A PHONE NUMBER - WERE YOU SUPPOSED TO CALL IF YOU RAN INTO ME?
Y'KNOW, HE DIDN'T EVEN SUGGEST IT.
OKAY, THAT'S HOW HE'D WORK. HE WOULDN'T TRUST YOU EITHER.
YOU CAN TRUST ME, MAL. WE'RE-
YEAH, I KNOW. FRIENDS.
YOU HAD HIM AND YOU LET HIM GO — NOW GET OUT THERE AND FIND HIM AGAIN.
SHIT, MAL, PLEASE-
I'M GIVING YOU A BREAK, SWEETIE. I'M GIVING YOU A CHANCE TO MAKE GOOD.
I--I'LL TRY, MAL.
DON'T TRY, SWEETIE, DO. NOW GET US A COUPLE BEERS.
SURE, MAL.
TWO BEERS COMING UP— MY TREAT.
YOU SEE ME REACHING FOR MY WALLET?

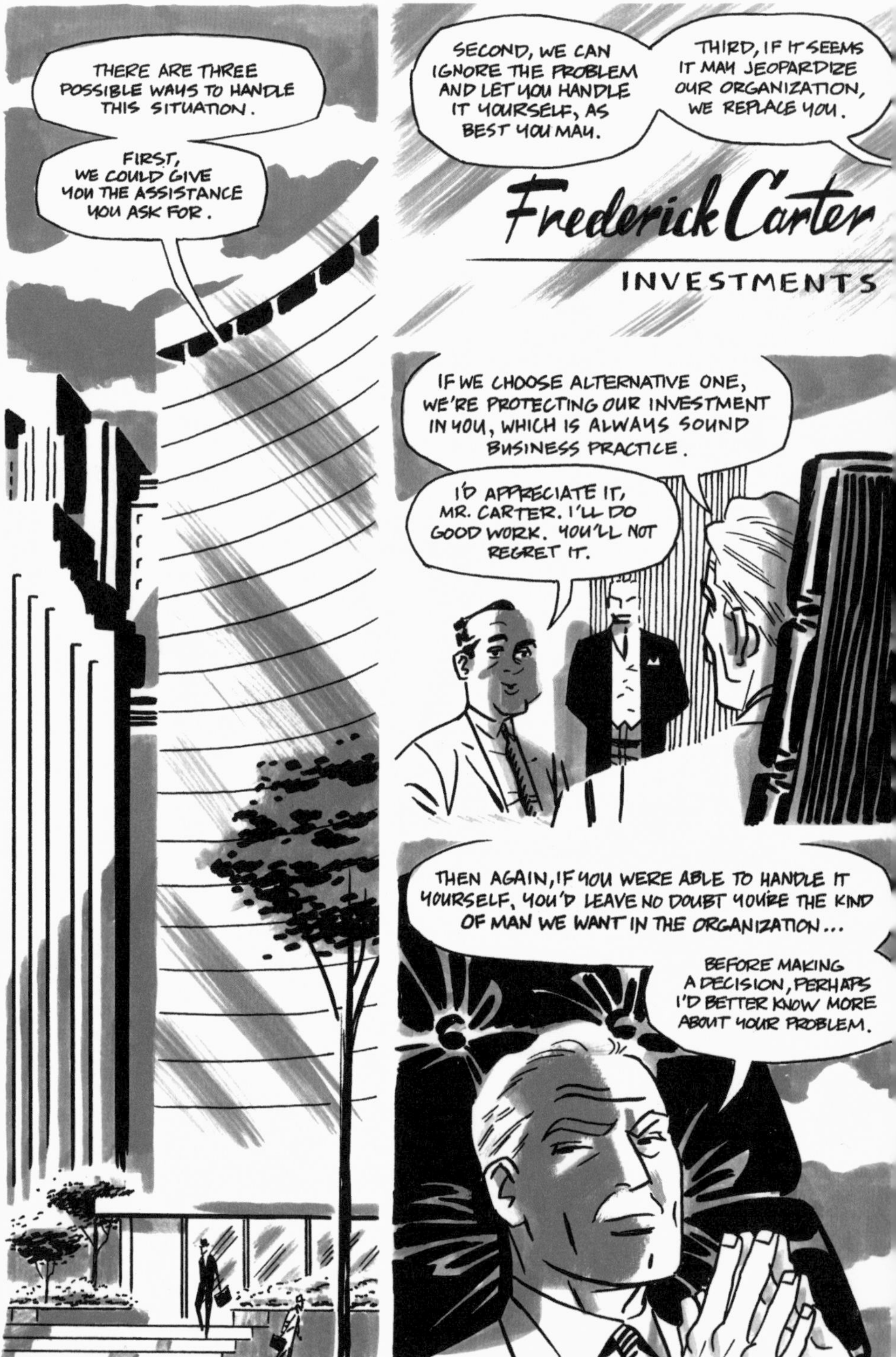
THERE ARE THREE POSSIBLE WAYS TO HANDLE THIS SITUATION.
FIRST, WE COULD GIVE YOU THE ASSISTANCE YOU ASK FOR.
SECOND, WE CAN IGNORE THE PROBLEM AND LET YOU HANDLE IT YOURSELF, AS BEST YOU MAY.
THIRD, IF IT SEEMS IT MAY JEOPARDIZE OUR ORGANIZATION, WE REPLACE YOU.
Frederick Carter
INVESTMENTS
IF WE CHOOSE ALTERNATIVE ONE, WE'RE PROTECTING OUR INVESTMENT IN YOU, WHICH IS ALWAYS SOUND BUSINESS PRACTICE.
I'D APPRECIATE IT, MR. CARTER. I'LL DO GOOD WORK. YOU'LL NOT REGRET IT.
THEN AGAIN, IF YOU WERE ABLE TO HANDLE IT YOURSELF, YOU'D LEAVE NO DOUBT YOU'RE THE KIND OF MAN WE WANT IN THE ORGANIZATION...
BEFORE MAKING A DECISION, PERHAPS I'D BETTER KNOW MORE ABOUT YOUR PROBLEM.

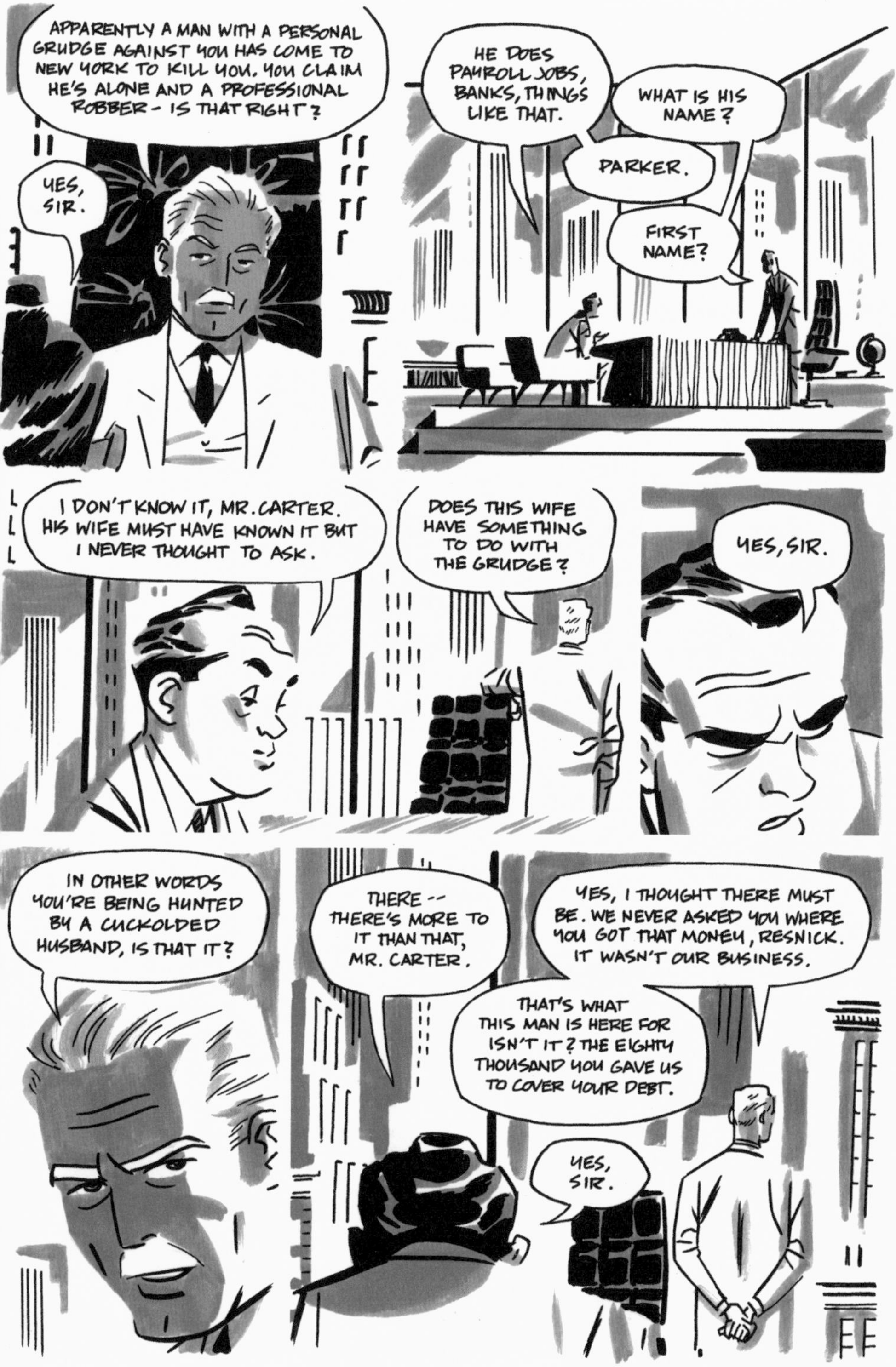
APPARENTLY A MAN WITH A PERSONAL GRUDGE AGAINST YOU HAS COME TO NEW YORK TO KILL YOU. YOU CLAIM HE'S ALONE AND A PROFESSIONAL ROBBER - IS THAT RIGHT?
YES, SIR.
HE DOES PAYROLL JOBS, BANKS, THINGS LIKE THAT.
WHAT IS HIS NAME?
PARKER.
FIRST NAME?
I DON'T KNOW IT, MR. CARTER. HIS WIFE MUST HAVE KNOWN IT BUT I NEVER THOUGHT TO ASK.
DOES THIS WIFE HAVE SOMETHING TO DO WITH THE GRUDGE?
YES, SIR.
IN OTHER WORDS YOU'RE BEING HUNTED BY A CUCKOLDED HUSBAND, IS THAT IT?
THERE -- THERE'S MORE TO IT THAN THAT, MR. CARTER.
YES, I THOUGHT THERE MUST BE. WE NEVER ASKED YOU WHERE YOU GOT THAT MONEY, RESNICK. IT WASN'T OUR BUSINESS.
THAT'S WHAT THIS MAN IS HERE FOR ISN'T IT? THE EIGHTY THOUSAND YOU GAVE US TO COVER YOUR DEBT.
YES, SIR.

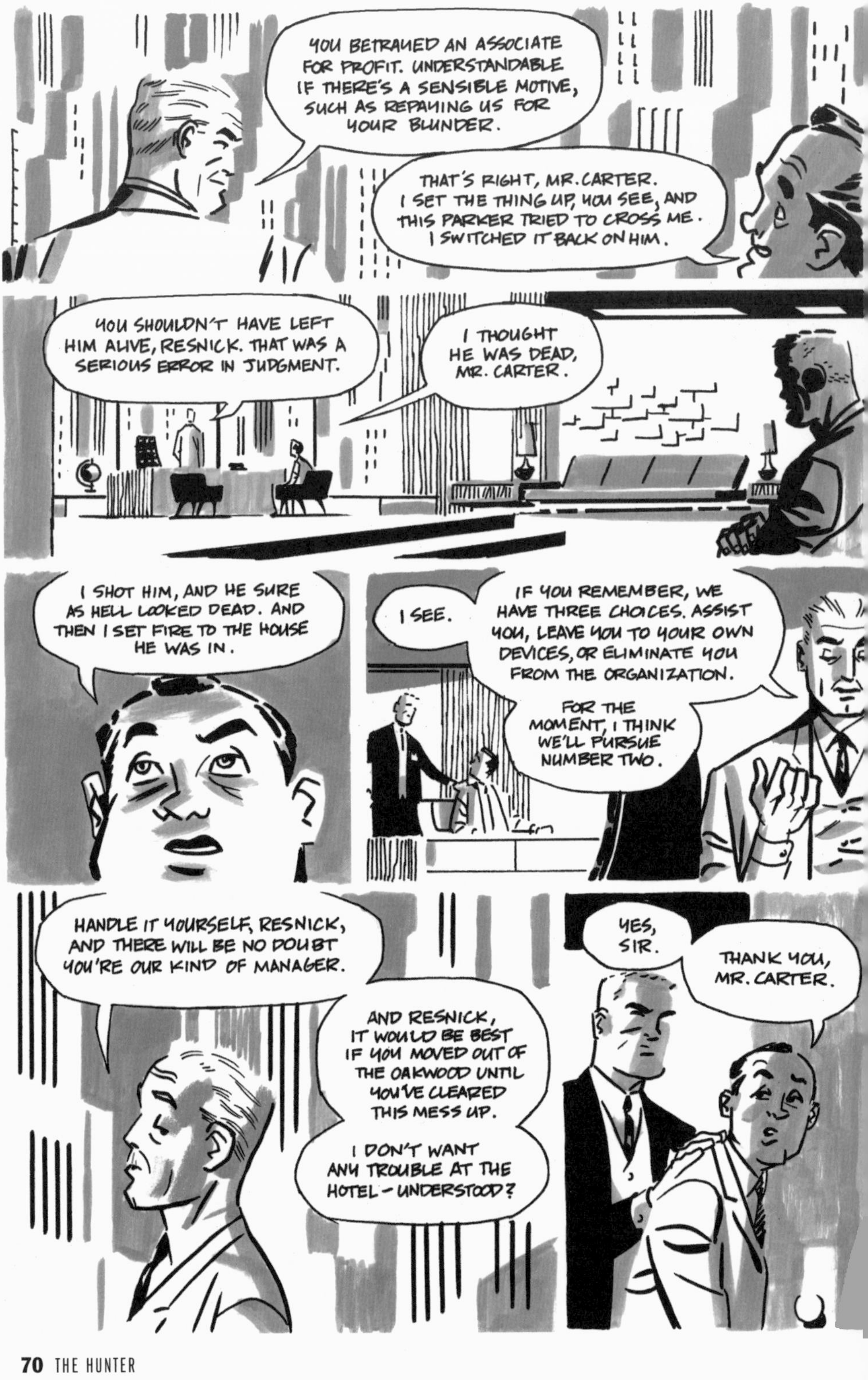
YOU BETRAYED AN ASSOCIATE FOR PROFIT. UNDERSTANDABLE IF THERE'S A SENSIBLE MOTIVE, SUCH AS REPAYING US FOR YOUR BLUNDER.
THAT'S RIGHT, MR. CARTER. I SET THE THING UP, YOU SEE, AND THIS PARKER TRIED TO CROSS ME. I SWITCHED IT BACK ON HIM.
YOU SHOULDN'T HAVE LEFT HIM ALIVE, RESNICK. THAT WAS A SERIOUS ERROR IN JUDGMENT.
I THOUGHT HE WAS DEAD, MR. CARTER.
I SHOT HIM, AND HE SURE AS HELL LOOKED DEAD. AND THEN I SET FIRE TO THE HOUSE HE WAS IN.
I SEE.
IF YOU REMEMBER, WE HAVE THREE CHOICES. ASSIST YOU, LEAVE YOU TO YOUR OWN DEVICES, OR ELIMINATE YOU FROM THE ORGANIZATION.
FOR THE MOMENT, I THINK WE'LL PURSUE NUMBER TWO.
HANDLE IT YOURSELF, RESNICK, AND THERE WILL BE NO DOUBT YOU'RE OUR KIND OF MANAGER.
AND RESNICK, IT WOULD BE BEST IF YOU MOVED OUT OF THE OAKWOOD UNTIL YOU'VE CLEARED THIS MESS UP.
I DON'T WANT ANY TROUBLE AT THE HOTEL - UNDERSTOOD?
YES, SIR.
THANK YOU, MR. CARTER.

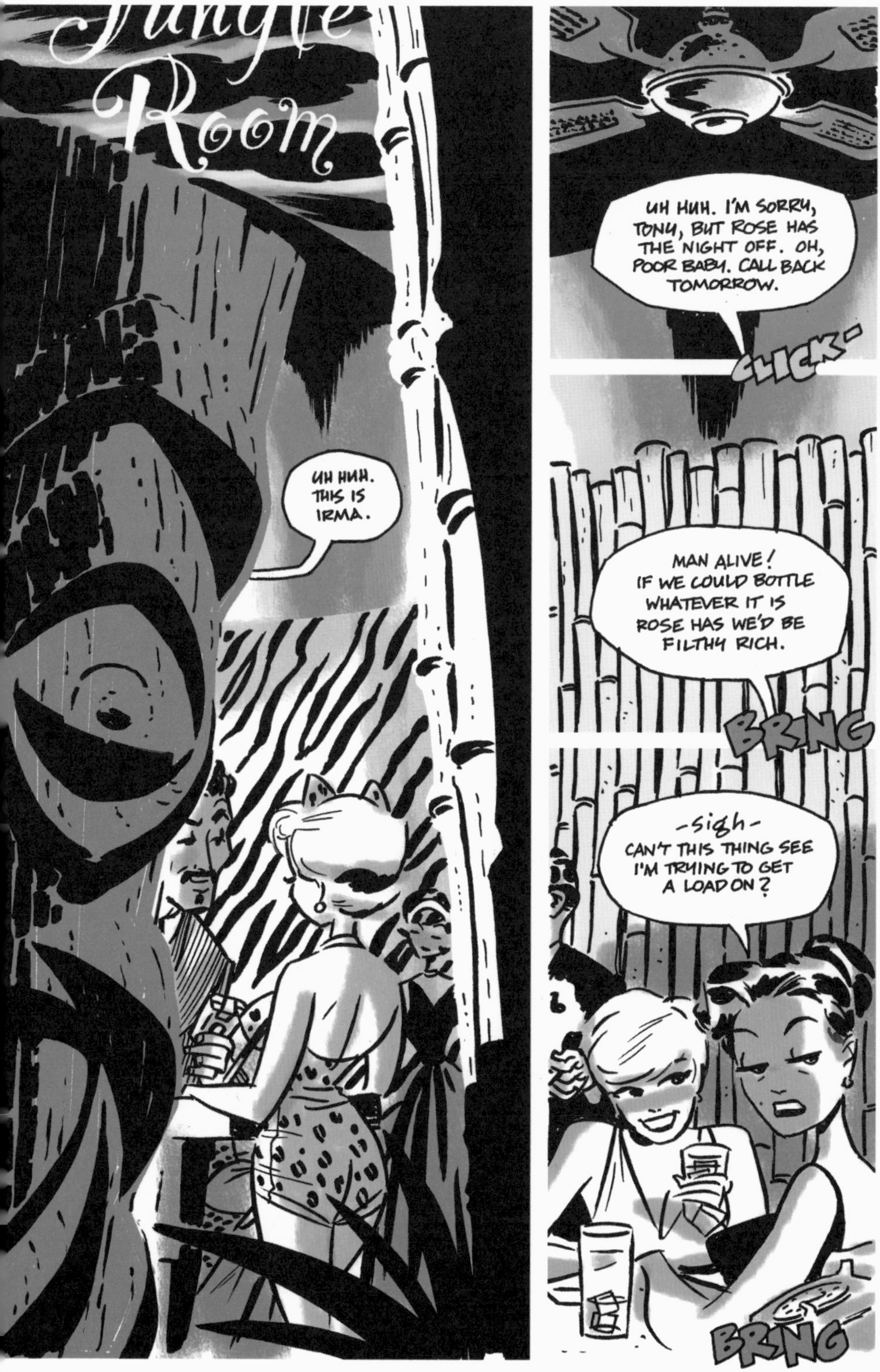
Jungle Room
UH HUH. THIS IS IRMA.
UH HUH. I'M SORRY, TONY, BUT ROSE HAS THE NIGHT OFF. OH, POOR BABY. CALL BACK TOMORROW.
CLICK-
MAN ALIVE! IF WE COULD BOTTLE WHATEVER IT IS ROSE HAS WE'D BE FILTHY RICH.
BRRNG
-sigh- CAN'T THIS THING SEE I'M TRYING TO GET A LOAD ON?
BRRNG

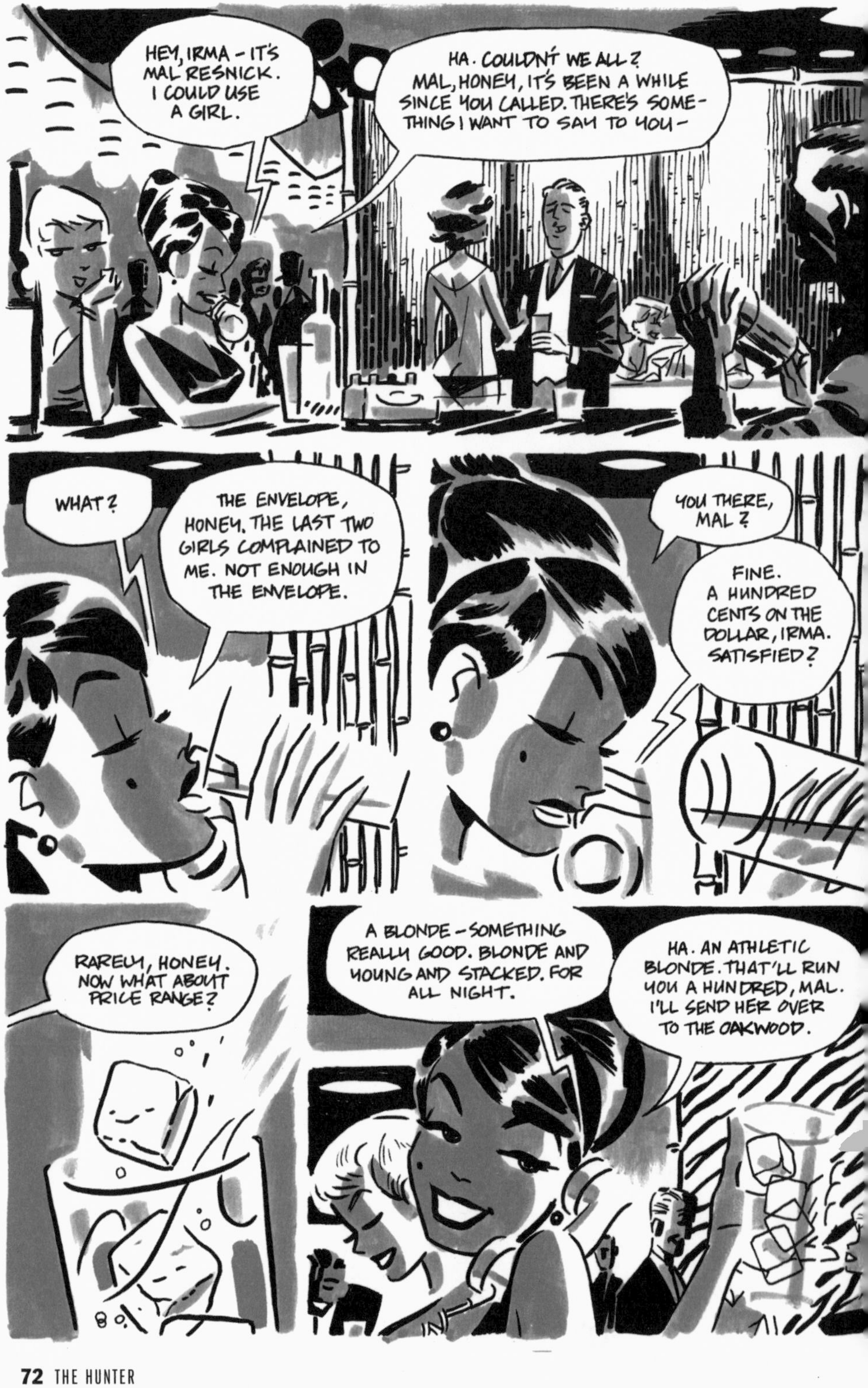
HEY, IRMA - IT'S MAL RESNICK. I COULD USE A GIRL.
HA. COULDN'T WE ALL? MAL, HONEY, IT'S BEEN A WHILE SINCE YOU CALLED. THERE'S SOMETHING I WANT TO SAY TO YOU-
WHAT?
THE ENVELOPE, HONEY. THE LAST TWO GIRLS COMPLAINED TO ME. NOT ENOUGH IN THE ENVELOPE.
YOU THERE, MAL?
FINE. A HUNDRED CENTS ON THE DOLLAR, IRMA. SATISFIED?
RARELY, HONEY. NOW WHAT ABOUT PRICE RANGE?
A BLONDE - SOMETHING REALLY GOOD. BLONDE AND YOUNG AND STACKED. FOR ALL NIGHT.
HA. AN ATHLETIC BLONDE. THAT'LL RUN YOU A HUNDRED, MAL. I'LL SEND HER OVER TO THE OAKWOOD.

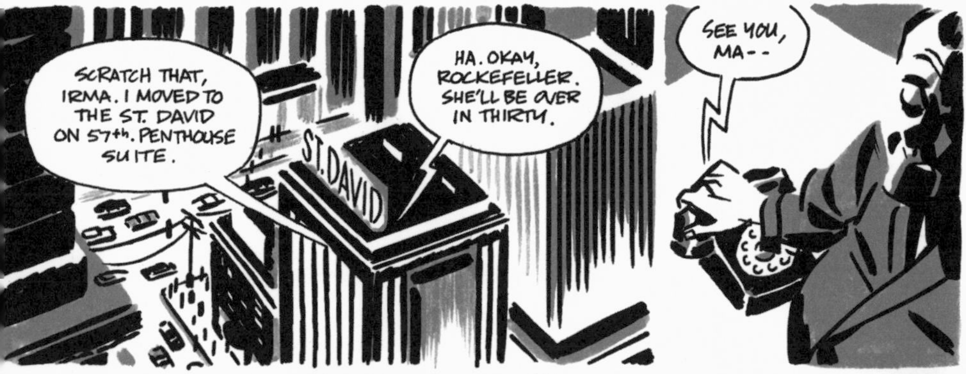
SCRATCH THAT, IRMA. I MOVED TO THE ST. DAVID ON 57th. PENTHOUSE SUITE.
ST. DAVID
HA. OKAY, ROCKEFELLER. SHE'LL BE OVER IN THIRTY.
SEE YOU, MA--

Mal was disgusted. He wasn't sure why he splurged on the penthouse suite any more than he was sure why he was throwing away a c-note on a broad who couldn't possibly do more for him than Pearl would- probably far less. Disgusted, he picked up the phone.

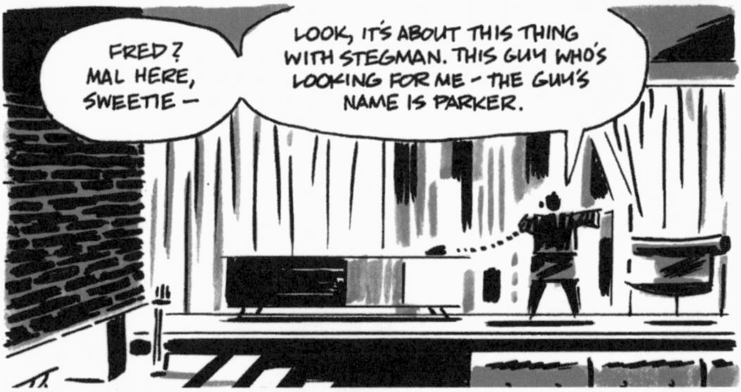
FRED? MAL HERE, SWEETIE -
LOOK, IT'S ABOUT THIS THING WITH STEGMAN. THIS GUY WHO'S LOOKING FOR ME - THE GUY'S NAME IS PARKER.

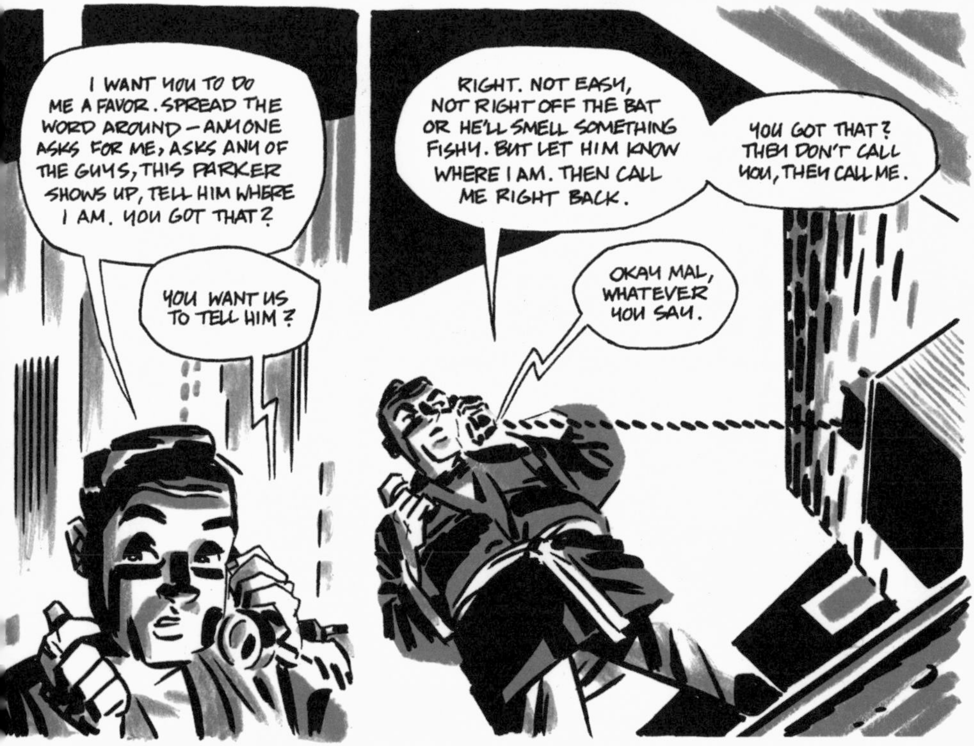
I WANT YOU TO DO ME A FAVOR. SPREAD THE WORD AROUND - ANYONE ASKS FOR ME, ASKS ANY OF THE GUYS, THIS PARKER SHOWS UP, TELL HIM WHERE I AM. YOU GOT THAT?
YOU WANT US TO TELL HIM?
RIGHT. NOT EASY, NOT RIGHT OFF THE BAT OR HE'LL SMELL SOMETHING FISHY. BUT LET HIM KNOW WHERE I AM. THEN CALL ME RIGHT BACK.
YOU GOT THAT? THEY DON'T CALL YOU, THEY CALL ME.
OKAY MAL, WHATEVER YOU SAY.

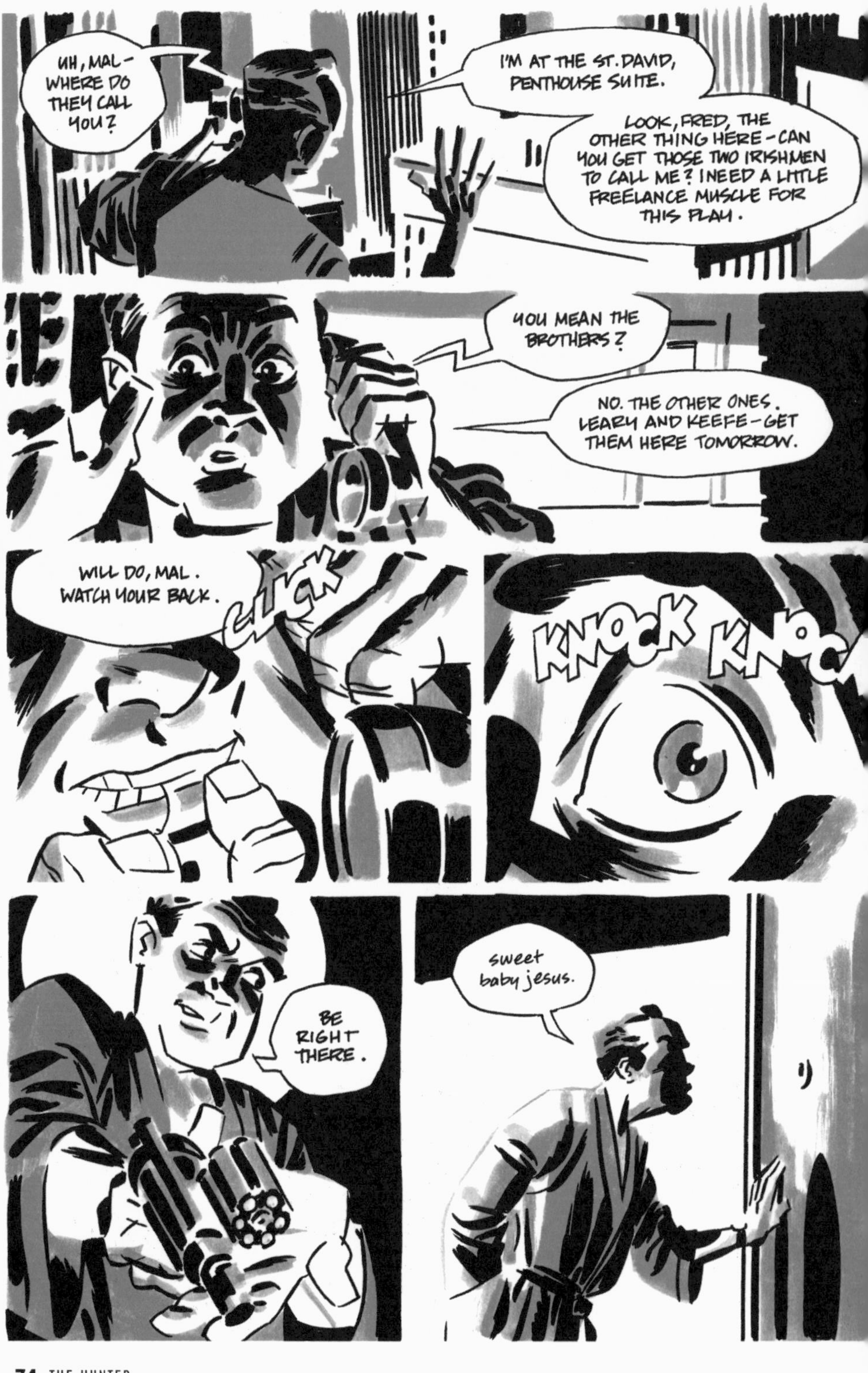
UH, MAL- WHERE DO THEY CALL YOU?
I'M AT THE ST. DAVID, PENTHOUSE SUITE.
LOOK, FRED, THE OTHER THING HERE - CAN YOU GET THOSE TWO IRISHMEN TO CALL ME? I NEED A LITTLE FREELANCE MUSCLE FOR THIS PLAY.
YOU MEAN THE BROTHERS?
NO. THE OTHER ONES. LEARY AND KEEFE - GET THEM HERE TOMORROW.
WILL DO, MAL. WATCH YOUR BACK.
CLICK
KNOCK KNOC
BE RIGHT THERE.
sweet baby jesus.

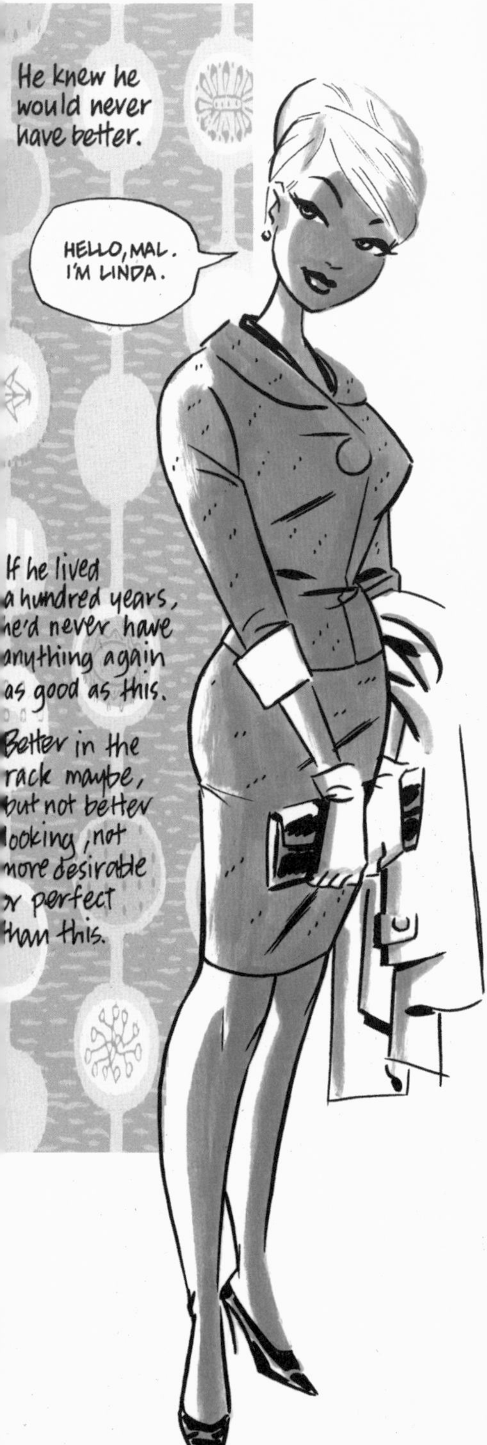
He knew he would never have better.
HELLO, MAL. I'M LINDA.
If he lived a hundred years, he'd never have anything again as good as this.
Better in the rack maybe, but not better looking, not more desirable or perfect than this.

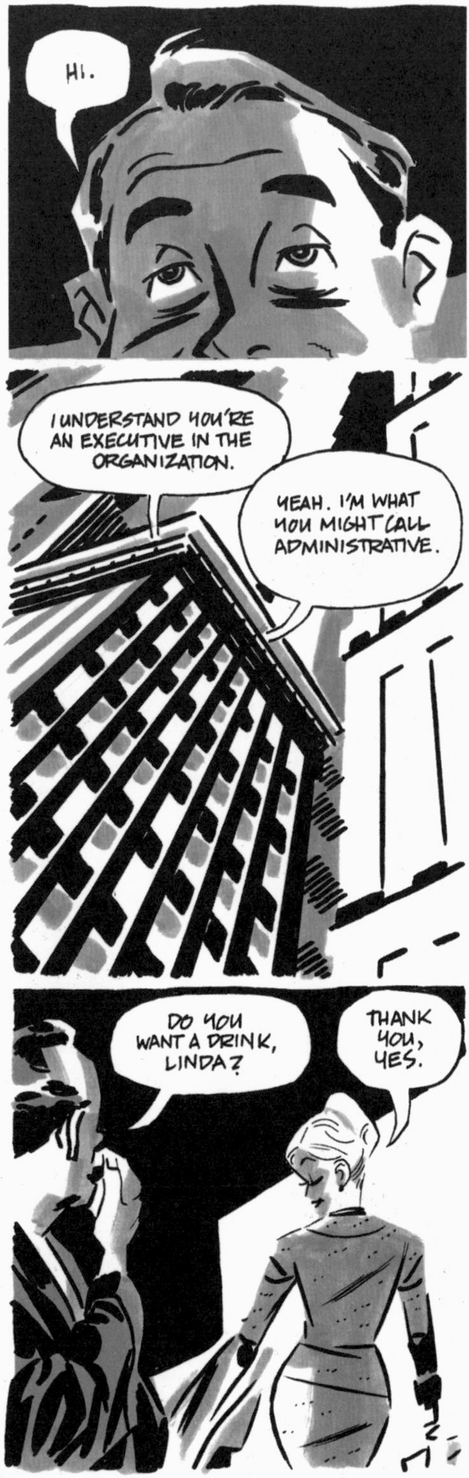
HI.
I UNDERSTAND YOU'RE AN EXECUTIVE IN THE ORGANIZATION.
YEAH. I'M WHAT YOU MIGHT CALL ADMINISTRATIVE.
DO YOU WANT A DRINK, LINDA?
THANK YOU, YES.

Excitement and expectation and her skill finished him almost at once. He lay startled and humiliated and enraged: the boy who got to the movie just as it was ending. But then he found out what it truly was he was paying her for.

To make him more a man than he was. With gentle, smiling urgency she made him ready again.

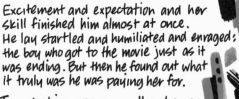

It was the best he ever had. Afterwards, he slept, content.

He was back in the movie star's house feeding Ryan the story about Parker and Sill planning a double cross.

Mal told a convincing lie and Ryan listened but he found it hard to imagine Parker crossing him.

That night Mal slit Chester's throat. He went to Ryan's room and claimed he'd found Chester after seeing Parker leave his room.

Ryan was incredulous but convinced.

They crept down the hall and Ryan stopped off in Sill's room for a minute.

Both men checked their guns and made their way to the bathroom connected to Parker's room.

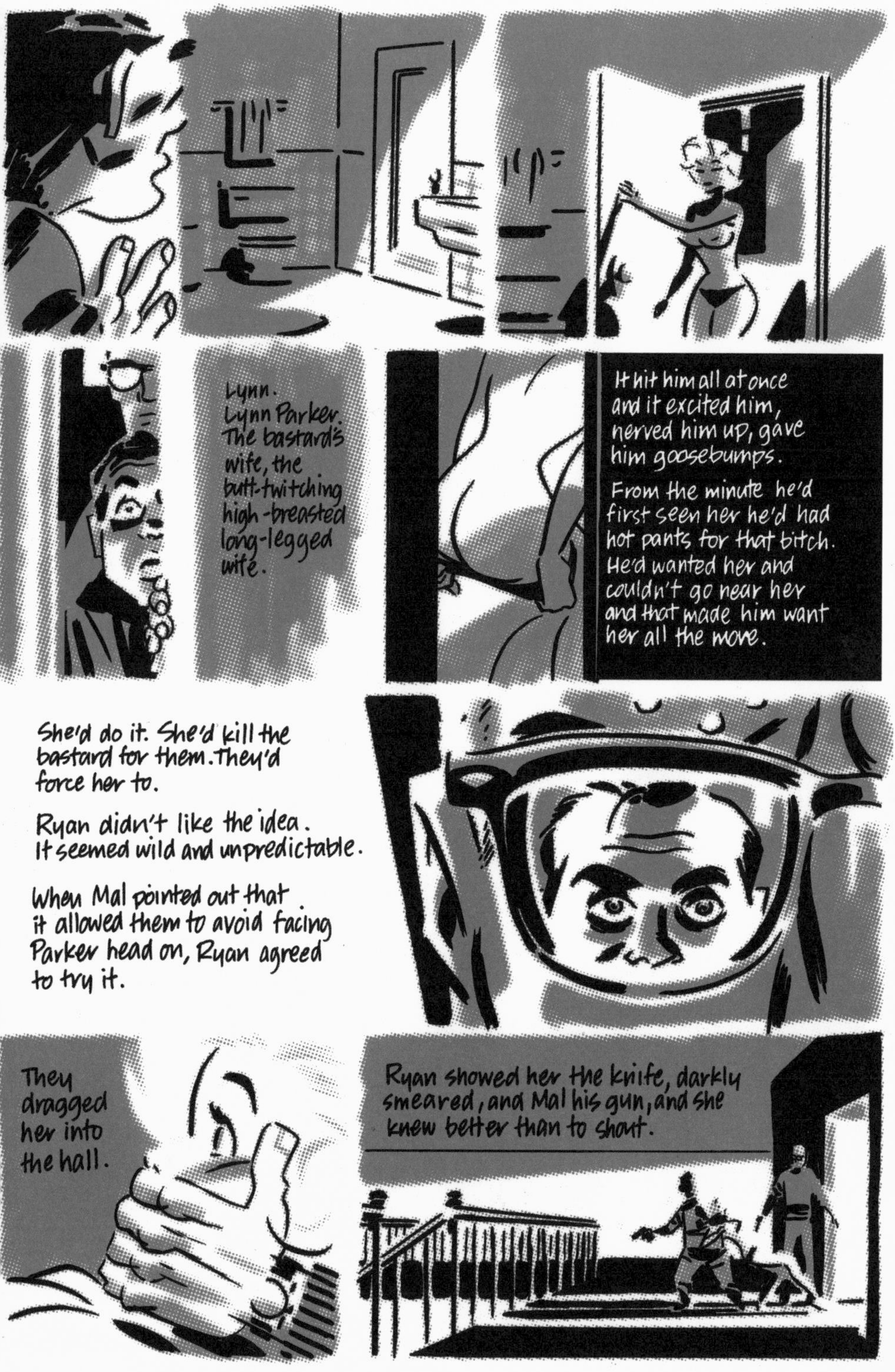
Lynn.
Lynn Parker. The bastard's wife, the butt-twitching high-breasted long-legged wife.
It hit him all at once and it excited him, nerved him up, gave him goosebumps.
From the minute he'd first seen her he'd had hot pants for that bitch. He'd wanted her and couldn't go near her and that made him want her all the more.
She'd do it. She'd kill the bastard for them. They'd force her to.
Ryan didn't like the idea. It seemed wild and unpredictable.
When Mal pointed out that it allowed them to avoid facing Parker head on, Ryan agreed to try it.
They dragged her into the hall.
Ryan showed her the knife, darkly smeared, and Mal his gun, and she knew better than to shout.

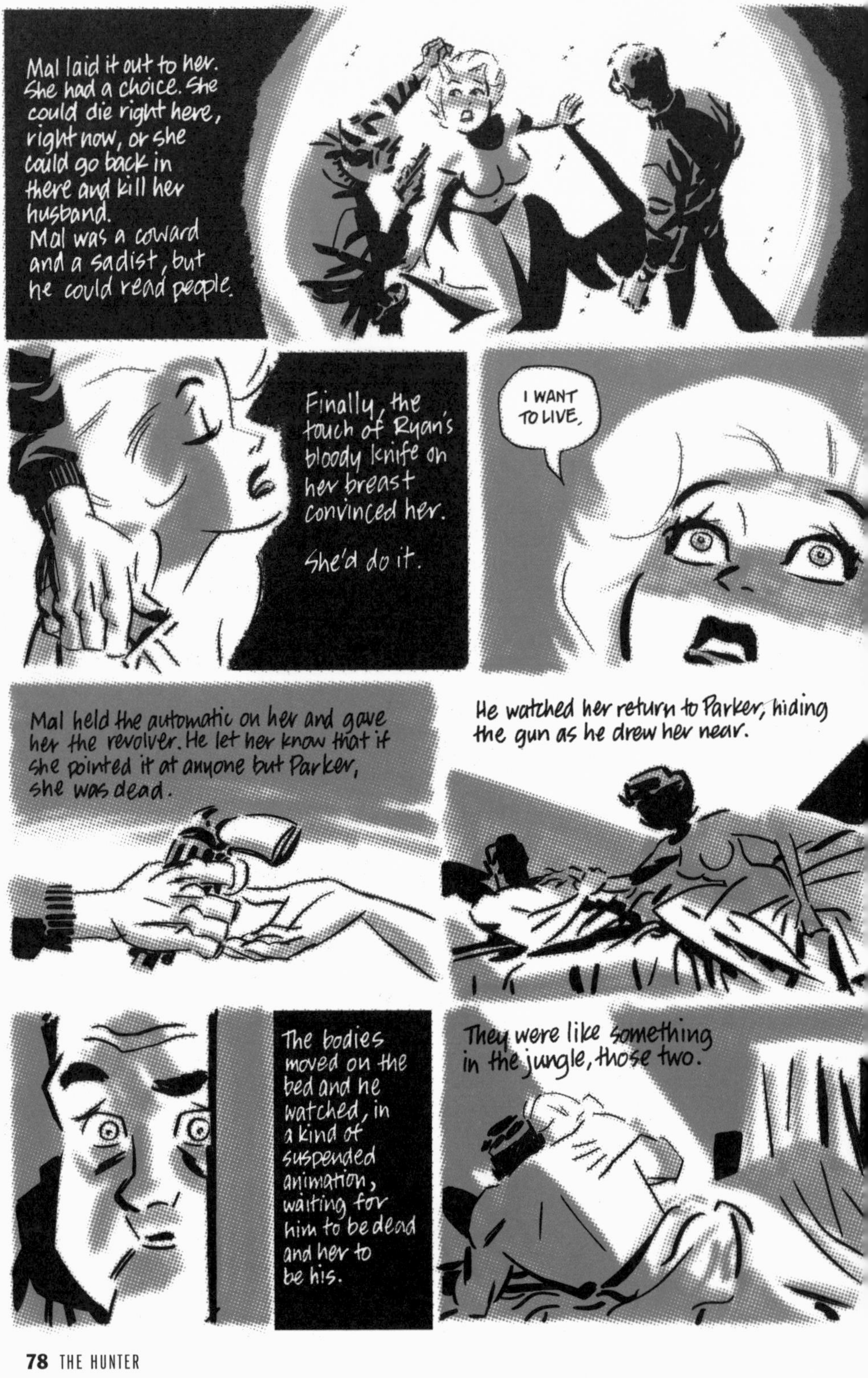
Mal laid it out to her. She had a choice. She could die right here, right now, or she could go back in there and kill her husband.
Mal was a coward and a sadist, but he could read people.
Finally, the touch of Ryan's bloody knife on her breast convinced her.
She'd do it.
I WANT TO LIVE.
Mal held the automatic on her and gave her the revolver. He let her know that if she pointed it at anyone but Parker, she was dead.
He watched her return to Parker, hiding the gun as he drew her near.
The bodies moved on the bed and he watched, in a kind of suspended animation, waiting for him to be dead and her to be his.
They were like something in the jungle, those two.

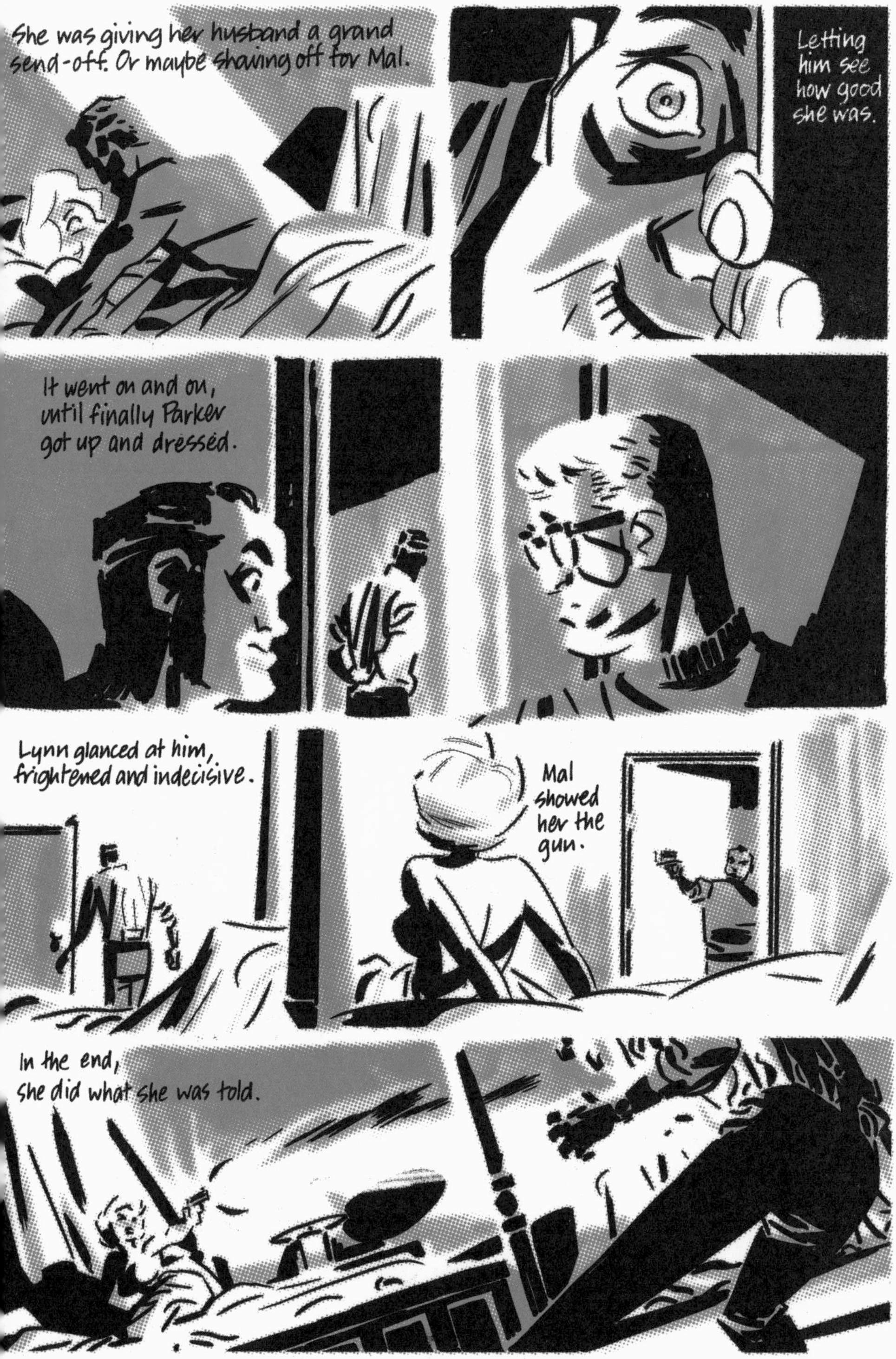
She was giving her husband a grand send-off. Or maybe showing off for Mal.
Letting him see how good she was.
It went on and on, until finally Parker got up and dressed.
Lynn glanced at him, frightened and indecisive.
Mal showed her the gun.
In the end, she did what she was told.

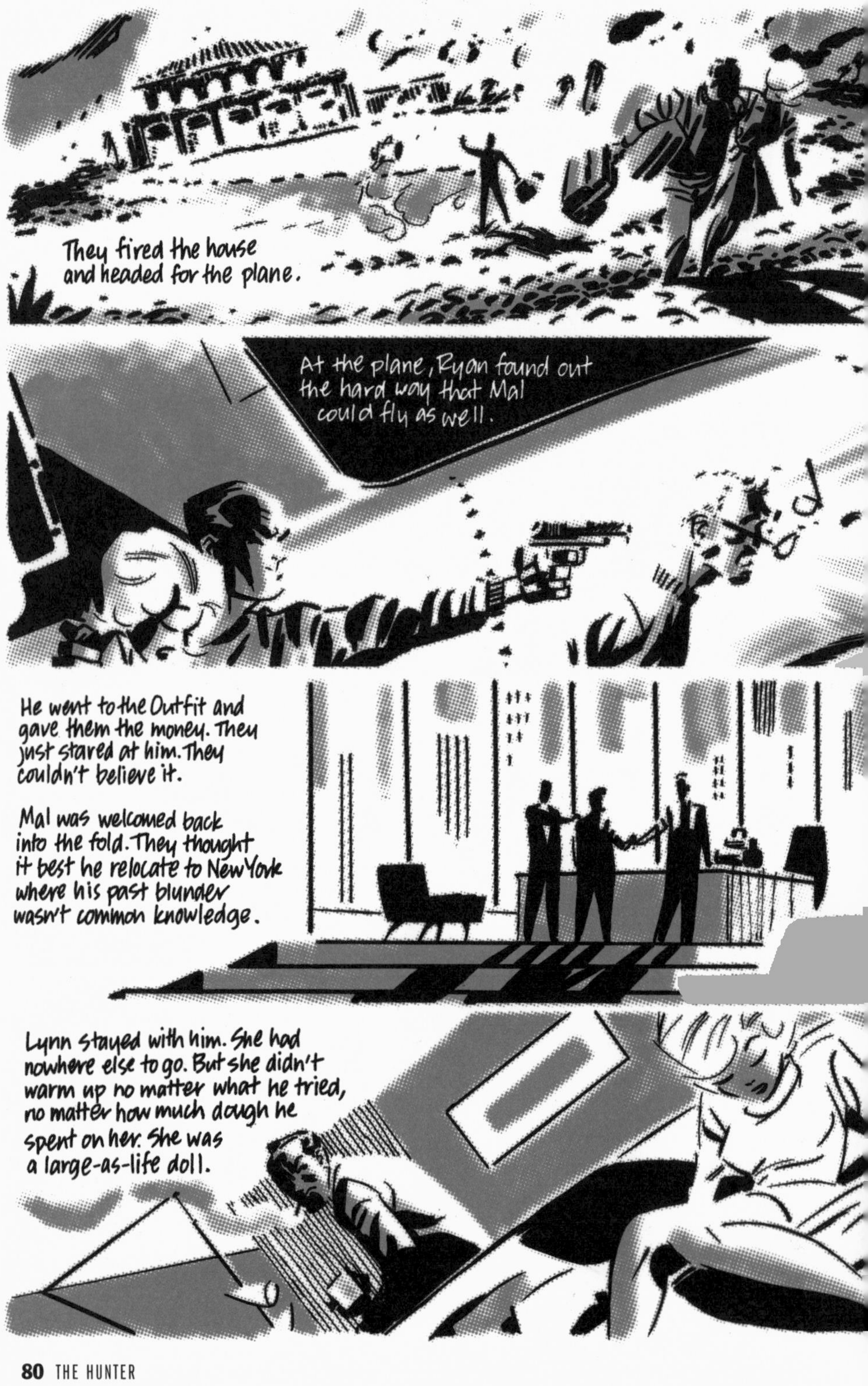
They fired the house and headed for the plane.
At the plane, Ryan found out the hard way that Mal could fly as well.
He went to the Outfit and gave them the money. They just stared at him. They couldn't believe it.
Mal was welcomed back into the fold. They thought it best he relocate to New York where his past blunder wasn't common knowledge.
Lynn stayed with him. She had nowhere else to go. But she didn't warm up no matter what he tried, no matter how much dough he spent on her. She was a large-as-life doll.

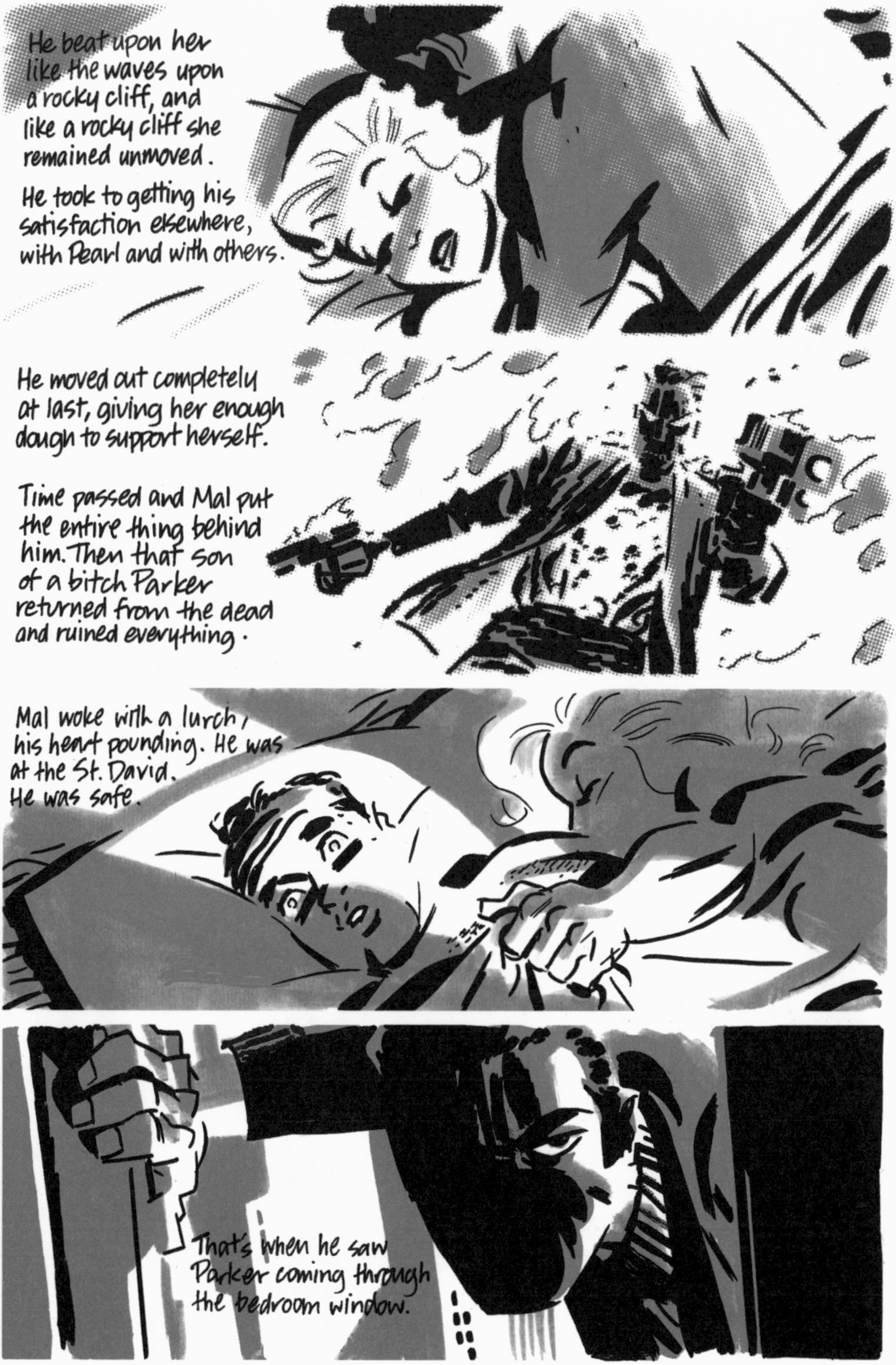
He beat upon her like the waves upon a rocky cliff, and like a rocky cliff she remained unmoved.
He took to getting his satisfaction elsewhere, with Pearl and with others.
He moved out completely at last, giving her enough dough to support herself.
Time passed and Mal put the entire thing behind him. Then that son of a bitch Parker returned from the dead and ruined everything.
Mal woke with a lurch, his heart pounding. He was at the St. David. He was safe.
That's when he saw Parker coming through the bedroom window.

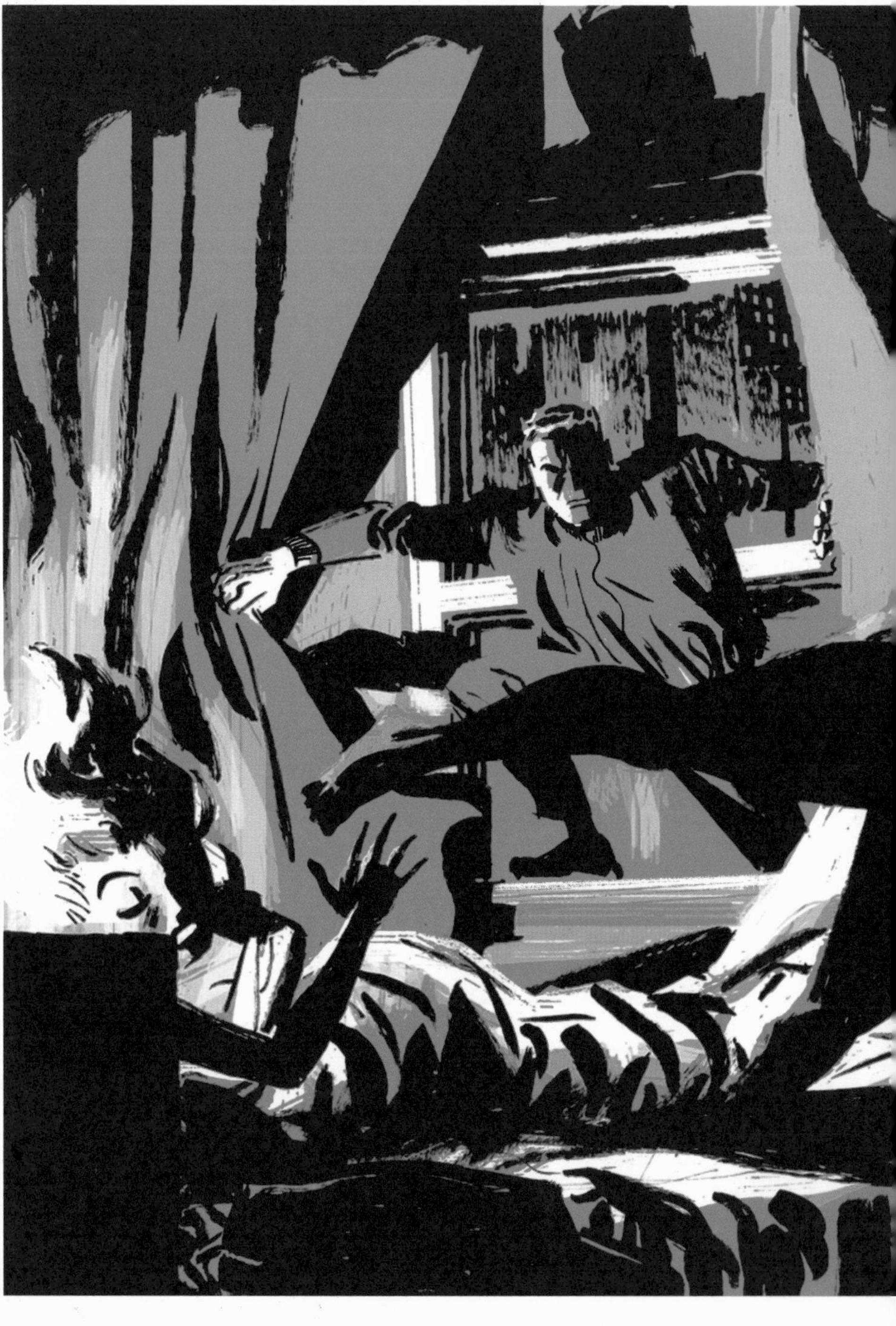

Mal had got himself the best hotel suite and the best professional lay.

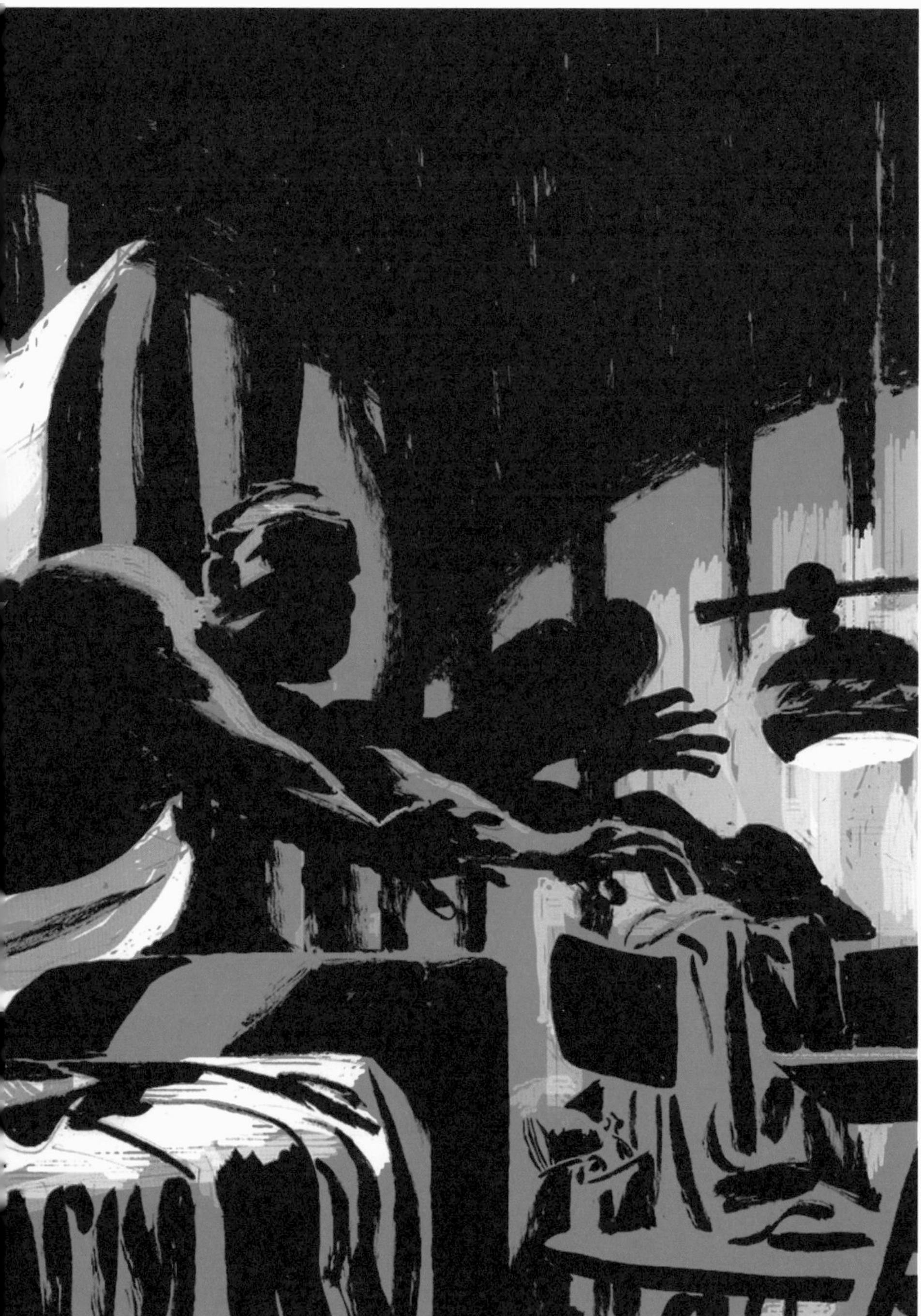

And he got them just in time.

BOOK THREE

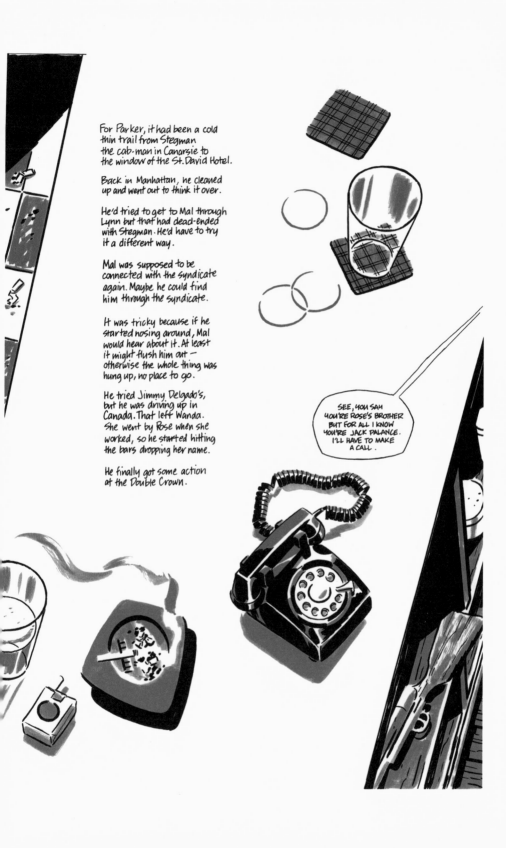

For Parker, it had been a cold thin trail from Stegman the cab-man in Canarsie to the window of the St. David Hotel.

Back in Manhattan, he cleaned up and went out to think it over.

He'd tried to get to Mal through Lynn but that had dead-ended with Stegman. He'd have to try it a different way.

Mal was supposed to be connected with the syndicate again. Maybe he could find him through the syndicate.

It was tricky because if he started nosing around, Mal would hear about it. At least it might flush him out — otherwise the whole thing was hung up, no place to go.

He tried Jimmy Delgado's, but he was driving up in Canada. That left Wanda. She went by Rose when she worked, so he started hitting the bars dropping her name.

He finally got some action at the Double Crown.

SEE, YOU SAY YOU'RE ROSE'S BROTHER BUT FOR ALL I KNOW YOU'RE JACK PALANCE. I'LL HAVE TO MAKE A CALL.

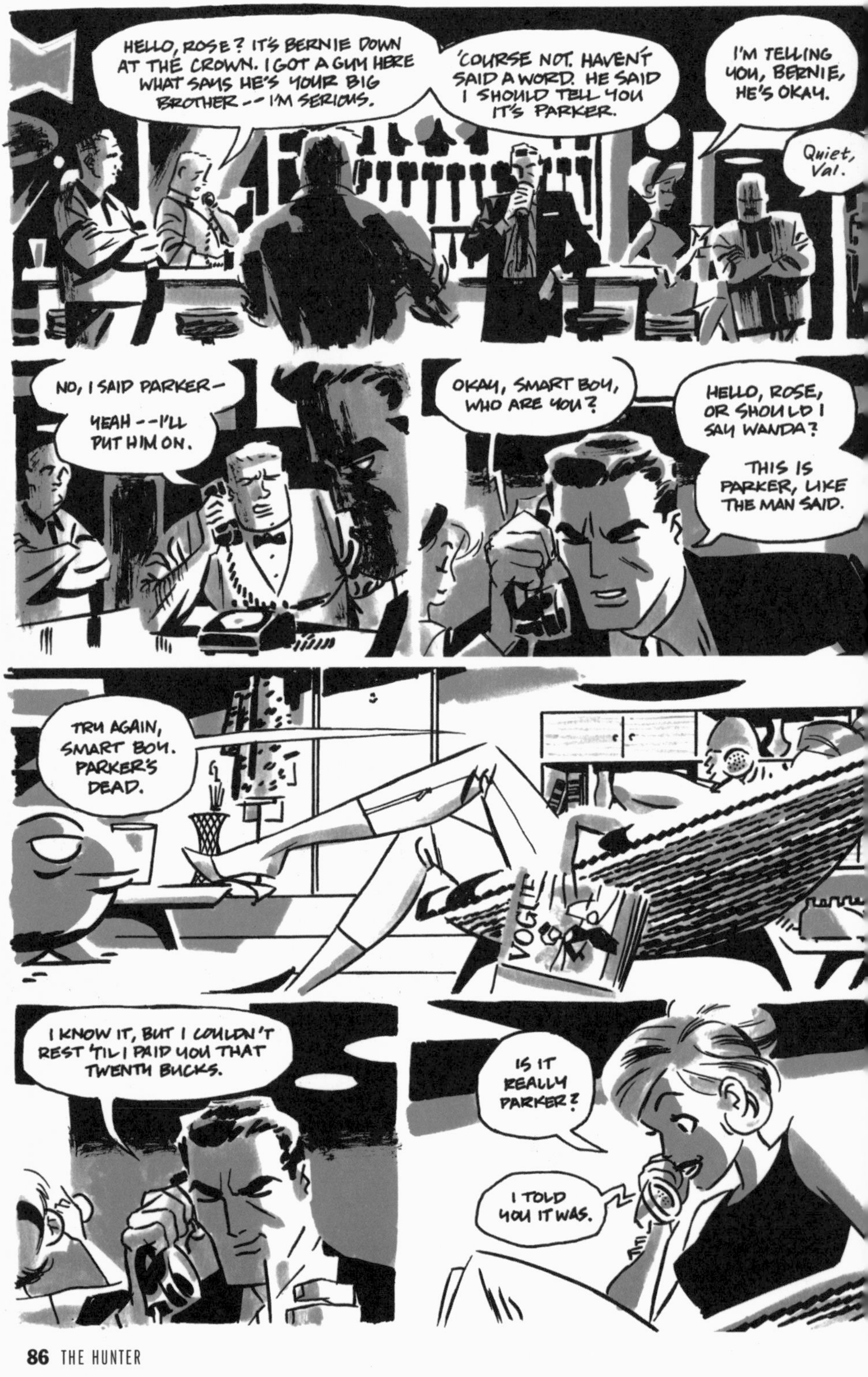
HELLO, ROSE? IT'S BERNIE DOWN AT THE CROWN. I GOT A GUY HERE WHAT SAYS HE'S YOUR BIG BROTHER -- I'M SERIOUS.
'COURSE NOT. HAVEN'T SAID A WORD. HE SAID I SHOULD TELL YOU IT'S PARKER.
I'M TELLING YOU, BERNIE, HE'S OKAY.
Quiet, Val.
NO, I SAID PARKER-
YEAH --I'LL PUT HIM ON.
OKAY, SMART BOY, WHO ARE YOU?
HELLO, ROSE, OR SHOULD I SAY WANDA?
THIS IS PARKER, LIKE THE MAN SAID.
TRY AGAIN, SMART BOY. PARKER'S DEAD.
VOGUE
I KNOW IT, BUT I COULDN'T REST 'TIL I PAID YOU THAT TWENTY BUCKS.
IS IT REALLY PARKER?
I TOLD YOU IT WAS.

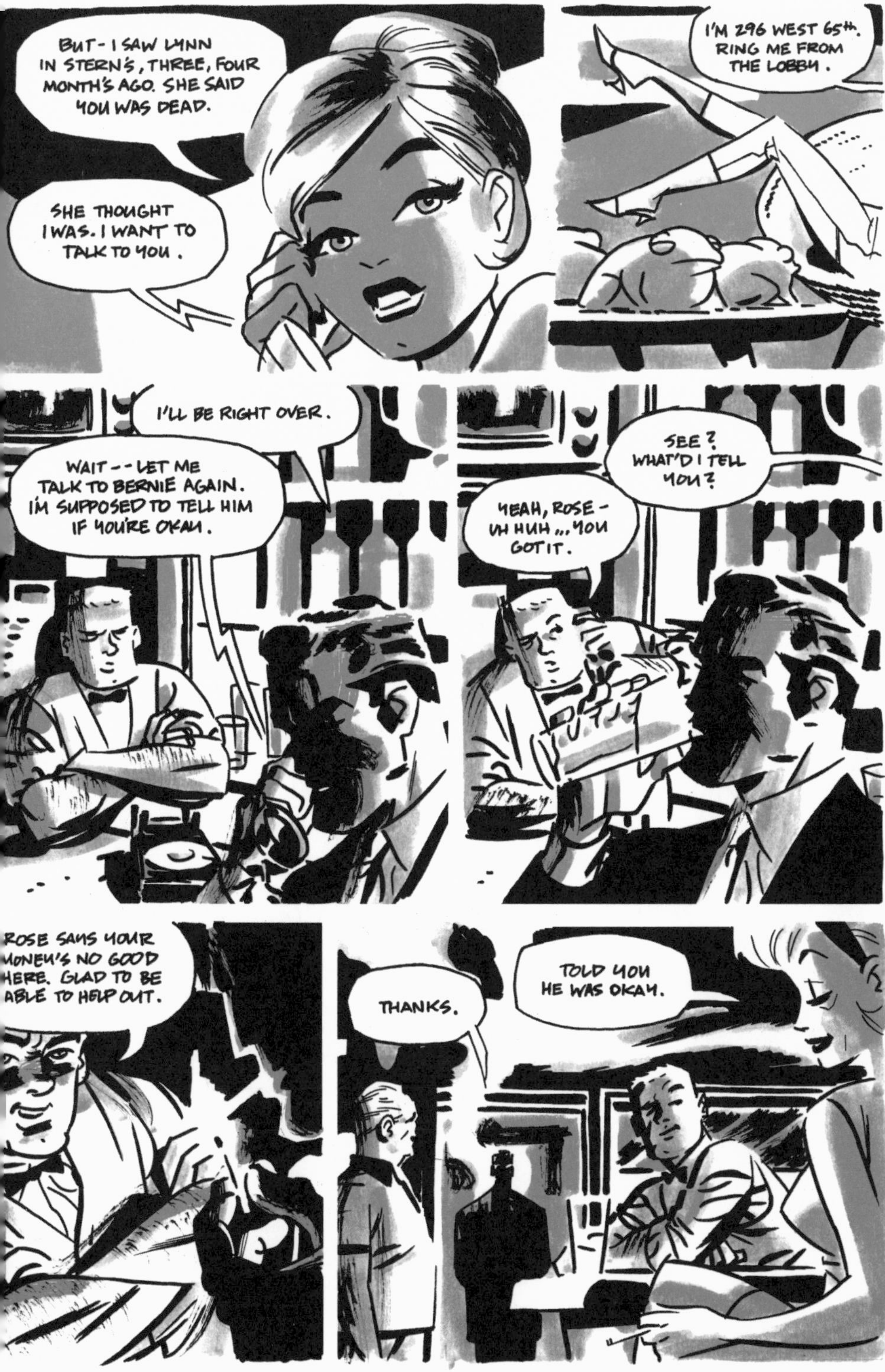
BUT- I SAW LYNN IN STERN'S, THREE, FOUR MONTH'S AGO. SHE SAID YOU WAS DEAD.
SHE THOUGHT I WAS. I WANT TO TALK TO YOU.
I'M 296 WEST 65th. RING ME FROM THE LOBBY.
I'LL BE RIGHT OVER.
WAIT-- LET ME TALK TO BERNIE AGAIN. I'M SUPPOSED TO TELL HIM IF YOU'RE OKAY.
YEAH, ROSE - UH HUH... YOU GOT IT.
SEE? WHAT'D I TELL YOU?
ROSE SAYS YOUR MONEY'S NO GOOD HERE. GLAD TO BE ABLE TO HELP OUT.
THANKS.
TOLD YOU HE WAS OKAY.

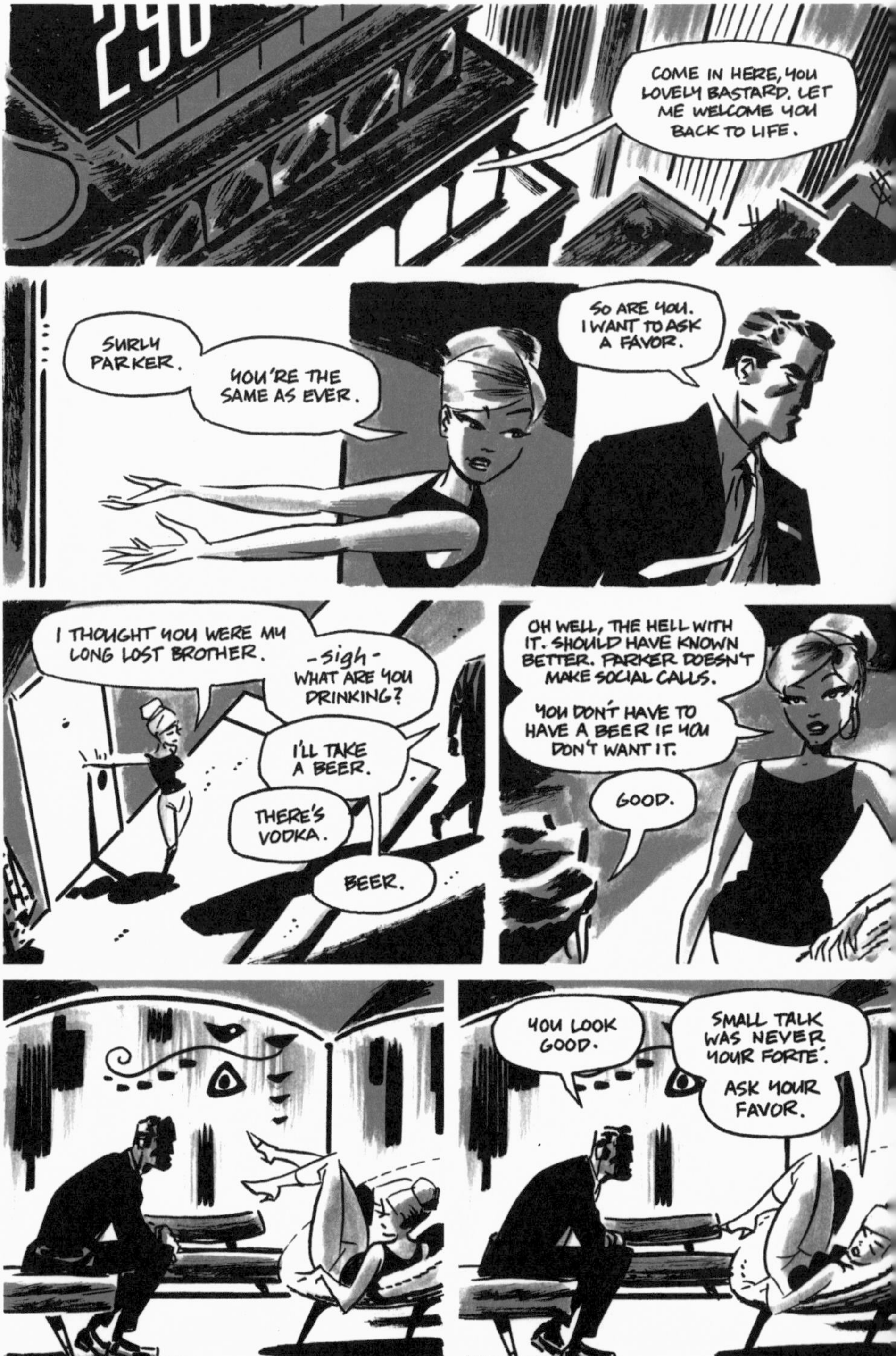

COME IN HERE, YOU LOVELY BASTARD. LET ME WELCOME YOU BACK TO LIFE.
SURLY PARKER.
YOU'RE THE SAME AS EVER.
SO ARE YOU. I WANT TO ASK A FAVOR.
I THOUGHT YOU WERE MY LONG LOST BROTHER.
-sigh- WHAT ARE YOU DRINKING?
I'LL TAKE A BEER.
THERE'S VODKA.
BEER.
OH WELL, THE HELL WITH IT. SHOULD HAVE KNOWN BETTER. PARKER DOESN'T MAKE SOCIAL CALLS.
YOU DON'T HAVE TO HAVE A BEER IF YOU DON'T WANT IT.
GOOD.
YOU LOOK GOOD.
SMALL TALK WAS NEVER YOUR FORTE.
ASK YOUR FAVOR.

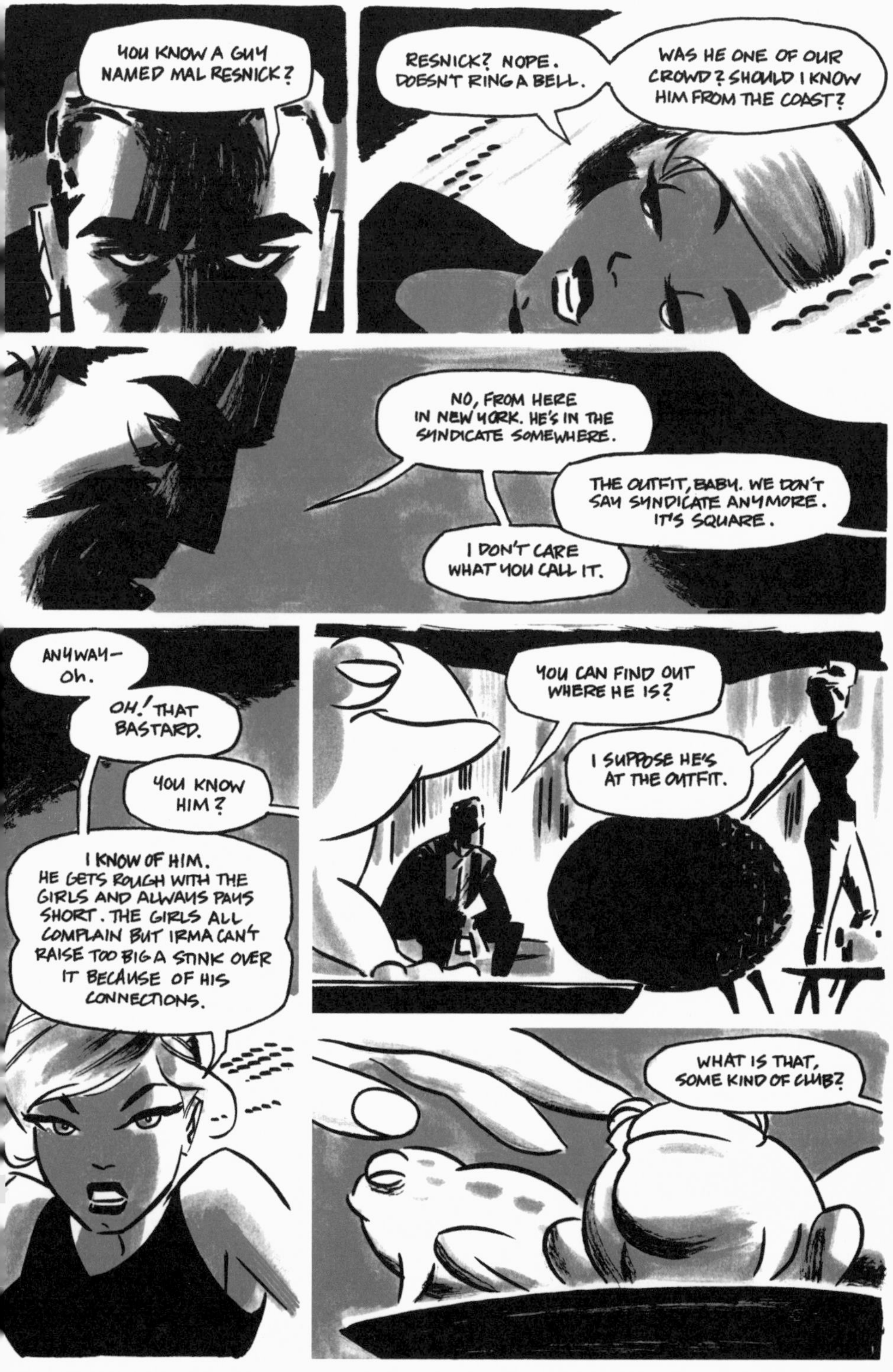
YOU KNOW A GUY NAMED MAL RESNICK?
RESNICK? NOPE. DOESN'T RING A BELL.
WAS HE ONE OF OUR CROWD? SHOULD I KNOW HIM FROM THE COAST?
NO, FROM HERE IN NEW YORK. HE'S IN THE SYNDICATE SOMEWHERE.
THE OUTFIT, BABY. WE DON'T SAY SYNDICATE ANYMORE. IT'S SQUARE.
I DON'T CARE WHAT YOU CALL IT.
ANYWAY— Oh.
OH! THAT BASTARD.
YOU KNOW HIM?
I KNOW OF HIM. HE GETS ROUGH WITH THE GIRLS AND ALWAYS PAYS SHORT. THE GIRLS ALL COMPLAIN BUT IRMA CAN'T RAISE TOO BIG A STINK OVER IT BECAUSE OF HIS CONNECTIONS.
YOU CAN FIND OUT WHERE HE IS?
I SUPPOSE HE'S AT THE OUTFIT.
WHAT IS THAT, SOME KIND OF CLUB?

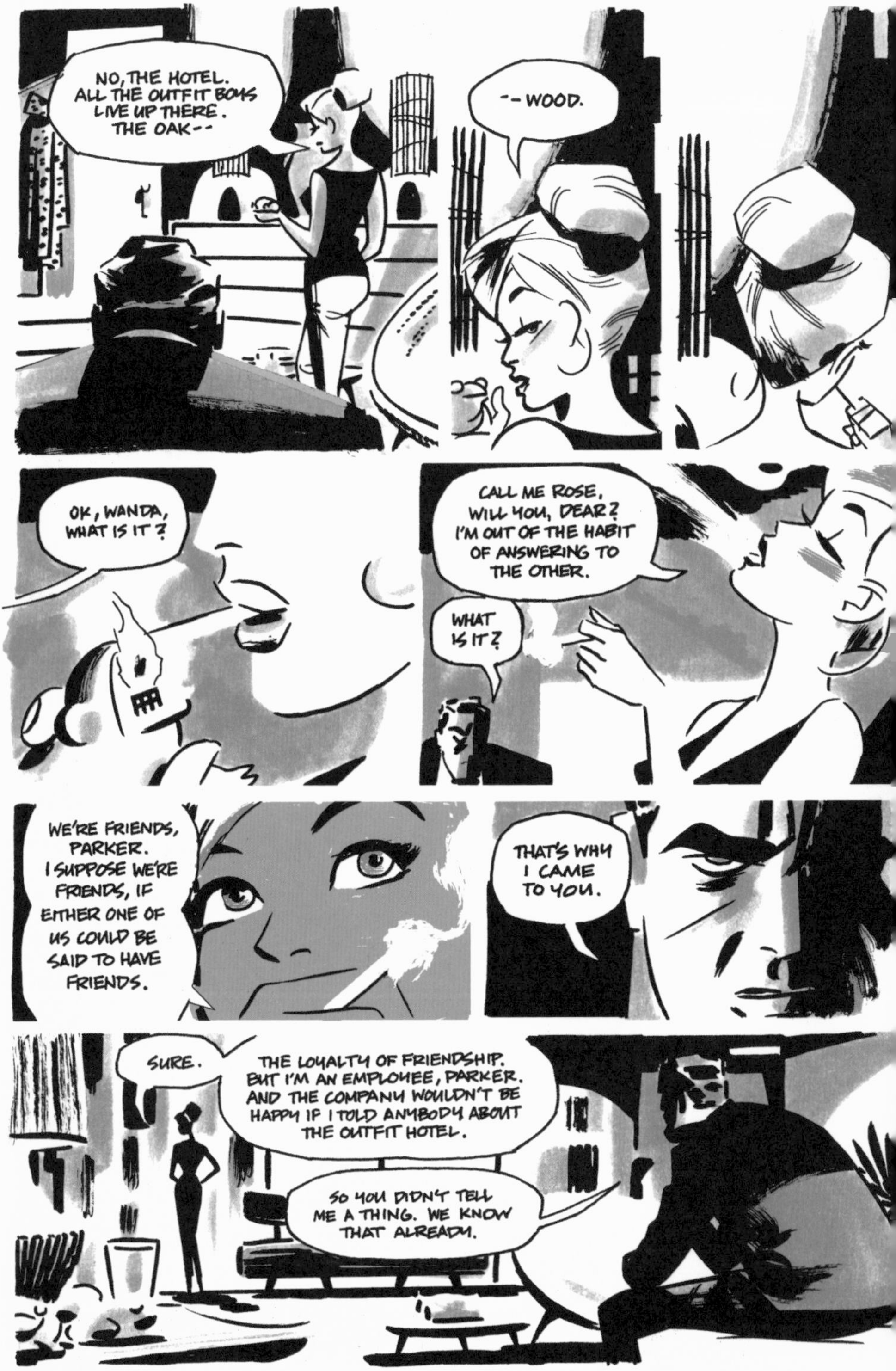
NO, THE HOTEL. ALL THE OUTFIT BOYS LIVE UP THERE. THE OAK--
--WOOD.
OK, WANDA, WHAT IS IT?
CALL ME ROSE, WILL YOU, DEAR? I'M OUT OF THE HABIT OF ANSWERING TO THE OTHER.
WHAT IS IT?
WE'RE FRIENDS, PARKER. I SUPPOSE WE'RE FRIENDS, IF EITHER ONE OF US COULD BE SAID TO HAVE FRIENDS.
THAT'S WHY I CAME TO YOU.
SURE.
THE LOYALTY OF FRIENDSHIP. BUT I'M AN EMPLOYEE, PARKER. AND THE COMPANY WOULDN'T BE HAPPY IF I TOLD ANYBODY ABOUT THE OUTFIT HOTEL.
SO YOU DIDN'T TELL ME A THING. WE KNOW THAT ALREADY.

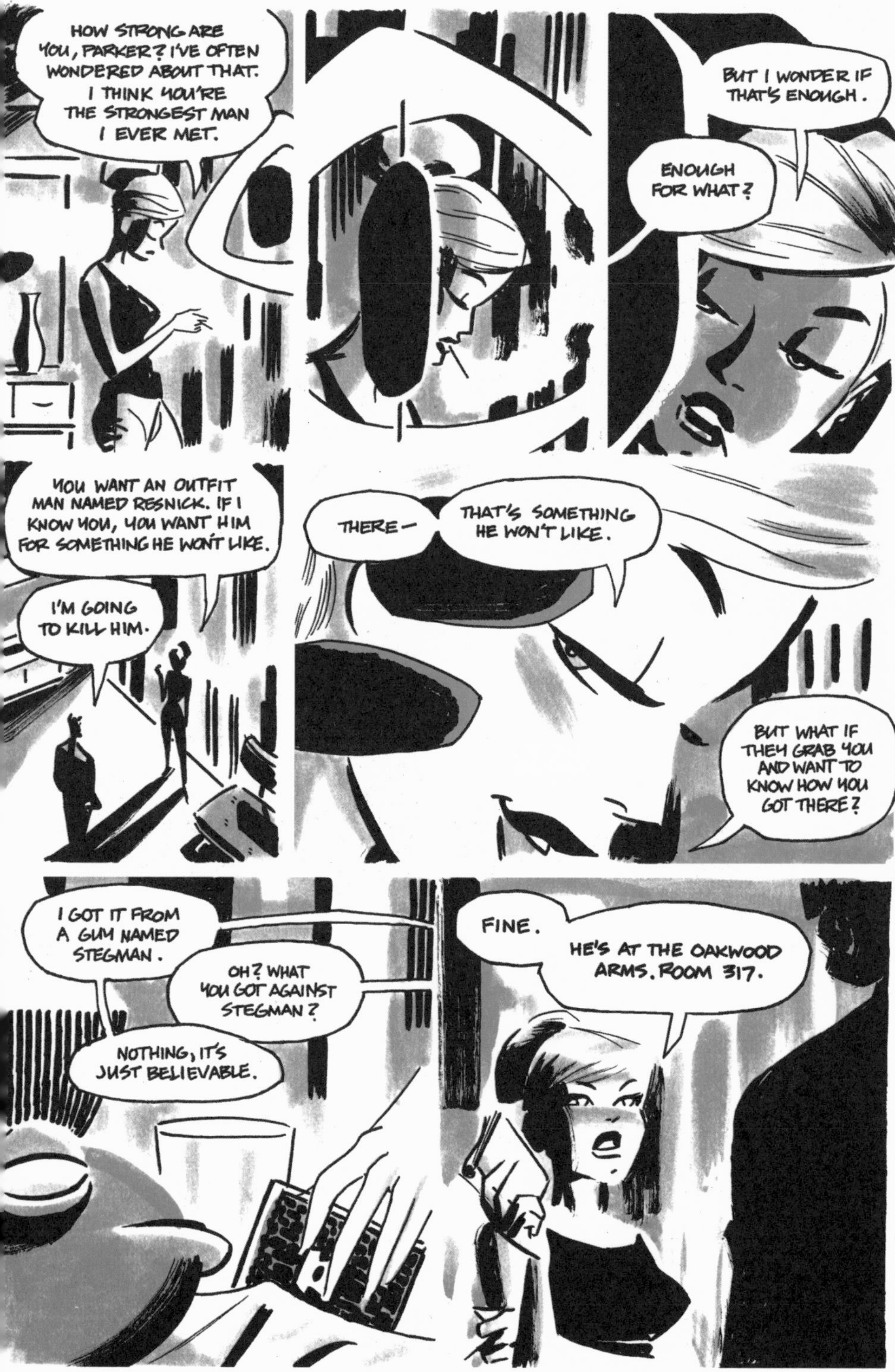
HOW STRONG ARE YOU, PARKER? I'VE OFTEN WONDERED ABOUT THAT. I THINK YOU'RE THE STRONGEST MAN I EVER MET.
BUT I WONDER IF THAT'S ENOUGH.
ENOUGH FOR WHAT?
YOU WANT AN OUTFIT MAN NAMED RESNICK. IF I KNOW YOU, YOU WANT HIM FOR SOMETHING HE WON'T LIKE.
I'M GOING TO KILL HIM.
THERE—
THAT'S SOMETHING HE WON'T LIKE.
BUT WHAT IF THEY GRAB YOU AND WANT TO KNOW HOW YOU GOT THERE?
I GOT IT FROM A GUY NAMED STEGMAN.
OH? WHAT YOU GOT AGAINST STEGMAN?
NOTHING, IT'S JUST BELIEVABLE.
FINE.
HE'S AT THE OAKWOOD ARMS. ROOM 317.

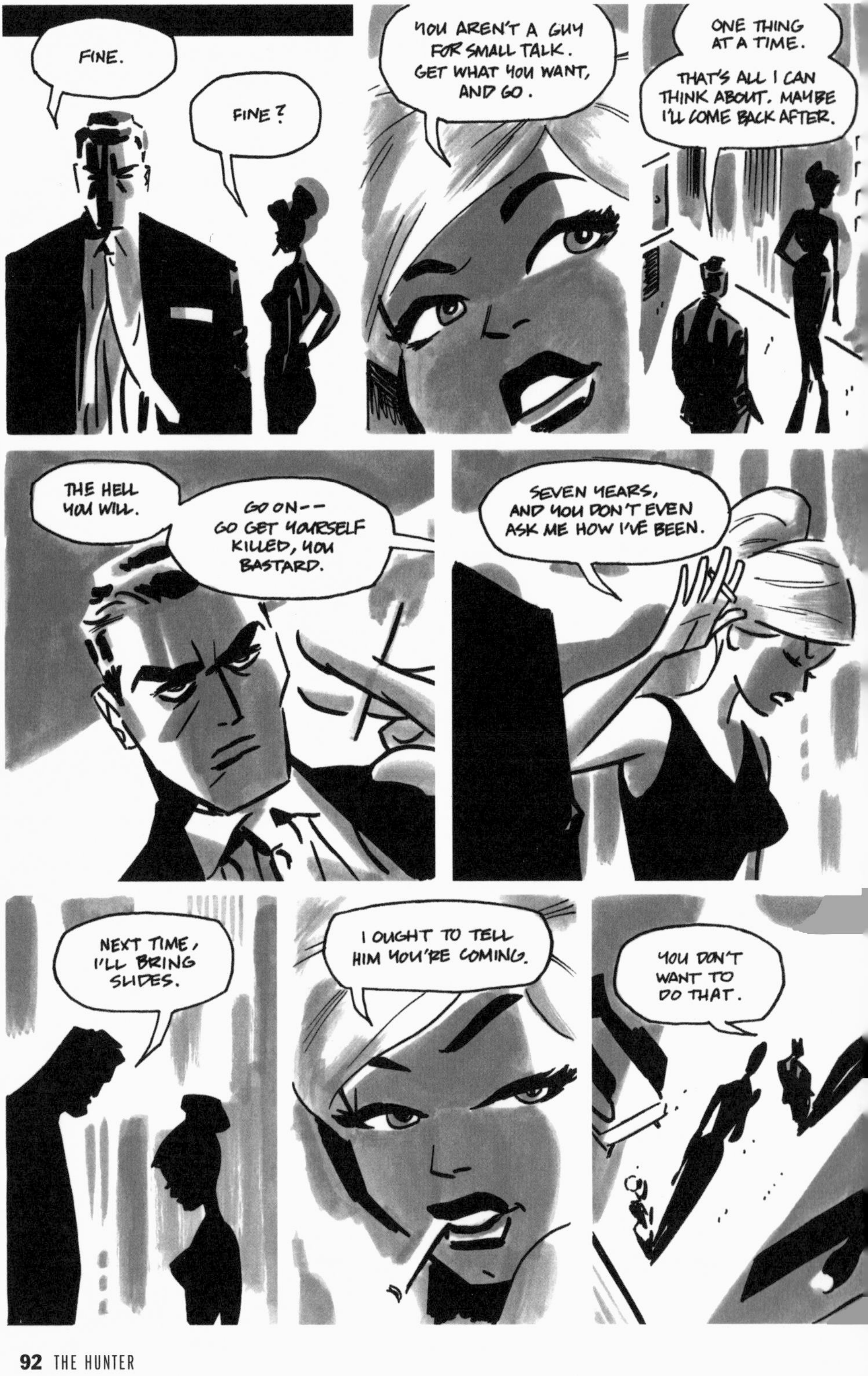
FINE.
FINE?
YOU AREN'T A GUY FOR SMALL TALK. GET WHAT YOU WANT, AND GO.
ONE THING AT A TIME.
THAT'S ALL I CAN THINK ABOUT. MAYBE I'LL COME BACK AFTER.
THE HELL YOU WILL.
GO ON-- GO GET YOURSELF KILLED, YOU BASTARD.
SEVEN YEARS, AND YOU DON'T EVEN ASK ME HOW I'VE BEEN.
NEXT TIME, I'LL BRING SLIDES.
I OUGHT TO TELL HIM YOU'RE COMING.
YOU DON'T WANT TO DO THAT.

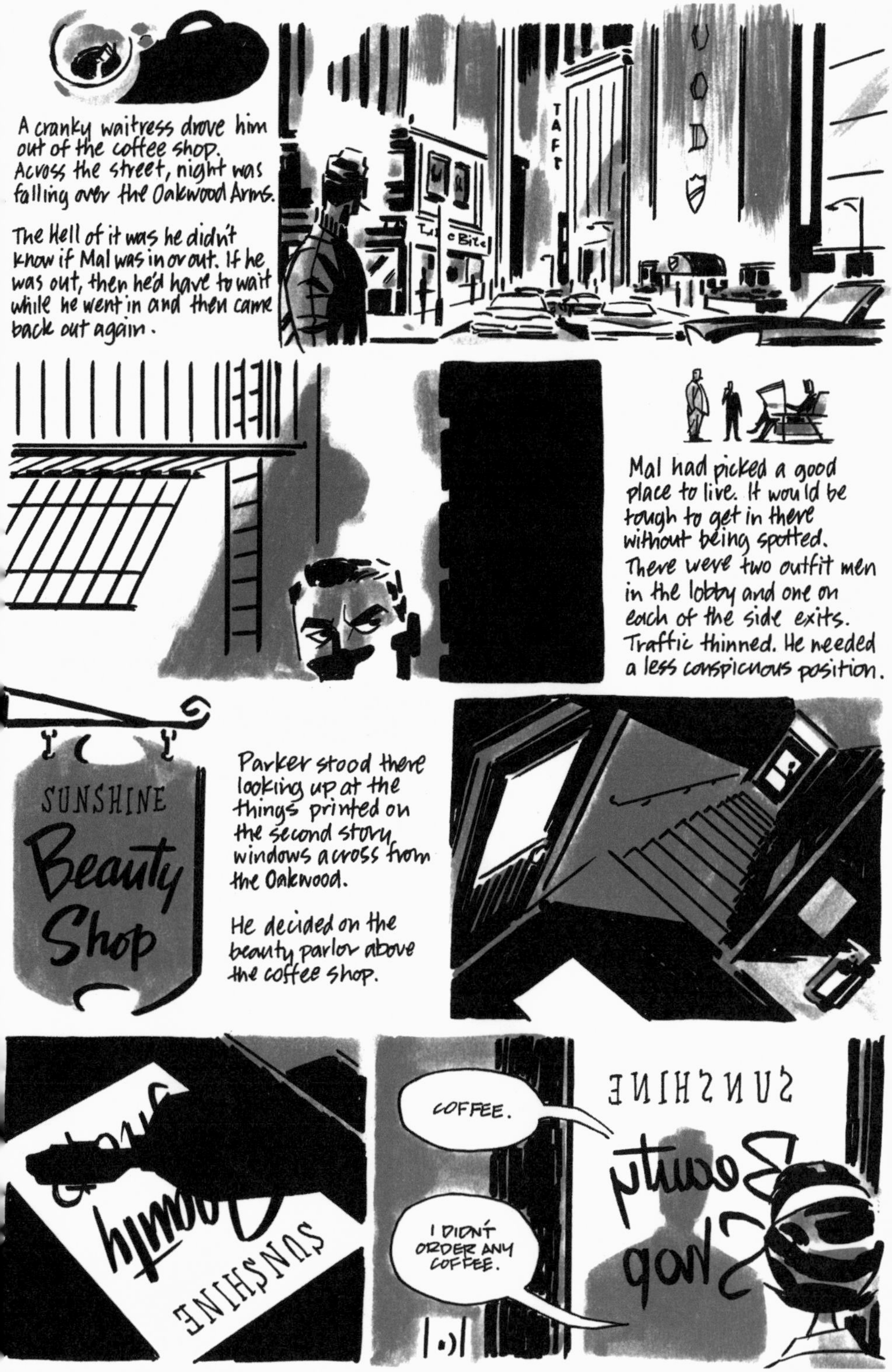
A cranky waitress drove him out of the coffee shop. Across the street, night was falling over the Oakwood Arms.
The Hell of it was he didn't know if Mal was in or out. If he was out, then he'd have to wait while he went in and then came back out again.
TAFT
Mal had picked a good place to live. It would be tough to get in there without being spotted. There were two outfit men in the lobby and one on each of the side exits. Traffic thinned. He needed a less conspicuous position.
SUNSHINE
Beauty
Shop
Parker stood there looking up at the things printed on the second story windows across from the Oakwood.
He decided on the beauty parlor above the coffee shop.
COFFEE.
I DIDN'T ORDER ANY COFFEE.

She opened the door and he clipped her, base knuckles against the tip of her chin. Her eyes rolled back and she fell like a piece of glass.

In the dark he unplugged two dryers and ripped the cords loose at their bases.

The woman hadn't moved. He tied her arms and ankles and used a piece of her slip to gag her.

She had good legs- but not now. After it was over and Mal was dead- he'd want somebody then.

He went back to the window in the other room and smoked.

It was a bad position. If Mal came out and flagged a cab, then what? He might have to wait for the cab, long enough for Parker to get downstairs- but maybe not. If Mal came out and walked, that would be better. If he didn't come out at all, that would be worse.

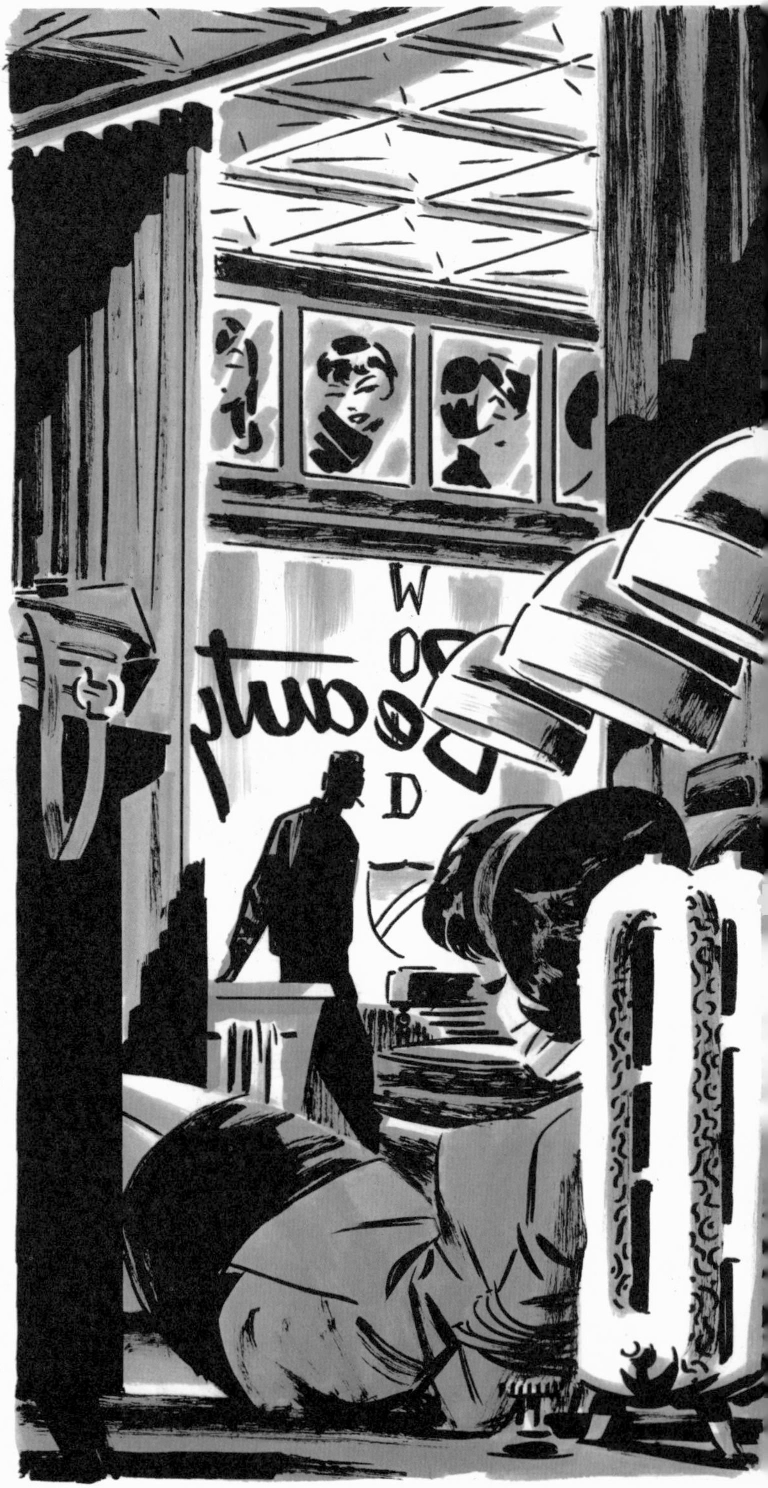

People came in, people came out. He finished his last cigarette and that made him nervous. He found the woman's purse and inside was a half pack of filters.

He glanced over at her. She was still out. That bothered him.

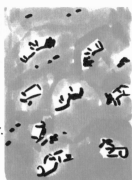

He went over and looked more closely. Her eyes bugged halfway out of their sockets and her skin was a bluish red. He'd seen an inhaler in her purse.

It was stupid. There wasn't any reason for a mouth gag to make her dead.

nger fueled his impatience. Parker was done waiting. He wiped down the room and then dialed the police.

YEAH, HEY ?
I- I'VE FOUND A WOMAN—

I-I THINK SHE'S DEAD. NEVER MIND WHO I AM -- JUST SEND THEM TO THE BEAUTY PARLOR ON 57th AT 8th.

Parker slipped out the back way and circled two blocks, coming up in the alley behind the Oakwood.

As long as the cops showed up, the rest should be easy.

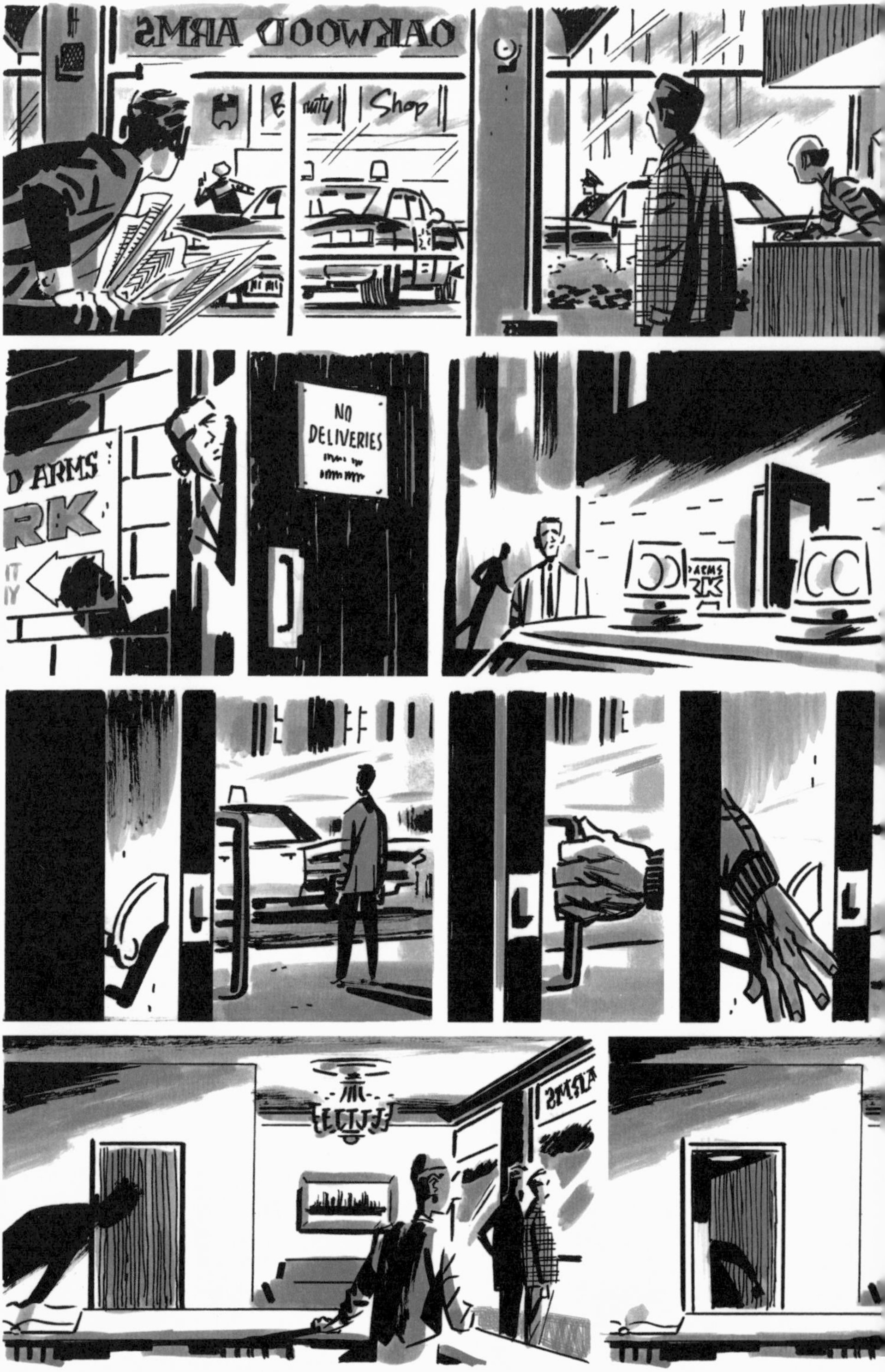
OAKWOOD ARMS
Shop
NO DELIVERIES
D ARMS

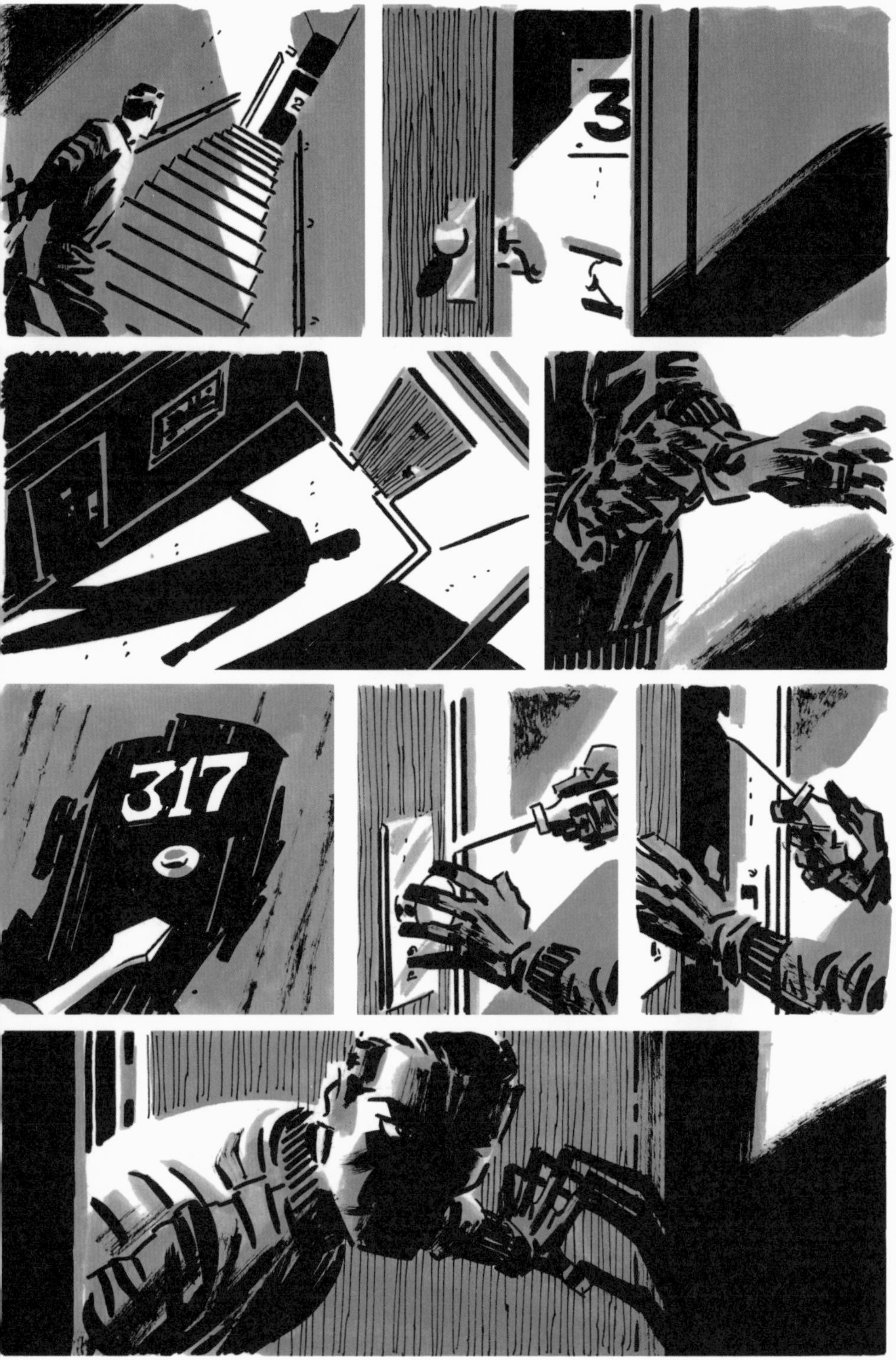
3
317

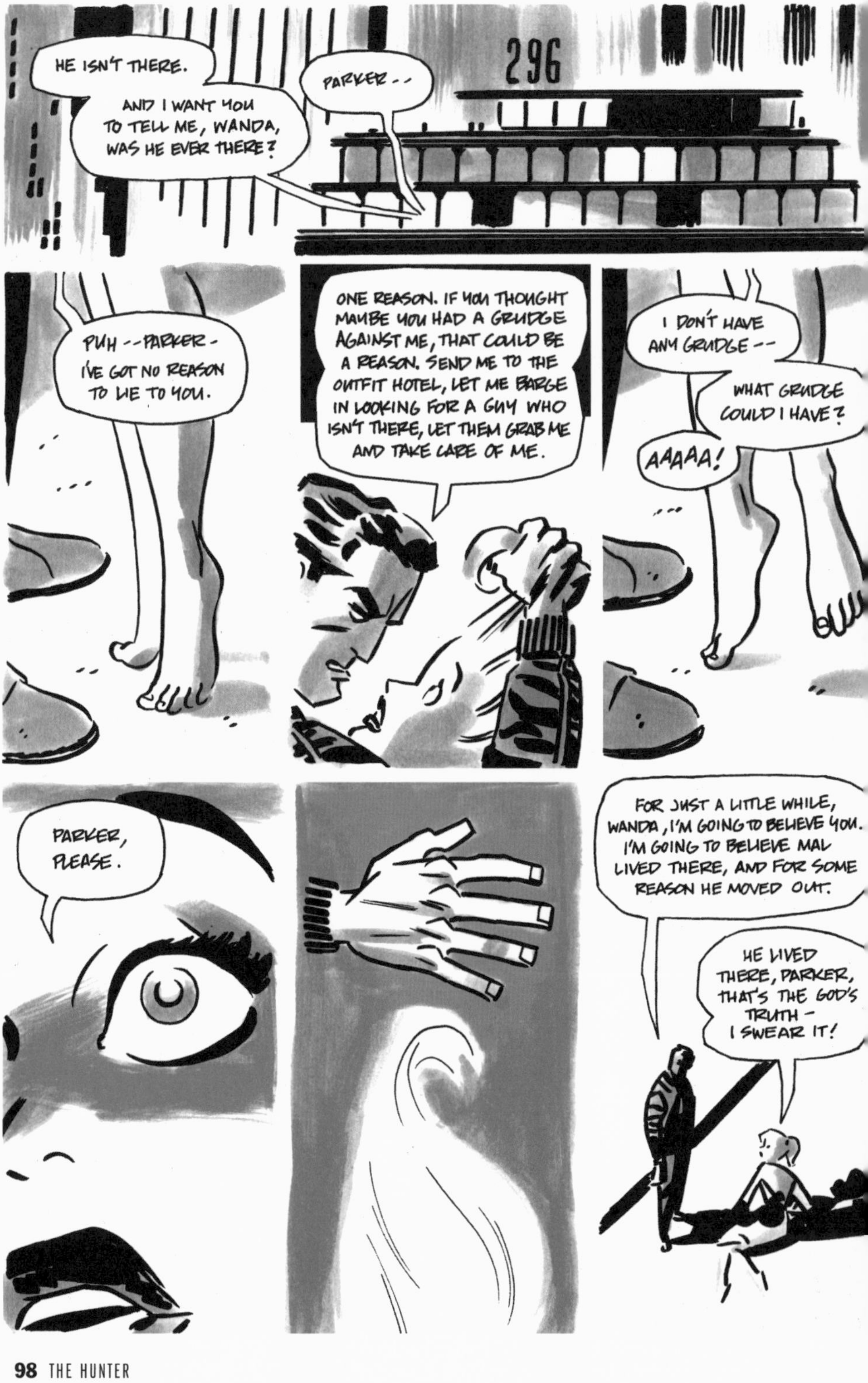
HE ISN'T THERE.
AND I WANT YOU TO TELL ME, WANDA, WAS HE EVER THERE?
PARKER --
296
PUH -- PARKER - I'VE GOT NO REASON TO LIE TO YOU.
ONE REASON. IF YOU THOUGHT MAYBE YOU HAD A GRUDGE AGAINST ME, THAT COULD BE A REASON. SEND ME TO THE OUTFIT HOTEL, LET ME BARGE IN LOOKING FOR A GUY WHO ISN'T THERE, LET THEM GRAB ME AND TAKE CARE OF ME.
I DON'T HAVE ANY GRUDGE --
WHAT GRUDGE COULD I HAVE?
AAAAA!
PARKER, PLEASE.
FOR JUST A LITTLE WHILE, WANDA, I'M GOING TO BELIEVE YOU. I'M GOING TO BELIEVE MAL LIVED THERE, AND FOR SOME REASON HE MOVED OUT.
HE LIVED THERE, PARKER, THAT'S THE GOD'S TRUTH - I SWEAR IT!

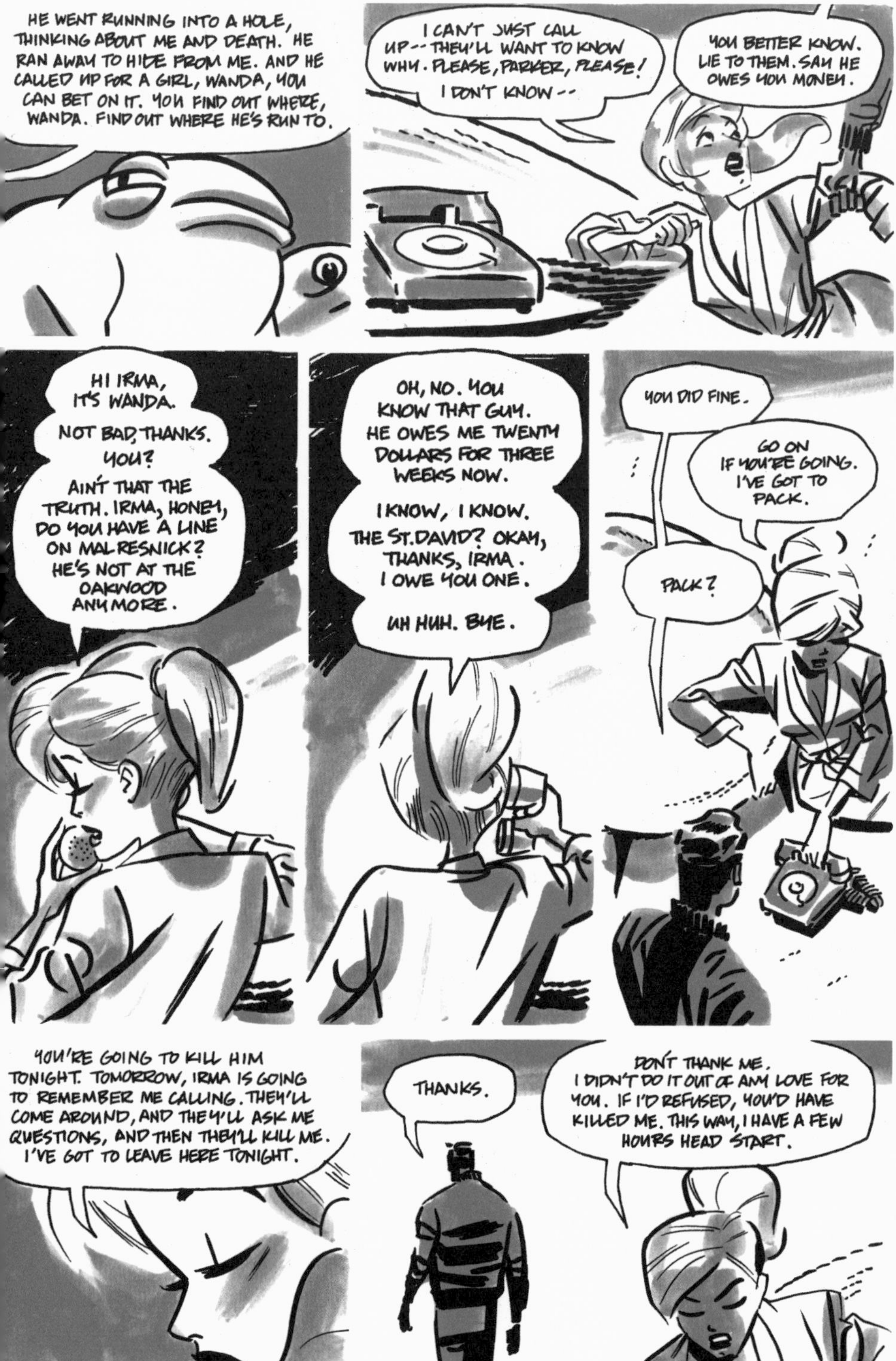

HE WENT RUNNING INTO A HOLE, THINKING ABOUT ME AND DEATH. HE RAN AWAY TO HIDE FROM ME. AND HE CALLED UP FOR A GIRL, WANDA, YOU CAN BET ON IT. YOU FIND OUT WHERE, WANDA. FIND OUT WHERE HE'S RUN TO.
I CAN'T JUST CALL UP-- THEY'LL WANT TO KNOW WHY. PLEASE, PARKER, PLEASE!
I DON'T KNOW--
YOU BETTER KNOW. LIE TO THEM. SAY HE OWES YOU MONEY.
HI IRMA, IT'S WANDA.
NOT BAD, THANKS. YOU?
AIN'T THAT THE TRUTH. IRMA, HONEY, DO YOU HAVE A LINE ON MAL RESNICK? HE'S NOT AT THE OAKWOOD ANYMORE.
OH, NO. YOU KNOW THAT GUY. HE OWES ME TWENTY DOLLARS FOR THREE WEEKS NOW.
I KNOW, I KNOW. THE ST. DAVID? OKAY, THANKS, IRMA. I OWE YOU ONE.
UH HUH. BYE.
YOU DID FINE.
GO ON IF YOU'RE GOING. I'VE GOT TO PACK.
PACK?
YOU'RE GOING TO KILL HIM TONIGHT. TOMORROW, IRMA IS GOING TO REMEMBER ME CALLING. THEY'LL COME AROUND, AND THEY'LL ASK ME QUESTIONS, AND THEN THEY'LL KILL ME. I'VE GOT TO LEAVE HERE TONIGHT.
THANKS.
DON'T THANK ME. I DIDN'T DO IT OUT OF ANY LOVE FOR YOU. IF I'D REFUSED, YOU'D HAVE KILLED ME. THIS WAY, I HAVE A FEW HOURS HEAD START.

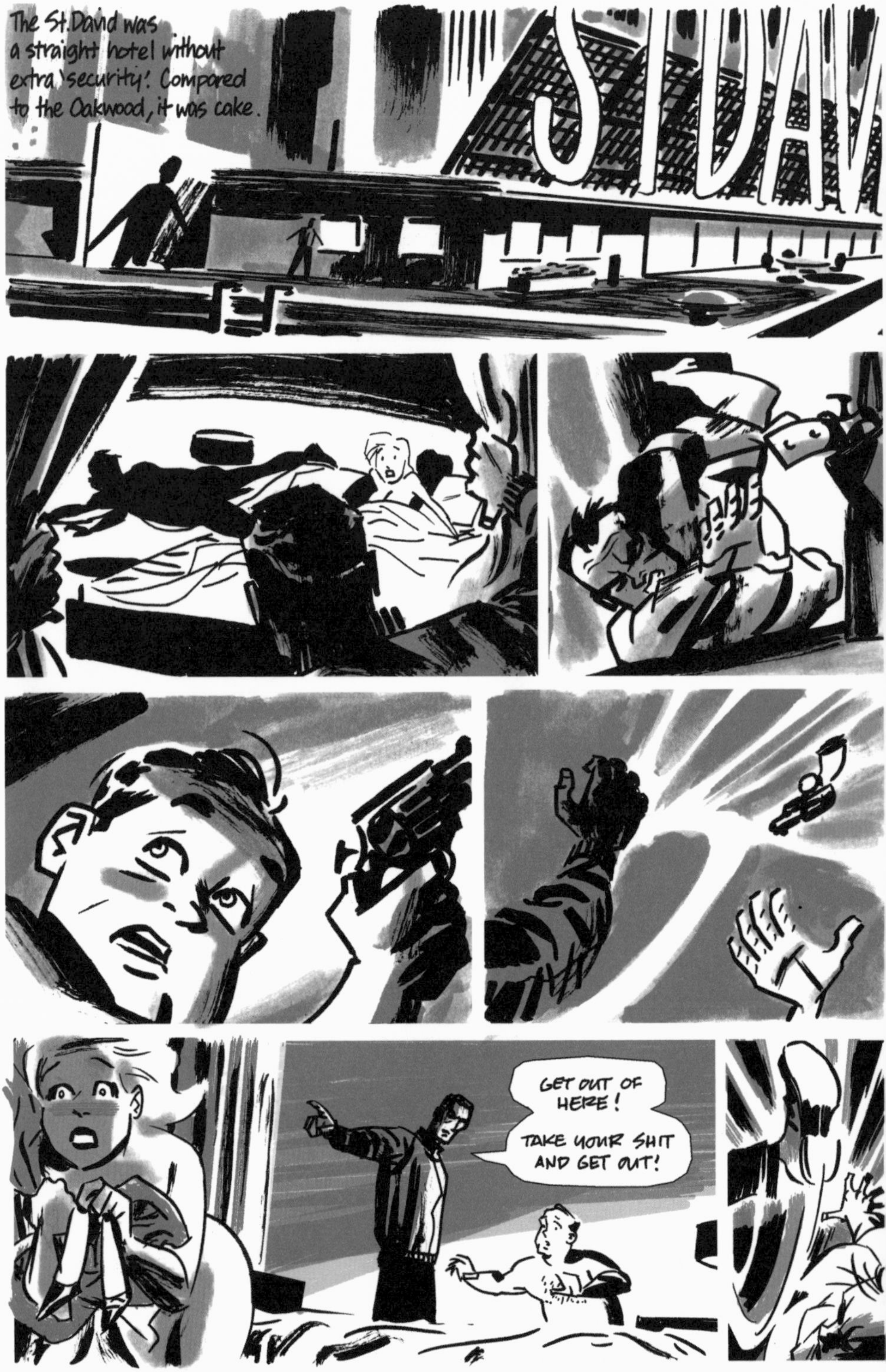
The St. David was a straight hotel without extra 'security'. Compared to the Oakwood, it was cake.
GET OUT OF HERE!
TAKE YOUR SHIT AND GET OUT!

Parker stood over him, and it was too easy.

And it wasn't enough.

He didn't want to torture Mal, he wouldn't have got anything from that but wasted time.

Ending his life quick and easy with his own hands, that was the way.

But it was too easy, and it wasn't enough.

Killing Mal would leave a hole in the world. Once he killed the bastard, what then?

He wanted the money. He wanted his share.

He had less than two thousand dollars to his name. He had to go on living, get back into his old groove.

The resort hotels and the occasional job, the easy and comfortable life he'd had til this bastard came along in his taxicab and told him about the job on the island.

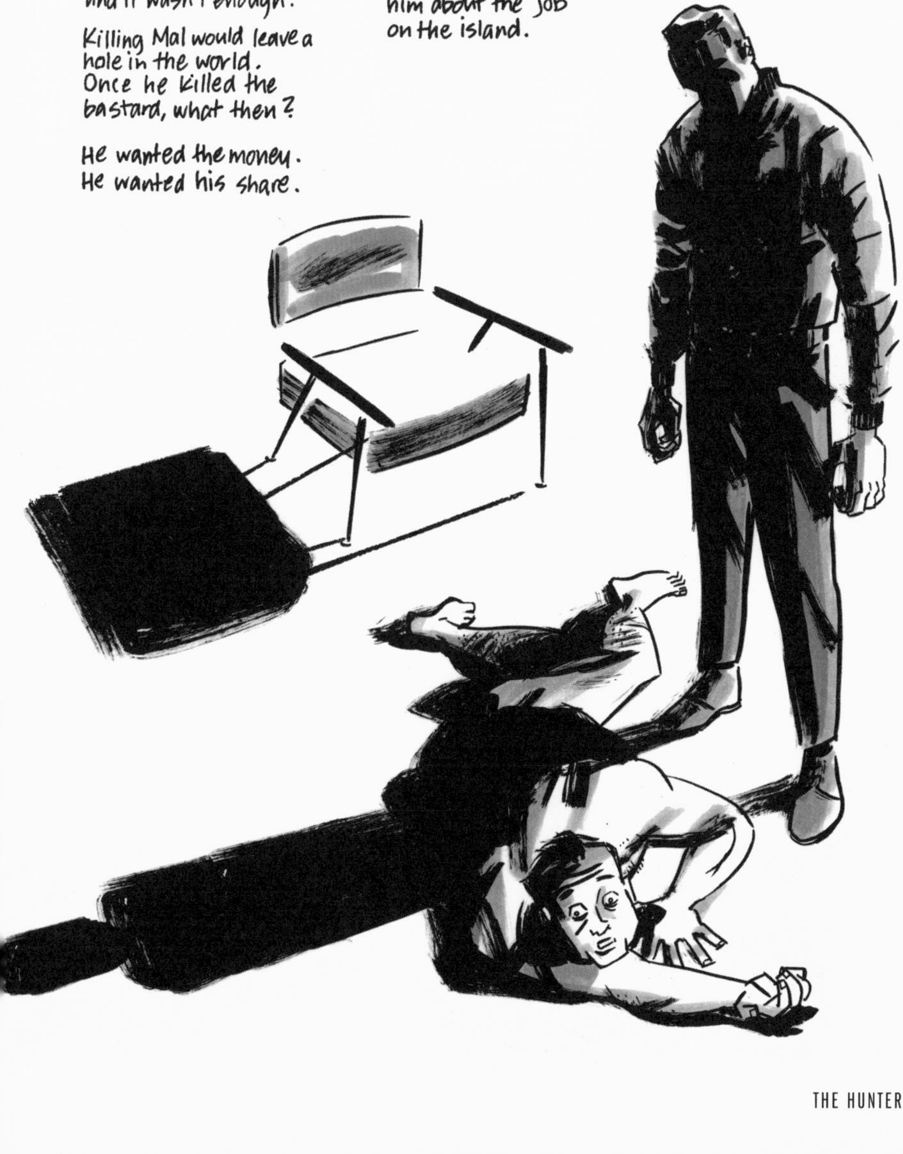

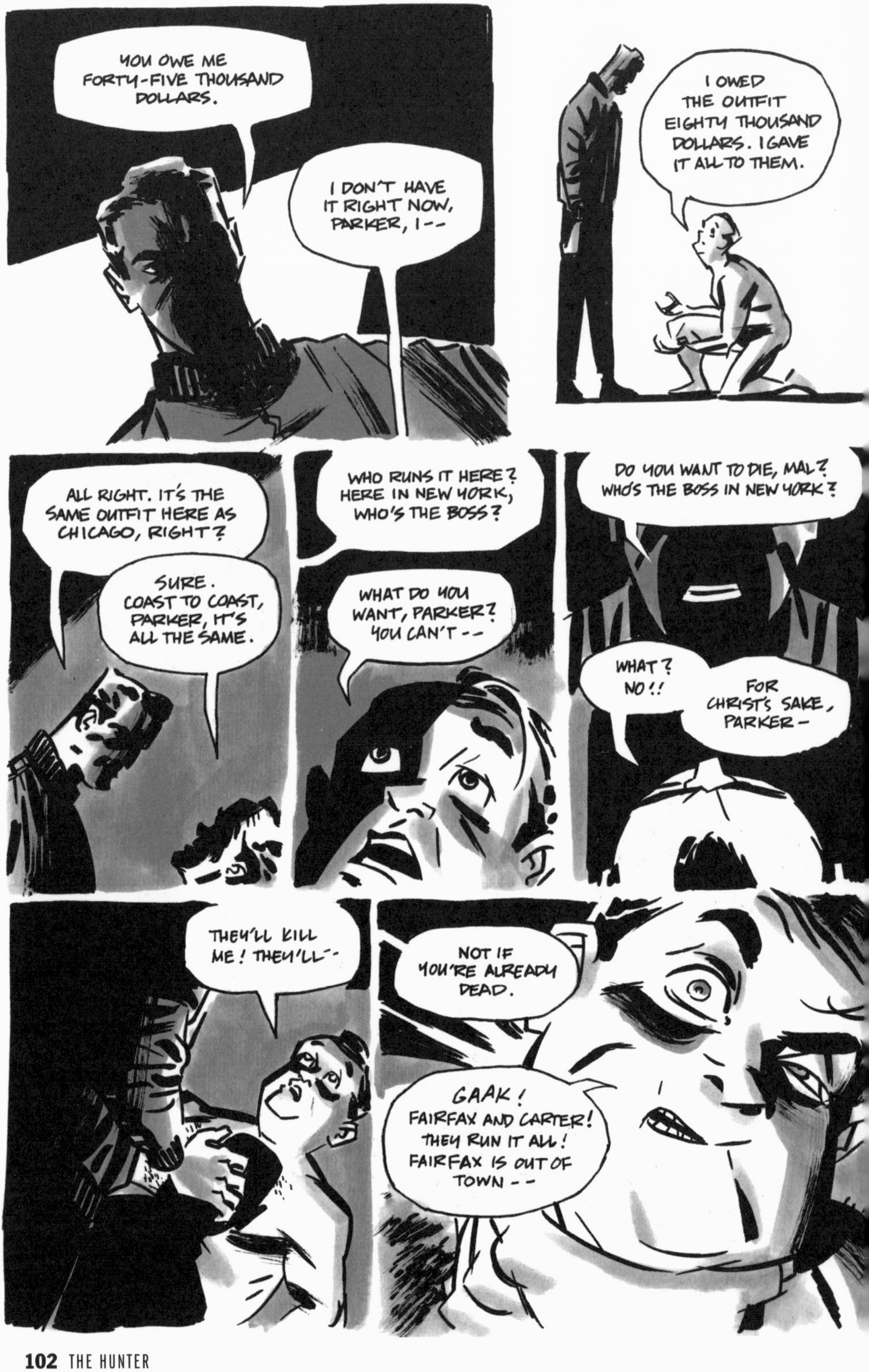
YOU OWE ME FORTY-FIVE THOUSAND DOLLARS.
I DON'T HAVE IT RIGHT NOW, PARKER, I--
I OWED THE OUTFIT EIGHTY THOUSAND DOLLARS. I GAVE IT ALL TO THEM.
ALL RIGHT. IT'S THE SAME OUTFIT HERE AS CHICAGO, RIGHT?
SURE. COAST TO COAST, PARKER, IT'S ALL THE SAME.
WHO RUNS IT HERE? HERE IN NEW YORK, WHO'S THE BOSS?
WHAT DO YOU WANT, PARKER? YOU CAN'T--
DO YOU WANT TO DIE, MAL? WHO'S THE BOSS IN NEW YORK?
WHAT? NO!!
FOR CHRIST'S SAKE, PARKER-
THEY'LL KILL ME! THEY'LL--
NOT IF YOU'RE ALREADY DEAD.
GAAK! FAIRFAX AND CARTER! THEY RUN IT ALL! FAIRFAX IS OUT OF TOWN--

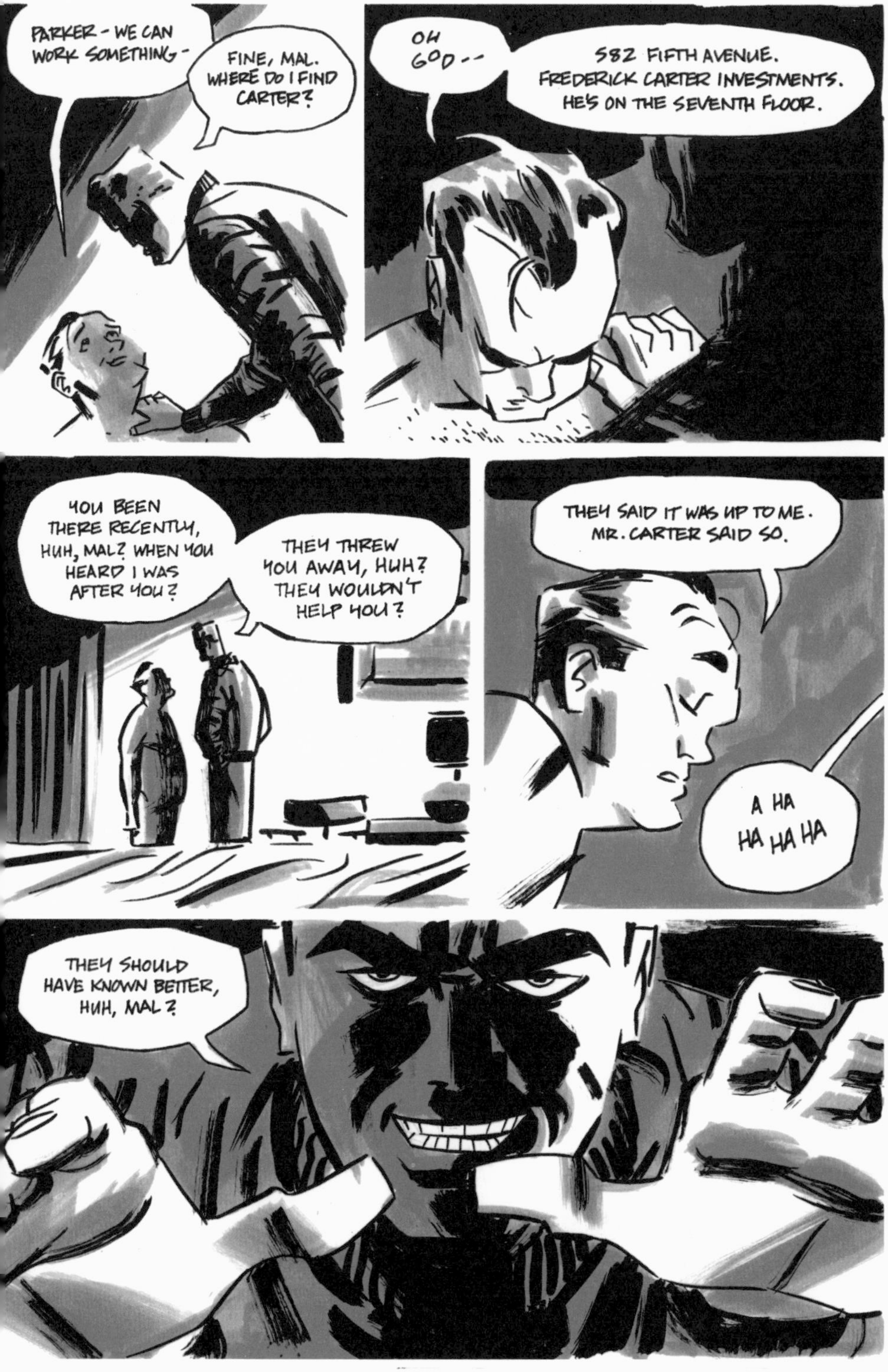
PARKER - WE CAN WORK SOMETHING -
FINE, MAL. WHERE DO I FIND CARTER?
OH GOD --
582 FIFTH AVENUE. FREDERICK CARTER INVESTMENTS. HE'S ON THE SEVENTH FLOOR.
YOU BEEN THERE RECENTLY, HUH, MAL? WHEN YOU HEARD I WAS AFTER YOU?
THEY THREW YOU AWAY, HUH? THEY WOULDN'T HELP YOU?
THEY SAID IT WAS UP TO ME. MR. CARTER SAID SO.
A HA HA HA HA
THEY SHOULD HAVE KNOWN BETTER, HUH, MAL?

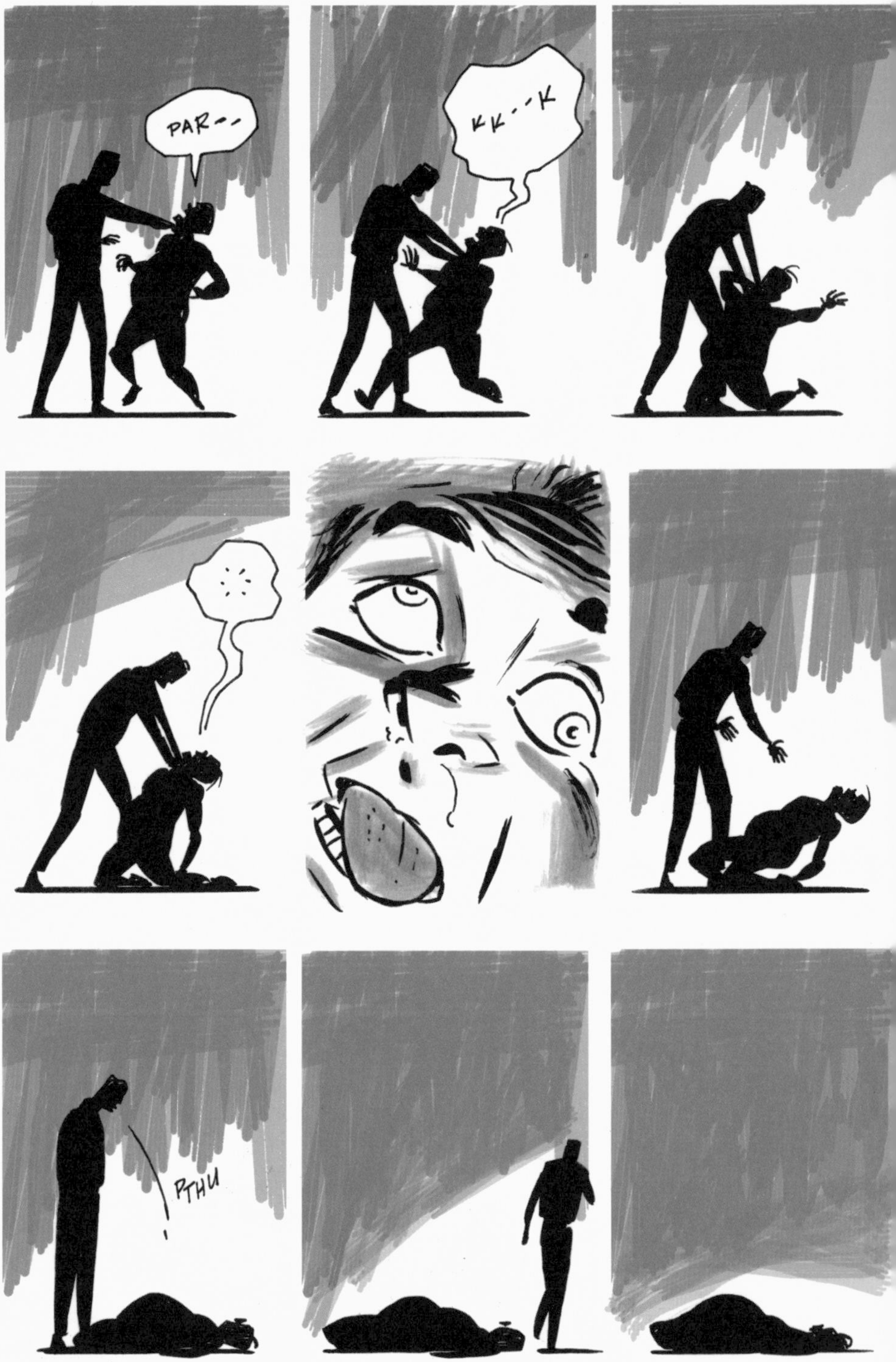

PAR--
KK--K
PTHU

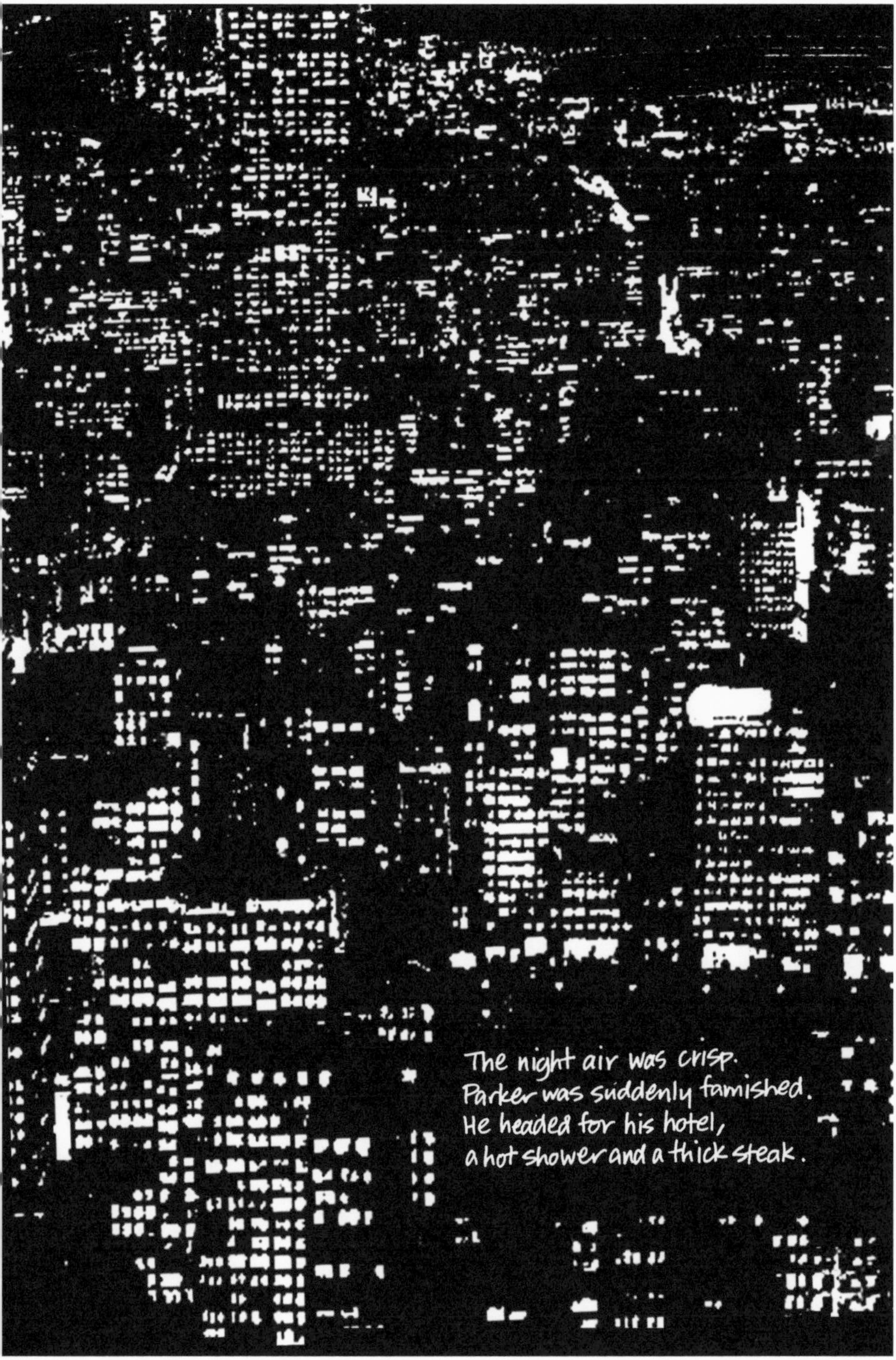
The night air was crisp.
Parker was suddenly famished.
He headed for his hotel,
a hot shower and a thick steak.

BOOK FOUR

The silent man at the door sounded puzzled. He didn't recognize Parker as an outfit man, but he didn't look like an investment customer either.

When Parker said "Tell your boss the guy who killed Mal Resnick is here", the puzzlement on the man's face shifted subtly from real to fake.

Parker sat down and when he didn't look up, the man shrugged and disappeared behind a thick door.

Five minutes went by and the silent man came back, looking mistrustful.

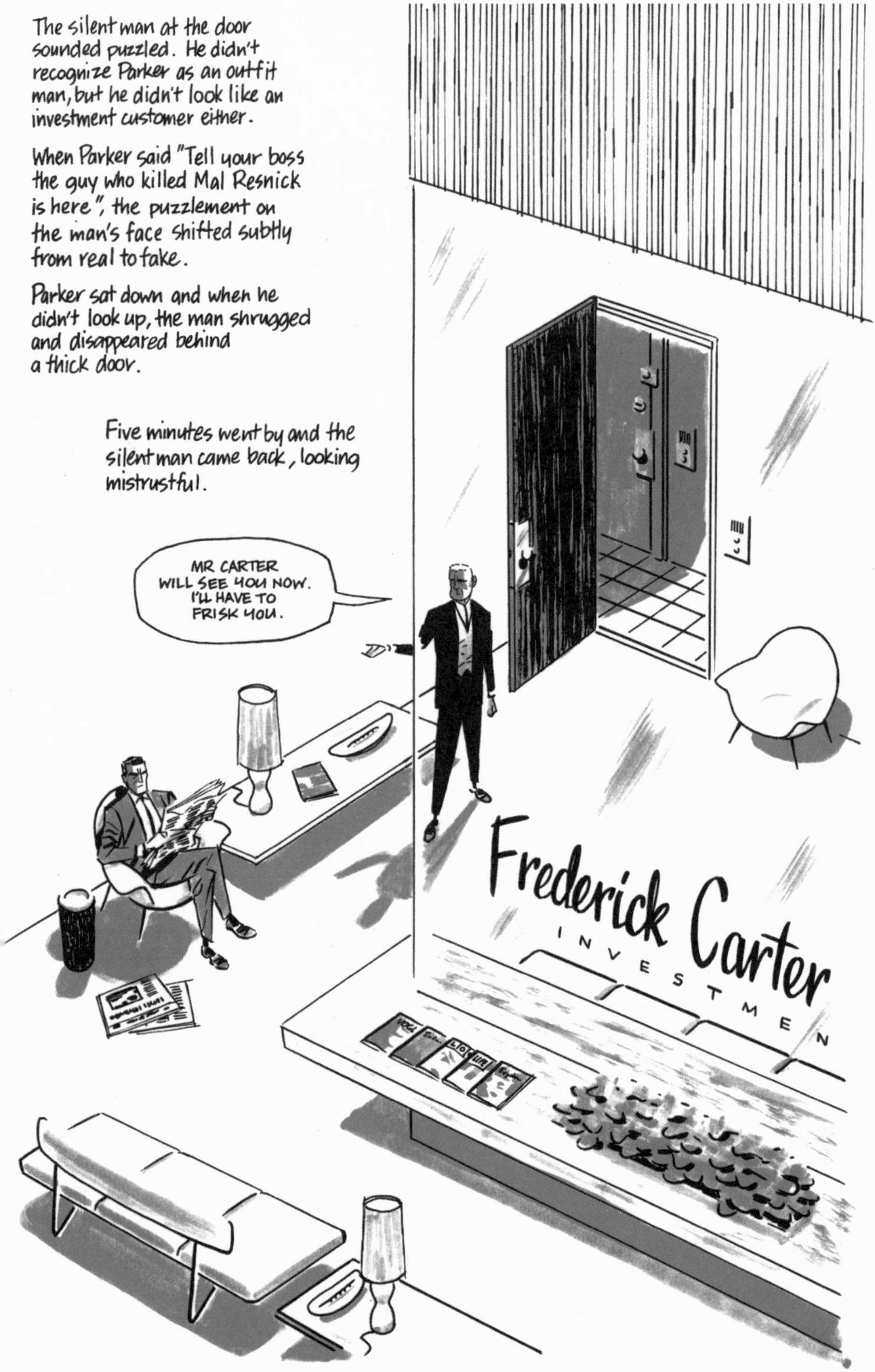
MR CARTER WILL SEE YOU NOW. I'LL HAVE TO FRISK YOU.
Frederick Carter
INVESTMEN

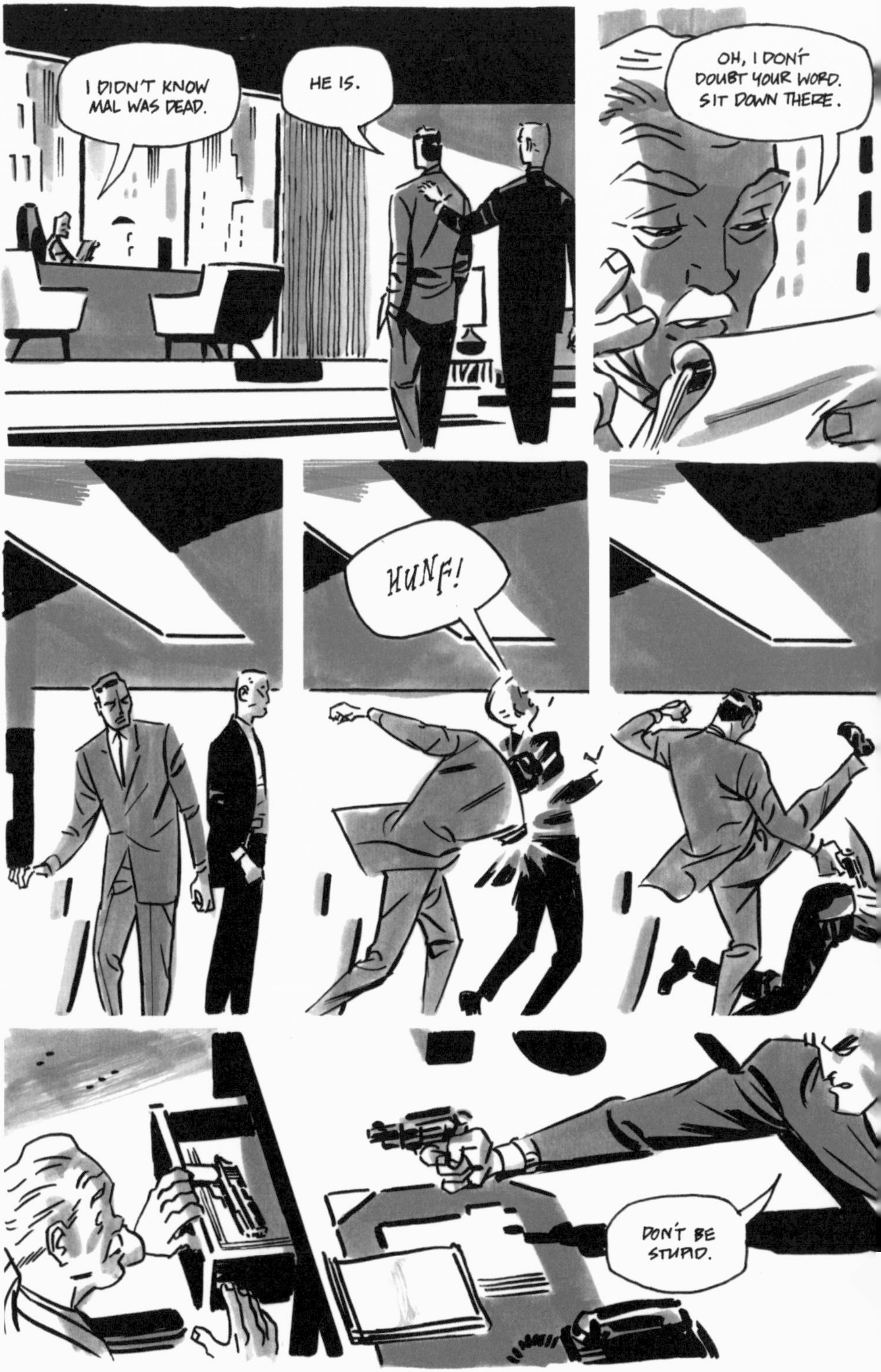
I DIDN'T KNOW MAL WAS DEAD.
HE IS.
OH, I DON'T DOUBT YOUR WORD. SIT DOWN THERE.
HUNF!
DON'T BE STUPID.

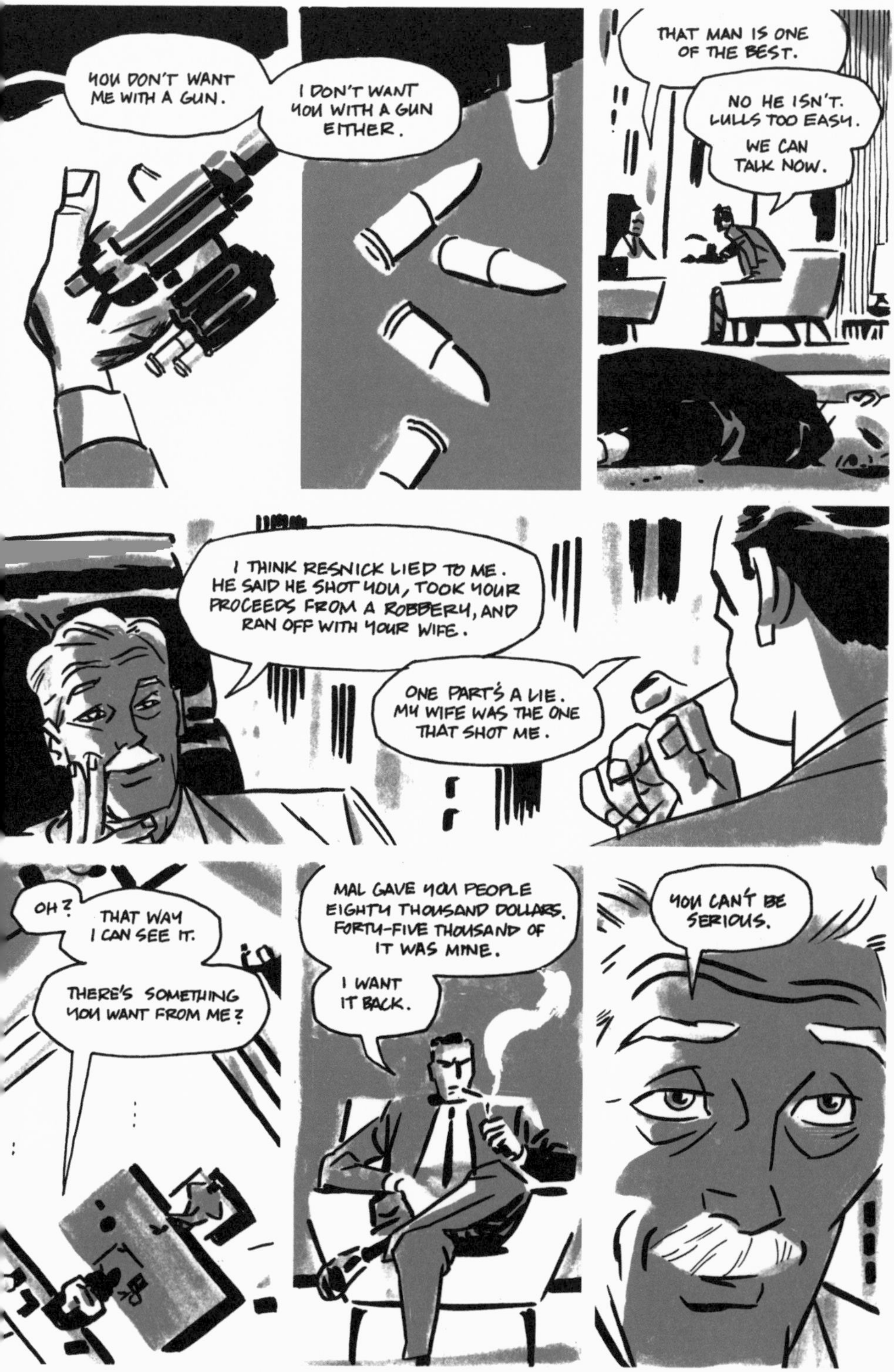
YOU DON'T WANT ME WITH A GUN.
I DON'T WANT YOU WITH A GUN EITHER.
THAT MAN IS ONE OF THE BEST.
NO HE ISN'T. LULLS TOO EASY.
WE CAN TALK NOW.
I THINK RESNICK LIED TO ME. HE SAID HE SHOT YOU, TOOK YOUR PROCEEDS FROM A ROBBERY, AND RAN OFF WITH YOUR WIFE.
ONE PART'S A LIE. MY WIFE WAS THE ONE THAT SHOT ME.
OH?
THAT WAY I CAN SEE IT.
THERE'S SOMETHING YOU WANT FROM ME?
MAL GAVE YOU PEOPLE EIGHTY THOUSAND DOLLARS. FORTY-FIVE THOUSAND OF IT WAS MINE.
I WANT IT BACK.
YOU CAN'T BE SERIOUS.

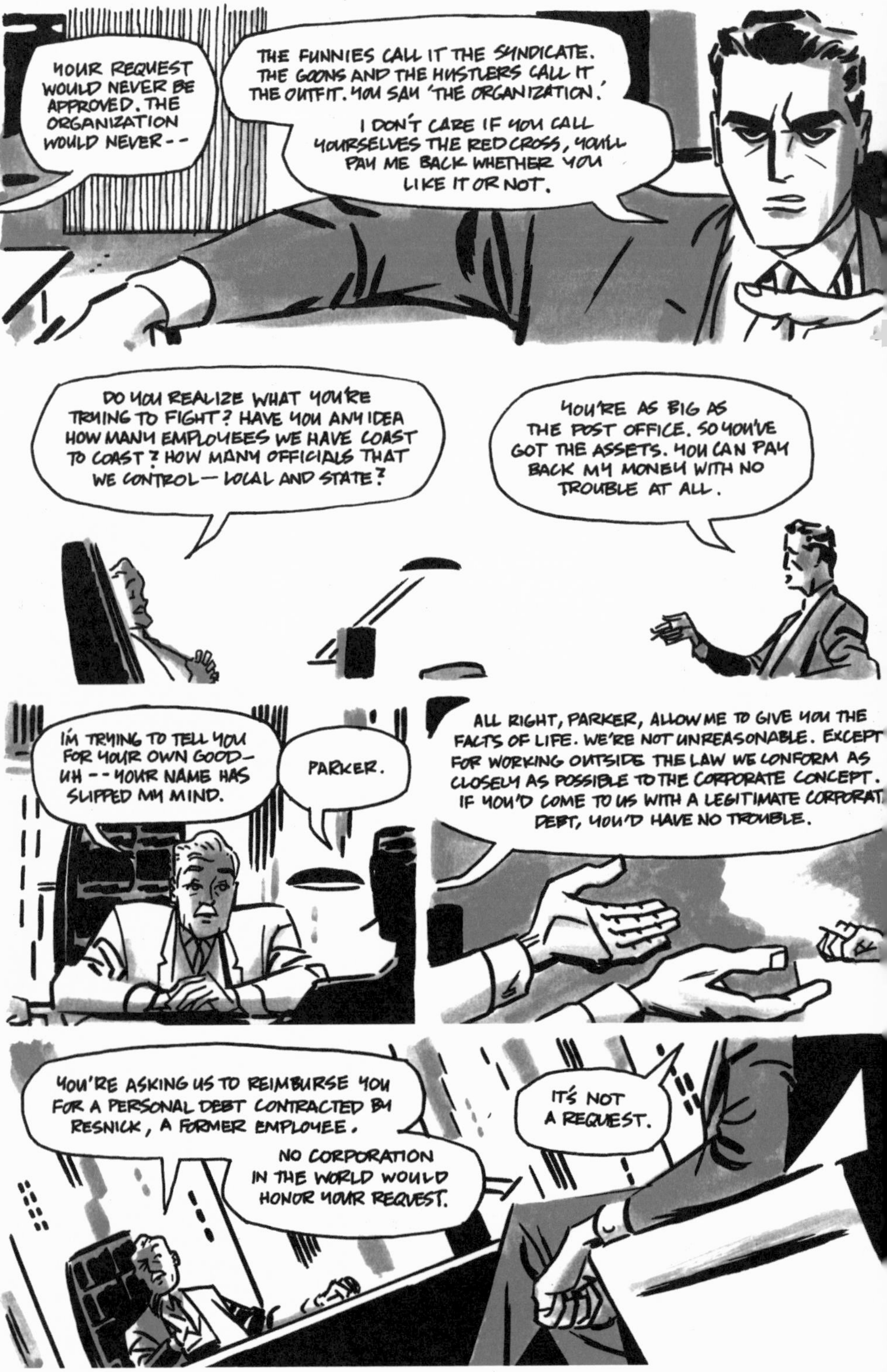
YOUR REQUEST WOULD NEVER BE APPROVED. THE ORGANIZATION WOULD NEVER--
THE FUNNIES CALL IT THE SYNDICATE. THE GOONS AND THE HUSTLERS CALL IT THE OUTFIT. YOU SAY 'THE ORGANIZATION.'
I DON'T CARE IF YOU CALL YOURSELVES THE RED CROSS, YOU'LL PAY ME BACK WHETHER YOU LIKE IT OR NOT.
DO YOU REALIZE WHAT YOU'RE TRYING TO FIGHT? HAVE YOU ANY IDEA HOW MANY EMPLOYEES WE HAVE COAST TO COAST? HOW MANY OFFICIALS THAT WE CONTROL— LOCAL AND STATE?
YOU'RE AS BIG AS THE POST OFFICE. SO YOU'VE GOT THE ASSETS. YOU CAN PAY BACK MY MONEY WITH NO TROUBLE AT ALL.
I'M TRYING TO TELL YOU FOR YOUR OWN GOOD-UH --YOUR NAME HAS SLIPPED MY MIND.
PARKER.
ALL RIGHT, PARKER, ALLOW ME TO GIVE YOU THE FACTS OF LIFE. WE'RE NOT UNREASONABLE. EXCEPT FOR WORKING OUTSIDE THE LAW WE CONFORM AS CLOSELY AS POSSIBLE TO THE CORPORATE CONCEPT. IF YOU'D COME TO US WITH A LEGITIMATE CORPORAT DEBT, YOU'D HAVE NO TROUBLE.
YOU'RE ASKING US TO REIMBURSE YOU FOR A PERSONAL DEBT CONTRACTED BY RESNICK, A FORMER EMPLOYEE.
NO CORPORATION IN THE WORLD WOULD HONOR YOUR REQUEST.
IT'S NOT A REQUEST.

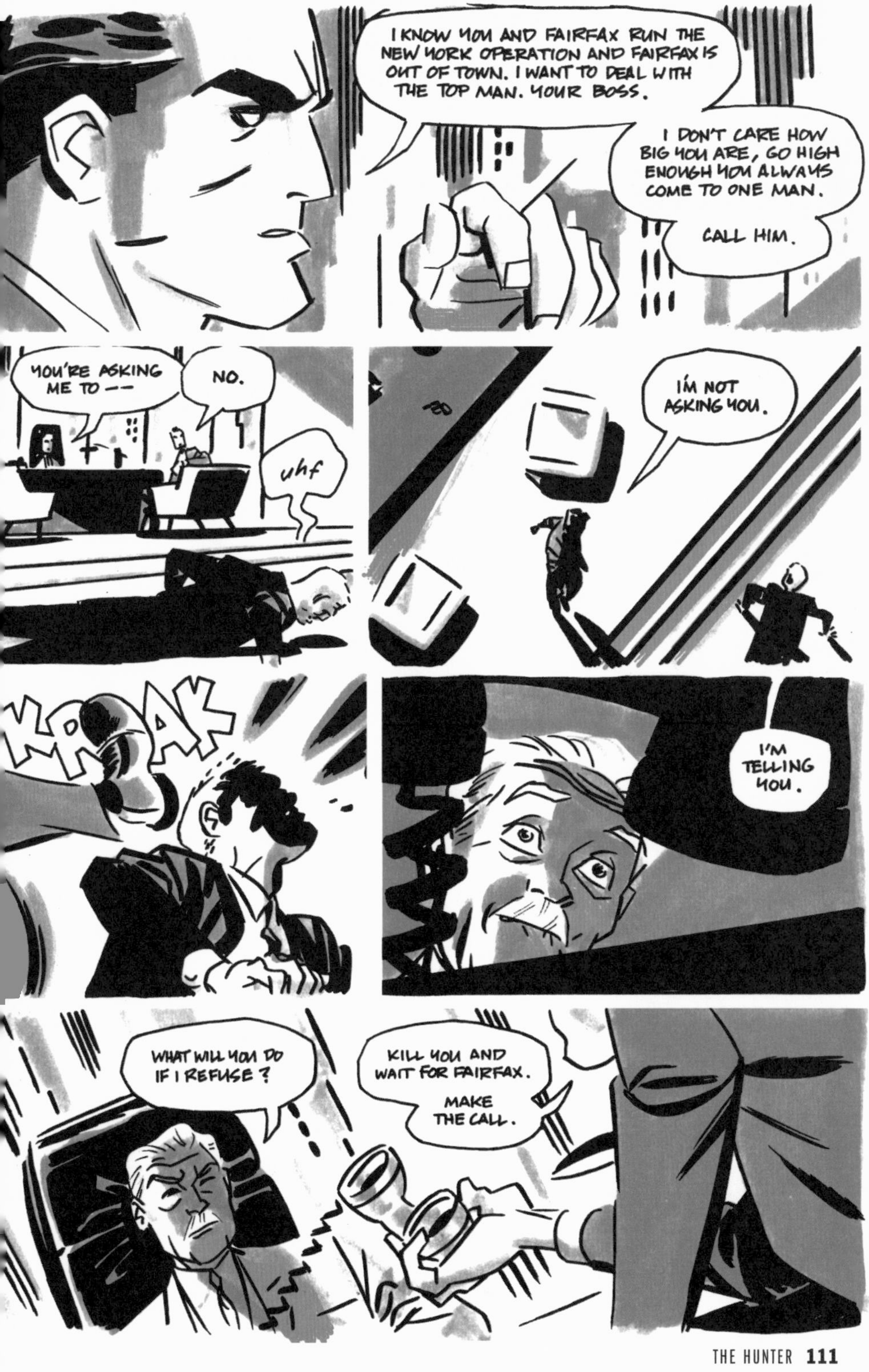

I KNOW YOU AND FAIRFAX RUN THE NEW YORK OPERATION AND FAIRFAX IS OUT OF TOWN. I WANT TO DEAL WITH THE TOP MAN. YOUR BOSS.
I DON'T CARE HOW BIG YOU ARE, GO HIGH ENOUGH YOU ALWAYS COME TO ONE MAN.
CALL HIM.
YOU'RE ASKING ME TO --
NO.
uhf
I'M NOT ASKING YOU.
KRAK
I'M TELLING YOU.
WHAT WILL YOU DO IF I REFUSE?
KILL YOU AND WAIT FOR FAIRFAX.
MAKE THE CALL.

FRED CARTER TO TALK TO YOUR BOSS, SWEETHEART. TELL HIM ITS FRED CARTER -- GODDAMMIT! BRONSON -- I WANT TO TALK TO BRONSON.

CARTER HERE. SORRY TO BE CALLING LIKE THIS. YOUR GIRL MADE ME SAY YOUR NAME -- YES, WELL I'M NOT ALONE.

THAT'S THE PROBLEM.

IT'S THE INDEPENDENT FROM THE RESNICK MATTER. NO, HE INSISTED I CALL OR HE'D KILL ME HE'S ALREADY KILLED RESNICK, HIS WIFE AND GOD KNOWS HOW MANY MORE.

NINE.

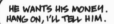

HE WANTS HIS MONEY. HANG ON, I'LL TELL HIM.

BRONSON SAYS HE'LL LOOK INTO IT AND CALL US BACK.

NO. WE DO IT IN ONE CALL.

IN THAT CASE HE SAYS THE ANSWER IS NO.

GIVE ME THE PHONE.

HOW MUCH IS THIS GUY CARTER WORTH TO YOU?

WHAT DO YOU MEAN?

EITHER I GET PAID, OR CARTER IS DEAD.

I DON'T LIKE TO BE THREATENED.

NO ONE DOES. IF YOU SAY NO, I'LL KILL CARTER AND COME AFTER YOU. THEN WE'LL CALL YOUR BOSS. IF HE SAYS NO, I'LL KILL YOU TOO.

YOU CAN'T STRONGARM US, YOU ASSHOLE.

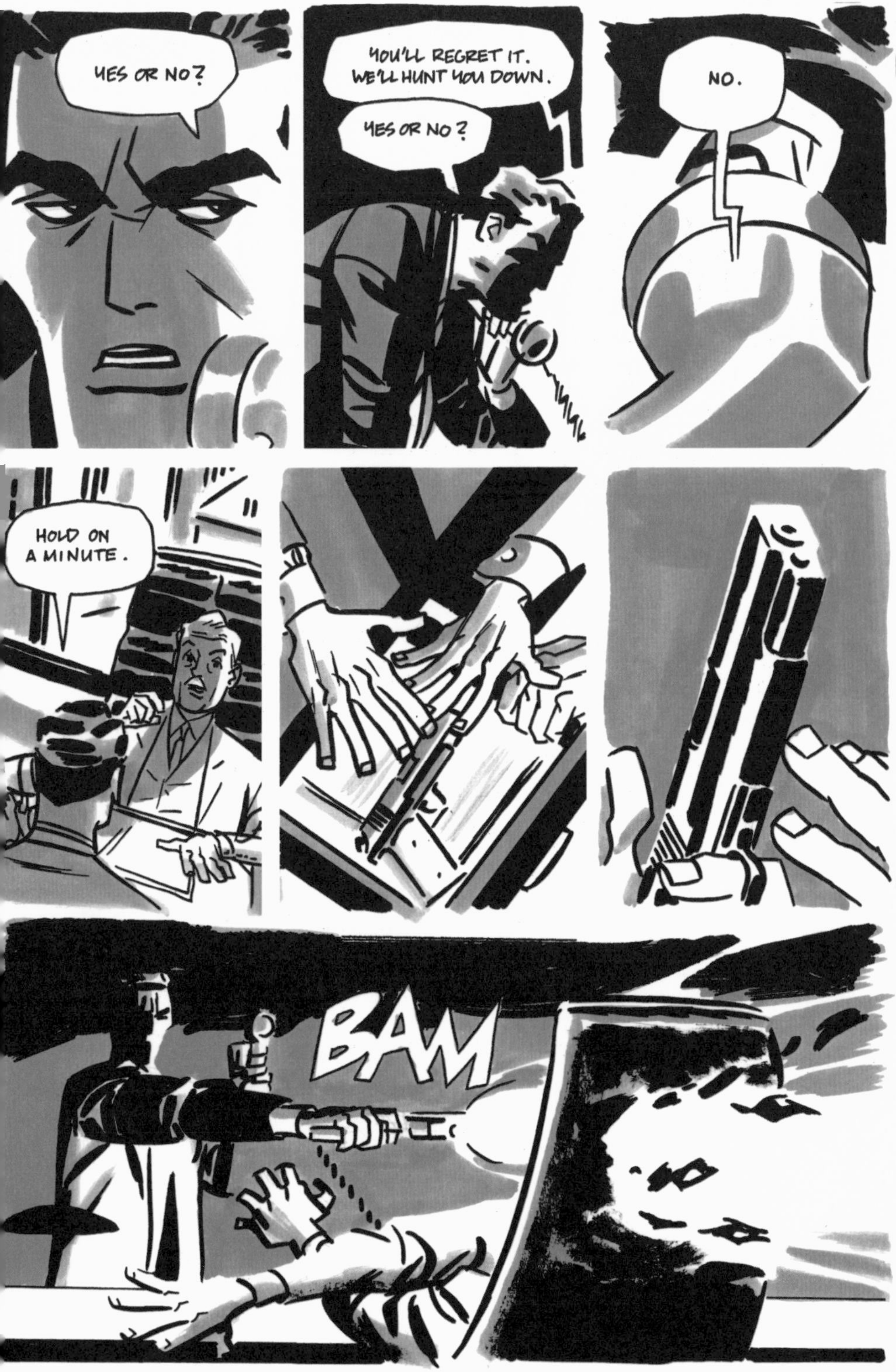
YES OR NO?
YOU'LL REGRET IT. WE'LL HUNT YOU DOWN.
YES OR NO?
NO.
HOLD ON A MINUTE.
BAM

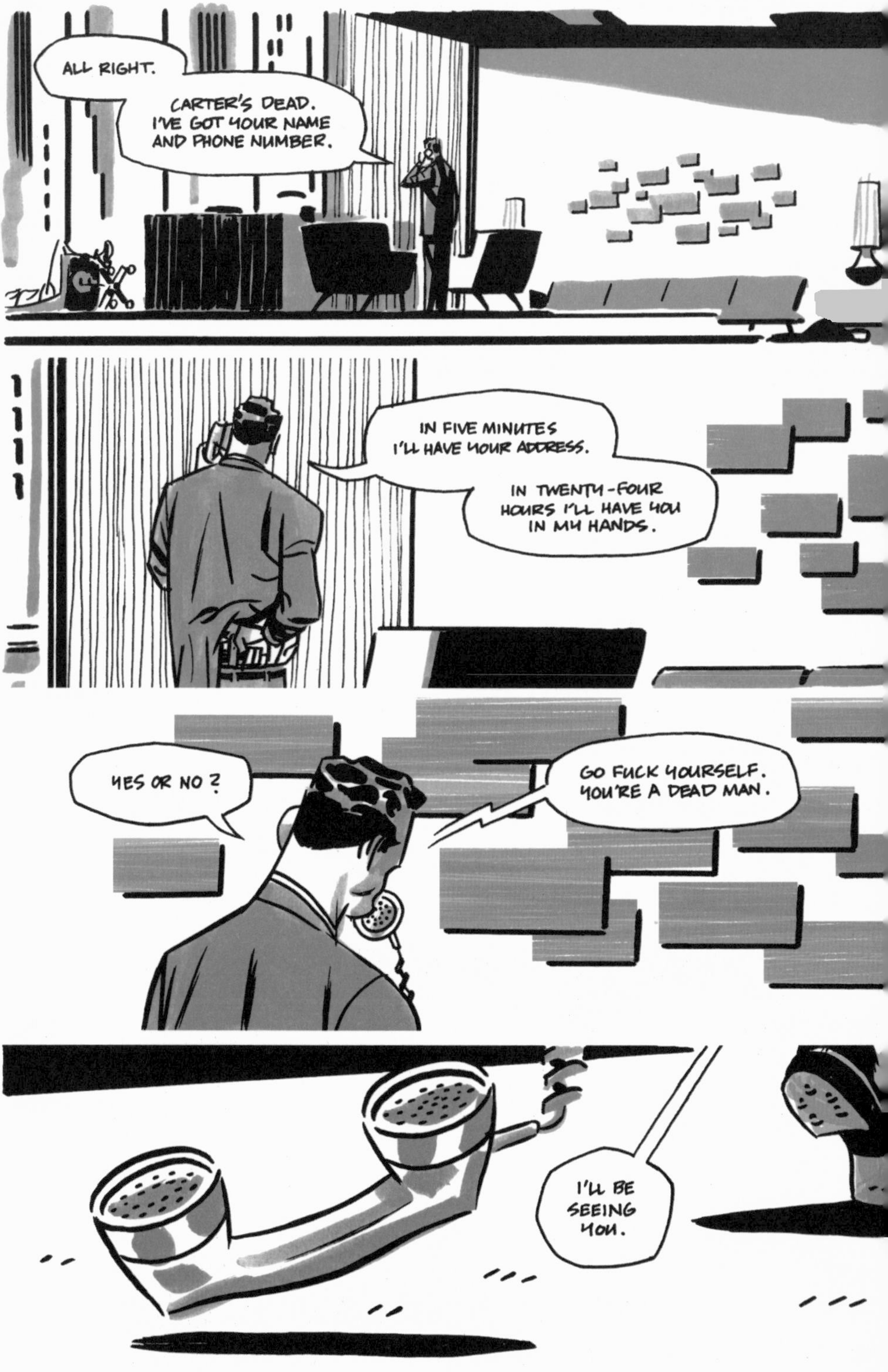
ALL RIGHT.
CARTER'S DEAD. I'VE GOT YOUR NAME AND PHONE NUMBER.
IN FIVE MINUTES I'LL HAVE YOUR ADDRESS.
IN TWENTY-FOUR HOURS I'LL HAVE YOU IN MY HANDS.
YES OR NO?
GO FUCK YOURSELF. YOU'RE A DEAD MAN.
I'LL BE SEEING YOU.

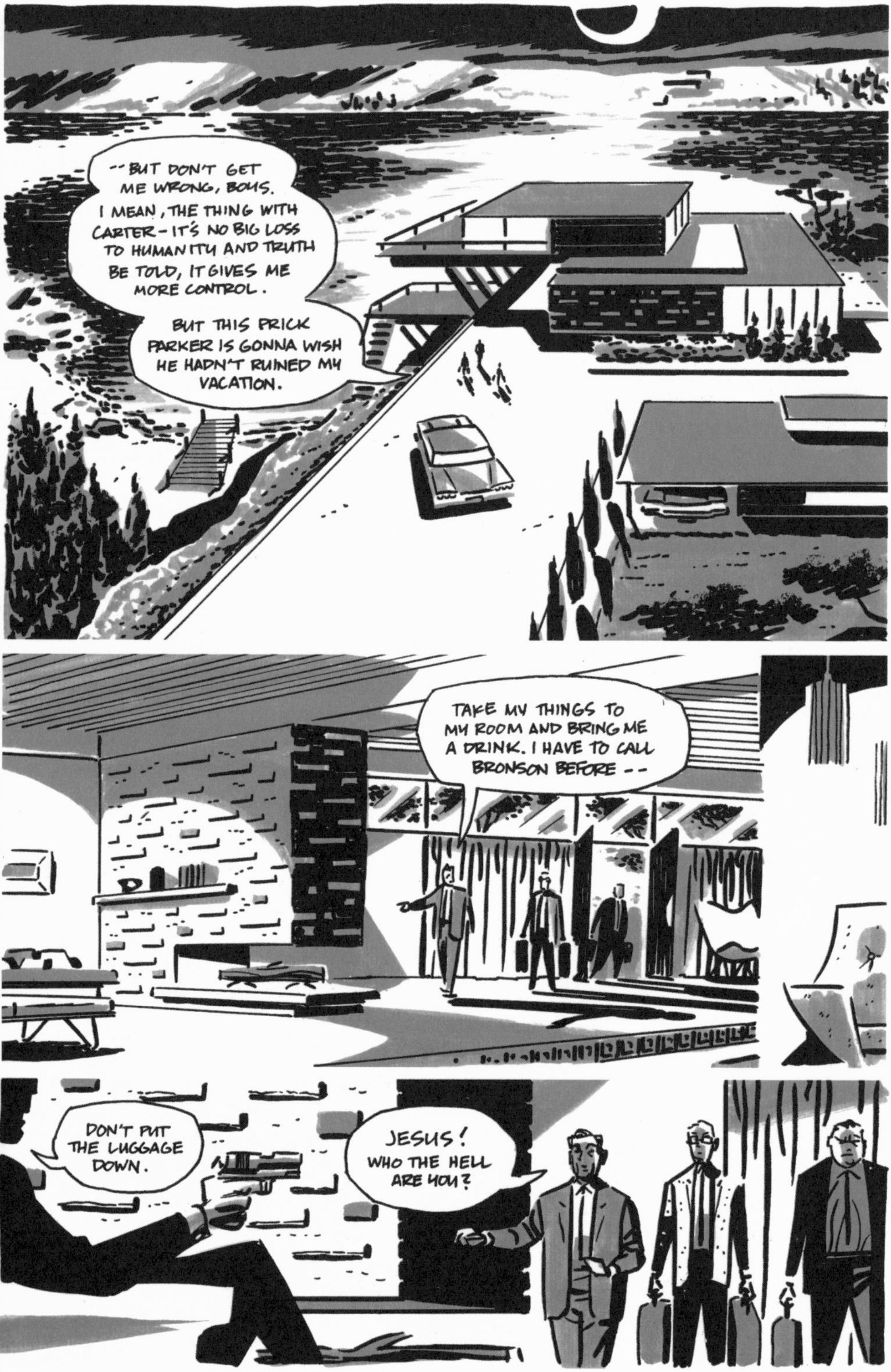
--BUT DON'T GET ME WRONG, BOYS. I MEAN, THE THING WITH CARTER - IT'S NO BIG LOSS TO HUMANITY AND TRUTH BE TOLD, IT GIVES ME MORE CONTROL.
BUT THIS PRICK PARKER IS GONNA WISH HE HADN'T RUINED MY VACATION.
TAKE MY THINGS TO MY ROOM AND BRING ME A DRINK. I HAVE TO CALL BRONSON BEFORE --
DON'T PUT THE LUGGAGE DOWN.
JESUS! WHO THE HELL ARE YOU?

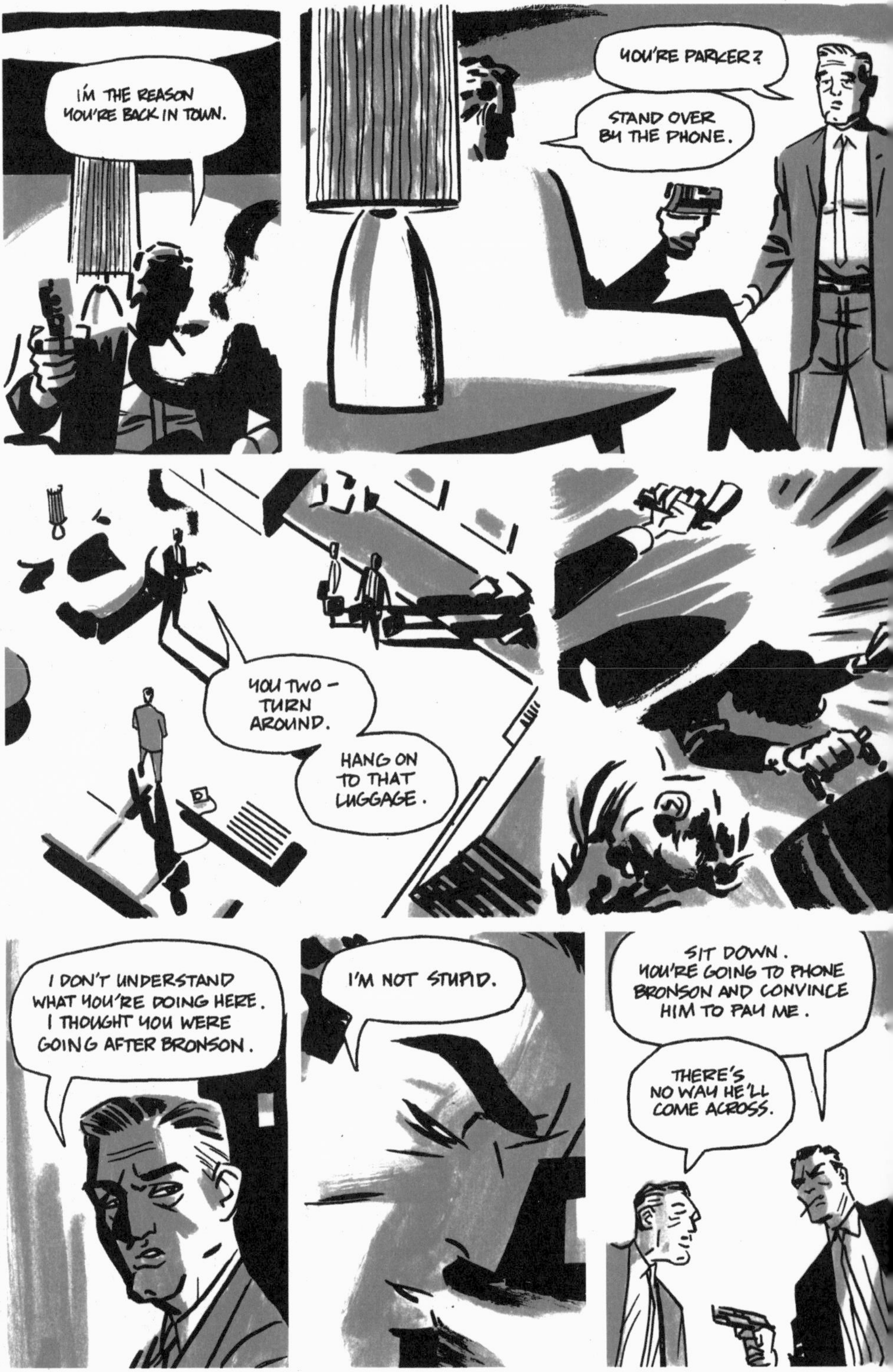

I'M THE REASON YOU'RE BACK IN TOWN.
YOU'RE PARKER?
STAND OVER BY THE PHONE.
YOU TWO - TURN AROUND.
HANG ON TO THAT LUGGAGE.
I DON'T UNDERSTAND WHAT YOU'RE DOING HERE. I THOUGHT YOU WERE GOING AFTER BRONSON.
I'M NOT STUPID.
SIT DOWN. YOU'RE GOING TO PHONE BRONSON AND CONVINCE HIM TO PAY ME.
THERE'S NO WAY HE'LL COME ACROSS.

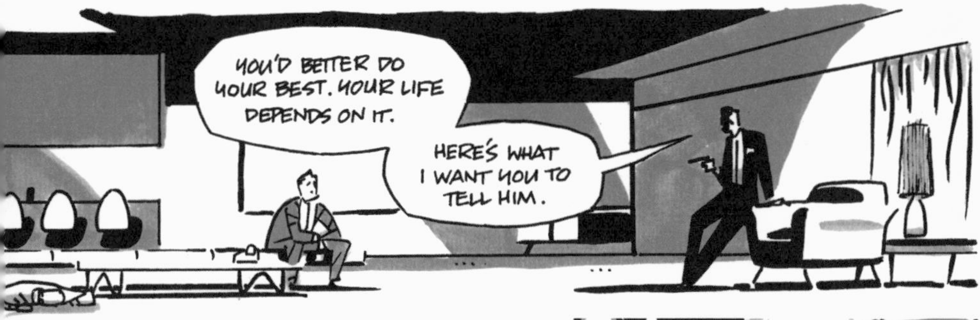
YOU'D BETTER DO YOUR BEST. YOUR LIFE DEPENDS ON IT.
HERE'S WHAT I WANT YOU TO TELL HIM.

Parker explained the type of business he was in. He and fellow independents hit banks, payrolls, armored cars, jewelers – anything worth the risk.

They never hit casinos or layoff bookies or narcotics caches. The syndicate was left alone even though they were wide open. The people Parker knew weren't organized. They could hit an outfit operation and vanish without a trace.

If Bronson didn't come across with his money, Parker would keep chopping off heads, starting with Fairfax.
He'd also write letters to every man he'd ever worked with. He'd tell them the outfit hit him for forty-five G's – Do him a favor and hit them back when you get the chance.

At least half these men were just like Parker – they already had an outfit job cased. All they needed was an excuse to go take it.

Parker handed Fairfax the phone and made him call Bronson.

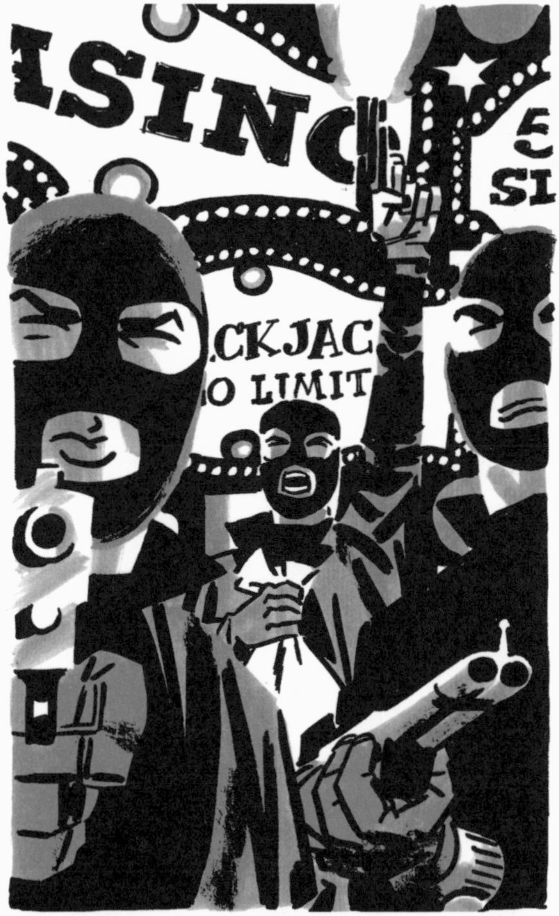
SINC
.CKJAC
O LIMIT

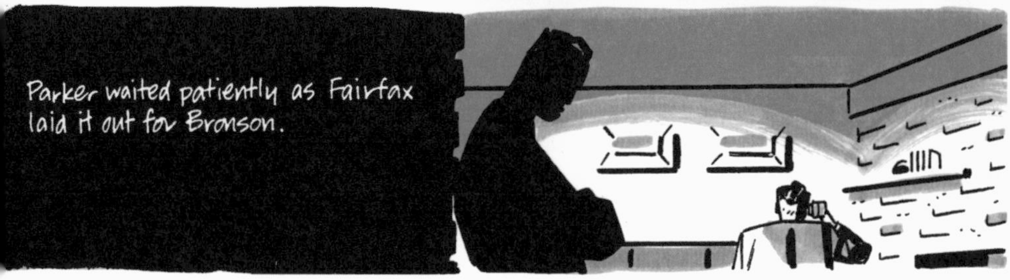
Parker waited patiently as Fairfax laid it out for Bronson.

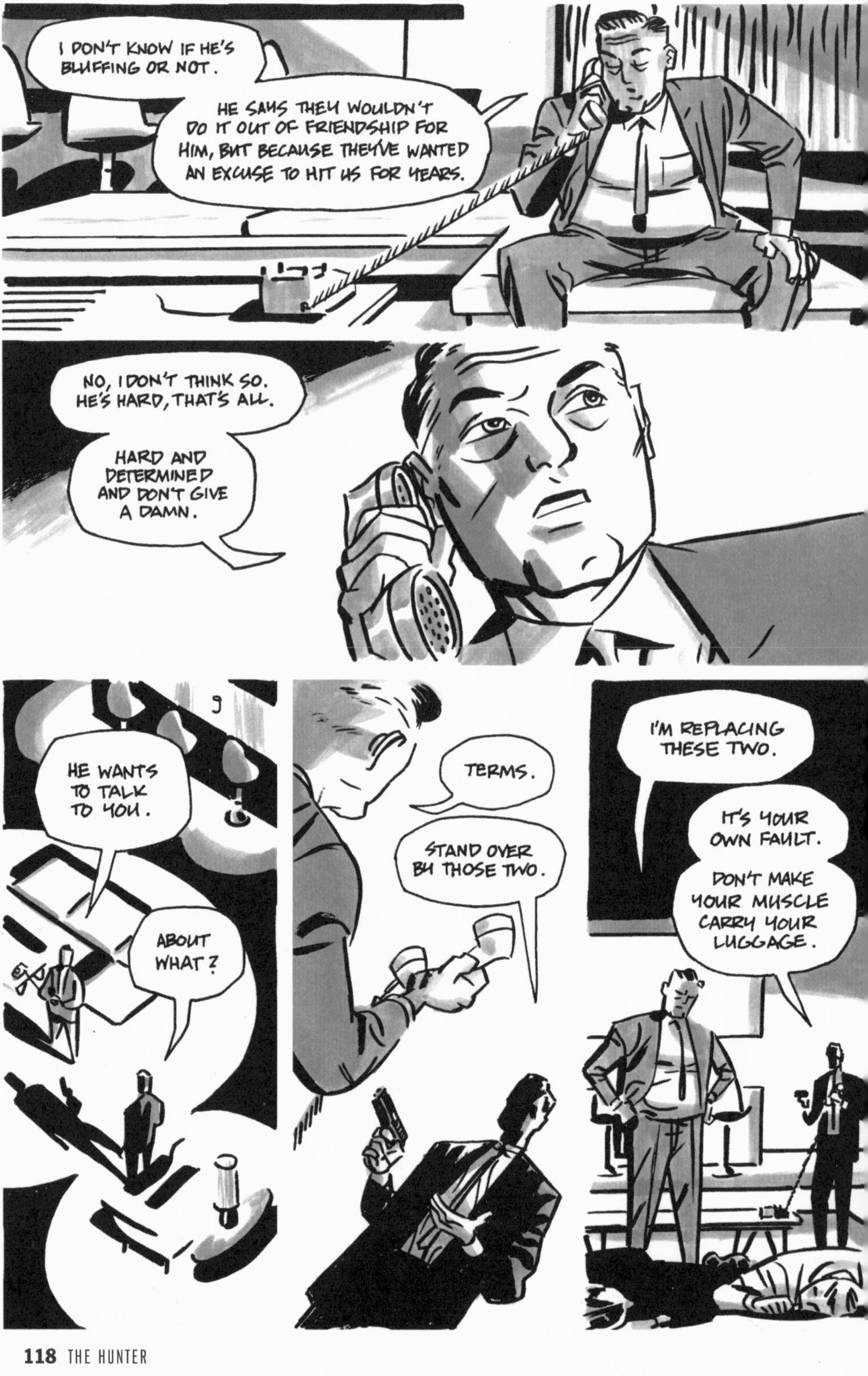
I DON'T KNOW IF HE'S BLUFFING OR NOT.
HE SAYS THEY WOULDN'T DO IT OUT OF FRIENDSHIP FOR HIM, BUT BECAUSE THEY'VE WANTED AN EXCUSE TO HIT US FOR YEARS.
NO, I DON'T THINK SO. HE'S HARD, THAT'S ALL.
HARD AND DETERMINED AND DON'T GIVE A DAMN.
HE WANTS TO TALK TO YOU.
ABOUT WHAT?
TERMS.
STAND OVER BY THOSE TWO.
I'M REPLACING THESE TWO.
IT'S YOUR OWN FAULT.
DON'T MAKE YOUR MUSCLE CARRY YOUR LUGGAGE.

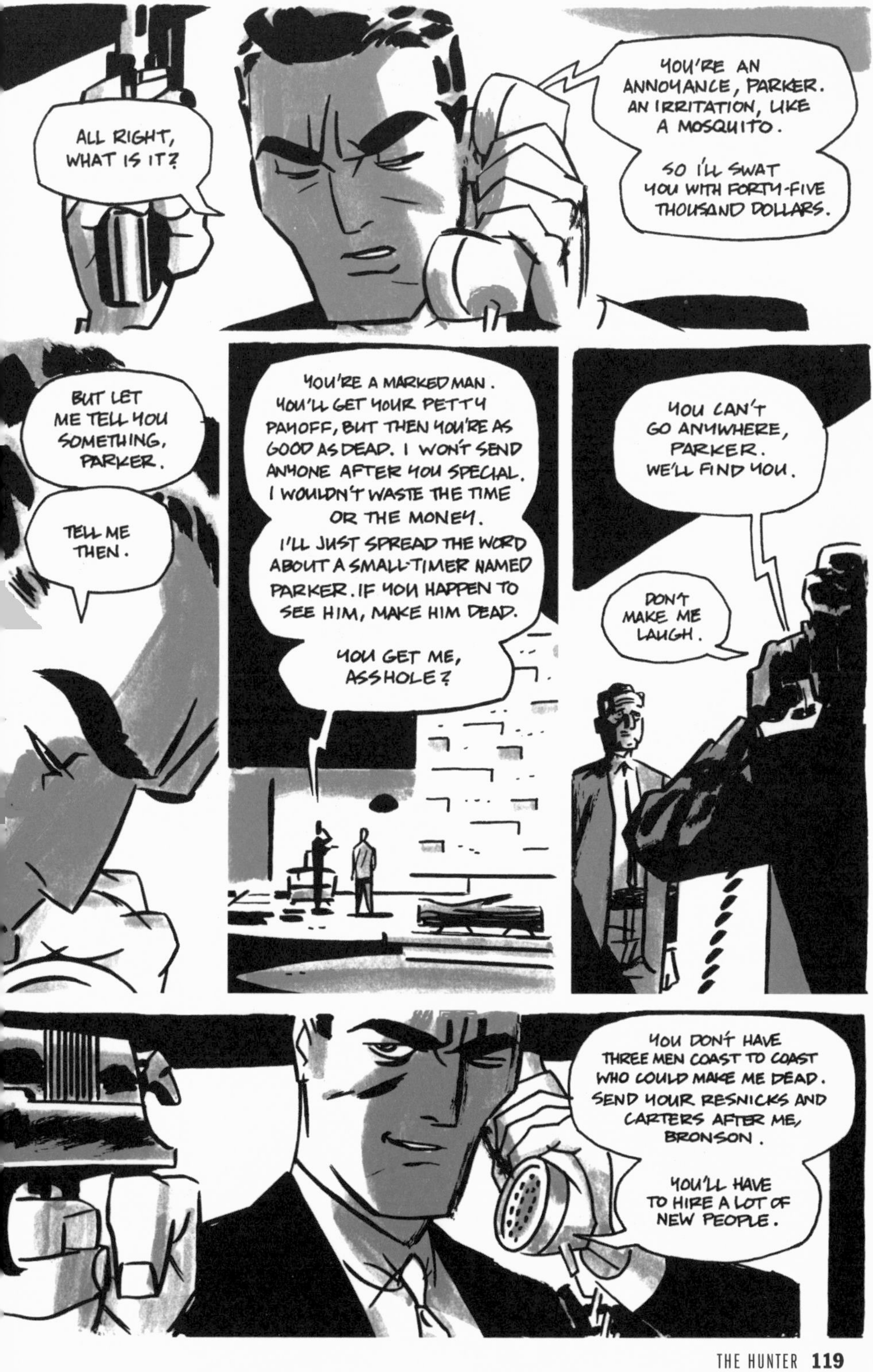
ALL RIGHT, WHAT IS IT?
YOU'RE AN ANNOYANCE, PARKER. AN IRRITATION, LIKE A MOSQUITO.
SO I'LL SWAT YOU WITH FORTY-FIVE THOUSAND DOLLARS.
BUT LET ME TELL YOU SOMETHING, PARKER.
TELL ME THEN.
YOU'RE A MARKED MAN. YOU'LL GET YOUR PETTY PAYOFF, BUT THEN YOU'RE AS GOOD AS DEAD. I WON'T SEND ANYONE AFTER YOU SPECIAL. I WOULDN'T WASTE THE TIME OR THE MONEY.
I'LL JUST SPREAD THE WORD ABOUT A SMALL-TIMER NAMED PARKER. IF YOU HAPPEN TO SEE HIM, MAKE HIM DEAD.
YOU GET ME, ASSHOLE?
YOU CAN'T GO ANYWHERE, PARKER. WE'LL FIND YOU.
DON'T MAKE ME LAUGH.
YOU DON'T HAVE THREE MEN COAST TO COAST WHO COULD MAKE ME DEAD. SEND YOUR RESNICKS AND CARTERS AFTER ME, BRONSON.
YOU'LL HAVE TO HIRE A LOT OF NEW PEOPLE.

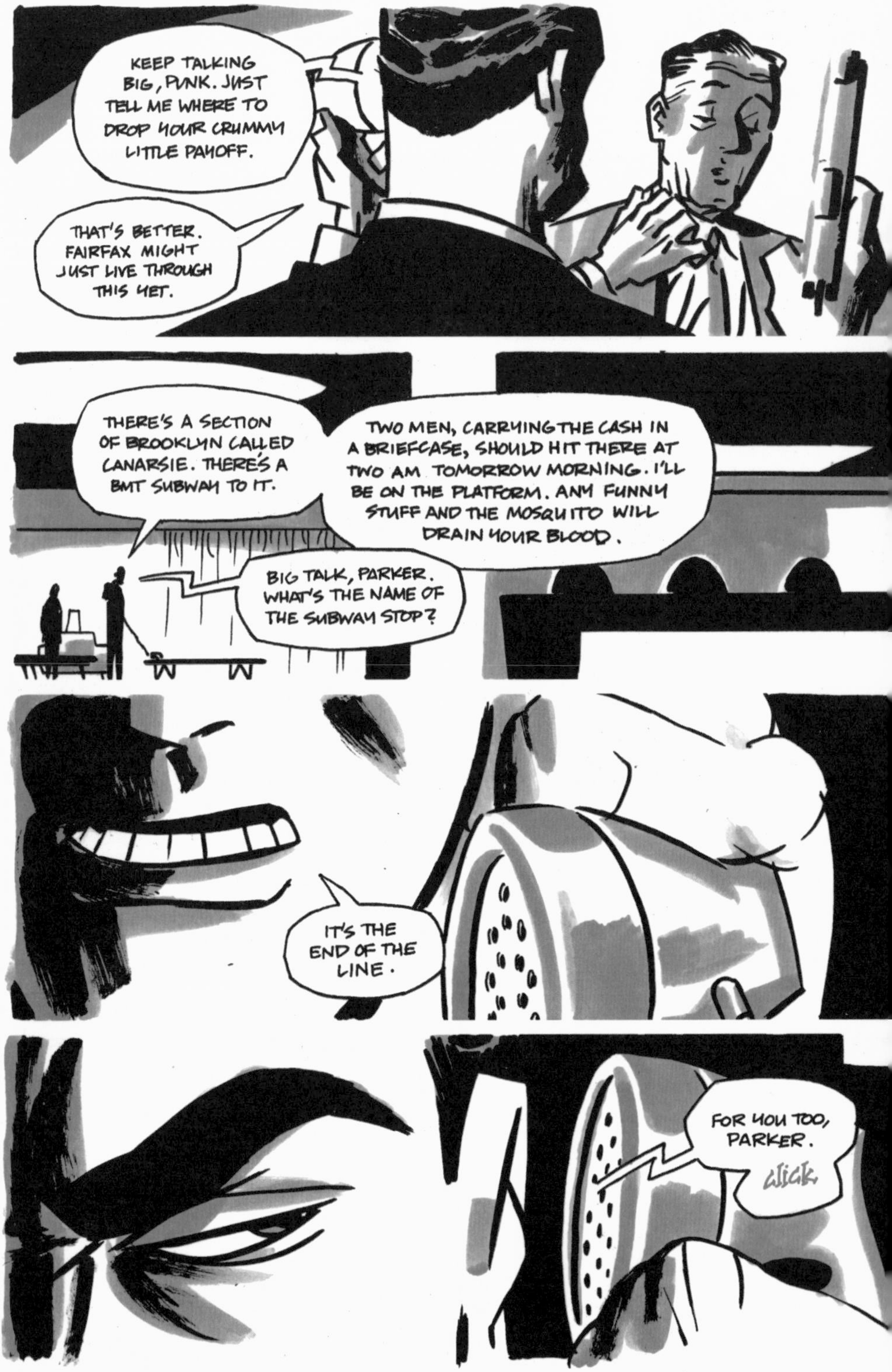
KEEP TALKING BIG, PUNK. JUST TELL ME WHERE TO DROP YOUR CRUMMY LITTLE PAYOFF.
THAT'S BETTER. FAIRFAX MIGHT JUST LIVE THROUGH THIS YET.
THERE'S A SECTION OF BROOKLYN CALLED CANARSIE. THERE'S A BMT SUBWAY TO IT.
TWO MEN, CARRYING THE CASH IN A BRIEFCASE, SHOULD HIT THERE AT TWO AM TOMORROW MORNING. I'LL BE ON THE PLATFORM. ANY FUNNY STUFF AND THE MOSQUITO WILL DRAIN YOUR BLOOD.
BIG TALK, PARKER. WHAT'S THE NAME OF THE SUBWAY STOP?
IT'S THE END OF THE LINE.
FOR YOU TOO, PARKER.
Wick

lomentum kept him rolling.
e wasn't sure himself anymore
ow much was a tough front to
npress the organization and
ow much was himself.
le knew he was hard, he knew
e worried less about emotion
han other people, but he'd
ever enjoyed the idea
f killing.

was momentum, that was
ll. Eighteen years in one
usiness, doing one or two
lean simple operations
year, living relaxed and
asy in the resort hotels
ith a woman he enjoyed.
hen Mal had come along.
he woman was gone,
he pattern was gone,
verything was gone.

e spent months as a
agrant on a prison farm -
pent weeks coming across
e country like an O. Henry
ramp - He devoted time
nd effort and money to a
ob that didn't net a dime -
inding and killing Mal.

nd now this. Bucking the outfit
ore for the mean Hell of it
han anything else, as though
or eighteen years he'd been
toring up all the meanness,
ll the viciousness and now
had to come rushing out.

e didn't know if he would
ake it and he didn't really
are. He was doing it, and
olling along with the
omentum, and that was
ll that mattered.

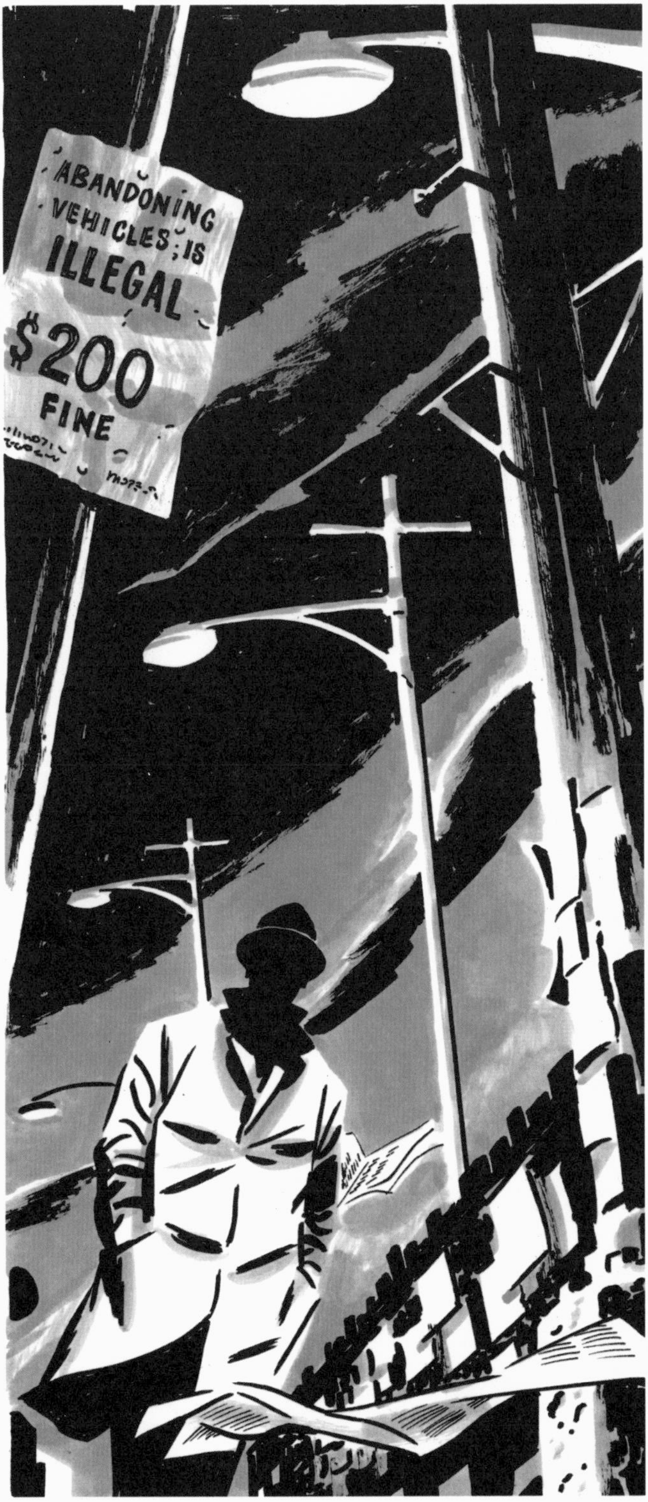
ABANDONING VEHICLES; IS ILLEGAL
$200 FINE

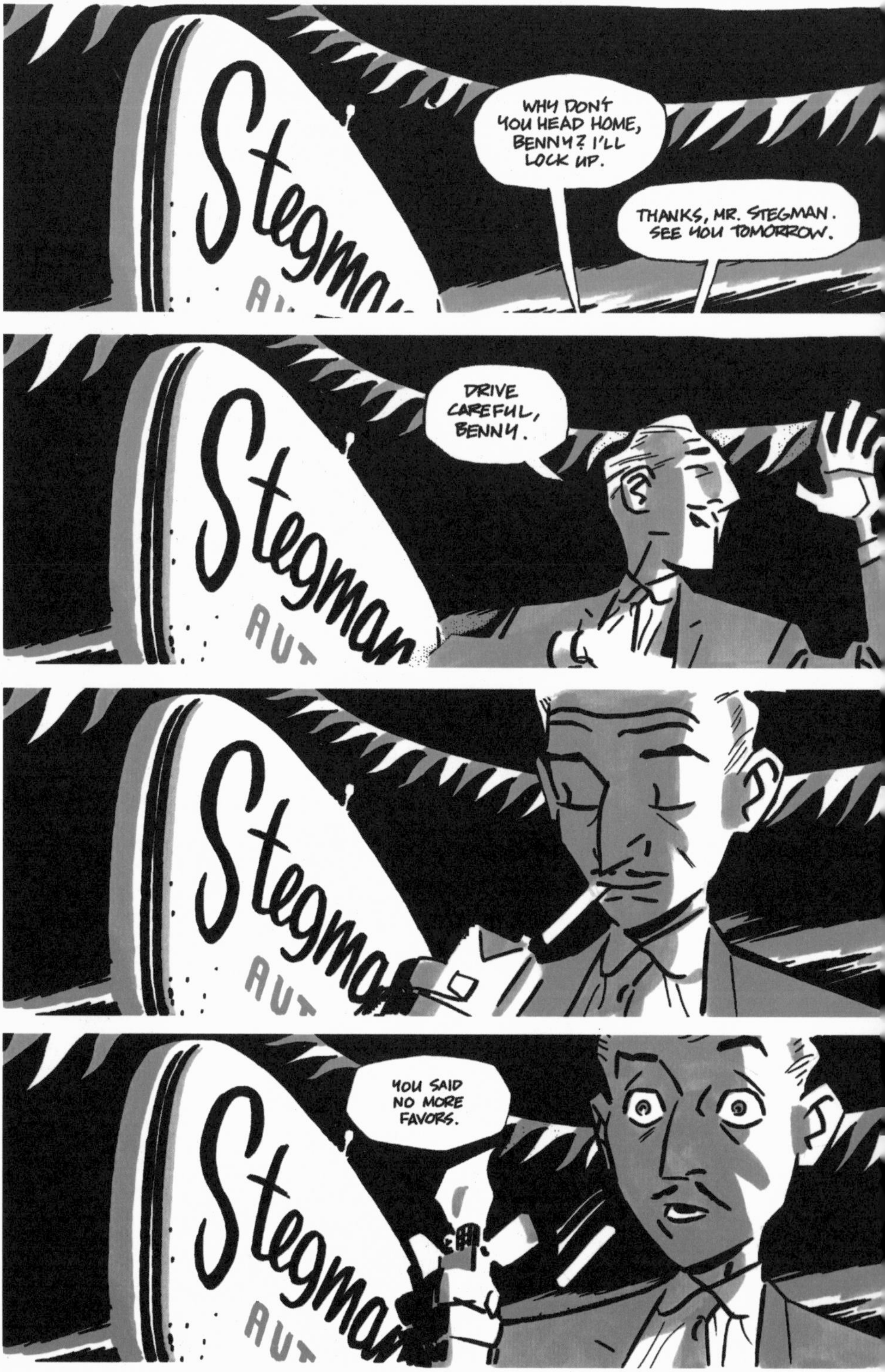
WHY DON'T YOU HEAD HOME, BENNY? I'LL LOCK UP.
THANKS, MR. STEGMAN. SEE YOU TOMORROW.
Stegman
DRIVE CAREFUL, BENNY.
Stegman
Stegman
YOU SAID NO MORE FAVORS.
Stegman

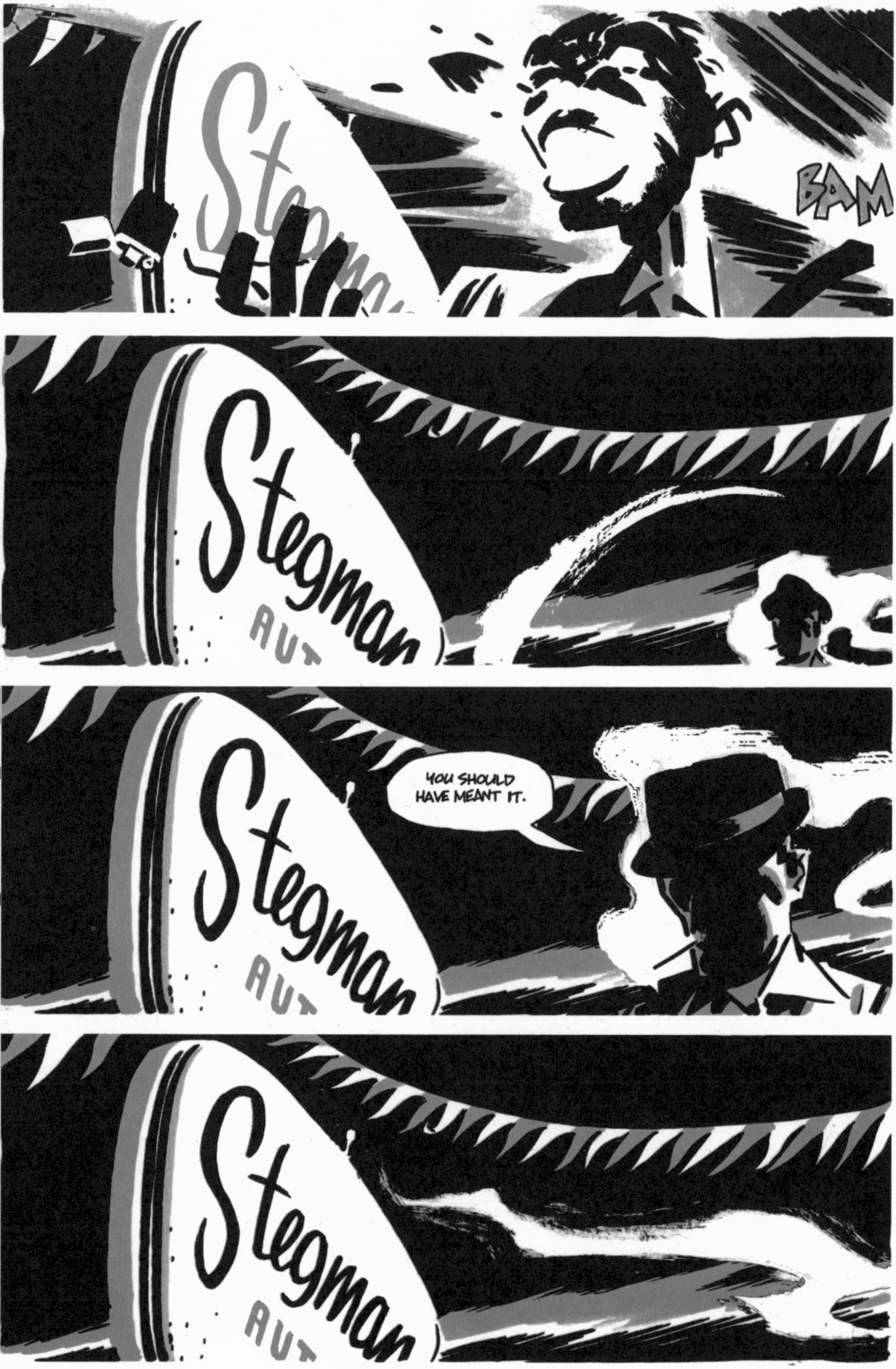
BAM
Stegman
Stegman
YOU SHOULD HAVE MEANT IT.
Stegman

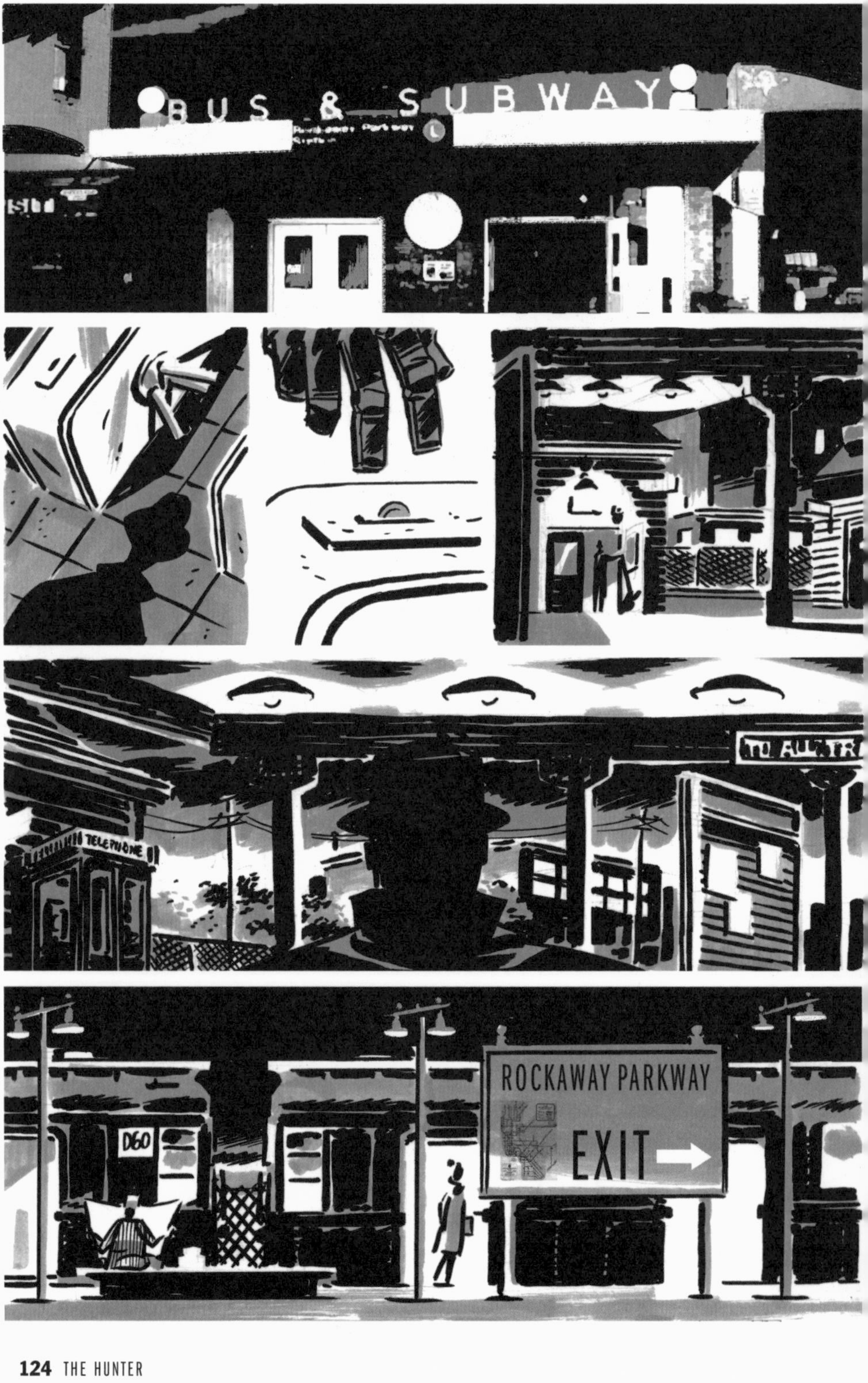
BUS & SUBWAY
TELEPHONE
D60
ROCKAWAY PARKWAY
EXIT

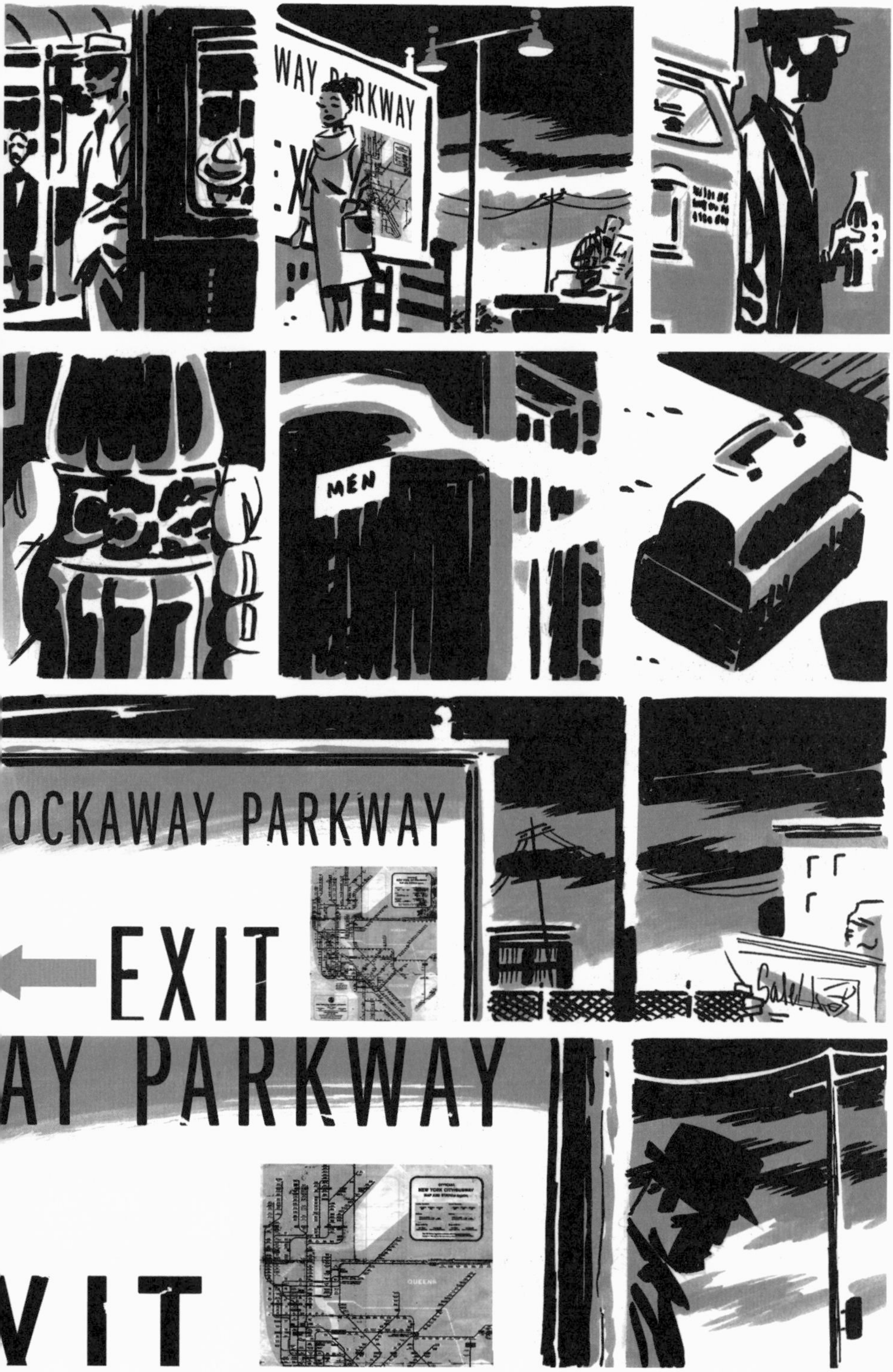
MEN
OCKAWAY PARKWAY
EXIT
AY PARKWAY

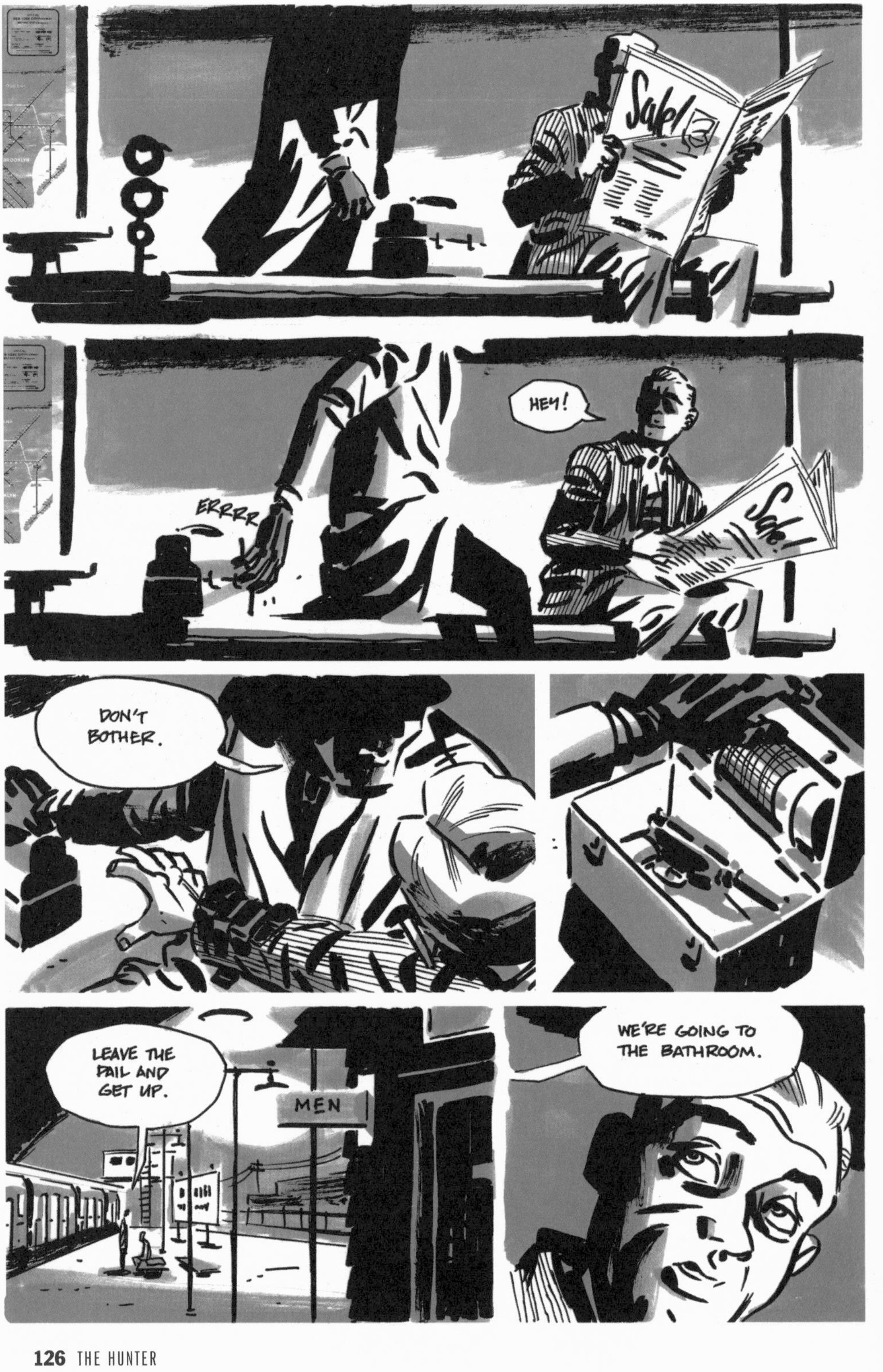
HEY!
ERRRR
DON'T BOTHER.
LEAVE THE PAIL AND GET UP.
MEN
WE'RE GOING TO THE BATHROOM.

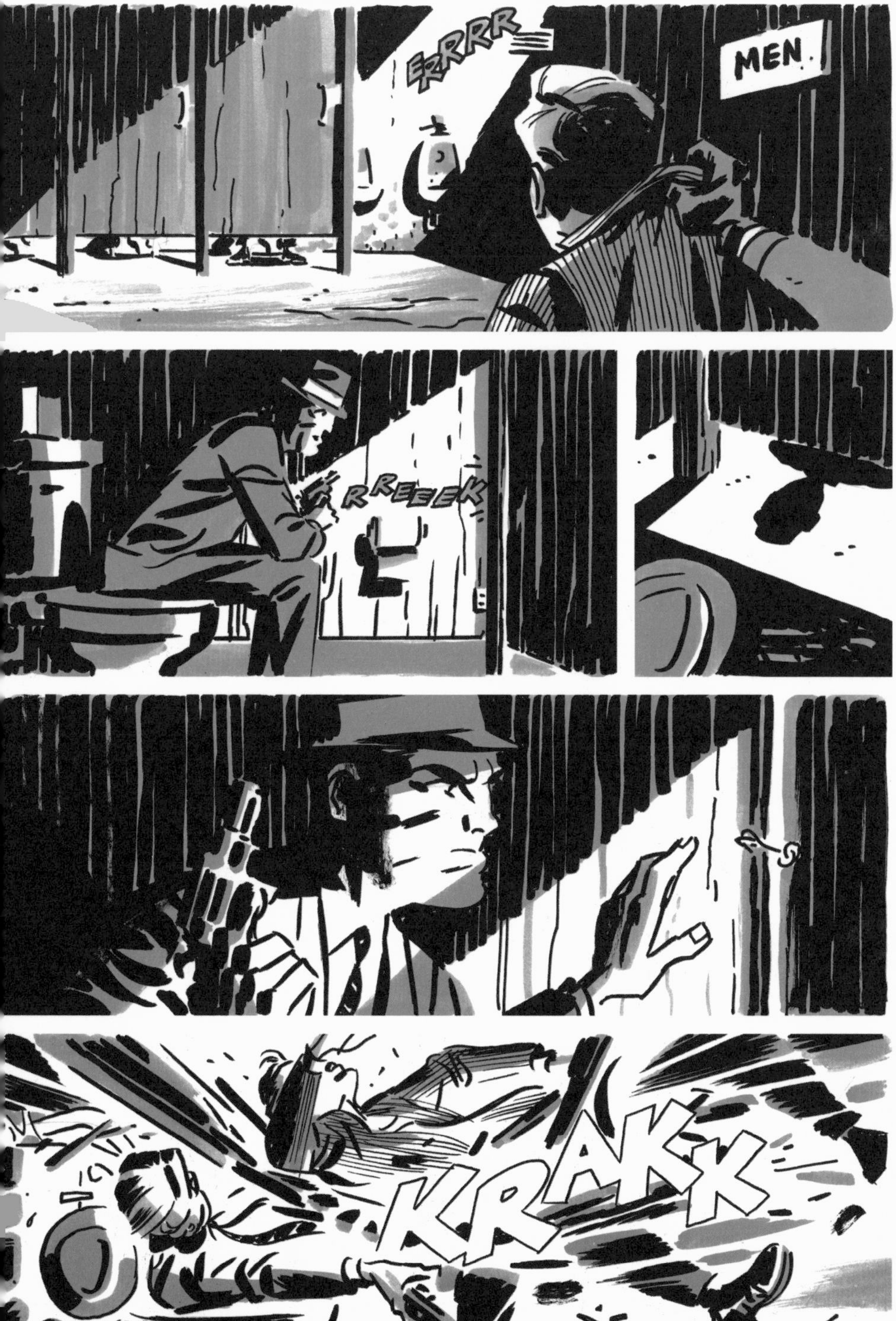
ERRRR
MEN
RREEEEK
KRAKK

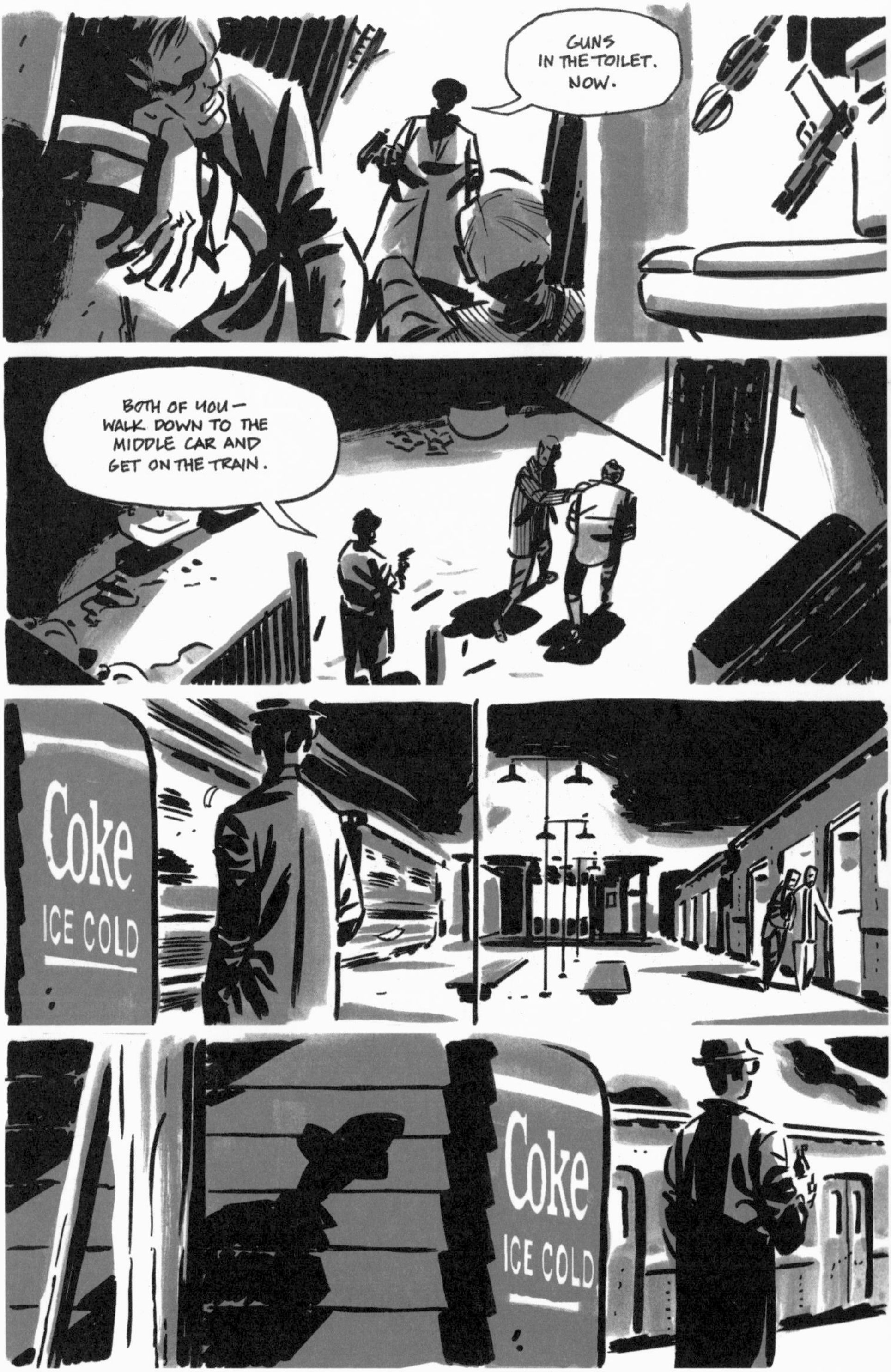
GUNS IN THE TOILET. NOW.
BOTH OF YOU— WALK DOWN TO THE MIDDLE CAR AND GET ON THE TRAIN.
Coke
ICE COLD
Coke
ICE COLD

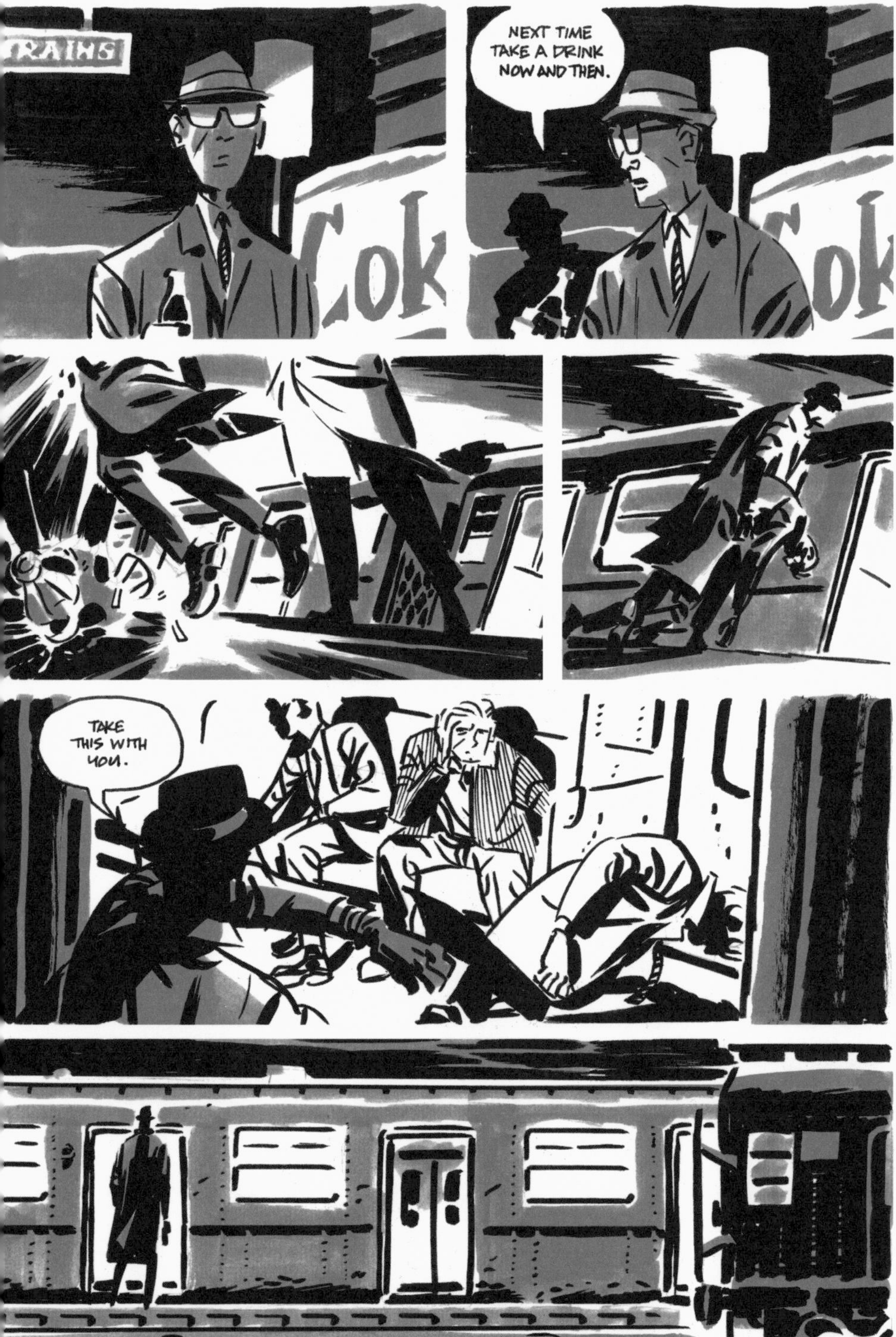

TRAINS
NEXT TIME TAKE A DRINK NOW AND THEN.
Cok
Cok
TAKE THIS WITH YOU.

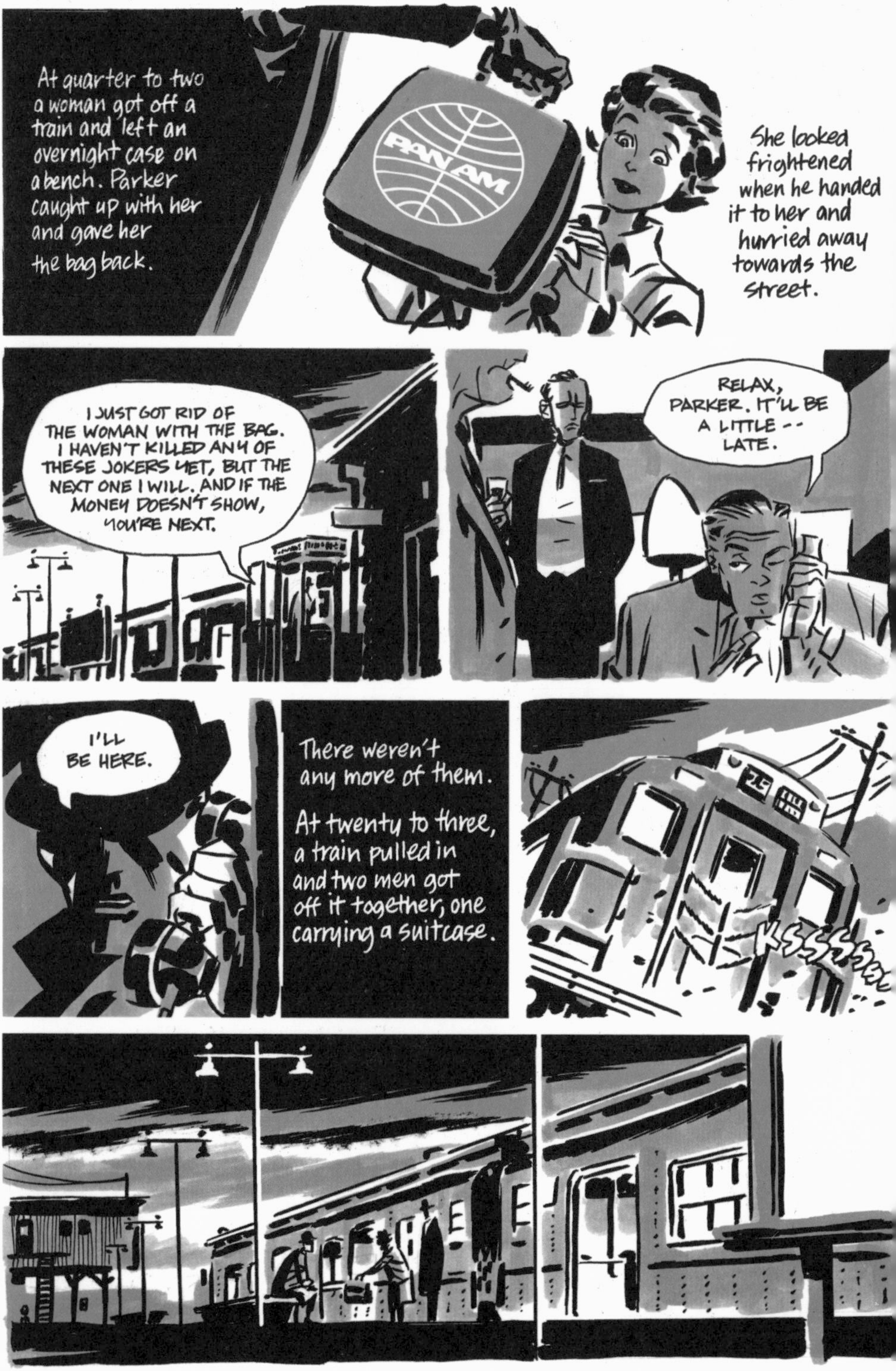
At quarter to two a woman got off a train and left an overnight case on a bench. Parker caught up with her and gave her the bag back.
PAN AM
She looked frightened when he handed it to her and hurried away towards the street.
I JUST GOT RID OF THE WOMAN WITH THE BAG. I HAVEN'T KILLED ANY OF THESE JOKERS YET, BUT THE NEXT ONE I WILL. AND IF THE MONEY DOESN'T SHOW, YOU'RE NEXT.
RELAX, PARKER. IT'LL BE A LITTLE -- LATE.
I'LL BE HERE.
There weren't any more of them.
At twenty to three, a train pulled in and two men got off it together, one carrying a suitcase.
KSSSSS

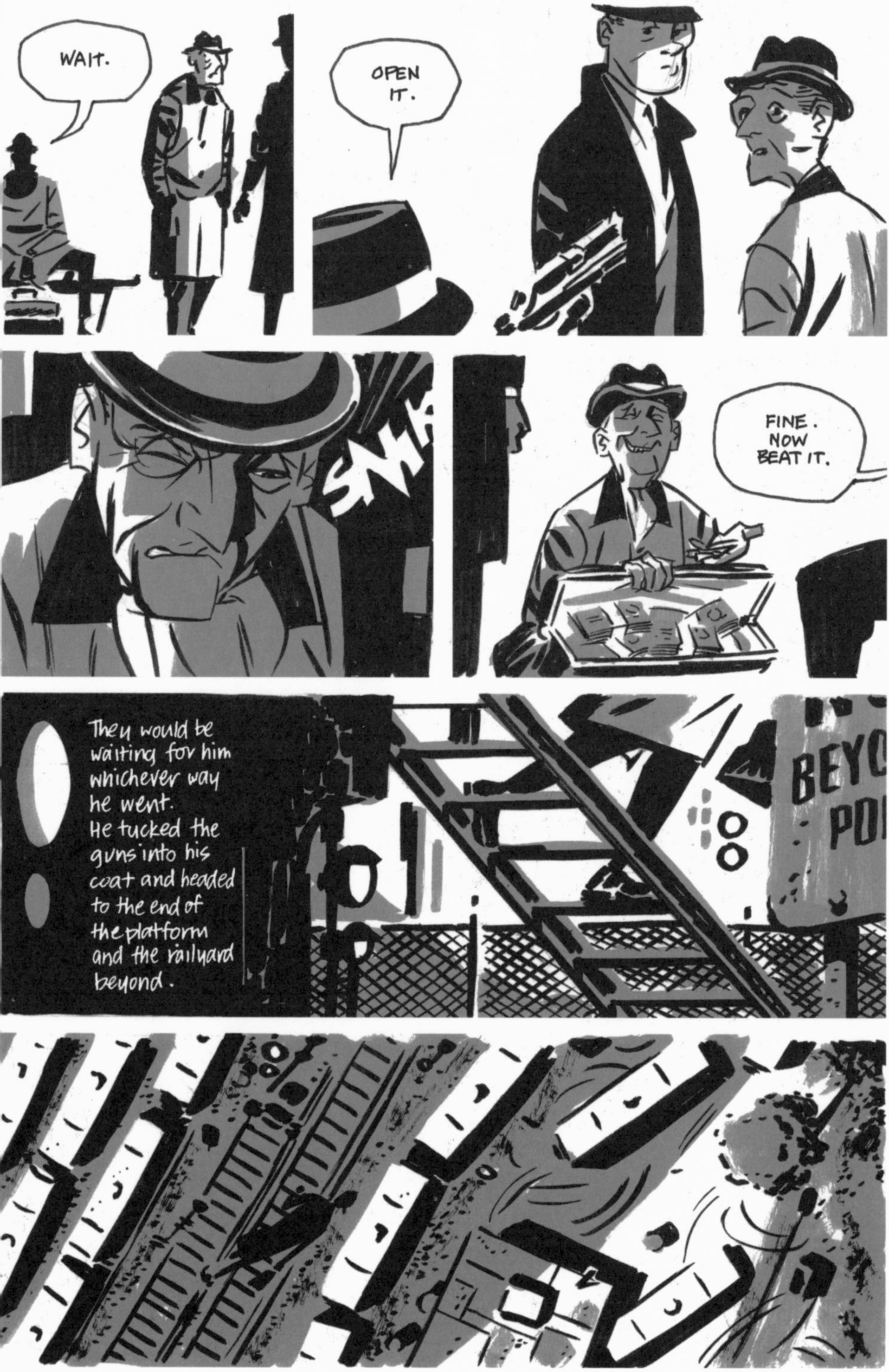
WAIT.
OPEN IT.
FINE. NOW BEAT IT.
They would be waiting for him whichever way he went. He tucked the guns into his coat and headed to the end of the platform and the railyard beyond.

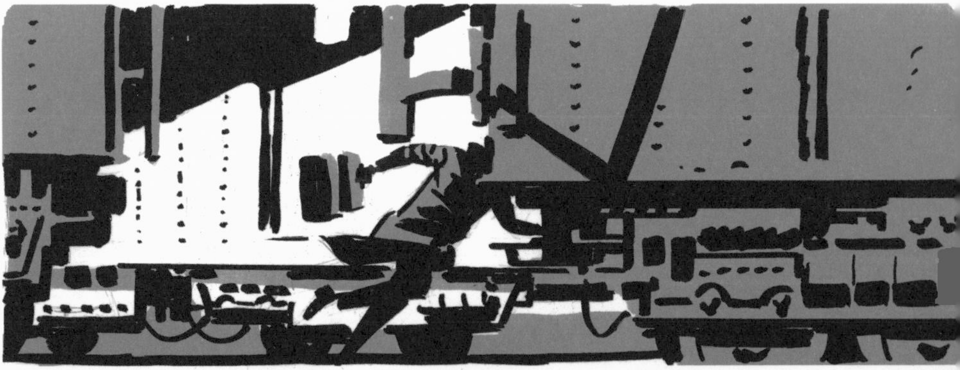

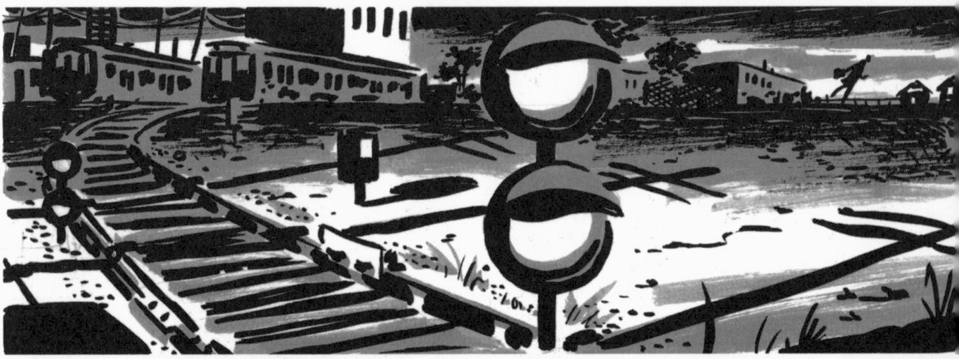

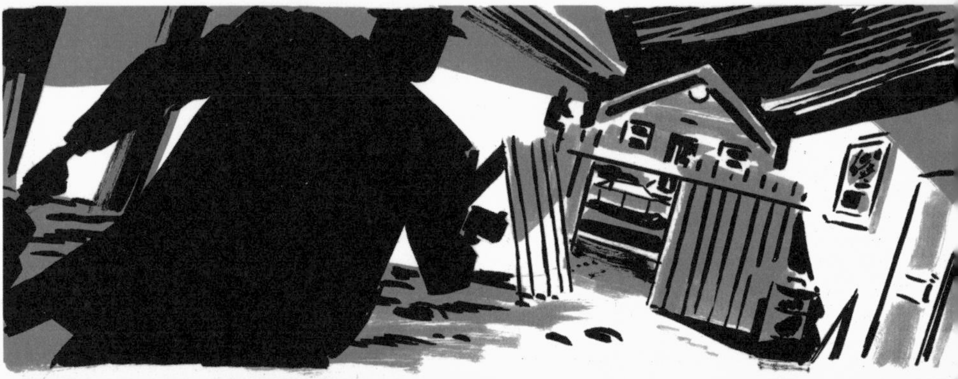

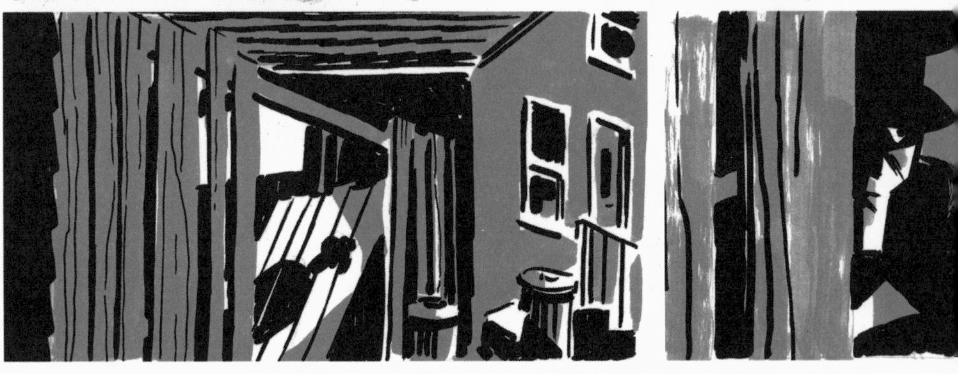

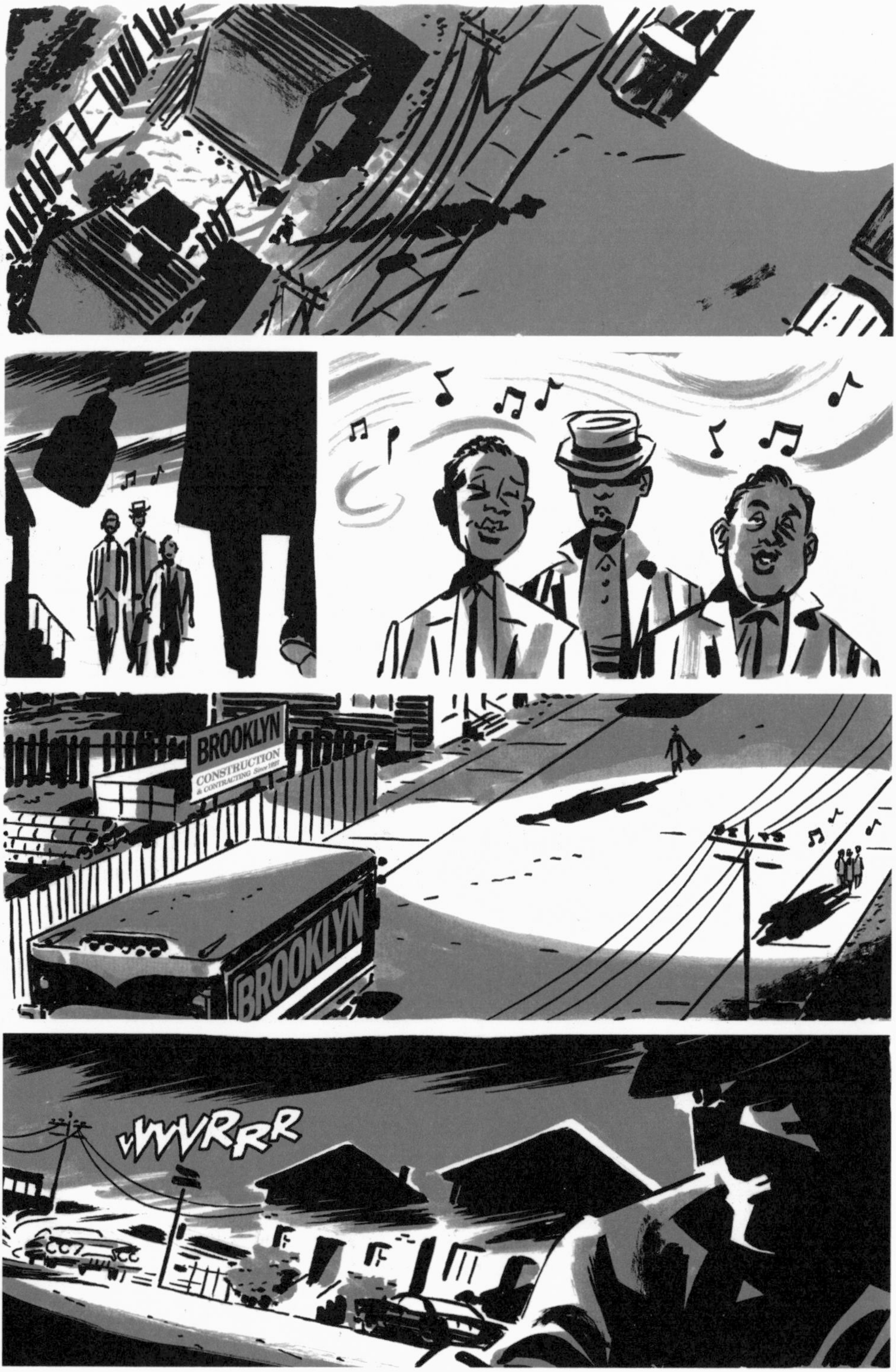
BROOKLYN
CONSTRUCTION
& CONTRACTING Since 1897
BROOKLYN
VWRRR

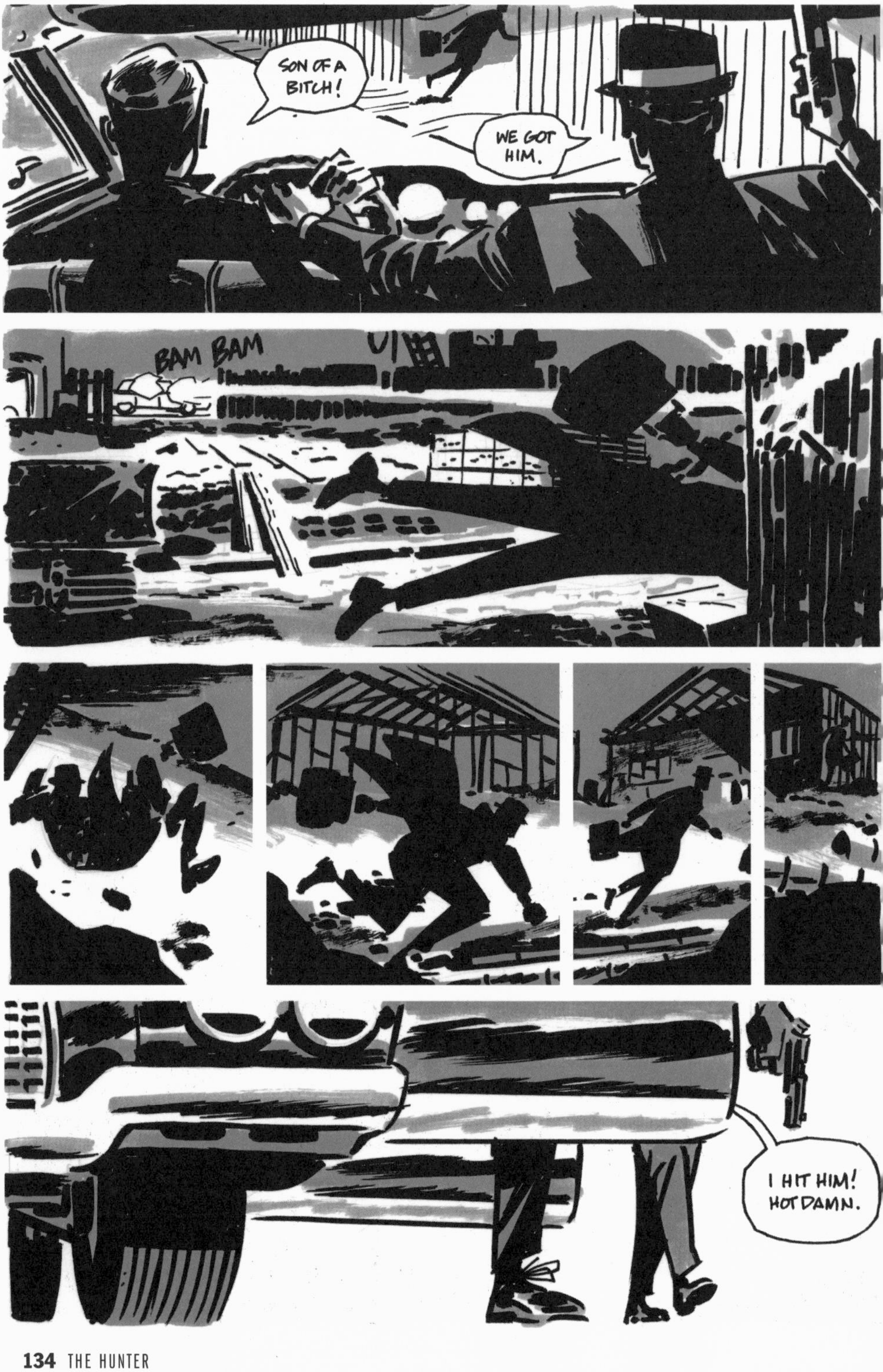
SON OF A BITCH!
WE GOT HIM.
BAM BAM
I HIT HIM! HOT DAMN.

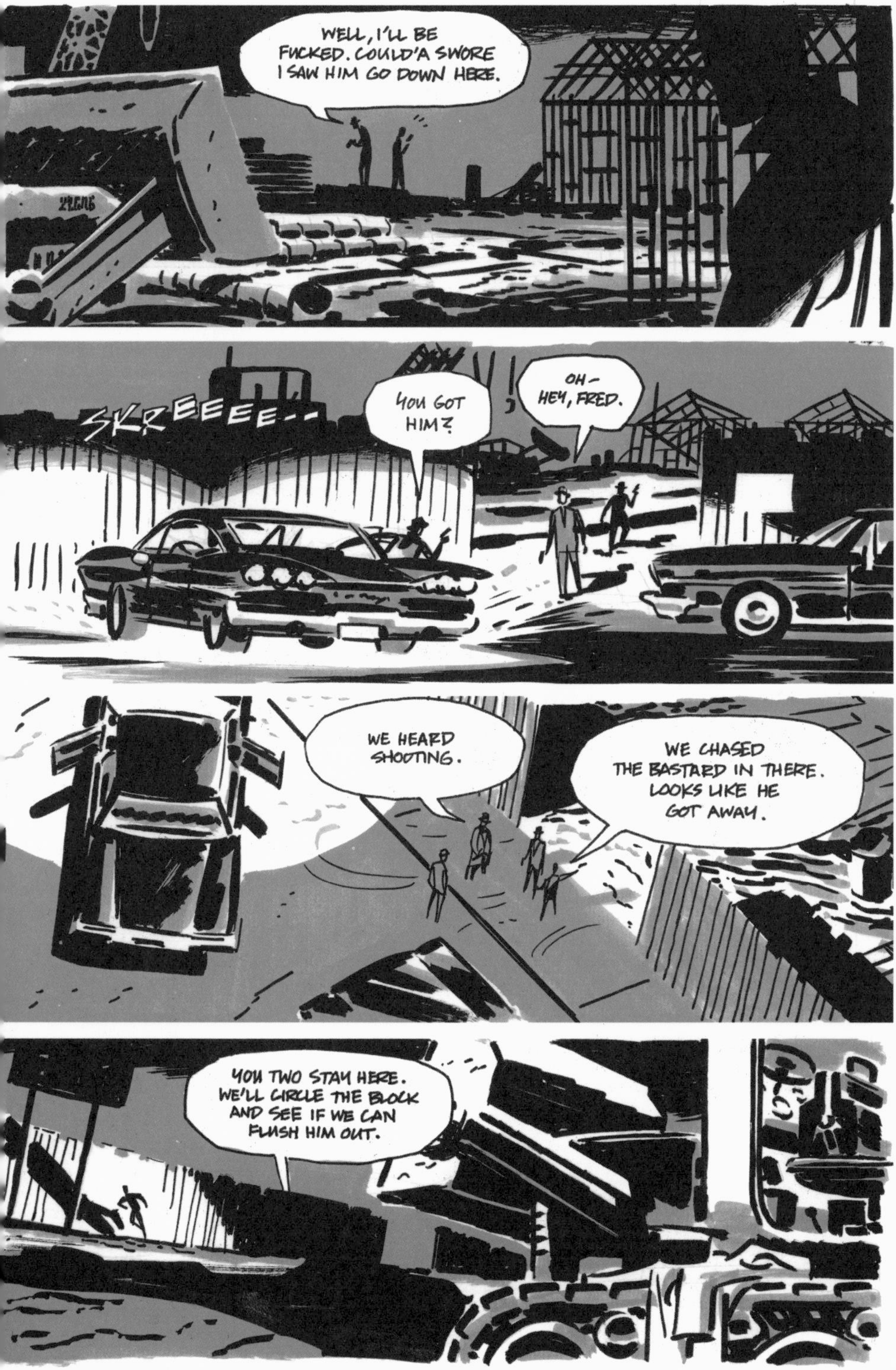
WELL, I'LL BE FUCKED. COULD'A SWORE I SAW HIM GO DOWN HERE.
SKREEEEEE...
YOU GOT HIM?
OH— HEY, FRED.
WE HEARD SHOOTING.
WE CHASED THE BASTARD IN THERE. LOOKS LIKE HE GOT AWAY.
YOU TWO STAY HERE. WE'LL CIRCLE THE BLOCK AND SEE IF WE CAN FLUSH HIM OUT.

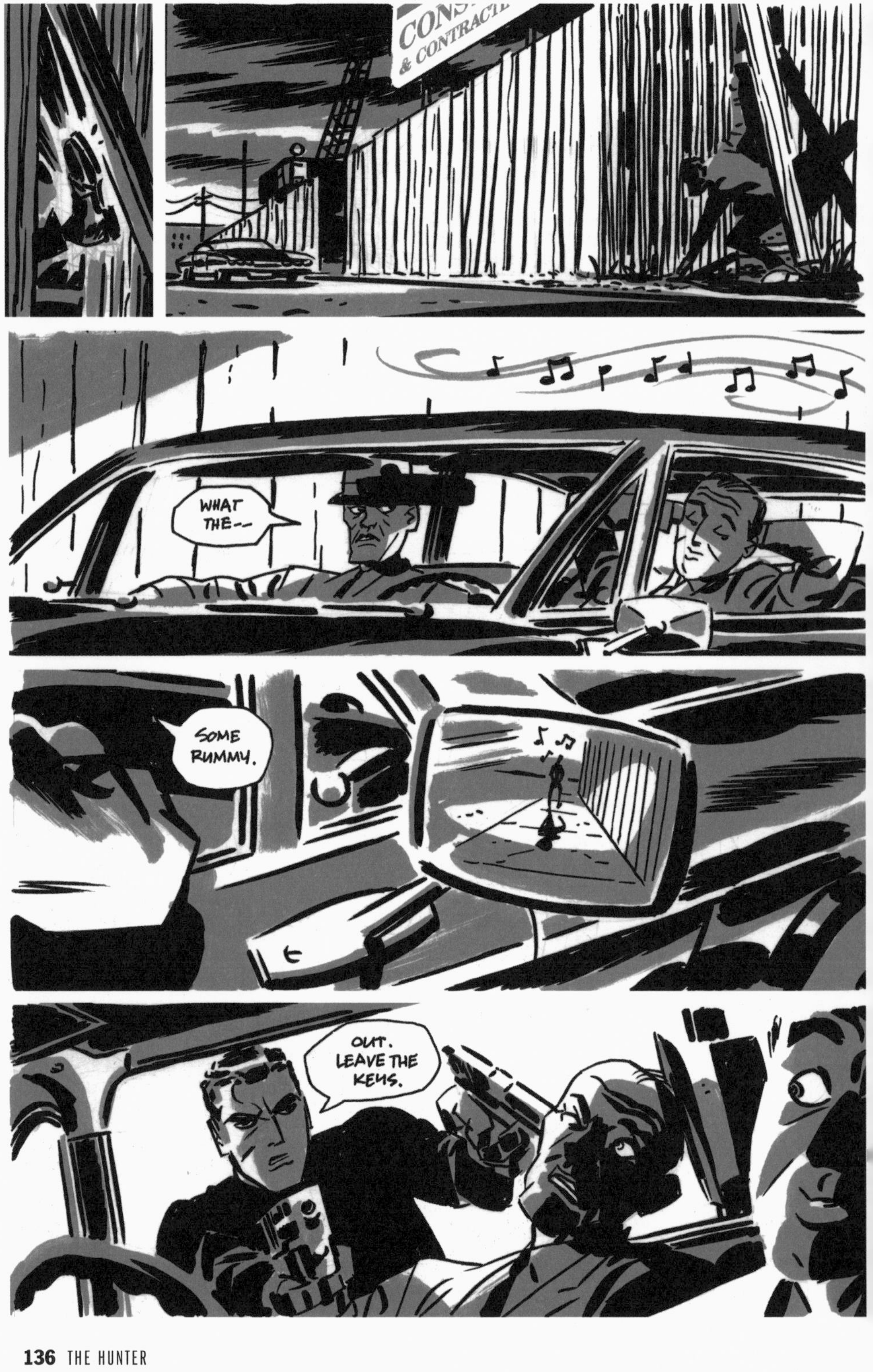
WHAT THE--
SOME RUMMY.
OUT. LEAVE THE KEYS.

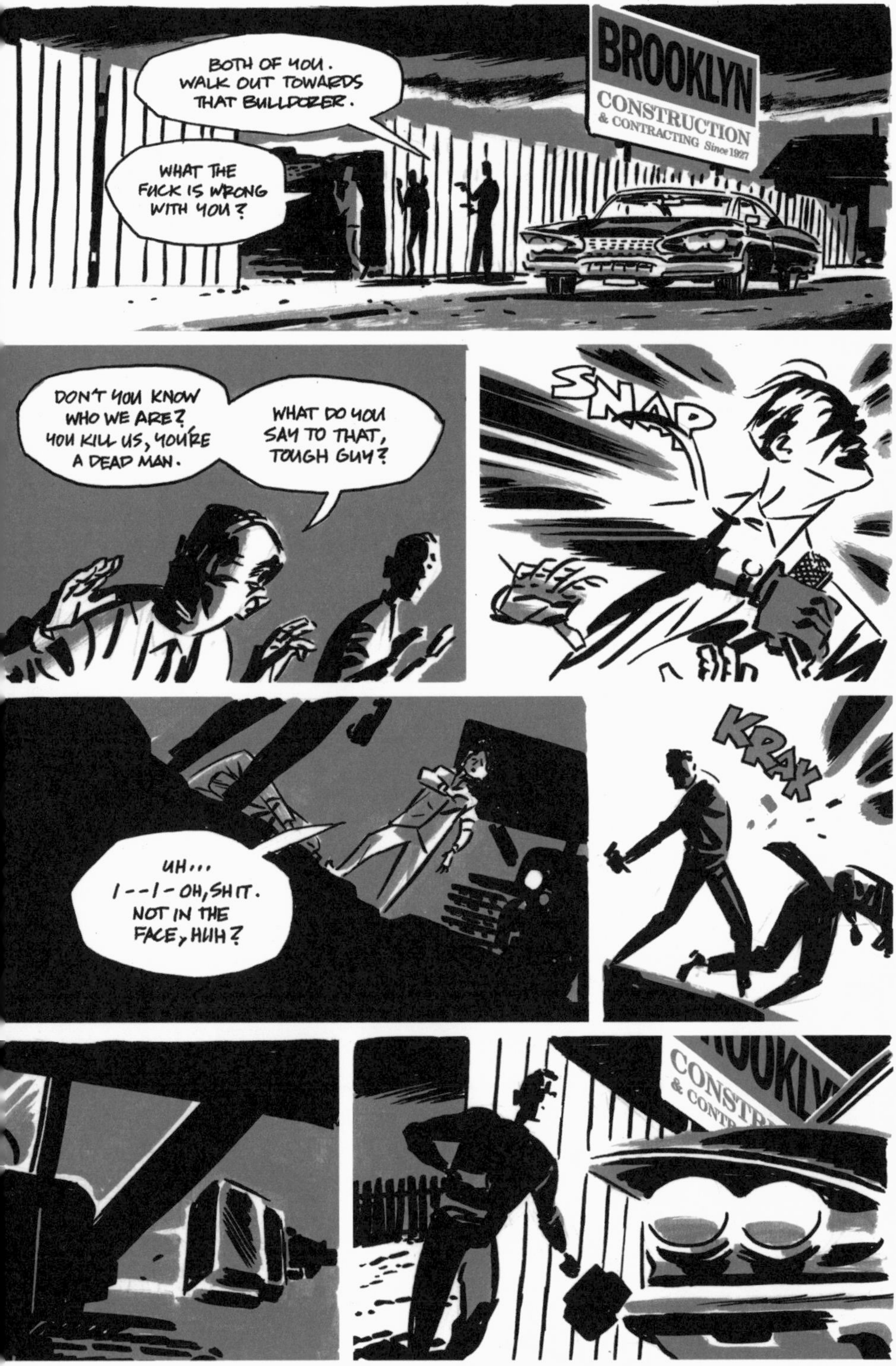
BROOKLYN
CONSTRUCTION
& CONTRACTING Since 1927
BOTH OF YOU. WALK OUT TOWARDS THAT BULLDOZER.
WHAT THE FUCK IS WRONG WITH YOU?
DON'T YOU KNOW WHO WE ARE? YOU KILL US, YOU'RE A DEAD MAN.
WHAT DO YOU SAY TO THAT, TOUGH GUY?
SNAP
UH... I--I- OH, SHIT. NOT IN THE FACE, HUH?
KRAX
BROOKLYN
CONSTR
& CONTR

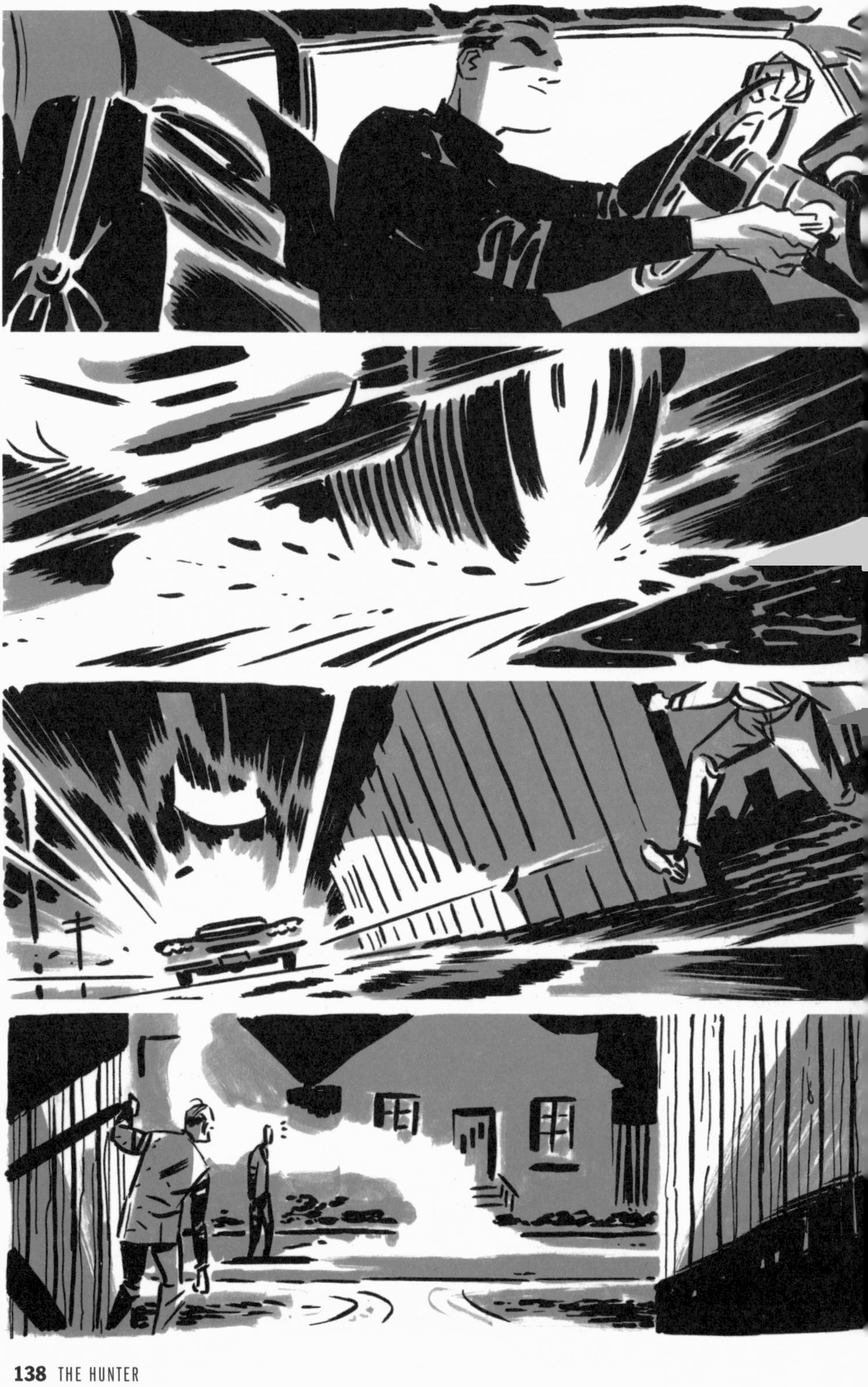

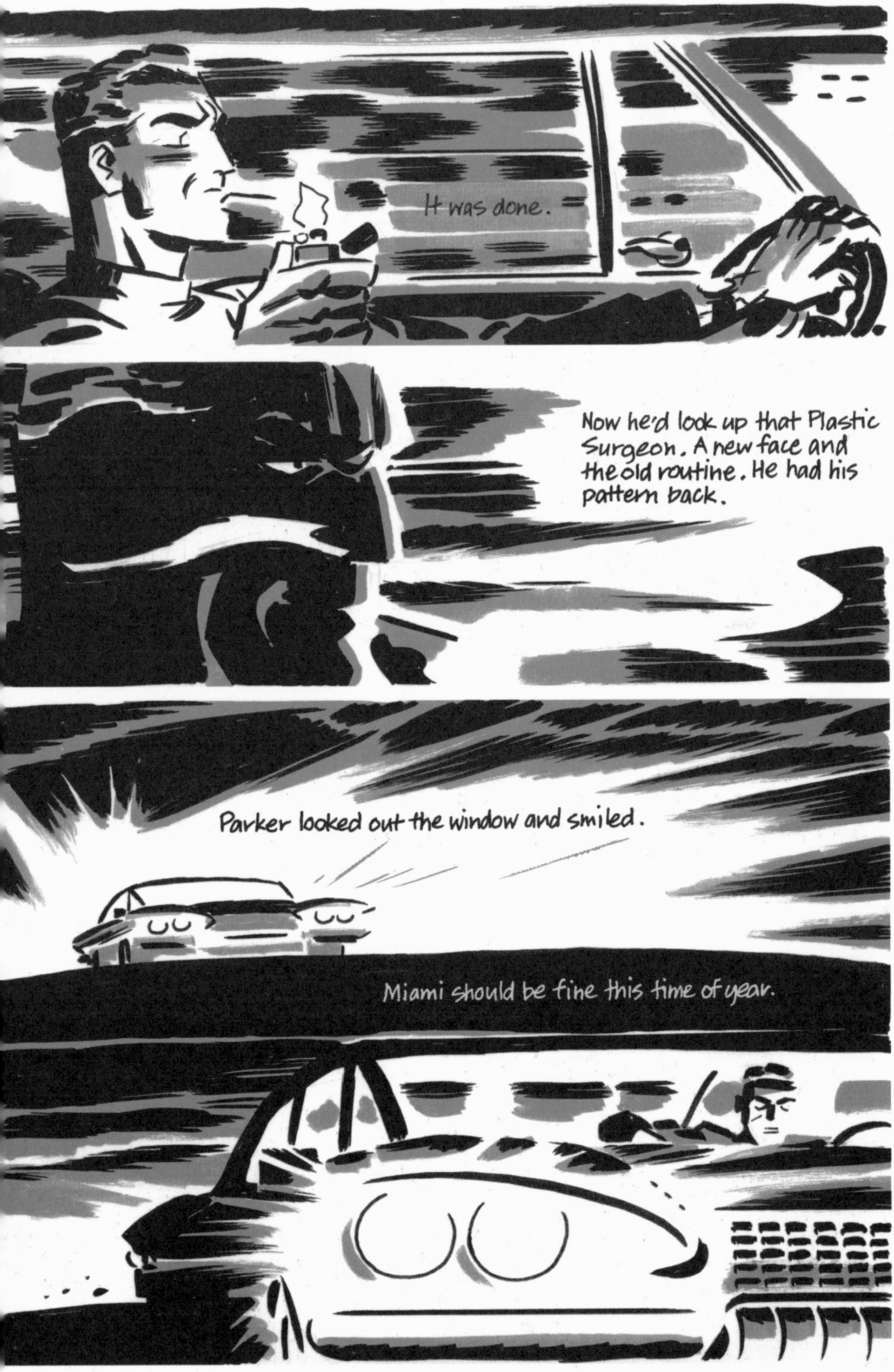
It was done.
Now he'd look up that Plastic Surgeon. A new face and the old routine. He had his pattern back.
Parker looked out the window and smiled.
Miami should be fine this time of year.

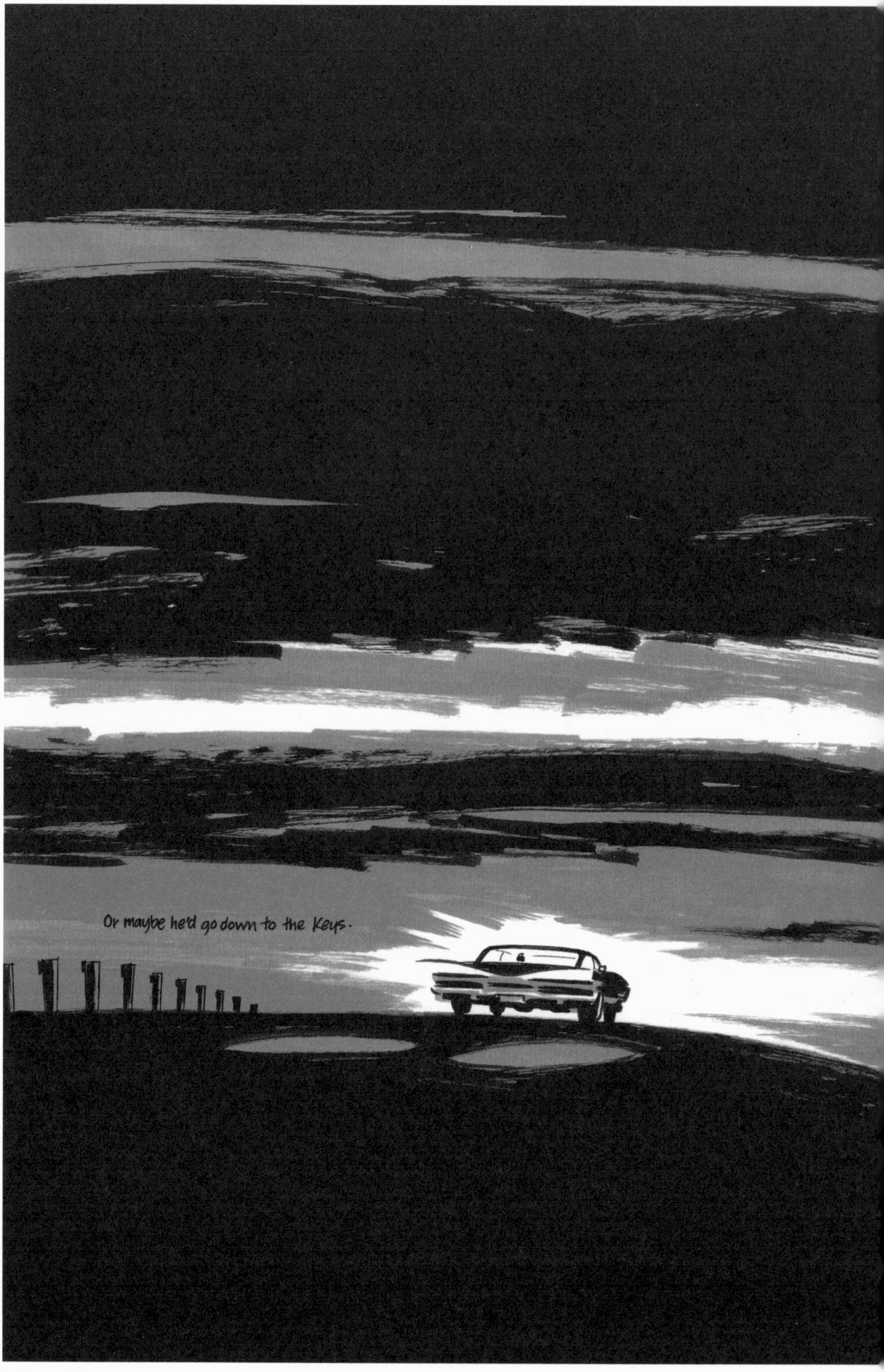
Or maybe he'd go down to the Keys.

Special Thanks

Abby Westlake
Paul Westlake
Charles Ardai (of Hard Case Crime)
Susanna Einstein (of LJK Literary Management)
Heidi MacDonald
Jimmy Palmiotti
Marsha and Amanda
Tom Spurgeon
Ed Brubaker
Chris Stone
Will Kane
Mike Stratford

PARKER
WILL RETURN

SUMMER 2010

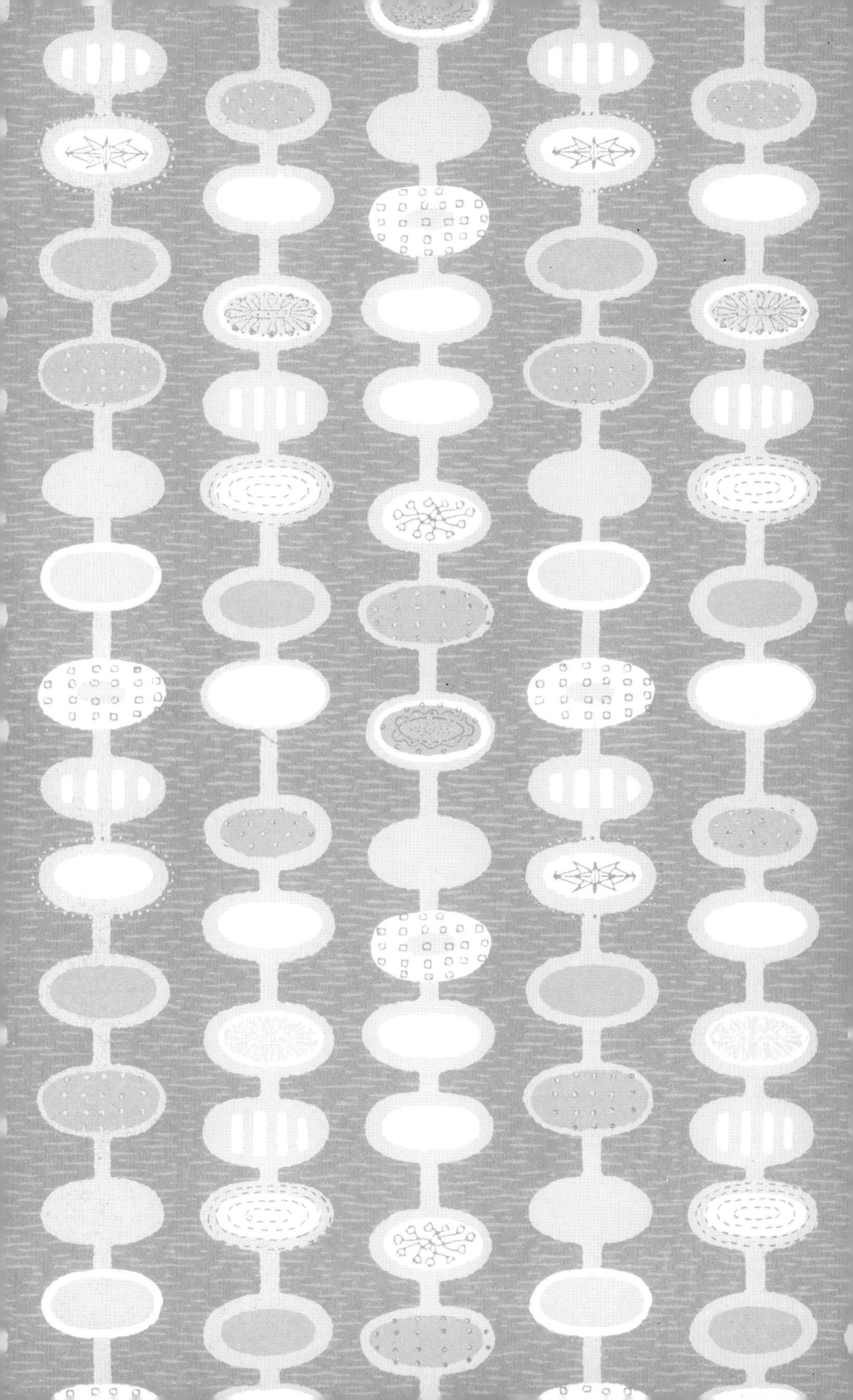